LODESTAR

LODESTAR

Sarie Mackay

LANTERN LODGE
PUBLISHING

2 0 0 6

Library of Congress Catalog Card Number: 2006910388

ISBN 978-0-9789259-1-8
ISBN 0-9789259-1-2

Cover design, illustration, and production: Joe Heins
Book design and production: Judy Gilats

SPRING 1880

Persis bent low, digging to find one more crevice in the trunk. There, along the right hand side. But the bundle of silk chemises wouldn't go in easily; they required a fierce shove, and with that, the hairpin that had threatened to slip all afternoon fell out at last, releasing blond curls that tumbled over her eyes.

Whipping back her hair with one hand and tamping the ivory fabric into place with the other, she muttered, "Absence makes the heart grow fonder, does it? God knows it has for me, but how much fonder for him? Not fond enough to come and get me; only fond enough to send a summons."

She sucked in a breath of muggy air, feeling the oppression of both her corset and the humidity rolling in off the lake. "Damn Alex," she gasped into the rising tide of her trousseau. "Cocksure, that's what he is. And furthermore, it's too hot to be doing this."

As she straightened up, darkness on the periphery of her vision rushed in and, unlike all the other times that day, did not abate. Staring into a sepia tunnel lashed with white sparks, she flailed for the bedpost, caught it, and let her hand slide down as she melted onto the bed.

The pressed linen was cool against her damp neck. Blood slowly ebbed back into her head, fanning the flames of her anger. Tears welled up. There are a hundred things to consider, and he is so cavalier! Father was like that. Alex, the man who is supposed to love me, simply waves his hand and says, "It's all right for you to come now, so get on the train, come across the continent, and be quick about it."

"Yes, damn Alex MacKinney!" she spat.

The second-story bedroom, despite its high, plastered ceiling and wide-open casements, was stifling. Much too hot for May. She thrashed on the bed, conjuring a strange pleasure in thoughts of stripping off her dress and grabbing the shears on her bureau to lop off the thick, golden knot of hair at the base of her neck. No, she thought, instead I shall fling myself, fully clothed, into the lake. But I wouldn't sink, like Ophelia. I would float. Forget about all this worry and just float, for the rest of the afternoon.

Several layers of ivory paper, creased with the folds of many readings, lay on the marble-topped commode next to the bed. Placing her hot palm on the smooth-polished stone, she drank its coolness through her skin. How familiar was that pale-veined marble, as was everything in her room—how familiar and safe. From Ireland the ornately carved commode had come, forty years before, when Grandfather Gallagher had settled in America. Her eyes moved from the gray depths of the ancient stone to the folded letter. Stirred by a breeze off the lake, its pages quivered as if answering her gaze.

Her gray-green eyes focused on Alex's bold hand. Reaching for it, ready to read it for the fiftieth time, she snatched back her fingers when a light tap sounded on the partly open door.

Millie, the housemaid, peered in, a frizz of gray hair issuing like steam from a rent in her cap. Persis whisked a tear from her cheek and sat up.

"You've a visitor, Miss. And I was near done with the chicken salad," Millie said, wiping her furrowed brow with a handkerchief.

"Is it Constance?" Persis brightened at the prospect of talking to her best friend.

Millie raised her eyebrows. "No, it's that Windham fellow."

Persis covered her face with her hands. "Gilbert Windham? What could he possibly want?" Flopping back on the bed, she dug her fingers into the crocheted coverlet.

"He said to tell you he only wants to see you this one last time."

"Is this why he's been staring at me in church lately?" She sat up stiffly. "I shouldn't have been so kind to him. I tried to let him down easily. This is all Mama's doing. Imagine, trying to foist me off on that mildewed banker!"

Millie shrugged. "Shall I send him away? Make up your mind, Miss Percy; I've got to get back to the kitchen."

"It's all right," Persis said, flinging her hands in the air. "I'll just have to confront him with the facts. Again." She went to the mirror, involuntarily reaching for the pot of rouge she kept hidden behind her jewel case. But the humidity and her agitation had already colored her cheeks. Her hair was nicely disheveled, she decided, so she simply ran her hands over her bodice, smoothing the dress of deep rose—a color that always intensified the green in her eyes.

"I'd rather be dazzling Alex, damn him, than that dreadful Windham, damn him as well." She straightened the large emerald engagement ring on her finger and went downstairs. With each footfall on the carpeted steps, she silently mouthed the words, "Damn, damn, damn."

Gilbert Windham was in the drawing room, gazing out the window and turning his hat around and around in his slender hands. His right forefinger was stained with ink.

A life of ciphers, thought Persis. God spare me.

Taking a few tentative steps toward her, Windham bowed slightly. "Miss Allen, I am delighted to see you again. We seldom chat anymore."

There was something about him that revived in Persis the ire she had felt toward both Gilbert Windham and her mother at that awful dinner party a year ago. The supercilious aura of condescension she had discovered before finishing the first course was oozing from his every pore.

"Hello, Mr. Windham," she replied. Before he opened his mouth, she knew he was going to compliment her on her appearance.

"You . . . ah . . . are looking especially lovely today," he began haltingly, then glanced away as he continued. "I feel it my duty to tell you, Miss Allen, something that you will doubtless not want to hear."

Persis steeled herself. It is his last chance, she thought; I will let him speak.

". . . and you may not choose to believe me, but in light of the high regard in which I hold you and my concern for your safe and happy future . . . I feel my conscience must be my guide."

There was an unusual sense of resolve in him this time around. *Out with it*, she thought, picking at a ruffle on her sleeve.

He glanced at her eyes. "I have come by some information acciden-tally, and it gives me a great deal of pain to be the bearer of such . . . intelligence, so to speak. But I . . . er, I really have no choice."

This was strange talk. "Please, Mr. Windham, be quick about your news."

"Yes, well then, here it is. My business associates in Syracuse, whom I recently had occasion to visit, just returned from St. Louis, where they happened to be in the company of your fiancé one evening at a local entertainment hall. He—Mr. MacKinney, I mean—well, he was, according to their reports, of which I do not doubt the veracity, for they would have little reason to prevaricate on this matter—Mr. MacKinney was in the rather intimate company of a well-known . . . businesswoman, and according to my associates, had frequently been so, during his recent visit to that city."

Persis's heart pounded and the blood surged into her cheeks. She wanted to blurt out that these friends of Windham were idiots, ped-dling claptrap. Instead, she turned away by a few degrees. Caution, caution, she urged herself, concealing a ragged inhale. He thinks I'm about to have an attack of the vapors.

In an odd way, she was pleased that he had brought her, albeit indi-rectly and with a trace of maliciousness, in touch with Alex. Instead of dwelling on the darker implications of Windham's story, she thirsted for news of Alex, to know what he was wearing, what he dined on, and what the rooms were like at the Queensbury Inn. Six months! Six months is too long to be apart! If there was another woman—she could hardly brook the idea—something drove her to know more.

She turned fully upon Windham, taking care to show not the frightened girl but a composed young woman. "I realize it must have been difficult for you to present this to me, Mr. Windham. I appreciate your concern for my well-being. Thank you. I have a great deal of faith, however, in my fiancé, and I am certain beyond any doubt that there is a very legitimate explanation for the scene you describe."

Straightening a lamp chimney on the sideboard, she wondered how she might get the woman's name. The situation required a direct approach. "Your friends—did you say they knew the woman?"

Windham, fidgeting again with the brim of his hat, replied, "Did I say that? Well, they do know her. Her name is Daltry. Elizabeth, I think."

Shifting her approach, she asked lightly, "Did they say whether or not Alexander looked well?"

Windham's sidelong stare made the whites of his round eyes appear even larger. "Well, no. They wouldn't have had cause to mention anything pertaining to his health. They said they had seen him, and mentioned that he appeared to be in the company of Bess . . . Miss Daltry."

Bess, thought Persis. *If he does have any kind of friendship with this woman, it is nothing for me to fear. The nickname "Bess" is rather telling. Sounds like a bit of livestock.*

"Again, I do appreciate your gesture of concern," she said, taking a step toward the hall. *I believe in Alexander and in his love for me.* But I will always remember your honesty and forthrightness in this matter, Gilbert."

Her sudden use of his Christian name caught Windham off guard. Dismissed, he rose and straightened his collar. "Well, Miss Allen, you are still planning your trip?"

Of all the pathetic audacity! "Yes," she said in an offhand but firm voice. "Yes, of course I am. In fact, it appears I'll be leaving even sooner than I thought." This was a fabrication, but she didn't care. "As soon as my brother graduates from the Columbia School of Mines. We'll leave three weeks from today."

"How serendipitous that both you and your brother are going to Montana Territory. Please tell Charles I wish him every success in his mining career. I always liked him."

Persis tilted her head, smiling genuinely. "Everyone likes Charlie. Constance misses him very much. I hope to see her today, in fact, and I am sure much of her thoughts will revolve around her husband, as they always do. As you can imagine, this final college term has been hard on the newlyweds. They are eager to see one another—a feeling I understand very well."

This remark landed just as she intended, making Windham flinch. "We will miss you here," he said. "I do hope you will be happy with Mr. MacKinney, and that you will find your new life in the West to be all that you deserve and more."

"We Allens have always had a spirit of adventure," she said, extending her arm toward the foyer. "I am sure you and I will see one another again—at church, I mean—before I leave. Have a good day, Mr. Windham, and give my regards to your family."

She closed the wide front door as quietly as she could, then turned and climbed the stairs. The banister was sticky beneath her palm. By the time she got to her room, she was awash in the anxiety she had striven to conceal.

Unable to aim her anger at anyone in particular, she kicked at the steamer trunk. What does Windham know! Well, there's one thing he *doesn't* know and surely never will, and that's the heady delirium of passionate love. He couldn't, in a million years, understand what is between Alex and me.

Then, twisting her handkerchief into a damp rope, she stared out the window. Her hands came up to her cheeks as she stared vacantly through the trees, catching sight of the weathered shingles of the Gascogne cottage, where her best friend Constance lived with her crone of a French grandmother.

It's perfectly within Windham's nature to want to "regulate" my romantic fervor. To him, it would be more seemly if I had a more prudent kind of love affair. Thank heaven it has been anything but that! I *have* been delirious. And I probably have overlooked Alex's faults. But he's never given me any cause for concern! An occasional pout, but he's a darling, he's my hero, in spite of that. That's the stuff of love. Constance knows. And now, at last, I know.

She was down the stairs and out the door in less than a minute, running along the deer trail that led to the Gascogne cottage. The light breeze off the lake came through the thin batiste of her dress like a caress. Then, through the green web of sassafras and beech leaves, she saw a slim figure coming down the trail.

"Percy! How peculiar! I was just coming to see you," Constance called out with a laugh. Corkscrews of fine, pale hair floated at her temples and her face was lit with pleasure.

"Isn't that the way it has always been with us?" Persis said, taking her friend's hand. "Here's our old rock. Come and sit down. I need to talk to you."

"Nothing has happened? Not to Charlie?" Constance caught her breath.

"Oh! No, no! Your beloved Charlie is just fine, I am sure. I know you are counting the days. No, this is about Alex."

After hearing the report, Constance was silent. The thrush piped from deep in the woods and the languid water slapped at the lakefront rocks.

"Well," Constance said at length, "I won't act as though this is nothing to be upset about. But think about it. Alex is thirty-three, ten years your senior. He's been a man of the world since he was seventeen. All that traveling, finding money to build railroads and then his own shipping business. He has lived large. Remember that night he said you were to be 'Mistress of the MacKinney Manse?' He was being clever, but all romanticizing aside, he has built an empire on the frontier. He wants you and needs you to be his partner. He said so."

Persis picked at a clump of moss.

"He's marrying you," Constance went on almost fiercely, "not some colorful strumpet from a beer hall. How many letters have you gotten from him since he went back to the Territory in January?"

Persis bit her lip. "I've gotten one almost every week," she said.

"There! And now you have the letter you've been waiting for. It's time to go to him. And by-the-by, here on your finger is the monument of an emerald he gave you just six months ago." Constance tapped the square-cut stone with her fingernail.

Heaving a sigh, Persis let her head fall back. "But things are never like this with you and Charlie," she said. "You're both so . . . calm." Her eyes ran across the fluttering canopy of leaves and came to rest on the battered old owl's nest they used to spy on as children.

"You mustn't compare us, Percy."

Persis took Constance's chin gently and aimed her friend's face at the owl's nest. "Where do you suppose Aristotle is? How long do owls live, anyway?" She let go. "As far as not comparing myself to you, *ma petite choux,* all I have to say is *ha!* We've always done that, you and I."

Constance lowered her eyes and smiled. "Yes, I guess we have. But maybe it's time to do less of that," she said. "You know what an old crone Grandmere is. Crotchety, but wise. I have to tell you something she said when I quarreled with Charlie last March. You know, when I visited him in New York City. Grandmere said, 'When you have the bad times, you must remember why you thought you would be able to manage it all. *Pourquoi? Pour l'amour.*"

Persis nodded. "She always finds the truth, that old girl. I'll miss Grandmere," she said. "But I won't miss her sticking me with that bony finger every time she makes a point."

They both laughed.

"Oh, I can't stay," Persis said, jumping up. "I need to get back to the house. Mama wants to talk to me about our shopping trip to Buffalo tomorrow. I wish you could come."

Constance shook her head. "You know very well I haven't got a penny to spare."

"You are an inspiration," Persis said, kissing her friend on the cheek. "I guess you and I can talk ourselves to death on the train. Three whole days to talk while the entire country passes by the window. Charlie will abandon us for the saloon car."

Constance's blue eyes twinkled. "I can't wait."

Persis's step was lighter on the way home. There were few things in the world she loved more than spilling her ponded thoughts to Constance.

There's someone else I need to visit just now, she realized. I must make the time. She dodged into some low-hanging sassafras branches, down past the old mill that gave the community its name, through a small pasture to the horse barn her father built the year before he died. It was still the home of two or three of the Allen family horses, one of them a dapple gray Persis had, in a moment of romantic fancy, named Astarte, after a goddess of love. But the name suited the animal and the bond between them was deep. Persis stood with her horse for fifteen minutes, rubbing her down and exchanging long inhales and exhales an inch or two from Astarte's muzzle. This secret language of breath never failed to renew the trust between them. The steamy caress, the long, white whiskers, the velvet skin; she loved every aspect of their communion. When the time came to go, tears were streaming down Persis's cheeks.

Resolutely climbing the path, she stopped and looked back, even though she knew she shouldn't. Astarte's dark, liquid eyes stared for a long moment and then blended into the shadows.

She turned her step homeward. Astarte trusts me, there is no doubt of that. But what of trust between the sexes? Love between a man and a woman is such an uncertain thing, she thought, scuffing at the papery leaves along the narrow path. Will I ever be released from the maddening fear that my love for Alex may not be reciprocated? Are there women who never have cause to worry? If there are, I have not known them.

Alex MacKinney didn't notice the wild plum blossoms in the creek bed or the red-winged blackbirds darting among the cattails along the Nebraska rails. He was deep in thought, trying to calculate how many times he had ridden the Union Pacific. The cross-country railroad had been completed in May of 1869, almost eleven years ago to the day, when the golden spike was driven at Promontory, Utah.

The UP was still a young railroad by anyone's standards, yet in the last seven years, he estimated, he had traversed the country at least thirty-two times, in balmy spring weather like this and in December blizzards that had stalled the train for days. This trip to meet some St. Louis financiers had been number thirty-three, and he was glad to be returning to Montana Territory, where he could keep the contractor moving on the construction of his new home on Helena's north side.

A nervous smile spread over his handsome face. He tugged in a boyish, unconscious way at his stiff white collar, then drained his drink. I'm to be led to the altar at last, he mused. Married to Persis Madeleine Allen, a beautiful woman who suits me perfectly. How can a woman be so demure and so piquant at the same time? She is remarkable.

She had captivated him with a combination of naiveté and sophistication. And in addition to her good looks, there was something about her, a suggestion of sensuality that seemed almost improper, but not quite. No man could miss it.

He kept thinking of how she looked that night after Christmas. He had never insisted with her, the way he had some of the others. But there had been moments, like that late December night on the stairs at her mother's house. He had studied her all evening, taking in every seam of her green silk dress, noting how it revealed the form of her breasts and the slight convexity of her belly. When they met by accident on the steps, she was standing one riser above him, making their eyes nearly level. He had grown hoarse with desire and had wanted to whisk her off her feet—how easy it would have been—and stare into her eyes as he pressed her into the nearest bed.

He dashed away a trace of perspiration from his upper lip as the memory of her came fully back to him. He had been bold enough to take her in his arms that night, to feel her tremble. He had felt that quiver in plenty of women, but seldom in respectable young ladies like Persis Allen. Her breath came quickly and he watched the shadow of her hair as it moved on her skin with the rise and fall of her breasts. No one was anywhere near. Her lips were open and she smelled of currant wine.

"More whiskey, Mr. MacKinney?" The porter was at his elbow.

"Uh, sure." Alex blinked and shook his head slightly. "Glenmorgan, you'll remember."

"Right away, sir."

It was good the porter had come by, because Alex could never have stood up and gone to the saloon car, not with such a bulge in his close-fitting trousers. His chest swelled beneath his silk damask waistcoat as he took a deep breath, shaking off the reverie. Yes, a gateway was opening for him, leading him to a new period of life that would bring joys of an entirely different kind.

No marriage is entered into without some risk and some compromise, he pondered. But I know Persis will match my efforts, and I will be everything I can be for her and for our children. I hope there are children!

The trip to St. Louis had been fruitful, he reflected as he waited for his Scotch whiskey. Old friends, fine horses. He had even purchased a matched pair who were, he hoped, weathering the trip relatively well in one of the stock cars at the rear of this very train.

What a luxury, moving livestock by rail! It's happening all over the states, finally. But still unheard of in Montana Territory, at least for now. It would be a good many years, he speculated, before he and his fellow rail promoters could start using the Utah and Northern to move the Territory's cattle to market.

Still, the progress they had made in the past year constructing the little narrow gauge railroad through the mountains was astounding. It'll reach Butte City within a year, a year and a half at the most, he vowed.

Railroads! His lips curved into a proud smile as he glanced around at the regal appointments of the Pullman car. How old was I when my folks took me to visit Dad's old friend George Pullman up north of Rochester? I was a tyke, maybe eight at the outside. George lit the boiler fire in me, no doubt about it. If he—and my father, for that matter—had only known back then that I would fall in with a league of Mormons to build a railroad in the wilds of the American West! And then to find a bride in New York State, a scant hundred miles from where I spent my boyhood. Life takes such peculiar turns.

His eyes sparkling with anticipation, he turned his thoughts to the new house on Gilbert Street in Helena, trying to look at its functional layout from a woman's point of view. He wanted to make Persis Allen happy, and vowed to do everything in his power to arrange the best possible kind of family life.

* * *

Genevieve pulled out all the stops in Buffalo, outfitting Persis with every imaginable trousseau item. They acquired almost too much cargo to carry: linens and clothing, sterling-handled hairbrushes and boot-hooks, apothecary items, and books that Genevieve deemed "helpful in making the adjustment to wedded life." Persis gasped with relief when the clerk finished wrapping the more embarrassing volumes in several layers of brown paper.

That afternoon, a rustic but handsome man—a frontiersman of sorts—stopped to help them as they struggled to hail a cab. He was lean and tall, taller even than Alex, Persis noticed. She compared every member of the male species to Alex and was consistently pleased to find most of her subjects wanting. But this man was attractive in a silent, capable way. His whiskey-colored leather coat conformed to his broad shoulders and muscular arms, and he wore peculiar heeled boots. Cowboy boots, Persis realized. Absently studying his dark, back-swept hair and tanned cheekbones, she was caught off guard when he suddenly turned and looked at her.

"May I?" he asked, extending his hand to help her into the cab. As he took her arm, she smiled briefly at him and saw his eyes, granite-gray with sparks of hazel. A small sensation of heat crept up from her lace collar when their eyes met. She was barely seated, however, when the cab jerked forward, leaving him behind. She felt the urge to turn around and take one more look at him, but she was too well-bred for that.

Chance meetings, she reflected, keeping her eyes forward. Our lives are full of them. Sometimes, as with Alex, they change our lives—but sometimes they flicker past us and are gone forever.

And how close she had come to missing Alex entirely! That day at the Dunkirk Harbor Station—what if she hadn't gone with Charlie to pick up Genevieve's horticultural shipment? What if they had gone the day before, or the day after? She stared out at the hordes of people milling through downtown Buffalo. Chance, pure chance.

The horticulture supplies weren't even at the Harbor Station when she and Charlie arrived that cloudy afternoon ten months ago. Faced with the disappointing news that the shipment had, for reasons un-clear, been loaded off the barge in Rochester, Charlie decided to take advantage of the station's supply of cast-off crates and wooden boxes.

While he rummaged, Persis wandered back toward the gate. She breathed deep, enjoying the languid morning, the mewing gulls, and the faint fishy scent of everything along the shore. On her left, a long dock stretched out into the gray expanse of Lake Erie. Two small boys were silhouetted at the very end. Mesmerized by the way the water and the hazy air blended into one pale, humid fabric, she watched the boys tossing sticks into the water.

Turning to the right, she could see all the way down the platform, where the manager was packing a crate, and on up the road. A loud rumbling caught her attention and suddenly a huge wagon appeared at the top of the hill, rattling down the road toward the dockyard at breakneck speed. The elderly manager looked up from his work, pushed his hat back on his head, and resolutely placed his hands on his hips.

Alarmed, Persis opened the gate and walked through, stepping over a cat and up onto the platform. The wagon, a huge dray, was piled high with something concealed beneath a dirty canvas cover. It was barreling straight toward the platform.

No one should drive that way, she thought with disgust, especially on the streets of an established community. The freight station may lie on the outskirts of town, but there are homes all along the station road, with children and livestock to consider.

The careening freight wagon came on, drawn by a team of four frothing horses. At first glance, an observer might have judged it a runaway, but two men sat high in the driver's box, one of them clearly wielding some influence over the horses. This man was now shouting and reining the team in sharply. The horses strained against the harness in an effort to stop, and the wagon came grinding and squealing up to the platform. Sparks flew as the horses' shod hooves clattered on the bricks. The wagon shuddered, groaned, and finally shifted into a resting position.

Persis was transfixed. The driver's management of the team was astounding. Never had the arrival of a wagon been so frightening and yet so spectacular. But what required such drama and haste? The horses looked fit, but their mouths were chafed and their eyes rolled anxiously from side to side.

A tall, hatless man with tousled light brown hair jumped down and called some instructions to his companion, who began tending the horses. As the manager maintained his stiff posture on the platform, the driver stepped to the rear of the wagon to search for something beneath the canvas cover. Grinning, he pulled out a hat, dusted it on his thigh, and clapped it on his head as he leaped up onto the platform. Although he was still some distance away, Persis could see that he was strikingly handsome. Concealed in the shadows, she was able to watch the scene with unselfconscious interest.

"You the manager?" the driver called out, his eyebrows raised in an expression of friendly inquiry.

"That would be me." Then, in a slow, steady voice, he added, "We don't drive like that around here."

The driver smiled, his entire face radiating good humor. He was without a doubt the most attractive man Persis had ever seen. As his generous smile flashed, she saw his even, white teeth and a liveliness in his eyes.

"Alex MacKinney," he said to the manager. Then he saw her. It was a long, electric moment. His brown eyes rested heavily on her and his lips parted in soft surprise. Taking off his hat and holding it waist level with one hand, he stepped toward her.

Everything that followed was a rapid jumble. Charlie elbowed rudely past her, greeting the stranger. The two of them recognized one another from New York City and were soon in enthusiastic conversation about Montana Territory, smelters, and a silver mine called the "Neversweat."

Charming, Persis thought as she tamped a splinter with the toe of her shoe. The stranger stopped talking and stared at her over Charlie's shoulder. She did not raise her eyes to meet his, but she could feel him appraising her, and dared to believe he was favorably impressed.

Charlie, seeing the man's gaze drift, at last took the hint. "Oh, I'm sorry. Alex—Alexander MacKinney, may I introduce my sister, Miss Persis Allen."

When their eyes met this time, Persis felt the world shift a half-degree. She knew in that instant that even if she never saw him again, she would remember this moment forever. As he reached to take her hand, her heart thumped wildly. But that thump was instantly replaced by a terrible pounding, a pounding layered with screams.

As soon as she heard the panicked voices and the frenzied sound of feet on the dock, Persis knew what had happened. "Two boys," she gasped. "One must have fallen in!"

Alex's hat was now in her hands. In four long strides he had gone from the depot platform to the dock and was running along its sturdy boards, casting his leather coat onto a weathered piling. Persis watched his every stride, how his loose sleeves billowed as he ran, and how his muscular legs powered him into the air as he dove from the end of the dock.

The boy was fished from the lake, and none too soon, for the little fellow did not know how to swim. He was choking and flailing wildly by the time Alex got a good hold on him.

Back at the depot, by means of some rags, Persis got the boy, whose name was Timmy, as dry as possible.

Water beading at the tip of his nose, Alex squatted down and looked at him, saying, "Now, Timmy, my friend, why don't you and your chum walk home the long way and get nice and dry. That way you'll avoid getting scolded by your Ma and Pa."

As the two boys ambled up the road in conspiratorial discussion, Alex slicked back a lock of wet hair and watched them go, murmuring under his breath, "I love children." A moment later, he grinned at Persis and Charlie and said, "God love a rascal, you know? Twenty years ago I was just like him."

"I rather fancy you still are," Persis said, suppressing a coy smile.

By the time her thoughts drifted back to the present, Persis and her mother were rattling briskly along Pershing Avenue toward the Buffalo Depot. Chance and choice, she thought. Alex and I met by chance, and have continued by choice.

They had missed the mid-afternoon train for Dunkirk by a long shot, but another one would come through in less than an hour. The sheet-iron sky cast spatters of rain on the brick streets and on the clog of dusty black carriages around the depot.

A leg of lightning shot down from the clouds over Lake Erie, followed by a clap of thunder loud enough to lay the horses' ears back. Persis peered out from under the scalloped black edge of the hansom's canopy. Thunder. It will always remind me of him, because he literally thundered into my life ten months ago. August 14, 1879. And now I can't imagine life without him.

* * *

The appointed hour came. On Saturday morning, June 5, Persis, Charlie, and Constance found their seats on the 10:15 Baltimore & Ohio. Persis had kept her good-byes brief; after all, she and her mother had been exchanging anticipatory farewells for several weeks. The hiss of steam and the chatter of other passengers sent a shiver of excitement through her. Tears welled up as she saw her mother and Millie waving from the platform, but when she saw the baggage handlers shaking their heads over her eleven trunks, she couldn't suppress a giggle of delight.

Their destination was Montana Territory, but they would stop in Chicago to visit Constance's parents, the Parments. Then it would be on to Cheyenne, where she would be reunited with Alex.

Constance went to her compartment, complaining of a *petite malaise.* Persis stayed in the parlor car, reading several chapters in *The Ideal Woman: A Handbook for Brides,* then fell into a doze. When she woke, Charlie was gone. Probably sequestered with that fair-haired wife of his, she thought. She wandered restlessly through the passageway to the dining car. There he was, standing near a table, with maps and copies of *Harper's* strewn everywhere.

She stopped a few yards away, struck just now by how much he reminded her of herself. It must be the pensive posture, she reasoned, that is emphasizing the hollows in his cheeks and making his high cheekbones more pronounced. His lips have that—what is the French word Constance has used to describe my mouth and Charlie's too? *Embouchure,* that's it. As if we were each about to pick up a flute and start playing. And inside this train, that faint auburn cast the sun brings out in his hair is all but gone. Right now it's the same gold-blond as my own. As she approached, she could see that he was peering closely at a mining claims map entitled, *Butte City.* "That looks like a haphazard mosaic," she said.

"Hmmph," he grunted, barely acknowledging her.

Sitting down, she inspected a simpler map for a while and then fell to watching the summer foliage flutter past the window. Sugar maple, oak, beech, the occasional spray of hemlock or the satin-smooth needles of white pine. Last year, after she made little botanical studies of each in watercolors, her mother had proudly framed them.

"You're a few thousand miles away," Charlie commented, not looking up.

"Well," said Persis, pulling herself back into the car, "so are you. Does that map really make sense to you?"

He smiled down at the pattern of multi-colored squares and trapezoids. "Yes. This is what I need to be thinking about, if I'm to provide for myself and my bride, also known as your best friend. This, and mine shaft structure, assaying, and the like."

"I don't understand it, but would you teach me about it someday? You know, mining?"

He looked up and pushed back a dangling curl of hair. "Well, of course I can, but what on earth for?"

"Charlie! I want to learn about so many things! Don't you? It will be vastly different where we're going."

"There's truth in that," he said with a little laugh.

"You seem so certain of your . . . destiny," she said, leaning forward with her elbows on the table.

"Yours is as clear as mine," he responded. "I should think you will have your hands full doing other things. Women things. Like Constance will."

"Life is easier for men," she announced, leaning back now and folding her arms over her chest.

"Oh, is it? How do you justify that observation?"

"Women," she said, warming to her subject, "are expected to find almost all of their adventure close to the hearth. I mean, most women. It's as if the confines of home, dooryard, and family must hold as much excitement and variety for women as the outer world holds for a man."

"I have always said, dear sister, that you are not the average girl. I still can't believe you got away with wearing trousers when you went riding."

"Dearest Charles, you rascal, you share some responsibility for that occasional—and I emphasize occasional—habit of mine! You're the one who taunted a skinny little twelve-year-old girl for an entire summer about not being a good enough rider to join your elite Pony Express Club. You knew very well no one could make it across Mill Creek Flats in less than two minutes riding sidesaddle. Tell me you weren't proud of me that day. Tell me!" She grabbed his elbow and put her nose up to his, laughing.

His face broke into a grin. "You know damn well I was, but it didn't help either of us when Father saw you barreling down the lane—" he stopped, sensing someone in the aisle. Both he and Persis turned and saw a tall, suntanned man wearing a broad-brimmed hat.

"Pardon me," said the man, nodding to Charlie, "my name is Avery Burke. I walked by earlier and couldn't help noticing that you had a real good map of Montana Territory. No, not the claims map," he said, shaking his head as Charlie touched the brightly-colored patchwork. "I'm a rancher. I was hoping to look at the rangeland map—that one," he said, pointing across the table to a large, folded map. "I'll just sit down right over there, and I'll return it to you pronto, just as soon as I get a sense of how the surveyors think things are laid out."

Charlie gathered up the map and handed it to the man. "Be my guest," he said. "I'm not using it right now."

"Thank you," said Burke, with a nod. "I live in Montana Territory, but it's a real different experience living on the land than seeing it from a bird's eye view. Sometimes I agree with the cartographers and sometimes I don't. Like I said, I'll bring it back. Thanks."

He nodded to Charlie, then looked at Persis intently. He knew it was an ill-mannered look, but he couldn't help it. Aside from her beauty, there was an elusive charm about her that simply made him stare. Green eyes. Very green.

Persis gave him a perfunctory smile and picked up a copy of *Harper's*. "Excuse me, Mr. Burke," she said, standing up. Her arm brushed his jacket lightly as she moved past him and stepped into the aisle.

"Please, call me Avery," he said quickly, lifting his hat.

When the hat came off, Persis was struck by something familiar. What was it? The dark hair shot with gray at the temples? The cheekbones? She almost asked him if they had met, but thought better of it. She tore her gaze away from his dark eyes.

"It was nice to meet you . . . Avery. Good day," she said, and made her way toward her compartment.

Settled there, her thoughts left Avery Burke and drifted to the topic she had nearly beaten out of her mind: St. Louis, the Queensbury Inn and the infamous Bess Daltry. She imagined the Queensbury as a busy place, teeming with settlers, traders, miners, and immigrants. Alex would stand out among them, of course, in his well-tailored frock coat and moleskin pants. In the evening his chin would bear a shadow of stubble, but this would only add to the sculpt of his jaw and make his smile flash more brightly. Pewter tankards of ale or cups full of Scotch whiskey, Alex's favorite, would be everywhere on quaint plank tables. Would he sit at a small table with Bess Daltry? Or would they stand together, his strong arm around her waist?

Finally, fury swept over her like a hot wind. Visceral anger, stirred up with teeth-gritting jealousy, grew palpable enough to make her sick to her stomach. Her hand shook as she reached for the water bottle.

Taking a sip, she counseled herself with a drilling fierceness that would have made Grandmere Gascogne proud.

I can spend my time torturing myself, or I can give my full attention to remembering why I thought my love for Alex could surmount any challenge. I refuse to spend the next ten days like this. Bess Daltry! She is a fiction, and nothing more.

Persis stared across the car at Constance, who was deeply engrossed in her book. Only a few feet separated them, but it felt like a hundred miles. There are so many differences between us, she brooded. Constance and Charlie, what a portrait of convention and stability, like a magazine article. And just as banal. She jerked her head away.

What made her able to choose such a life, while I am drawn to—no, utterly transfixed by—the mystery and excitement I have with Alex?

As unable to repress this impulse as any other, Persis scooped up her full green skirt and bustled across the car. Constance's sapphire eyes peered up from the book, *A Lady's Life in the Rocky Mountains*.

"Hello," Constance said, smiling.

"May I interrupt?"

"Of course," said Constance. "I'd rather be talking to you than reading a book." The smile was still there, but weaker than usual.

"I . . . I wanted to tell you that I believe things will be all right between Alex and me, and I wanted to thank you for being so fair in your judgment of him."

Constance's eyes widened. "Of course I am fair, Percy. I like Alex. And I know without a doubt that he loves you and means to be a devoted husband."

"You do?" Relief welled up in Persis. "Well, yes, of course he does love me," Persis said, tracing a design on her skirt. "It occurred to me this morning that you seem a little—detached. I thought perhaps you were worrying about my future and didn't know how to share your apprehension with me."

"Oh, Persis!" Constance's hand flew to her forehead. "I think I've got a touch of the ague, that's all. I've never been on a train for so many hours continuously."

"Can I get you some tea? Ginger ale?"

"I'm fine. But please stop worrying about what I think of your fiancé."

"Oh Constance, I love him so much!" She leaned in and rested her head on Constance's shoulder. "Memories of our time together keep coming back to me, like the first time we were forced to part. You know, last fall, when business called him back to Montana Territory.

Her eyes brimmed as she drifted back to that crisp October evening. "I can still smell the air and feel that kiss!" That night, a mist had settled on Canaqua Lake, but high above, the stars twinkled. She and Alex were standing on the porch. She was trying not to think about the next morning, when he would take the railroad to Utah and from there drive a MacKinney Freight wagon north to Montana Territory—a place too far away to comprehend.

"I regret I can't stay on as the Allens' resident *raconteur* any longer," Alex had said softly, meshing his fingers with hers. "I've postponed business long enough." Then, with a half turn of his hand, he drew her slowly, deliberately toward him.

A faint waft of smoke from a neighbor's bonfire mingled with the warm Bay Rum scent of his skin. Desire and fear burned through Persis. Their physical closeness made it impossible to imagine him gone. Her throat tightened.

"It's dark," he said softly, "but I think I see a tear in your eye."

She turned her head away but his left hand stopped her, gently grazing her face. "Nothing could make me happier than knowing that you care whether I am here or not, Persis."

Her eyes fully on him now, she let the tear slip down her cheek.

Still holding her hand, he pulled her to his chest and slowly bent forward, kissing her parted lips.

Her free hand flew to his arm, clutching hard, pulling the soft wool of his sleeve into a knot. She felt his embrace tighten as his tongue brushed fiercely against her mouth.

Their teeth bumped together as he kissed her hard and deep. She was lost, insensate, knowing nothing but her ache for him. For a long, liquid moment, there was only the dark, whirling cosmos where their passions met.

Alex pulled back and the cold air rushed between them. She teetered, unable to come to herself.

"We—" he began, "If I stay any longer . . . I can't. We can't. Persis, I have to go. I'll be back." The words came hoarsely as he held her away.

Before she could utter a word, he was gone. Leaning against the tall windows that flanked the front door, she covered her ears so that she wouldn't hear the receding sound of his boots on the gravel.

He *had* come back, of course; and her front-porch sorrow seemed quaintly absurd in retrospect, especially when he presented her with an engagement ring at Christmas.

Now, as a light spatter of rain began to streak the windows of the Baltimore & Ohio, she looked down at the ring and plucked a fiber of lint from the gold setting.

"It sounds ridiculous now," she said, "but that night I didn't know if I would ever see him again. It has been a peculiar courtship at best, don't you think?"

"I don't know that I would call it peculiar," Constance said. "But I think it has been hard on you. Waiting is hard. I know that very well. But the wait is over for both of us, at last."

Persis was only partly attentive. "It is a beautiful ring, isn't it?" she said, making a quick arc through the air with her hand, watching the emerald flash.

"Yes," Constance said, "beautiful enough to remind you of Alex's love every time you look at it."

* * *

Late in the day, the train stopped at Ashtabula for water and coal. Persis swept down the iron steps, eager to get away from her cramped compartment and breathe some fresh air. On the crowded platform, she shook out her skirt and turned her stiffened neck both left and right. Her spine loosened with a series of tiny, satisfying cracks.

The depot doors swung open and closed, disgorging new travelers.

She watched the newcomers with their carpetbags and leather valises, wondering where they were bound. As she scanned the platform, her gaze was arrested by the tall figure of Avery Burke stepping off the train some twenty yards away.

What is it about him that stirs me? she puzzled. Whatever it is, I am in no mood for a conversation with him. She walked briskly to the far end of the platform and then down the luggage ramp where she could get a glimpse of the Ohio countryside.

Dairy cattle grazed in the blue-green pastures and a buggy moved silently along a distant yellow road. The scene eased her spirits and separated her from the irritating chatter of the crowd and the shouts of the baggage handlers. Who knows when I will next look upon an eastern landscape, she wondered, inhaling the scent of rain-dampened grass.

The shouting on the platform grew strident. Annoyed, she focused on the bucolic view before her. A rumble came from behind her and grew so loud that she whirled around in alarm. An enormous baggage cart was hurtling straight toward her.

She felt a backward jerk, as if someone had punched her in the stomach. Like a rag doll, she was spun around into the side of the building, cushioned by a strong pair of arms. The baggage cart shot past, crashing into a board fence and sending splintered wood, trunks, and dirty canvas bundles all over the cobbled pavement.

With the wind knocked out of her, Persis could only gasp for breath. Finally, squirming around to see the owner of the arms that restrained her, she looked straight into the eyes of Avery Burke.

In the space of a second, she assessed those eyes. Deep gray, but not leaning in any way toward black. Hazel flecks softened the darkness and made her think of wood smoke on an autumn day.

He released her, then extended a callused hand.

With that tiny gesture, a memory unlocked with a nearly audible click. She stared at him, dumbstruck with recollection.

"It . . . it was you," she stammered. "In Buffalo that day. When I was shopping with Mama."

He smiled and cast his eyes down.

His lashes are criminally long, thought Persis.

"I remembered too," he said. "Before you did, though."

He lifted his eyes and looked into her face. It seemed to Persis that she knew him, not just from the chance meeting in Buffalo. She had even felt a peculiar familiarity with him that day on the street. There was some kind of current moving between them. It was a bit like her feeling for Alex, but easier and less urgent.

And he was attractive; there was no arguing that. He wasn't the sartorial type, like Alex, who wouldn't be caught dead without a silk brocade waistcoat. No, Burke had an entirely different kind of physical charm. His stovepipe canvas pants fit him trimly through his slim but muscular thighs, then crumpled slightly at the instep of his polished boots. His tanned, clean-shaven chin made a pleasing contrast with his white shirt and loosely knotted indigo scarf.

While she took all of this in, he hooked her arm through his and took hold of her hand, his rough fingers closing on hers.

"I didn't hurt you, did I?" he asked.

"Oh, no, not in the slightest. Thank you so much."

"I don't think you would have been killed by that cart, but you may have had a broken bone or two by the time both axles got through with you."

Then they were laughing and walking up the ramp, the wreckage and melee behind them. Working through the tide of passengers and porters, they found Charlie and Constance in the dining car.

Constance jumped up. "Persis! You're as white as a winding sheet! What happened?" Her head went from left to right, looking first at Persis and then at Avery Burke.

"I heard a crash," said Charlie, smirking. "I suppose you either caused it or were right in the middle of it." He tipped his chair back and raised his brows.

"It was a runaway baggage cart," Persis said glacially. "And yes, I was most desperately in the middle of it, or would have been, had it not been for Mr. Burke. Constance, this is Avery Burke, whom Charlie and I met while you were resting."

Constance nodded a greeting.

"Mr. Burke and I met briefly in Buffalo a week ago," continued Persis, "although neither of us remembered it until the fracas with the baggage cart. Truly, he snatched me from disaster just now. The ramp . . . the ramp was slippery—" Dizzy, she reached for the back of one of the seats.

Constance slipped a quick arm around her shoulders, lowering her onto the upholstery. Charlie lost his mocking expression and quickly poured a glass of water.

"I'm fine, I'm fine," Persis said. "Mr. Burke, please tell us about your place in Montana Territory."

"Avery," he said, sitting down next to her. "Please call me Avery."

Persis smiled. "Of course. Avery."

"Well," he began, "I figure you're familiar with the two principal cities, Helena and Butte City."

Seeing everyone nod, he continued, "I live on a ranch outside of a town called Cottonwood, very near Butte City. They've just changed the name of Cottonwood to Deer Lodge, after the Indian way. I'm trying to get used to it. We run cattle," he concluded simply.

"Your family runs the ranch?" asked Charlie.

"After a fashion. I'm unmarried. My parents are deceased. Fate brought me to the Territory seven or eight years ago. My little brother and I came there for the first time back in '73, driving cattle up from Mexico." His voice softened as he added, "They call it God's country. When you get there, you'll see why."

"Cattle, eh? Sounds as though I won't be able to pump you for much information about the mining trade," Charlie said, smiling.

"No, I'm afraid not. I could regale you with stories of cattle drives and vigilantes and maybe a little gold-dust drama, but that's it. Now I'm just trying to grow my herd and keep the rustlers away."

"Rustlers?" said Constance.

"Unfortunately," said Avery, "some men think they're entitled to build their herds using other men's cattle. It's easier, I'll allow that much, but the end result often involves a little too much rope." He reached a finger into his shirt collar. "If you know what I mean."

Constance's eyes widened.

"That part of cattle ranching is ugly work," Avery said quickly. "Not fit for polite conversation. Say, I'm entertaining a few friends at the Midwestern Hotel in Chicago. Mostly livestock people I've known for years. But I'd be pleased to have you join us. It's just dinner and a little libation. Will you be stopping over in Chicago?"

Persis stiffened. Was this an advance? However warm their relations had suddenly become, she had to keep things from becoming too cordial. Somehow, she had to tell him about Alex, and the sooner the better.

"Yes," she said, before Charlie or Constance could speak. "We'll be staying with Constance's parents, the Parments, for a few days. However, I'm afraid our time will be taken up with family. And I have more shopping to do to complete my trousseau. Since you live in Montana Territory, perhaps you have heard of my fiancé, Alexander MacKinney?"

It was brutal, far more brutal than she had been with Gilbert Windham. But it had to be done. She breathed a silent exhale.

Avery stared at her. "You're engaged to Alex MacKinney?" His eyes flew to her left hand, where he spotted the noteworthy emerald.

"Yes. We're to be married in August, in Helena. Do you know Alex?"

"I do." Burke nodded, looking off to the side. "Yes, I'd wager nearly everyone in the Territory knows—of him," he said with measured courtesy. "And of his tireless efforts to bring in the Utah and Northern rails."

These were wooden comments, but Persis decided he was disappointed by the news that she was engaged.

Charlie stared at her with barely concealed dismay. She swallowed, realizing too late that he had been interested in the dinner invitation. Given her intuition about Avery's inclinations, however, she held to the opinion that attending such a soiree would not be prudent. Well, perhaps in the company of a married couple . . .

"Where did you say you were staying?" she asked Avery, trying to fill the sudden vacuum.

"At the Midwestern," he answered, without looking up.

"Well, if Charlie and Constance would like to attend your party," she said, "I certainly would not want to stand in the way."

"Oh Percy, you could come too," said Constance.

That was all Avery Burke needed. "I'll send a courier with the details," he said. "If you can't attend, just send your regrets. I understand."

"I'm sure we can work something out," said Charlie. He scribbled the Parments' address on a card and handed it to Burke. "Thank you for including us. We shall look forward to it."

* * *

Avery Burke made his way back to the passenger car and found his seat among the rows of maroon mohair. Pulling out a calfskin wallet, he fanned open a sheaf of papers and began reading, not so much out of a desire to study the information but as a means of avoiding any discourse with nearby passengers.

His eyes passed over several sentences of the stock description from the Chicago yards, but he was not really reading. He was thinking about Persis Allen. He didn't just vaguely remember her from that meeting on the street. The curve of her mouth and her gold-blond hair had burned themselves into his mind. And she had such an inquisitive, penetrating look. Since their chance encounter, he had repeatedly kicked himself for being tongue-tied, like a damn fool. He had walked down Pershing Street that afternoon muttering to himself, certain he would never see her again.

And now this turn of events. There was no doubt that Persis was completely smitten with Alex MacKinney. How could she not be? Even women who didn't have a chance of spending more than a few moments with him were dazzled by his good looks, his name, and his bravado.

His brow creased, however, as he recalled someone describing MacKinney as a "perfumed parlor snake." His own contacts with Alex had been brief but pleasant; still, he understood the sentiment behind the epithet. There's a trace of the dandy in Alex MacKinney, he thought, no question. And there was something else, something a little darker, but he had nothing to base it on.

What am I doing, he scolded himself, wondering about MacKinney and his pretty little fiancée? It's not my affair, and I'm plenty thankful for that.

He snapped the drooping papers back into focus and studied the description of the longhorns coming in from the Langley Ranch near San Antonio. "It'll be a slow drive," Langley had said, "so they'll be in excellent condition when you find them in Chicago."

It sounded good on paper, but Avery was familiar with the trail boss, a card player with a love for whiskey.

His thoughts drifted inexorably back to the young woman in the green suit. The suit, along with the ostentatious emerald, were forget-table, but not those green eyes.

She looks like a girl, he mulled. In spite of the upswept hair and the figure swelling beneath her fitted jacket, there was a complete lack of worldliness about her. If nothing else, this trip and some time spent in Montana Territory will make her grow up.

They were still a half-hour from Cleveland. Stuffing the papers back into the leather wallet and slipping it inside his coat, he cast a half-smile at the plump woman across the aisle. She put down her knitting, but before she could open her mouth, Avery slid his low-crowned felt hat over his eyes, hoping to empty his mind into the river of sleep.

On nights at the Double Diamond Ranch, sleep settled on Avery Burke like a Montana winter—deep, long, and still. But during cattle drives, train rides, or any other form of travel, sleep was a tangled rope, catching him up in knots of wakefulness and bittersweet memory.

Slumped in his seat on the train, those memories pulled him, as they often did, along a familiar road to the first cattle drive he and his younger brother Pete had ever made. Parts of the 1873 drive from San Antonio to Montana Territory were damned good to re-live—like the three days they had in Dodge City. We were no more than boys back then, Avery mused, every one of us on that drive!

Horse wrangler Deke Wakefield had baited and teased Avery for weeks about getting to Dodge City to "go in without knocking." Avery had no idea what the rawboned, prankish wrangler meant, but that evening in the spring of 1873, he found out.

It was their third and final night in Dodge. Most of the trail hands were clustered around tables at the Long Branch. The darker it got outdoors, the livelier the crowd became.

Avery pulled up a chair to join fellow trail hand Will Pokarney at a poker game. He was soon doing better than he had ever done at cards, but the man directly across the table from him, a local named Ruskin, made him nervous. Unable to shake the feeling that Ruskin was cheating, Avery shot stealthy glances at him whenever he could do so unobserved.

All the while, he kept one eye on his younger brother. About the time he thought Pete would pry a certain blond dancer away from the bar and move upstairs, Pete instead grabbed a bottle and sauntered over to join the game. Avery breathed a sigh of relief. Pete would turn seventeen that summer and had never been with a woman before. While it was no comfort to see his younger brother drink and play cards with a low form of frontier society, it somehow seemed better than watching him climb the stairs with the blond.

Within ten minutes, Avery's luck began to turn and he knew he ought to fold. They had just finished a hand in which Pete took a sizeable hit. It was Ruskin's turn to deal.

Pete's dark brows were knitted into a scowl and he was working his jaw. Avery knew that look well. It seemed to Avery, as he watched Ruskin shuffle, that Pete was going to chew out the inside of his cheek.

As soon as the last card had fluttered into place, Pete said, "Hold on a goddam minute there, Rusty. I've seen that one before."

Ruskin looked up, peering over spectacles that suddenly seemed like pure artifice to Avery. "The name is Ruskin. Larry Ruskin. And I certainly should hope you've seen a jack of hearts before," he added with a brusque laugh.

"I don't care if your name is Larry Long Branch. I think this deck is weighing a little heavy. What do you think, Avery?"

"Why don't we all just put our cards in the middle of the table and ask that nice lady over there to come and count them?" said Avery, motioning to the oblivious blond, who couldn't have counted the cards if her life depended on it.

"Not a bad idea."

"Do you imply that I'm cheating?" asked Ruskin, his voice even and hard.

"You're crooked as a dog's hind leg, you bastard," piped up Will Pokarney.

Ruskin calmly placed his cards on the table and dropped his hands down alongside his chair as if to get up.

"Avery, on the floor, look!" snapped Pokarney.

Avery had second-guessed the situation and had already tilted back his chair to watch Ruskin's hands. A card slipped from the man's sleeve and slid into the darkness under the table.

Ruskin leaped up and belted Avery hard across the chest, knocking him over. As his chair shot out from under him, his head whipped back and thudded on the floor. The table overturned and chips, bottles, and money flew everywhere. Pokarney lunged across the toppled table and grabbed Ruskin by the coat. Two strangers tried to pull Will off Ruskin, to no avail.

Stunned, Avery rolled out of his shattered chair and scrambled to his feet. Suddenly, someone big was restraining him. He bent forward, grasping the arms around his neck, and with a quick, rolling thrust, pitched his assailant over his head and onto another table. As the fellow landed, Avery saw it was one of the Long Branch's henchmen. The table cracked loudly and split down the middle. The big man fell in, sandwiched between the two broken halves.

Outside, gunshots split the air. Avery was certain Marshal George Peck was coming to reap his due. The gunshots got louder, and as the blazing bursts lit up the night, Avery saw a man on horseback coming full speed ahead, right into the saloon.

The house henchman, whose back was to the door, barely had time to turn around when the wild-eyed, frothing horse reared up and pawed the air less than a yard from his face. He stumbled out of the way, making quickly for the edge of the room. The entire place dissolved into roaring pandemonium. More gunshots doused the lights, but in the semi-darkness, Avery saw the wiry shape of the rider and made out the grinning face of Deke Wakefield.

Deke was on Pug, his best horse, and now Avery knew why. Deke winked, then urged the wide-eyed Pug into a couple of pirouettes, fired two more shots into the wall, then rode straight through the saloon toward the back door. As he passed the bar, he tossed a small pouch to the infuriated bartender. It landed on the bar with a faint but distinctive clink.

The entire spectacle was a bizarre combination of disrespect and courtesy; for Deke Wakefield, a floorshow for which a bit of rent must be paid. As Avery watched Pug's hooves fly out the back entrance, he stood motionless for a moment. "In without knocking," he murmured, a slow smile spreading over his face. The smile disappeared when a piece of kindling flew through the air and struck him on the shoulder. Plainly, it was time to flee.

He grabbed his hat and scooped up some coins off the floor, spun the bartender around, and thrust the money into his apron.

"Pete!" he shouted. "Let's get out of here!" They dashed out the back door just in time to hear glass breaking as Ruskin catapulted through a window into the alley. The small window frame gave way during the propulsion and lodged around Ruskin's shoulders like a yoke. Wrestling free, he hobbled away into the darkness.

The half moon shining overhead gave a pitiful allowance of light as Avery and Pete slunk away. Without a word, they jumped up on their mounts and urged them quietly toward the edge of town. Two or three miles out, they found Deke, and the three of them managed a laugh in spite of the fact that each of them was worried about news of the episode reaching the trail boss.

Now, aboard the Baltimore and Ohio, watching the light summer rain drift down the Ohio hills, Avery remembered the sound of raindrops spattering on their tent canvas after the adventure in Dodge. That rain had muffled their laughter and soothed them to sleep that night. Pete, Pete! He saw his brother's face, happy, even giddy, as it had been that night. If only they had known what that rain would come to mean.

* * *

As the train neared Chicago, flat farmland gave way to clusters of houses. Persis looked at the floor, then averted her eyes. The drift of crumbs she had seen on the carpet yesterday morning was still there. She was weary of it all, especially of her tiny overnight berth and of the oleaginous smell of people who needed baths.

It was high noon when they pulled into the station. Waving summer gloves or handkerchiefs against the oppressive humidity, women in fashionable dresses walked along the platform, accompanied by men in lightweight coats and linen vests.

At last, a real change of scenery! Persis nearly left her compartment without her bags. "What am I about?" she scolded herself and spun around, scooping up books, gloves, and her handiwork bag. A ball of cotton escaped and rolled out of sight, so she sank to her knees and bent low, her eyes level with the unpleasant carpet.

A slight cough came from behind her. Whirling like a startled cat, she fixed her eyes on Avery Burke. How long had he been standing there, watching her bustled *derriere*? Jumping up, she smoothed her silk skirt and held out her hand, revealing the ball of crochet thread in her palm.

"Errant little things, these." She dashed a strand of hair from her face, and as she did, it seemed to her she was also trying to dash away the pesky notion that she wanted him to confirm the dinner invitation he had issued earlier.

"Seems there's always a stray to round up," he said with a playful smile.

"I've come to give you and your brother my card," he said, sobering. "He's a good man, that brother of yours. I hope you'll both be able to accept my invitation to dinner. Please extend it to your friend Mrs. Allen and her parents."

"Thank you kindly, Mr. Burke, for repeating the invitation. We will certainly contact you at your hotel—the Midwestern—if it is possible."

Shuffling back to collect her things, she raised a sticky palm to her forehead and murmured, "I guess I don't quite know what I am about, do I?"

* * *

She spent part of the afternoon walking along the elegant oak-lined avenue where the Parments lived, trying to wring the knotty tension of travel and anticipation out of her limbs. Returning to her room, she wrote industrious letters to both her mother and Alex, apprising them of the pleasantness of the journey and the amenities of the Parment home. The intelligence imparted by Gilbert Windham was still in the forefront of her thoughts, but she resolved never to allude to it in her letters to Alex.

The next morning, Persis and Constance managed to get away from Anne-Marie and Winston Parment long enough to take a buggy ride.

"You look so happy!" Persis said, grasping Constance's hand. "Both you and Charlie look happy. I feel that I have everything I could ever want, just seeing the two of you so full of hope and excitement. But Constance, there's something you aren't telling me. You seem different."

Constance colored and turned her eyes forward. "Well, I do feel a little different. I think it's because I've—gained a few pounds. And now that we're here with *Maman* and *Papa* for a few days, I'll get even fatter," she laughed. "It's the midwestern way of life. It makes no difference if you are a cow or a person, you come to Chicago to get fat!"

Persis laughed. "You are not fat. You look splendid."

They turned onto a level road heading west. The houses fell gradually away, and they found a quiet lane with a place to water the horse. Constance threw a Turkish rug onto the grass and the two of them were soon gazing up through the aromatic branches of a Russian olive tree. Aside from the horse's tugging at the grass, they heard only the murmurous buzz of bees and the soft plashing of the creek.

"We've made our decisions, haven't we?" Persis said softly.

Constance lifted her head and looked at the pale blue horizon, where farmhouses and barns dwindled gradually into the distance. "Yes, we will go forward."

There it was again—a trace of strain in Constance's voice. Persis reached over and rested her hand lightly on Constance's fingers. "What are you thinking?"

Constance looked up sharply, almost furtively. Then she laughed. "Oh, I love you! You're the only person who ever asks me that."

"Well?"

"Percy—I do have something to tell you."

As Persis stared at Constance, prescience poured into her. She knew the words before Constance spoke them.

"I—I am going to have a baby." Constance looked at her, wide-eyed and sober.

"What!" Persis shrieked. She flung her arms around Constance.

Constance pulled back. "No one is to know, do you understand? I have kept silent ever since I knew. *Maman* doesn't know, nor does Charlie. I want it this way, at least until we get to Montana Territory."

"But why? Charlie should know, shouldn't he? And why can't you tell your mother? And why can't I embrace you, for heaven's sake?"

"You can embrace me, but—" she grasped both of Persis's hands. "I didn't think I'd have to defend myself with you."

"Defend yourself!" gasped Persis. "What do you mean? Can't I be excited?" She gathered Constance in her arms again. This time, Constance's arms tightened around her.

"My dearest, beloved Persis," Constance said, pulling away gently this time. "What would I do without you?"

"I won't say a word, Constance, if that's the way you want it."

"Good."

Persis appraised Constance's physique. "Do you think your mother suspects—"

"Don't even say it. If she does have an inkling, it is only an inkling. She is not one to pry."

"Have you been sick? How long has it been?"

"I haven't had my flux for over three months. Seeing Charlie only once this past spring made it very simple to calculate when the child was conceived. It was the week of March 24."

"Good Lord, a baby. You are further than I thought," Persis added, "and safe, too, by now."

"Safe? I wish that was certain. I don't care about myself, mind you, but the baby—"

As Persis opened her mouth, Constance put two fingers across her friend's lips. "Don't say it. The main reason I don't want Charlie to know is that he would probably insist that I stay in Chicago for my confinement. And that's probably what you were about to say." She took her fingers away and looked at Persis.

Persis compressed her lips and looked aside.

"Charlie coddles me so," Constance went on. "You all do. I'm no doll, damn it. I certainly don't want him to sit here with me for six months. He'd go mad. I mean to teach that brother of yours that I can be his wife, his partner, and the mother of his children, wherever the two of us make our home."

Persis swallowed the concern welling up in her throat. "I do understand. I mean, as much as anyone could." She thought of the clean white nurses' uniforms at the maternity hospital only a few miles away.

Constance caught the look. "Ah, you are worried too." She sighed. "I need you to be brave with me. Every woman who ever has a child must confront her own death as a possible outcome of it all. That's what you're afraid of, isn't it?"

"Constance! I wasn't thinking of death," Persis lied. There was desperation in her friend's vivid blue eyes. "I was thinking of who will attend you, and of how to make certain you get the best care." She paused, then added, "Maybe I am as worried as you say. If this is my reaction, I can imagine how Charlie and your parents would feel. I see your point."

"Thank you," said Constance.

"What matters," said Persis, "is that I am your devoted friend and will do my best to be what you need me to be. I understand, believe me. If something posed even the faintest threat to my making the journey west to meet Alex, I wouldn't tell a soul. Despite my concerns, I do understand."

Fanning herself with a clutch of ferns, Persis watched an obviously more relaxed Constance allow the horse to move at its own pace on the drive home.

"You are still worrying about your Alex, *n'est-ce pas?*" Constance asked, giving the reins a brisk shake.

Persis sighed. "Even though we aren't married, I feel betrayed." Her brow creased as she examined the bouquet she had gathered. "I'm hoping it was nothing more than a little horseplay before going into double-harness. That's a nice, vulgar expression my father used to use."

"For what it's worth, Percy, I don't see Alex being unfaithful."

The ferns waved languidly. "Constance."

"Hmm?"

"Avery Burke came by my cabin again before we left the train. He re-stated his wish for us to join him at dinner on Thursday. That's tomorrow—"

"Did he flirt with you?" Constance interrupted.

Persis raised the ferns to her face and peered through them. "I wouldn't tell anyone else in the whole world, but yes, perhaps a little."

"Was he overbold?" asked Constance, brows raised.

"He is not the type of man to be overbold, as you put it. But really, there aren't that many people in the Territory, and shouldn't we make as many friends as we can?" Her gaze drifted.

"Percy, you're looking like a minx just now, but it makes all the sense in the world that we spend time with Mr. Burke. Charlie will be delighted; he asked me about the dinner party just this morning." She lifted the reins again and sent a light ripple along the horse's backside.

* * *

Finally buttoned into a blackberry-colored damask gown with a revealing square neckline, Persis took a look in the mirror and was pleased with the effect, although she knew the absent Alex would not approve at all. The dress was new; something she had bought in Buffalo as part of her trousseau. Its cut was becoming, no doubt about it, and the cherry cordial the two women had been sipping had brought a rosiness to her usually pale cheeks.

"Constance," said Persis, "have you—I mean, after you get married, do you—when there are other men who seem to want to pay rather gallant attention to you, men that don't know you are married, do you ever find them attractive?"

Constance laughed. "It has only been four months, Persis! I am no authority on the vicissitudes of married life."

"Well, I haven't seen Alex for—well, since Christmas. And when men look at me with interest, I feel myself inwardly—well, I don't know how else to say it—responding."

"I once had a talk with Grandmere about this very thing," Constance said. "Can you imagine? As if the old girl could even remember what it was like to be our age!"

"What did the venerable Madame Gascogne have to say?" asked Persis.

"It was before I met you and Charlie. She told me that, during the course of her life, she'd had a great many men interested in her, even when she was married. I was sort of half-listening; you know how she goes on. But I did hear her final comment. And of course she had to poke me with her finger when she said it."

Persis laughed. "Of course."

"She said, 'Mark my words, *jeune fille,* there will always be men, and there may be opportunities for you to have the *liaisons,* the choice will be yours. But you must remember, for your own protection, that these feelings always pass.'"

Snapping her fan open, Constance added, "We have a soiree to attend. We're going to go and make friends and enjoy ourselves."

"Maybe I'd feel more settled inside if I wore something more sober," said Persis. "Gray, with a high neck."

"Don't condemn yourself for being a woman," said Constance, "or for wanting to be noticed. If you want to marry Alex, you shall. Even if you were to become involved in some brief flirtation—after all, you aren't married yet—I have a feeling that the excitement of it would more than suffice to . . . well, shall we say, subdue you."

"You are your grandmother's daughter, aren't you?"

"Besides, there will be some women at this party, and they'll be disappointed if you come all whaleboned up to the neck. Even though *we* know that upstate New York is a long way from Paris, *they* don't know it. Don't disappoint them. Good grief, it's quarter to five. I've got to get dressed."

* * *

It was a fine June evening, with no breeze to ruffle hair or dress. They were in the Parment's best open carriage, and Winston Parment took pains to wrap his wife, who was recovering from the ague, in a wool-and-silk shawl large enough for a piano. Ann Marie patiently submitted to this, winking at Persis. "He's a dear," she said, patting her husband's knee, "always looking after me. The way I know you girls will look after one another out West. It is a wonderful thing, this love that grows between two women." It was a gracious side note, but the injunction was clear.

Persis nodded vigorously, reaching over to squeeze Constance's hand. "Please rest assured, Anne-Marie. It will be our greatest pleasure."

Looking at a park with a jewel-like lake in its center, Persis saw well-dressed mothers and their small children tossing breadcrumbs to some swans. Chicago is so incredibly civilized; it does give a person pause when considering our frontier destination. She kept these thoughts to herself.

"Since its founding as a fur trading center in the early 1700s," said Anne-Marie, "Chicago has had plenty of time to gain a foothold of respectability in every sense, from architecture to economics. We sometimes think of ourselves as rivals with Saint Louis, striving to be a cultural oasis between the two seaboards."

Persis's heart skipped a tiny beat at the mention of Saint Louis, but she smiled brightly.

"If this Avery Burke is the young man I think he is," began Winston, "his family owns a pleasant home on the lakeshore, a mile or two from here."

Persis was startled. Avery Burke, with his rough ways and cautious manner? The one who trailed cattle up from the Pecos?

"He has done well, then," she said simply.

"Oh, my dear, no. Let me explain," said Winston. "He came by this house through very unfortunate circumstances. Both his parents were killed in a hotel fire in Omaha. Seven or eight years ago, I believe."

Persis was silent. Losing her father had been difficult. She couldn't imagine the pain of losing both parents at once. "How horrible," she murmured.

"It's very sad, even now," explained Anne-Marie. "As I understand it, he owns the house but has turned it over to his sisters."

"Their father was a livestock trader of good repute here in Chicago," said Winston. "Avery and his younger brother somehow convinced their parents to let them join a cattle drive a few years back. The younger brother was severely injured on the Platte River, but he survived. An irony that both the young men came through that ordeal only to see their parents so tragically taken."

"What is the brother's name?" Persis asked.

"Oh, now, if you hadn't asked, I would have been able to tell you," said Winston, rolling his eyes. "One of those Biblical names, like Paul or Peter."

Anne-Marie said, "Floss Bradford told me—and this is pure rumor—that Avery is going to use most of the Burke money to keep his sisters in the family home." Anne-Marie was solidly grafted into the social grapevine of Chicago, and her recent illness and influx of weekly visitors had freshened the harvest of information.

The Midwestern Hotel, an imposing structure of brick, slate, and wrought iron, appeared. As their coach came to a halt, Persis noticed an ornate buggy tied up nearby. "Look at that little conveyance! What would you call something like that?" she asked Winston.

The trim little buggy, lacquered in a shiny brown with bronze striping, was drawn by a dapple-gray that reminded Persis of her own beloved Astarte.

"That's called a *fiacre*," said Anne-Marie. "Or at least that's what Grandmere always called those *petite barouches*."

As Charlie helped each of the ladies out of the coach, Persis mused aloud, "It's so feminine. I wonder who owns it."

"It belongs to a horse-breeder from Missouri," said Anne-Marie. "Dartman family, I think."

Persis was carried along as the group swept up the stairs of the Midwestern toward the tall, warmly-lit French doors of the dining room. As Winston made introductions, Persis felt both men and women begin to notice her, a sensation that flowed through her veins like an intoxicant.

Just as she spotted Avery Burke near the private dining room, he also saw her. Resisting the impulse to look away, she held his gaze for a moment and nodded a greeting.

Burke took the hand of the attractive woman he was talking to and held it between both of his, excusing himself. As the woman turned to watch Avery leave, Persis saw her in full view. She wasn't just pretty, she was stunning. She was regally tall, wasp-waisted, and had a bosom that threatened to spill over the top of her bodice. Her dark eyes smoldered, but the most striking feature of her face was her mouth, full and sensuous, with a distinct v-shaped indentation at the center of her upper lip.

Constance drifted past on Charlie's arm and detected the focus of Persis's stare. "That's Miss Daltry," she whispered, "you know, the Baroness de Barouche." Constance let out a mischievous laugh and moved on through the small crowd.

Daltry? Anne-Marie had said the little barouche belonged to the Dartmans. In a blinding flash, reality hurled itself at Persis. *Miss Daltry.* Bess Daltry? The room grew suffocatingly hot. That impossible conversation she had with Windham back home in Mill Creek—it all came billowing back, oppressive and horrifying. Windham's hesitant, long face and mincing manner. And the object of Alex's affections, at least for one poisonous evening, was here. The mysterious libertine from St. Louis—this is she!

Stupefied, she could hardly collect herself to greet Avery Burke, who was quickly approaching. Before she knew it, he had her hand in his, bowing slightly. She snatched her hand away; after all, his hands had only seconds ago held the fingers of that woman, fingers that had—if Windham was right—touched Alex in ways too intimate to contemplate.

She could think of nothing except getting outdoors, but the French doors to the veranda seemed a mile away. The sooner she made some polite conversation with Avery Burke, the sooner she could retreat.

"Miss Allen, are you well?" he asked. "You're looking . . . warm."

"I—I am warm, thank you, Mr. Burke." She tried to keep her breath even and inaudible, not an easy task, with her chest heaving and her head growing lighter by the second.

"I was just about to step outdoors for a few minutes," she said. "Allow me to compliment you on your taste in hotels. I have been very favorably impressed with the architecture of Chicago." She flashed him a quick smile. "The Midwestern is one of the city's finest ornaments."

"Take my arm, won't you? It is blasted hot in here. I don't know what possessed me to have so many people here tonight. It started out as a small party—in fact, when I invited you, there were only eleven. Somehow the list grew to more than thirty, and now it feels like three hundred." He stopped short and looked in her eyes. "Don't mistake me—I'm glad you came."

"Oh, please don't apologize." The more the better, under these circumstances, she thought.

They found their way to the front of the hotel, where twilight met them with its curtain of cool air. Escape was hers, even if it was just a reprieve. She loosened her lace shawl and felt the evening settle around her shoulders.

"We'll soon move into the dining room, which has windows on either side," said Burke, "and although there is no breeze tonight, the cross-draft helps."

Persis forced herself to concentrate on what he was saying. There will be another time to think about Madame Daltry, she admonished herself. Setting her tension aside, she took in Burke's physical aspect. He wore a fashionable gray jacket over a camel-colored waistcoat. There was no air of bodily constraint about him—none of the stiffness she saw in Charlie, who habitually tugged at his high collar.

Even Alex, despite his urbane aplomb, carried himself with a boyish puffery and a dash of swagger. There was an ease about Burke that Persis found both authentic and disarming.

"We drove past your family home today," Persis said lightly, hoping he had not noticed her assessing him. "I am so sorry about your parents. How hard these last years must have been on you and your sisters." She wanted to add, "and your brother," but refrained.

"I appreciate you mentioning it," he said. A spear of pain shot across his gray eyes. He shifted his drink from one hand to the other and back again. "I think it takes a little courage to bring it up. Thanks."

After a moment, she asked, "Will you keep the house in the family? It would be a shame to sell it."

"I've sold all of my parents' legacy I intend to," he said with conviction.

"It—not just the house or the stock business, but all of your family's history—must mean a great deal to you," said Persis.

Despite her resolve and her genuine desire to know this man better, her composure began to bend like a candle flame in the cold draft of Bess Daltry. Staring at the lengthening shadows on the lawn, she longed to drift into a meaningless discussion with anyone other than Avery Burke.

With a gush of gratitude, she saw Constance and Charlie moving toward them along the darkening veranda.

"Is this what they mean by 'gloaming'?" Persis called out, directing the question at no one in particular. "I mean, this hour of the day? I have always liked the expression."

The four of them clustered at the end of the wide porch where Persis shrank against the rail and allowed Constance to carry the conversation.

Fear nipped at her. What do you *think* would happen if you put a man of Alex's looks and charisma with a woman of her figure and magnetism? As the white heat of jealous passion boiled up, a strangely pleasant spite rose from her viscera.

Through the window, she saw Bess Daltry and her cortege of male admirers choose their table. She sighed audibly and made rapid plans to find a table on the opposite side of the room. "Let's go in now," she said, eager to put her strategy into effect. With an iron will, she vowed to illuminate the west side of the dining room more brilliantly than the celebrated Miss Daltry could shine on the east.

Constance tilted her head and gave her an interrogatory look. "Let's do."

Once seated, Persis took a sip of wine, endorsing the mischievous thoughts in her head. She was wittier than usual and before long was enjoying herself immensely. For the next two hours, she dazzled everyone at the table.

All the while she knew, deep within, that this flash of social efful-gence and coquetry was fueled by jealousy. Still, she moved on, grace-ful and unhurried, her spirits sailing. She let out a soft peal of laugh-ter at something Burke said and caught the knowing and suspicious gaze of Constance out of the corner of her eye.

"What do you hear of late from your fiancé?" asked Burke.

Persis had been trying very hard not to think about Alex. "I re-ceived a letter from him just before we left Dunkirk last week," she said lightly. "He intends to meet us in Cheyenne on the first of July. We'll celebrate the Fourth of July there and leave shortly afterward for Montana Territory."

She found herself twisting the corner of her napkin and dis-creetly set it aside. "Those are our plans at this time," she added, "but things are always subject to change when Alex is involved. Some people say he is impulsive, but those who know him realize it is his zest for life."

"I understand things are going better with the Utah and Northern railroad," said Burke, steering his remarks away from any characterization of Alex MacKinney. "When I left Montana last May, the terminus had moved quite a few miles north, all the way to Red Rock. That's progress, however slow it may seem to the impatient residents of the Territory."

"How far north from the Territorial line is Red Rock?" she asked Burke, hoping to gauge the progress of the little mountain railroad that so consumed the interests of remote westerners, Wall Street barons, and her future husband.

"Red Rock is, I'd say, about 30 miles north of the border. That means that the rails are going down at a rate of about four miles a week. I left Montana on May 6, seven weeks after the rails hit the border." Everyone in the Territory knew the snail's pace at which the rail construction moved. Burke watched this uncomfortable knowledge sink into Persis, who was staring at her wine glass.

Tapping her on the arm, he said, "Come with me; there is someone I'd like you to meet." He guided her with a light touch on the elbow across the room.

Persis had just begun shaking off her preoccupation with her uncertain future when she found herself confronted with the corporeal warmth of Bess Daltry. She was certain anyone looking at her chest could see the skin vibrating with every beat of her heart. Despite the heat, she pulled her lace fichu closer around her shoulders.

Avery greeted Bess, then turned to Persis and introduced her, saying, "May I present Persis Allen. She is engaged to Alexander MacKinney and is on her way to meet him in Cheyenne. She and I met on the train out of Dunkirk. Small world, isn't it?"

Persis was ready, studying Bess's reaction intently. The faintest flicker of dismay passed across the woman's alabaster features. My suspicions are validated at every turn, thought Persis.

She smiled brilliantly. "Are you from Chicago, Miss Daltry?" she asked circuitously, buying a moment in which to fortify her composure.

"No, though I sometimes wish I were," came the reply. "I live in St. Louis and I am here on business."

I won't ask her what kind of business, thought Persis, her eyes drifting for a split-second down to the dark blue satin that captured Bess Daltry's spectacular bosom.

Avery Burke put in, "Miss Daltry's work is similar to my own, in a way." He smiled as Bess let out a low laugh. "More refined, without a doubt, I hasten to add. She specializes in thoroughbred horses."

Persis raised her eyebrows with feigned interest.

Avery continued, "Her animals are much more remarkable than mine, and Bess is becoming very well known."

In the Biblical sense, no doubt, thought Persis, detecting attar of roses on Bess's white skin.

Bess laughed again, dropping her dark lashes for a moment and squeezing Avery's arm. They exchanged what Persis thought was a familiar glance. Perhaps she also numbers Avery among her paramours, thought Persis, feeling roundly defeated.

Unexpectedly, Avery was called away to another table. The full focus of Bess Daltry was upon her.

"You are on your way to a reunion with Al—Mr. MacKinney, then?" asked Bess.

"Yes. We're to be married in Cheyenne," Persis said with unconcealed pleasure. "On our honeymoon, we intend to visit the site of the proposed national park—Yellowstone." She didn't know if this was even possible, but she liked the sound of it.

"How wonderful!" said Bess. "I think you will find Cheyenne very pleasant. I have been there several times but have yet to see the wonders of Yellowstone. Someday soon, perhaps."

"Do you conduct business in Cheyenne?" asked Persis, adding, before she could stop herself, "Your horses, I mean."

Bess cast her a look that clearly meant she was stepping carefully. "Yes, I do. I recently sold several animals to Douglas Irwin there, and a pair of geldings to your fiancé."

This forthright acknowledgement of a pre-existing relationship with Alex was violently disquieting. Making a conscious effort to close her slack jaw, Persis glanced around and saw that the guests were beginning to disperse. To her immense relief, Constance was motioning to her.

"If you'll excuse me, my companions are ready to leave," she said, her breath coming in rapid little puffs. "It was . . . lovely to meet you, Miss Daltry. It is hard to say whether we will meet again."

"I'm going out that same way," said Bess. "I'll walk with you."

Suddenly, Bess laid a lace-gloved hand on Persis's arm with meaningful firmness. Startled, Persis turned to look at her. The violet eyes were wide and full of intent. "You are a very beautiful woman," said Bess. "Alexander is fortunate to have you." She paused. Her eyes flickered away and she compressed her full lips. "I—" she began, looking Persis straight in the eye again, "I don't know you at all, but please be assured that I would very much like to be a friend to you. If there is ever anything I can do for you, will you contact me? Do you feel that you could?"

Staring back, Persis nodded dumbly.

Bess grasped Persis's fingers tightly in her own for a long moment. Then quickly, with a rustle of satin skirts, she left the room.

Persis wandered toward the door, her hand trailing along the tops of the chairs as she tried to make sense of what had just happened. Bess Daltry was nowhere in sight, like Cinderella gone at the stroke of twelve.

Avery Burke was locked in a conversation with several cigar-smoking men. As his eyes met hers, he touched the brim of his hat in farewell.

Constance and Charlie were beside her now, walking her outdoors into the humid summer night.

Winston Parment met them at the carriage and announced, "There's a storm whipping up over the lake. These things come down from Canada on a regular basis, courtesy of Her Highness Victoria. I think we'll take the short route home."

Persis twisted the ends of her fichu and sank into a corner seat. Bess either wanted something from her or was trying to find a way to remain connected to Alex—through her—after the upcoming marriage. The woman had clearly been anxious, even fearful. Anxious about what? Persis had banked heavily on a solid, black-and-white dislike of Bess, and the enigmatic woman had made that impossible.

Her thoughts around Avery Burke were almost as disturbing. He seemed to be giving her new adventure a sort of gentlemanly benediction, yet there were innuendoes of restraint and ambivalence. I can't understand these new acquaintances of mine, she thought, shaking her head. Her mind drifted westward, dwelling more comfortably for the rest of the evening on Alex. She spun images of him past her inward eye, listening to the infectious laugh and the pragmatic wit that charmed both grimy laborers and white-handed men of money. She saw the honey-brown eyes and the flashing smile, she saw the dripping wet hero who plucked the tyke from the lake and who probably saw himself in every bad boy on the street. She imagined his arm around her waist and exulted in the intoxication of being with him, of being his chosen companion. Life with Alex would never be boring.

*   *   *

They arrived at Council Bluffs, Iowa, two days later. Before crossing the muddy Missouri to board the Union Pacific in Omaha, Persis called at the Council Bluffs postal desk, as Alex had instructed. There she was given a letter from him and a heavy oilskin envelope containing a dark-blue leather wallet full of large bills.

Persis read aloud, "'The three of you should spend the night across the river in Omaha. This way, you can rise early and have your pick of the sleeping berths on the Union Pacific the next morning.'"

"He has obviously done this a few dozen times before," Charlie observed.

Constance nodded her head. "It's good advice."

Persis continued, "'The quiet and refined company you've enjoyed up to this point will undoubtedly change. For this reason it's important to take steps to assure that your traveling companions are as agreeable as possible.'"

"The adventure begins," said Constance, taking in a quick breath and drawing her right hand unconsciously toward her belly.

"'You might be surprised to know how many Union Pacific employees I've forewarned that you three are en route to Cheyenne,'" Alex's message continued. "'Use my name as much as possible and tip the porters generously. It will make a difference. I will be waiting in Cheyenne on the first of July . . .'"

"The rest of the letter is rather personal," Persis said, stuffing it back into the envelope.

At the new depot, the people on the wooden platform were a jumble of races, cultures, and livelihoods. Persis saw Alex's signature in everything about her, from the shining brass rails under the lunch counter to the ivory vellum of the tickets she held in her kid gloves. Even the rhythmic clatter of the iron wheels on the rails repeated his name, "Al-ex, Al-ex." Proud of her attachment to this great endeavor, she looked around. This train would go all the way to San Francisco and would, prior to arriving there, stop at dozens of places, unloading miners, settlers, and adventurers.

* * *

The next morning, dressed in a dark gray poplin traveling suit with a matching straw hat, she felt that she looked very smart. As she reached up to adjust a hatpin, she saw one of the laggards near the end of the platform watching her. She stared back as coldly as she could, then raised her chin and turned away.

Constance and Charlie appeared with not one but two porters, each towing a large cart of baggage. Persis felt the eyes of the immigrants boring into her and her companions. Their expressions ranged from ennui to scorn.

The Pullman car was elegantly furnished in walnut with velvet draperies in dark blue and gray. Brass wall sconces appeared frequently along the aisle. The illumination was startling, almost excessive, thought Persis.

The porter made a short bow. "We received a telegram from Mr. MacKinney two days ago, who asked that these quarters be reserved for you. They are the finest the UP has to offer its westward-bound passengers. Which one of you ladies is Miss Allen?" he asked.

"I am," answered Persis.

"Please follow me," he said, ushering her down the narrow hallway into a small, bright room with a sofa, a slipper chair, and built-in chest of drawers. "Another porter will come in at bedtime and convert the seating space into a bed."

He quickly withdrew, disappearing before Persis even thought to tip him. I'll make up for it later, she resolved, wanting fervently to observe the rules of railway etiquette.

With ten minutes before the final whistle, Persis got off the train to have a look around. As she walked the length of the train, she saw that the shiny Pullman cars each had a name, like "Gypsy" and "Voyager," in bronze enamel on the sides.

She kept walking, somehow drawn to the last few cars, reserved for immigrants. They were nearly full, crowded with men, women and children, all looking for a seat on the wooden benches. The air was filled with the mingled smells of perspiration, tobacco smoke, and dried urine.

Coffee was brewing on a small stove at the end of one of the cars, providing the only pleasant odor. Nearby, a couple of men played cards on the floor. A few tin lanterns hung along the walls. At the far end was a boxed-in toilet, intended to serve the entire car.

A porter brushed by her carrying several straw-filled mattresses. He climbed aboard the car and began bargaining with the passengers. Persis saw a woman with a bruised cheek, holding a baby, trying to understand the porter.

"How much?" she said in a thick accent, holding her thumb against her fingers in the universal sign for money. She succeeded in getting a mattress for two dollars. A ridiculous price for a tick of straw, Persis thought.

Where on earth will they all sleep? Persis wondered, retreating toward the Pullmans. When she reached her compartment, it seemed lavish and sinful. She felt even guiltier when she saw the basket of food that had been stowed alongside her sofa. There was boiled ham, baked chicken, cream cake, nut bread, and a small crock of butter.

She looked down at her hand and stared at the emerald. Although her family had always been able to afford a lakeside home, fine horses, and household help, she had never felt rich. Now, away from the uncomfortable sights of the immigrant cars and looking at a bright future, a pleasurable sense of entitlement stole through her.

In my own way, she thought, I knew what that poor woman was feeling as she bargained for that mattress. But am I like her? In some ways I am, I suppose. But if I took everything I owned and divided it up among the poor people on this train, it wouldn't improve their lots in life by much. My own life has not been one of luxury, but there is nothing wrong with aspirations. I'm sure that young woman with the baby has aspirations of her own.

My life is blooming into prosperity, she averred. If this is any taste of what it will be like living with Alex in Montana Territory, I shall be just fine, she thought, taking a bite of cake.

* * *

As the UP threaded its way deeper into the frontier west, Persis thought infrequently of Avery Burke and at times had to struggle to remember what he looked like. As Burke's visage melted into the gaslight recollections of Chicago, she was able to think of him in nearly neutral terms and to wish him well.

Late on the second afternoon, the three travelers met a passenger who was on his way back to Montana Territory after visiting the family home in Pennsylvania. His name was Cyrus Dern. He explained that he and his wife Polly lived in Butte City, the mining camp that interested Charlie, and had been trying to make a go of it with a small silver mine.

"What can you tell us about Montana? Although you live in Butte City, can you tell us anything about Helena?" asked Persis, delighted to have a living testament who might sharpen some of the fuzzy images she had culled from the territorial newspapers.

"You're traveling to Cheyenne? I guess that gives me enough time to get started on it all," chuckled Dern. "It's a big territory, and a lot has happened in the last five or six years." He turned to Charlie. "What did you say you'd be doing there?"

"Mining," said Charlie. "I'm a structural engineer. We'll be in your area, Butte City, mostly. My sister will be settling in Helena with her husband-to-be, Alex MacKinney. It's about a two-day stage ride between Helena and the Butte mining camp, correct?"

"Less than two days, really," said Dern. "The road's better than it used to be, which is a relief. Not as much of a relief, obviously, as we will all feel when the Utah and Northern is finished," he added. "People squawk about the new railroad being narrow gauge, but it's probably the best design for snaking through all those mountains. No matter what they say, being connected by rails to Salt Lake City and the Union Pacific will change everything. We'll be part of the United States at last."

"Well," he said, rising from his seat, "my Polly doesn't like to be left alone for long. She's already homesick at having to leave Pennsylvania and head back to the Territory." He gave a half-smile and touched the brim of his hat. "I'm sure we'll talk again."

* * *

Evening came to the grasslands of Nebraska. Tall, wavy, grass extended as far as the eye could see. At times it looked deep green, yet when the wind laid it flat, a silver bolt shot through it and left traces of red. An occasional bird arced through Persis's field of vision, and sometimes a wisp of song lilted in. There was something hypnotic and beckoning about the endless continuum of the horizon and the texture of the open prairie. She wanted to touch it all—no, not merely touch it—she wanted to feel the satin softness of the tall grasses sliding along the length of her body, to let their verdant tide wash her cheeks, her lips, her soul. I thought I loved the rolling hills and silvery lakes of New York State, she marveled, but this! The landscape of the west is awakening something in me.

At dusk, just before the sun touched the horizon, each silhouetted blade of grass, every tree and fence post were rimmed with rose-gold. I hope it's like this in Montana, she thought wistfully. Or could it possibly be more beautiful? As she watched the sunset braze a coral red line along the horizon, an odd and yet deeply familiar feeling came over her. It seemed that she was not observing external objects but instead beholding some aspect of herself.

She placed her fingertips upon the glass, aching to comprehend it all more deeply. She knew that the long, sinuous grasses, the dark, diving swallows, and the roseate sky were all some kind of living fabric. Only a thin, diaphanous cloud separated her from being drawn into the beating heart of it all.

At the railhead just north of Red Rock, Montana Territory, Alex MacKinney heaved his suitcase into the baggage car of the southbound Utah and Northern Railroad, the first leg of his trip to Cheyenne.

After finding his seat, he snapped open a copy of the Helena *Herald*. He could only read a few sentences at a time, however, before someone stopped in the aisle to slap him on the shoulder or shake his hand. The conductor thanked him for locating two new locomotive engines, a merchant from Butte City asked about a shipment of nail kegs from Saint Louis, a highly-powdered woman from Helena introduced her seven-year-old daughter, and so on.

It was the same everywhere he went; he didn't mind it in the least. A born deal-maker with a prodigious amount of personal charm, he was equally at home behind the heavy doors of a boardroom as he was in a chair near the parlor hob.

His forthright manner and charisma made him perfect for working with the Mormons, who were among the Utah and Northern's top financiers. When they opened their business meetings with a prayer, Alex was the first to bow his head.

He had read just enough Mormon literature to understand some of their religious terms, and to the astonishment of Brigham Young's entourage, he once laughingly declared that the Mormon railroad men were more "stiffnecked" than all the Eastern capitalists combined. The dour patriarchs glanced at one another as tension filled the air. Finally, one elder began to chuckle and soon the whole room was laughing.

As Utah and Northern construction alternately flagged and progressed, Alex and Sam Hauser became the chief proponents of a Territorial subsidy. Combining their forces, they cajoled everyone from the Territorial Governor to the barons of Wall Street. Alex was everywhere, at dance halls and summer picnics, weddings and funerals, barn-raisings and Christmas balls, promising Montanans that the value of their real estate would double as soon as the U&N was finished.

He took advantage of frequent construction delays to establish MacKinney Freighters. At the very least, he reasoned, he could keep himself afloat while politicking for the rails. But with so much cargo moving in and out of the Territory, he did more than stay afloat. The business flourished. Hell, it even paid to haul scrap lumber into Butte City to fuel the smelting process.

Alex soon heard of Marcus Daly and his mining-town rival, Will Clark. The more competition, the better, Alex felt. His eyes shone with excitement as he saw the hills of Butte City burgeon with shanties, taverns, boarding houses, hoisting works and the infamous roasting pits, where tons of timber were burned to reduce raw silver ore. Stinks like the devil down there at times, he thought, but it's a hell of a good time. A glorified mining camp with big ideas, that's Butte City.

He had heard recent rumors about an elite men's club being formed. Someday, he vowed, I'll have a seat at those private games and drink late-night brandies with the likes of Daly and Clark.

The way Alex saw it, he had two enormous blessings. The first of these was an almost limitless ability to adapt, and the second was an unremitting serendipity that had opened doors for him all his life.

Drawing an ornately engraved flask out of his coat pocket, he took a quick pull of his favorite Scotch whiskey. And why, he asked himself, should marriage be any different? Things will go well for us. I'm thirty-two years old; God knows I looked long enough for the right woman.

Persis was beautiful and intelligent—perhaps a trifle bookish—but modern women were wearing that kind of sophistication well these days. Even bookishness could be fashionable, as long as it did not create a shrew. Persis was neither. She had a spark, a clearly independent spirit. He liked that, but he would not have liked it without the balancing effects of her compassion and devotion. She was a remarkable composition.

He had begun the New Year hungry for her, and now, at the end of June, these feelings burned within him again. The very rhythm of the rails stirred him to thoughts of the marriage bedchamber.

The train was now out of the mountains, rocking easily through the valleys of southern Idaho. Accustomed to napping through this uneventful stretch, Alex turned his thoughts to the White Horse Hotel and, speculating idly about who might be in attendance at that popular water hole, fell into a doze.

* * *

The next morning, Persis asked Constance to help lace her corset.

"You're as jittery as I have ever seen you," Constance said as she tugged on the laces.

"Of course I'm nervous. I'm not going to pretend. The excitement of seeing him all but overwhelms me. And then all that nonsense about Bess Daltry and possibly others; it's haunting. But I'm drawn to this brilliant, flickering flame of a man. What if I'm a stupid moth, about to get my wings singed?"

"Persis," said Constance, leaning forward, "You've got it backwards. You are the light. He is the moth. You don't see it, but I do."

Persis let out a little laugh. "Oh, Constance," she said. "How you look at things! I adore you."

Persis pushed Constance gently out the door and watched her navigate the aisle toward her compartment. Lately, Constance looked so vulnerable. Persis now had a powerful second reason for wanting to reach the Territory as soon as possible. Charlie needed to know about the baby.

She finished dressing, slipping into a white mull shirtwaist and finally the new tailored blue jacket with black piping and the full, bustled blue skirt. As she reached into her toilet case and pulled out a tiny pot of lip rouge, her heart began to pound furiously. I can't help it, she thought anxiously. I want Alex to be completely smitten with me.

It was nearly five o'clock when they pulled into the Cheyenne station. Her heart raced. Should I sit at the window, she wondered, or is that too obvious? But if I'm not near the window, perhaps he'll notice and think I'm not eager to see him.

She couldn't possibly sit down, she decided, so she stood, holding a handrail for balance as the train slowed. Her eyes scanned the platform, but a throng of discouragingly dusty people obscured her view.

Then she saw him. The moment her eyes found his face in the crowd, a surge of energy pulsed through her, and her entire body remembered how she felt that day in Dunkirk. He was like no other man. There was such a cheerful air of distinction and elegance about him. The contrast he created with the homespun surroundings was remarkable. There, among the drab tans and grays, the dull leathers, the linsey-woolsey and the canvas jackets, stood Alex MacKinney, nearly six feet tall, wearing a dark gray frock coat and straight, pin-striped trousers. He lifted his hat to a passing couple and the sun shone on his bronzed curls.

She said stiffly, "I see him."

Charlie put his arm around her quaking shoulders. Persis glanced up at him, breathing unevenly. He let his arm drop and Persis moved resolutely forward.

Constance said nothing, smiling serenely as her friend stepped down from the Union Pacific Palace Car into the waiting arms of Alexander MacKinney.

* * *

After breakfast, Alex pulled Persis into the shadows of the hotel cloakroom. "We're together," he murmured, his lips in her hair. "I can't believe it. I lay awake half the night thinking about you just down the hall."

Scandalously happy that he felt so free with her after their long months apart, all Persis wanted at that moment was to be kissed. With her eyes closed and her cheek against his lapel, she inhaled the citrus scent of his cologne and the just-pressed crispness of his collar. She laid her hand against his throat and traced his jaw with her fingertips.

His hand flew up and grabbed hers. "Stop," he said, "you're making me think impure thoughts."

"You scoundrel," she said, laughing. "You don't need any help in that regard."

"I can't wait to get you into the carriage after the wedding." He pulled her close again and took a wet, playful bite of her lower lip, holding it for a moment and then letting it slip away. "Speaking of the wedding," he said, holding her slightly away and looking in her eyes, "I met with the minister at the Methodist church in Helena last week. He suggested Saturday, August 7th."

Still dizzy from the feel of his mouth on hers, Persis trembled. Married, in less than a month. The idea was incredible, but she had given it more than enough thought. There would be no backward glances. "Yes," she said with a smile that she hoped looked more demure than anxious. "August 7th. That sounds wonderful."

"But just now," he said, "I'm afraid I have some business to take care of."

"Oh. Of course."

"I'll see you after lunch, then. That will leave you and Constance the entire morning to shop, discuss weddings, fashion, and other topics of interest to the feminine mind."

It was as if her ankle had been snagged by a hidden tendril of nettles. She looked at him, taking in his grin and his dancing eyes, and easily let go of her irritation. It was an affectionate comment, after all, she allowed. Alex knows full well that I have a mind capable of far more than poring over fashion plates.

"Wait," Alex said. "If you're going shopping, you'll need this." He pressed a tightly-folded wad of bills into her hand, saying, "Buy the most elegant things you can find. It might be a challenge here in Cheyenne," he added, "but it would be even more so in the Territory. Have you a good coat? It gets bitterly cold up North. Take me seriously."

Persis was startled. She still had at least a hundred and fifty dollars in the blue leather wallet she had picked up in Omaha. She looked at the folded money, then up at him. Her face broke into a grateful smile. "You are so kind! So generous! It isn't nec—"

He put his finger up to her lips, and she felt the core of her body twist with a strange sweetness at his touch.

"Hush, now. We are together. I love you and I'm going to take care of you always." He leaned down and kissed her once more. "I'll see you later this afternoon. No talking to strangers," he added, lightly chucking her under the chin.

As he walked away, Persis breathed out a long sigh. In spite of their delightful flirtation and immense attraction to one another, she felt like a bird circling an unfamiliar meadow, trying to find a safe place to perch.

Shopping proved a fine distraction. By noon, she and Constance had not only found several dresses but a fur-trimmed cloak. Then they combed the shelves of Marks & Myers Dry Goods and bought an assortment of what they both called "serviceable" clothing, including a supply of maternity smocks for Constance, which they requested be wrapped into brown parcels.

* * *

The next afternoon, on the last leg of their Union Pacific journey to Utah, a portly, garrulous woman from the Denver area seated herself across from Persis and Alex and began spinning tales.

"Oh, the Rocky Mountains is rough all right, but things is a lot better than they used to be," said the woman. "I come out in '69 with the Mister. Chauncey. Gold, you know, on Cripple Creek."

Persis, smiling politely, gave her a blank look.

"Colorado. Cripple Creek, the gold camp," the woman said, raising her eyebrows.

"Oh, of course," said Persis. She could feel Alex's amused eyes on her.

"Chauncey got the typhoid only three months after I got in. Gawd, what a place that was. Not an ounce of physick for a dyin' man. Did everything I could. When the doctor finally come, he said I done a good job but there weren't nothin' left to help 'im. I was glad to know I had done right by 'im, God rest his soul. Ground was so hard we had to leave 'im in the shed 39 days 'fore we could bury 'im. T'weren't no life for a woman, nor a man, for that matter, far as I'm concerned. Yes, things is better now."

Alex looked at Persis and winked. "A glass of wine?"

Persis hesitated. She wasn't accustomed to wine before dinner, but it sounded like a good idea. "Yes; that would be fine. Something lighter than port, though, if they have it."

Alex turned to Mrs. Chauncey, who smiled up at him eagerly. "Don't mind if I do, thank ye kindly," she said warmly.

After Alex had left for the saloon car with Charlie, Mrs. Chauncey resumed her narrative. "You'll find things a sight better than most women have found them. O' course, sensitive girls such as yourself will still find plenty to shrink from."

Persis couldn't stop the corners of her mouth from turning upward.

Speaking in a deeply maternal tone, Mrs. Chauncey leaned forward again. Persis watched the fabric of her travelling jacket strain against its large abalone buttons. It seemed a perilous proposition, that jacket. "Back East," said Mrs. Chauncey, "I never run into any twilight fairies 'tall, you know, just on average. But here ye will. They's everywhere."

Persis decided to dismiss this nonsense. The poor old thing must be addled.

"Twilight fairies?" asked Constance, never one to hide an ingenuous nature.

Mrs. Chauncey responded matter-of-factly, "Why, yer handmaidens of Terpsichore."

Constance and Persis exchanged baffled looks.

"Terpsichore," said Persis, "was the Greek goddess of song and dance. Oh, you mean—"

"Ladies of the evening," Constance said.

"I kin see yer sensitive to the subject," said Mrs. Chauncey with a look of prudent condescension. "But ye'd best be warned about this sort o' thing. As I was saying, they's everywhere out here. And ye can't blame 'em, really. There ain't enough fine homes for women to get work as domestics. There's a lot o' men, 'specially in the mining towns. A lot o' single men."

Persis's cheeks were burning. Contemplation of this sorrowful livelihood led to horrific images and to thoughts of Bess Daltry.

"I don't agree with you, Mrs. Chauncey," Persis said boldly. "There are plenty of other occupations available to young women who are in earnest about supporting themselves. Why, a young woman could be gainfully employed in a dressmaker's shop, or even as a seamstress out of her own home. Plenty of women teach. Even if schools are few in number, ladies can teach music or elocution."

"How old are ye, my dear?" asked Mrs. Chauncey absently, straightening the crumpled silk flowers on her hat.

"Twenty-three," said Persis quickly. Too quickly, she realized. "Why would you ask such a thing? Do you think me naive?"

"It don't matter what I think, dearie, not really. It's jus' that when yer as old as meself and ye've seen what I seen, 'specially out here. Well, I used to think them girls ought to get outen that pit and do something respectable. Now I think different. I mean, it'd still be good fer them—fer everyone, I 'spect—if'n they could be occupied otherwise. But I seen so many of 'em, and I'll shock ye when I say this . . . I've known a few of 'em too, quite personal, from the lowest lows in yer canvas and leather all the ways up to the feathered hat variety, with rooms o' their own. But I don't judge 'em. Not any more."

It was a relief to see Charlie and Alex coming down the aisle. A steward followed close behind, carrying a silver tray full of cocktails.

"A *kir*, my dear? Ah! I am a poet!" Alex said with a laugh. "It's very light. White burgundy with a splash of cassis—or in this case, port. It was the best I could do."

The steward handed a glass of wine to Mrs. Chauncey, who threw caution to the wind and downed it in a few short gulps. Within minutes, Persis noted with profound gratitude, Mrs. Chauncey was nodding over her well-corseted chest.

* * *

At last the train pulled into Corinne, Utah. Alex was animated, visibly excited to show Persis and the others his freight office and other favorite haunts. After meeting the MacKinney Freighters manager, Carl Preston, and seeing the newest wagons and fleet of draft horses, the group lunched at the White Horse Hotel.

Over her lunch of oyster stew, Persis ventured an observation about one of the draft horses. "It was one of the bay-colored Belgians," she said to Alex, when he could not remember the beast.

"I forgot you knew your horses," Alex said. "Yes, now I recollect the one. You didn't fancy him, did you?"

"As a pleasure horse? Of course not," Persis said, a little indignant. "I mention him because I saw a wound about the left hind fetlock. It looked to be festering. With everything Carl must keep track of, will he notice this?"

Alex raised his eyebrows. "If you wish, we can ride back to the office and you can tell him yourself."

Alex's tone was deferential, but Persis had the uncanny sense that she was treading where perhaps she shouldn't. "No," she murmured. "It's all right. If it continues to trouble me"—she cast a glance at Alex, who was intent on his fried chicken—"I will post a letter to Carl. That is, if you think he won't be offended."

"I should think he would be delighted that you have taken such an interest," Alex smiled. He looked around the table and shifted the subject. "We'll take a Gilmer and Salisbury coach to Helena. A *Concord* coach, mind you. The best there is."

In the morning, they made ready by lantern light. When they emerged onto the street, the cool air was thick with the smell of wood smoke, bacon, coffee, and the sweat of horses and oxen. The piles of freight at the stage station were astonishing. There weren't just a few boxes and sacks, there were mountains of crates, furniture, barrels, canvas and leather bags, nail kegs, and casks, all stacked into tall, precarious columns. A line of wagons stood nearby, where a half dozen unshaven men were strategically stuffing as many articles as they could into each wagon.

These wagons were not the buckboard conveyances that she had seen in the East. They were true freight wagons, like miniature box cars, each one manned with a driver, two attendants, and a large team of horses or oxen. Full, they towered with articles of all shapes and descriptions jammed into place and lashed with ropes.

Persis saw that three of the six wagons were emblazoned with "MacKinney Freighters." Alex, talking with his drivers, was doing what he did so well, making each of them think he was the best of the lot. She smiled as she remembered her first glimpse of him hunched in the driver's box of the dray that rattled down the hill into the brick-paved lot of Dunkirk station.

Watching the bustling scene, she wondered how the upcoming change—the transition to rail freight—would affect Alex. His was an extremely lucrative livelihood, and it would be a major loss when the rails reached the big mining camps of Montana Territory. She reminded herself that Alex was friends with banker and politician Sam Hauser, who had dropped numerous hints to Alex about a future position with the Helena-based bank.

A slight smile crossed her face. How had the last five years' worth of profit tallied up for Alex? She knew he was well-off, but it began to dawn on her that perhaps she would be greeted in Helena by an even higher standard of living than she had imagined.

She shook her head, quickly discarding images of polished floors and a smartly-attired staff at her beck and command. The "MacKinney Manse" is a figure of speech, after all.

From the corner of her eye, she saw a short, grizzled man tip a small keg of whiskey to his lips and hold it there for what seemed at least half a minute. Whiskey at sunrise? Apparently. Another man, whom she assumed was the drinker's companion, grabbed at the keg.

"Hold on thar, Burt," said the small, unkempt man. "Where's going with that whiskey!" he exclaimed, snatching the keg back again.

The other man yielded, looking around furtively. "Near empty, anyhow," he said. "Where'd it all go?"

"Wall," said the wiry, unshaven man, "I guess it leaked down my gullet."

"Down your gullet! You drank the whole thing?" his companion said in disbelief.

"Th'entire keg were only half to start," said the little man. "What's half a tiny l'il keg to a tired ol' stage driver, anyhow?" he said petulantly, and walked toward the horses.

Persis's eyes widened with horror as she realized this man was the driver of their stagecoach. Alex, who had arrived at her side in time to watch the same exchange, gave her a brusque hug, saying, "They all act like that, sweetheart. A strange lot. They say the whiskey makes them better at it. The only way to stay on schedule is to drive the horses hard and fast."

Persis didn't believe "hard and fast" was the best way to accomplish anything, especially where horses were concerned. She thought back on the way Alex dismissed the Belgian's wound and began to realize that she and her betrothed felt quite differently about animals. He may be like Father in some ways, she mused, but Father would have tended to that animal. I should have gotten down on my knees and looked at that injury, she thought bitterly.

"Can't we wait for . . . for another one?" Persis stammered. She was suddenly frightened to the core, both for herself and for Constance. Even though the Concord coaches' egg-shaped bodies were suspended on leather straps for a rolling, rocking ride, a drunken driver boded ill.

A Concord coach could crash just as easily as any other. Persis's ire rose and filled her with determination to exert some control over their fate. She nervously tapped her lips with her fingers.

Alex laughed heartily. "You see, my dear, the other drivers—" He gestured toward a cluster of men leaning against the rough board-and-batten stage station, "are the same as ours. In fact, our Pie Eye is one of the best. I asked for him."

"*Pie Eye?* You asked for him?" She recoiled, then turned to assess the other drivers standing under the eaves. To a man, they were filthy. Their clothes were tobacco-stained and so covered with dust that it was impossible to tell what color their shirts were, except in an occasional crease or seam where sweat had dampened the fabric. Two of them were sitting down, dozing, and another was lying on his stomach, dead asleep in the dirt.

Persis caught Constance's eye and bored into her with a meaningful stare, but Constance turned her head. She turned to Alex and gripped his arm. "Aren't there any sober, respectable men in this line of work?" she blurted out.

Alex spun around. The moment she saw it, she wanted the cloud of annoyance in his eyes gone. "You see," she stammered, "there is something—I mean, are you quite certain there are no others?"

Alex sighed patiently. "Back when the terminus was in Idaho, there were some that you might have called 'genteel'. They were Mormon farmers turned stage drivers. But since the Mormons recently sold most of their stock in the Utah and Northern, those men have gone back to farming." He patted her hand and smiled.

She swallowed. Lightly retracting her hand, she picked up her skirts and hurried over to Constance. "I must talk to you," she said, staring hard into Constance's wide blue eyes. "*Now.*"

Persis led her behind one of the mounds of freight. "You've got to tell Charlie. I think this stage ride is going to be horrendous. The driver is drunk and Alex swears he's the best of the lot." Persis stopped, knowing that she was pushing their friendship to the limit.

Constance was silent.

"I know you don't want to," Persis said anxiously, "but what if something happens? Don't you want him to know? I need him to help me care for you in the event of—of an emergency."

Constance lowered her chin and peered up at Persis through her lashes. "This is not what I need from you." There was hoarfrost in her voice. "There is no problem right now and there will more than likely be no problem for the remainder of this journey."

Persis felt as if she had been slapped. She stared at her friend, not knowing what to say or even what Constance really meant. She saw a liquid brightness in Constance's blue eyes and a furrow of pain between her brows.

"Don't you see," began Constance, "that whatever fears you have for me and the child have already been expressed a hundred times inside my heart? I won't be the first pregnant woman to travel a rocky, rutted road in an overland coach driven by an intoxicated rustic."

She lifted her face and looked Persis full in the eye, adding, "It would be fine if you were apprehensive for yourself. But not for me, and especially not because of the baby. Don't try to move me away from where I am. People do that out of love, or the impulse of what feels like love, but it's seldom the right thing to do."

Persis flung her arms around Constance and held her breath as tears tumbled down her cheeks. "I'm sorry. I am selfish." She struggled to even out her voice. "I think only of what it would be like if anything happened to you, and of my own sense of loss. It's wrong of me, but can't you understand?"

"Of course. Don't let them see you like this," Constance urged. She stroked the tears off Persis's face. "You can't say things in little ways, Persis. You never have. It always comes out like a storm or a sunrise."

"But you need an ally, not a tempest," said Persis, sniffing hard.

The driver was shouting and the stock tender was fastening the final tug. The man named Tom, who had lost out on his fair share of whiskey, hoisted himself up into the driver's box next to Pie Eye.

Persis caught Charlie looking at her. He knows I've been crying, she thought, and made haste to scramble into the oval-shaped body of the dusty, dark red coach. She took a seat near the window, resolutely craning her neck to look out, letting the light wind cool her face. Once the tug was fastened, they set off at a quick pace.

Around mid-morning, they started their ascent into the Ruby Mountains. The roads were dry, and Persis was soon covered with a light sift of dust.

"Trail talc," said one of the male passengers from Helena, chuckling.

Persis smiled. After several more miles, the dust had become more than an irritation. All six passengers were covered with a pale ochre-colored film that settled into nostrils, hair, and in every fold of cloth. It took all Persis's concentration and goodwill to remain pleasant. They had been on the road only a few hours and she was already irritable and nauseated. Sandwiched between Alex and the side of the coach, she was at least able to keep herself from flopping into another passenger's lap. As it was, her neck was sore from the twisting and bobbing of her head.

By mid-day, her stomach stopped churning and she felt well enough to converse. They were getting closer to Alder Gulch, where Charlie would leave them for a few days to look at the more successful gold claims and to assess the progress of stamp mining.

"Stamping," he explained to Constance, "is the process by which larger chunks of ore and promising rock are crushed as preparation for reduction and shipping. It means a higher yield."

In the shanty town of Alder Gulch, Charlie kissed Constance good-bye, assuring her that he would meet her at the International Hotel in Helena in three days' time.

Persis watched as Pie Eye, who had been missing for some time, emerged from the Alder Gulch Saloon. A more forlorn-looking man she had never seen. The fight drained out of her and she resigned herself to whatever the trip held in store. As the sweat-covered horses set off determinedly, Charlie waved them on.

Two hours later, the stagecoach pulled up at the newly-constructed Ruby Hotel in Sheridan. The hotel was a simple but impressive frame structure, three stories tall, with wide white verandas bracketing each floor. Persis stepped down from the coach immediately behind Alex. Her attention was quickly drawn to the third story of the Ruby Hotel, where two well-rouged women in gaudy dressing gowns waved down and laughingly called to the men. As soon as the women saw Persis and Constance, they retreated through an open doorway. Persis wasn't sure, but it appeared that they were clad only in corsets and chemises beneath their long, flowered wrappers.

She heard their suppressed murmurs and laughter tinkling down from above. Then she froze. She distinctly heard one of them say, "Alexander." Then the balcony door closed and the voices were gone.

Alex did not hear it, or if he did, he elected to ignore it. Persis's heart sank. They know him. Who *doesn't* know him, she thought, noticing that her swift anger was becoming a habit.

Inside the Ruby Hotel, a middle-aged woman came out from behind the counter to greet them. She was attractive, with high cheekbones and a long, straight nose. Full-figured without being fleshy, she was simply clothed in a black poplin skirt and a plain white shirtwaist. The mistress of the house, no doubt, thought Persis with a tiny sniff.

"How are you, Mr. MacKinney?" she said.

Her diction was precise and clear but was heavily accented. It sounded British, but not quite. Welsh, perhaps?

The woman put a confident hand out to Alex and gave his arm a quick, vigorous shake. "It's nice to see you again. This is your party from the East, I see. And one of these ladies must be your fiancée."

She turned to Constance first, and then Persis. "Let me guess. It is you," she said to Persis.

Persis smiled.

"My name is Ruby," she said. "Let me show you women to the washroom."

"Ben!" she called out. "A glass of whiskey for Mr. MacKinney. Scotch. He'll take it in the dining room."

"She's not a proprietor," whispered Persis as they closed the washroom door. "She's a madam. I'm sure of it. Did you see how familiar she was with Alex? And those women upstairs, you saw them—those awful women. They knew him."

Constance closed her eyes and shook her head. "You can't change anything that has already happened. Try to look ahead. It's clear that these people know—or at least the hostess knows—that Alex is spoken for."

Looking woefully into the mirror, Persis dropped her face into her hands.

"Alex doesn't love those women; the very idea is absurd. You're pale. Wash your face."

In the dining room, they found Alex seated with a carriage merchant from Helena. There was a big buffet with roast duck, baked potatoes, green beans, biscuits with chokecherry jelly, and lemon curd pie. Persis watched Constance eat, but she herself could barely swallow a few bites of biscuit. Her entire body was working to digest the latest bitter glimpse into Alex's colorful past.

They had scarcely finished when they heard the stage driver's call for boarding. As Persis swallowed the rest of her tea and got up, the wobbly feeling returned. She tried not to reach for the sideboard.

As they left the dining room, Ruby came close to Persis and said, "How is she doing?"

Confused, Persis stared back at Ruby. "What? I'm sorry. . . ."

"Constance? Is that her name? How is she feeling?"

"Whatever do you mean? I'm sure she's quite well." Persis felt a strange, damp coolness rising up her neck.

Ruby tipped her head and gave Persis a look that was at once penetrating and gentle. "You don't know?"

Persis looked back, amazed. She searched the handsome, weathered face. Could she trust this woman? "Y—Yes," she said haltingly, "I know about her. But how did you—"

"Never mind. You don't know me, and I can see in your eyes that you don't think you can trust me. This is all new and you've got good reason to be suspicious. But take this anyway." She pressed a tiny waxed envelope into Persis's hand. "It's some powders I use to settle the stomach. Don't worry; there's no laudanum in it or anything else to question. If your friend feels sick, mix this in a few ounces of water."

"Are you a nurse?" asked Persis.

Ruby smiled. "After a fashion. People often come to me with their medical problems, and I've physicked quite a few, as they say. Most of what I know I learned from my mother. . . ." she stopped. "You look a little pale yourself. You have found the coach ride difficult."

"Yes," Persis breathed. "But I must be going. The others are waiting. Good bye, Ruby."

Resolutely, Persis walked into the heat of the July afternoon. Alex and Constance were waiting for her a few yards away on the shaded walkway. Pie Eye, who had thus far done a good job of keeping them out of the Beaverhead River, was there, jawing with his replacement, a huge, redheaded man who looked quite civilized next to the disheveled drunk.

"You take keer of Mr. MacKinney's ladies, too," drawled Pie Eye, instructing the new driver.

Persis stepped down into the dusty street and felt sun blaze on her shoulders. Pie Eye's voice sounded queer and metallic. As she looked around toward Alex and Constance, a dark fog forced its way into the periphery of her vision. She saw them looking at her. She wanted to speak, to tell them that she felt strange, but her lips wouldn't form the words. Their forms began to recede into the brown fog, and they drifted further and further away.

"Yep, them poor ladies think this Concord's takin' 'em to the marble farm," said Pie Eye. His loud guffaw was the last thing Persis heard as she crumpled in a heap on the street.

"**N**ever use them," came a soft female voice. "No one should have to wake up out of a dead faint to the smell of ammonia. Smells like Butte City, come to think of it! The whole town reeks from all that roasting ore."

Persis heard soft laughter and opened her eyes.

"Draw that shade a minute, Alex," the voice drifted in again. "I think it's a lot of things; could even be the change in altitude. Different folks react different ways."

Persis's eyes focused on the hair and the gray-black eyes of Ruby Cornish.

"Not much of a nurse after all," the older woman went on, looking into Persis's eyes. "I'm no credit to the profession. Should have seen you needed something."

"The stage—" began Persis.

"The stage can wait a few more minutes," said Constance. "How do you feel?"

"I'll be fine. We can go now."

Alex leaned over her with mock sternness and shook his finger. "You're going to lie there for ten more minutes. I'll be back."

Persis realized she was lying, appropriately enough, on a fainting couch. The quaintly furnished room had an Old World flavor. Nothing elegant, just homely things, many of which were burnished with age and wear. A spinning wheel, a stuffed rooster, a paisley shawl hanging from a hook near the door, and a row of blue and white china on the mantel. There were chemist's bottles here and there, either filled with powders or serving as vases for small bouquets of sweet peas and wild roses.

"This is where I live," said Ruby, reading Persis's face.

In a nearby chair, Constance was chewing the inside of her cheek, trying not to smile. Persis knew full well what that was about. She gave her head a little wag and widened her eyes in defiance, which only made Constance smirk and look away.

"Ruby is from England," said Constance. "While you were—indisposed—she told me that her mother and grandmother were both midwives in Cornwall. One of them actually trained at a famous midwifery hospital in Vienna."

Persis looked sharply at Ruby, but the woman's eyes were downcast as she wrung out a cloth for Persis's forehead. It seemed that Ruby had not revealed her prescience to Constance.

There was something soothing, almost hypnotic, about the sound of the lavender-scented water trickling into the basin.

Pulling her chair closer, Constance glanced at Ruby and said, "It's nice to have a midwife in the area." Turning her attention back to Persis, she went on, "It turns out that one of the reasons Ruby settled in this area was that the mountain range and the river both bore her name. But she says she doesn't believe in coincidences."

"Curious," said Persis, smiling.

Ruby laughed. "Do you know what the Indians used to call the Ruby River, not too long ago? To them, it was the 'Stinking Water.' I'm glad I didn't learn that until after I had been here for over a year."

Persis laughed, and Alex appeared in the doorway. Relief immediately gave way to flattered embarrassment as he swept her up in his arms and proceeded toward the door.

"Don't be ridiculous, Alex! I can walk!"

"Be quiet. I've telegraphed the Whitehall Inn and made arrangements for us to stay the night. This kind of travel is too hard on you ladies. Constance is as pale as you are."

Persis stewed for a moment about the impression she was making, but the idea of spending another twenty-four hours in the coach was enough to silence her. Resigned, she put out her hand to Ruby and said, "Good-bye. If you ever come to Helena, I hope you will call on us."

"We will see one another again," said Ruby matter-of-factly, as if she were reading tea leaves.

Persis felt both edgy and intrigued. There was nothing of the slattern about this woman. She kept her eyes on Ruby's until their gaze was broken as Alex swung her through the open door.

Hours later, Constance said, "I liked her. I don't know what there is about her. She's rather mystical. And it's not just because she's foreign born." She lowered her voice for Persis only to hear. "You know, I had the strangest feeling by the way she looked at me that she knew . . . you know." She cautiously motioned toward her belly.

"She *did* know."

"What?" Constance stared.

"She knows. She told me."

"How could I have not heard? I was there the whole time."

"She told me before I fainted, when you and Alex left the hotel and went out on the street. See?" she pulled the small packet of powder out of her bag. "She gave me this for you. She said she knew you were with child and she thought you might be feeling ill."

"That's incredible," Constance murmured, staring out the window. "Well, her female forebears were midwives. I suppose you learn to look at a woman's figure and discern these things. Still, that is remarkable, to say the least." She fell silent and looked at Persis, who raised her eyebrows and said nothing.

* * *

For thirty miles, the Boulder River glittered a stone's throw from the road, disappearing briefly into the woods and then coming back into view. Far ahead, they could see several small mountain ranges. "That's our destination," said one of the passengers, pointing to the darkly-thatched slopes in the distance.

Alex gave out a short, "Um-hmm."

He had been quiet for over an hour. Was something bothering him? Persis wasn't sure. She herself was in good spirits, moved by the beauty of the country. She began chatting easily with Constance about it, occasionally posing a question to Alex, and before long, the dark pointed firs surrounding Helena came into view. As they drew close to town, Persis was amazed to see lawns and gardens, with young shade and fruit trees growing on either side of the streets.

Alex's spirits seemed to lift as they left the stage station in his barouche-style carriage.

"The house is nearly done," he said. "I think they'll still be working on the floors and finishwork inside. But maybe I'll be pleasantly surprised. I told them it had to be ready for the lady of the house."

Persis beamed, her fears melting under the warm July sun.

As the barouche rolled slowly up Gilbert Street, Persis saw that they were entering an exclusive part of the city. The houses were large, with broad, sloping lawns and well-tended gardens. Many were surrounded by solid brick or stone walls, banking up the earth around the homes to create wide terraces.

They came to a halt before a large, red brick mansard villa on the west side of the street. Surrounding the yard was a low brick wall. Along the top of this wall, like a piece of stiff black lace, ran a spine of decorative wrought-iron grillwork.

"My builder tells me the design is a combination of Second Empire and Gothic," said Alex. "That's America for you—no respect for purity. We're always mixing things up. Do you like it?"

"Like it?" Persis gasped. "It's so . . . Eastern." She glanced at him to see how this blunt summation landed. If she had told the truth, she would have said that she had expected something more regional, but she astutely noted that the entire neighborhood had Victorian aspirations.

"I was hoping for that effect," he said, putting his hands on his hips and studying the structure. "Do you really think so?"

"It combines the best of both worlds," she went on diplomatically. "Set against these mountains, well, it is just magnificent." She laid her hand on his arm and smiled. "I can't believe it. To come into the frontier and to find a house rivaling the finest homes of New York or Boston—"

"Hah!" cried Alex. "I wouldn't go that far!" But he was visibly flattered. "Come ladies, let's go in."

The heavy front door opened on a large central hallway with stairs leading to a spacious, windowed landing halfway up.

"Donny," called Alex, "come and meet the ladies."

There was the sound of footsteps muffled by thick Turkish rugs. As Persis turned, a short, slender Chinese man appeared. She had never met anyone from China and had no idea what to say or do.

"Donny, this is the lady I am going to marry," said Alex slowly. "Her name is Miss Allen. And this is her sister-in-law, Mrs. Allen."

"Welcome to Mr. MacKinney house, Missy Allen and Mis-sus Allen." A lock of black hair fell over his forehead and was quickly smoothed back into place.

"Thank you, Donny," said Persis, trying to enunciate. "I am sure I will be happy here." She turned to Alex, who ushered them into the kitchen.

Persis instantly liked the room. A row of windows on the east wall let in the morning light, and a large Monarch stove gleamed brightly in the corner. Two women, one middle-aged and one still in her teens, both in simple black dresses, stood erect near a polished maple work table.

"Persis Allen," said Alex, "I'd like you to meet the other members of your—our—staff. This is Grace Mitchell and her assistant, Nora O'Brien."

Persis was relieved when the two women warmly greeted her in thick Irish brogue. If I can win their hearts, she thought, we'll make this house a home.

As Constance examined a stained glass window in the hall, Persis turned to Alex. "It is a truly lovely house, Alex. You seem—" She hesitated. "You seem to have spared no expense. I hope it has not put you in an uncomfortable position."

Alex looked at her with mild surprise. "Uncomfortable position? Get that thought out of your head right away, Persis. I can't have my bride doubting my ability to establish and maintain a position in the community. You just worry about the things to which your fair sex is suited." Avoiding her eyes, he kissed her on the forehead.

A spark flew in her, but Alex was walking away, excusing himself to attend to some neglected interests in the business district known as Last Chance Gulch.

That afternoon, as she and Constance unpacked linens, Persis noticed a little room between the library and veranda. Except for a quaint tiled stove in the corner, it was devoid of furnishings. She wondered if Alex had any particular use in mind for the odd little room. It struck her as a perfect little place for her writing or sewing. As soon as Alex's mood improves, she vowed, I will ask him about it.

Later that day, Alex took them both to the International Hotel, Helena's finest, where he secured a large suite for the two women to occupy until Charlie got back, at which point the hotel suite would be entirely at Persis's disposal—that is, until the wedding a mere six days away.

"Don't worry, I am not abandoning you ladies," Alex said. "I'll be back in the morning to give you a tour of Last Chance Gulch and the city environs." Touching the brim of his hat, he went quickly down the stairs.

* * *

Their tour of the Gulch and the nearby mining district took up most of the following day. Toward the east edge of the downtown area were several blocks of saloons and dance-halls which Alex offhandedly referred to as the "Tenderloin," or red-light district.

"It's not exceptionally dangerous, but you certainly do not want to wander into this area, especially after dusk," he said, flicking the reins and turning west.

Their last stop was the Helena office and corrals of MacKinney Freighters. Persis found the office and its south-facing windows very pleasant, but it was the barn that captured her heart. As they entered the barn, the horses—mostly Percherons—raised their heads and pricked their ears. Constance stopped to stroke their velvety noses while Persis quickly assessed the animals and judged them healthy.

The new barn was only partly raised, with much of the east wall still wide open. Sunlight poured around the heavy post framework and motes of straw-dust danced in the air. The air was rich with warmth, the ooze of sap from damp new pine, and the distinctive, fresh tang of a well-kept stable.

In the shadows was a man down on one knee. He was huge, but all Persis could see was his broad back, which was covered with a taut stretch of muslin shirt soaked through beneath the arms. The place was calm and still, with only the soft, grinding sound of a horse working his grain and the cooing of pigeons in the rafters. Persis came closer and saw that the man was examining one of the oxen. Big as he was, like an ox himself, he leaped agilely to his feet and snatched the hat from his nearly-bald head.

"Good Morning, Mr. MacKinney," he said with a slow smile. It was a thoughtful smile that felt all the more sincere to Persis because it never broke into a full grin. "Is it her, sir? The one we have been waitin' for? Aye, it must be."

Alex laughed and turned to Persis. "This is Angus Blaylock, my Helena freight office and stock superintendent." Then, turning back to Angus, who was making a slight bow, he said, "Yes, Angus, this is the one. I present Miss Persis Allen, my fiancée, and her sister-in-law, Mrs. Charles Allen."

Persis blushed slightly but extended her hand eagerly and felt the broad, callused grip of the Scot. He seemed to blush himself. She asked a few intelligent questions about the livestock, which he answered with unpretentious confidence.

On the way back to the house, she found her spirits lightened by the knowledge that a man like Angus was in Alex's employ. With his active concern for the animals, he might make up, at least somewhat, for the apathy she had noted in Carl and even in Alex. She sighed. To my husband, business is most definitely business.

* * *

That evening, Grace Mitchell and Nora O'Brien served dinner with timeliness and agility. Both women had fair skin and grey-blue eyes, Persis observed, but there the similarity ended. Nora was like a bottle of shaken soda, bursting with stories, laughter, and good spirits. She was slightly taller than Grace, but the advantage was a thin one. Grace outweighed Nora by a good forty pounds and was twenty years ahead of her in experience.

"What wonderful help you have found," Persis said.

Alex took a sip of his wine before replying, "Yes."

He then turned to Constance and asked, "Have you any contacts in Butte City to help you locate a house? I know several people there who would be happy to assist you, and would also be charmed to meet you."

Persis listened as Alex began paying more attention to Constance than he ever had in the past. As the minutes passed, she became convinced that this was not out of a genuine interest in Constance, but rather a pointed means of making her aware that she had somehow displeased him. She caught herself toying with her food and immediately put down her fork.

As they waited for dessert, Alex went to the sideboard and returned with a glass of port for each of them.

"How did you possibly keep your admirers at bay, Constance, while Charlie was so long at school in New York City?"

Persis felt her neck burn with a furious blush. She could not look at either of them.

"I employed the same tools that Persis used while you and she were separated," Constance said mildly, pushing her glass of port an inch away.

God love you, my sweet Constance, thought Persis.

As soon as they finished, Constance excused herself, explaining to Alex that she was utterly exhausted and asking that Donny please take her back to the International.

With Constance gone, Persis and Alex adjourned to the library. Now, at last, Persis thought, I can get to the bottom of this. She picked a chair close to him and said, "It really is wonderful to be here, Alex. Everything about this house enchants me."

Alex stared at a collection of papers on the coffee table, sipping a fresh brandy.

As the minutes ticked by, Persis's desperation mounted. Why won't he tell me what's wrong? We are all alone, and he could easily pour out his heart, whether he is worried about railroad or bank affairs or—if I've offended him somehow.

After three or four minutes she could stand it no longer. "Alex, are you distressed about something?" She waited, her heart thumping and her hands folded tightly together.

He looked at her straight on. A response! Her heart leaped.

Another half minute passed before he finally said, "I don't know, Persis. Maybe this is all wrong."

Her mouth went dry. His tone clearly meant the unthinkable: that perhaps they might not belong together after all. Now that she had come clear across the country, now that he had brought her "home," she was incredulous. 'All wrong.' How could he say such a thing? He was a mature man who should know enough to give them a chance to get started!

With breathless caution, she asked, "What do you mean?"

He held his glass a half-inch above the table for a long, maddening moment and then set it down. Placing his palms together in an almost supplicating way, he looked down at the floor. "How can I say this—" He glanced briefly at her and then away.

"Just say it, please," she responded, repressing her rising indignation.

"Persis . . . I don't want to hurt you," he said.

She hoped he could not see that she was holding her breath. Go ahead and hurt me, if you must, she was thinking, but in God's name be quick about it!

". . . but I don't want to be hurt either," he was saying. "I have been looking for years for a woman who will truly take care of me."

Persis didn't see how anyone could be more focused on caring for him than she. None of this made sense.

"I've known other women before you, you know that," he said gently.

She nodded, strangely grateful to have him broach this forbidden topic.

"I never wanted to marry any of them because they all became preoccupied with things that didn't matter—parties, Europe, furs, flirtations—you know the type. I asked you to marry me because I thought you were different."

What was this about? Did he want someone who never even ventured outdoors? She wasn't a floozy, but she liked a reasonable social life. She was a prudent, thoughtful person, and although Alex's wealth was a tantalizing aspect of his life, it certainly wasn't what attracted her to him. She loved him. She loved his eyes, his boyish humor, and his *joie de vivre,* as Constance had so aptly put it.

He looked at her, raising his eyebrows and compressing his lips.

"And now? How do you feel now?" She felt a rising impatience.

"As I said, I felt that I had found someone who would take care of me, and that at long last I might come first instead of fourth or fifth to a woman. You are so—God, I don't know how to say it. It is so awkward."

He looked at her and saw the intense, searching look in her eyes. "Oh, out with it," he finally said, raking his hands through his hair. "To be perfectly frank, I think you are preoccupied with Constance. Oddly so, in fact."

She felt her head draw back ever so slightly and a furrow of confusion form on her brow.

There was a pause. He looked at her. "Now, don't react. Think about it for a moment, Persis. Do you see how an extremely—entangled female friendship might make a man feel? Especially the man to whom you are engaged?"

Persis's lips parted in sheer astonishment. A flood of relief passed through her as she realized that this was a problem about which something could easily be done. Her relief, however, quickly gave way to mortification. What did he think about her and Constance? Did he think that they were—that they might be carnally familiar?

He may think what he chooses, she quickly resolved. I must demonstrate to him how farfetched this is. If this weren't so bizarre, it would be humorous. He has only one younger sister, so he may never have seen any innocent, intimate feminine companionship. His mother, from what he has said, tends to keep to herself.

"I am glad that you told me of your feelings," she said, arranging her words like figures on a chessboard. "I hope you will always do that. I am sure you have good reasons for feeling the way you do, but I wish you would not judge my suitability on the basis of the last two weeks."

"But Persis! I had such hopes about the beginning of our life . . . I wanted these last two weeks to be perfect, to be a herald of what was to come." His voice grew soft and hoarse, almost pleading. "Put yourself in my position, just for a moment. You've shown me what is important to you. These last few days especially have been very painful for me."

"But I am devoted to you, don't you know that?" She fell at his feet, her upturned face searching his.

Clutching tightly at the chestnut curls on either side of his head, he replied, "Actions speak louder than words."

With tears in her eyes, Persis got up and walked to the mantelpiece. She didn't know whose agony was worse. Staring vacantly at the feathery black veins in the white marble, she stood there, disheartened and alone. The dark, threadlike designs on the mantel looked like lightning, little jagged shafts coming down to jolt her perfect life.

She heard Alex's glass again as it came down quietly on the table behind her. He stood up and she thought to herself, dear God, don't let him leave the room! I want him to come over here and touch me and tell me that he forgives me. If only he can do that, I'll never give him reason to feel this way again. I'm not one of those women who've disappointed him, I am not!

As his fingers touched her shoulder, gently, tentatively, she spun around and flung herself into his arms.

"Persis! My Persis!" he breathed, burying his face in her hair.

Her heart leaped as she felt his strong arms fold her close. Silent, not knowing what to do, she clung to him and waited for him to say something forgiving, something hopeful.

At last, he pulled away slightly, his hands holding her upper arms. "I'll try again if you will earnestly try too." His eyes bored into her like augurs.

"Yes, of course, yes. I love you, Alex! My God, if you only knew! With time you will come to realize how much I do, and that you never ever need doubt me. If only you could sense what is in my heart for you; how much I care for your feelings. I think of little else but you. If I've paid more attention to Constance lately it's because she's pregnant—" She sucked in her breath.

He placed both hands on her shoulders, holding her away from him. "She's what? *Pregnant?* This is the first I have heard of this," he said, scanning her face. "For heaven's sake, why hasn't this subject come up?"

"Oh, no! I shouldn't have told you!" she cried.

He stiffened and pulled away.

"It's better that you know, really," she said, filling up the tense space. "But please don't say anything. I know Constance plans to tell Charlie very soon."

"Well," he said, tapping his hand on the marble and shaking his head. "I am happy for them, but I confess to some pure selfishness— I am happy for myself as well. With a new baby and a new household in the mining camp, your bosom friend will be a busy girl."

Smiling now, he pulled her close again and held her against him. As they stood quietly in the dark, their embrace lost its terror. Awash in relief, Persis nestled her head into his shoulder.

The only sound was the distant clatter of dishes in the kitchen and the thump of Alex's heart beneath his waistcoat. Persis grew more conscious of his physical presence and the smell of his warm skin. Energy began to move between them, vibrating in the air wherever their bodies were not touching. Somewhere inside her, most certainly not in her head, she knew beyond question that he was feeling exactly the same thing.

He murmured into her hair, "I love you." She felt his hand, warm against her upper back. There was a new gentleness in his touch as his hand moved down, grazing her shoulder blades and then coming to rest just above the small of her back.

As his hand settled into her, she became aware of his fingers and realized they no longer merely held her to him. His hand conformed to her as it moved over the soft contours of her waist and ribs.

He tipped his head back slightly, just enough to look in her eyes. There was a trace of a smile on his full lips.

The minute their eyes met, she knew what they were both thinking: what lay beneath the layers of clothing that covered them both, and what it would be like to have him unfasten the buttons at her neck.

Her breath was coming in soft puffs. His forefinger slid under her chin and lifted her face upward. The first kiss was hesitant, respectful. Persis could taste the brandy on his lips. He pulled back to look at her again.

She felt the wetness of his kiss cooling her lips and wondered what she looked like to him. Her heart raced and her breasts began to ache.

His mouth came down on hers with an eagerness that made her lips part to receive his tongue. She was not thinking anymore; she was only aware of the soft stroke of his tongue.

She thought of the bed that waited for them upstairs. *Their bed.* Now that the terrible distance between them had closed, she wanted nothing but to melt into him, to cover him with herself. Passion surged in her as his fingers went quickly to work at the long row of black buttons on her bodice.

His lips were on her throat and the heat of his kisses penetrated her skin. One tug at the ribbon on the gathered neckline of her chemise made it slacken and gap, revealing the shadow between her breasts. His hands curved tightly around the front of her ribs, then slid slowly and firmly upward, his fingers fanning over her breasts.

She drank in the mingled scents of castile soap, sweat, and brandy. Leaning into him, she shivered with desire.

Then, in that intensely heated moment, he hesitated. The split-second lull in the energy between them was all it took. Rational thought splashed over her like ice water.

"We . . . we have to wait," she gasped, and as soon as she uttered the words she was filled with panic. Would he understand? Would he let her have the time that she needed, that she deserved?

He stopped his caresses but did not sulk. Instead, he smiled and pulled the ribbons on her chemise back into a loose knot. He looked pleased, almost relieved. "It's all right," he said thickly. "It's only a few days." She heard him swallow hard as he pulled her clothing back into place. "This is not how I want it to happen. Nor do you."

Thoughts swam in her head. She also knew that if he had not hesitated, she would have given herself to him and been glad of it. As her heated feelings began to ebb, she was overwhelmed with gratitude that he had been able to exercise restraint.

"It's best if you take me back to the International now," she said, then quickly added, "But in five days you won't have to take me anywhere but upstairs."

He kissed her lightly. "I am keenly aware of that," he said, wearing a pout that easily broke into a smile. "I'll bring the small buggy around."

She let out a giggle and watched him go. How infinitely charming he can be, she mused.

A warm wind blew as they drove to the hotel. The few trees that had grown tall enough to provide shade rustled overhead as the shiny buggy spun along Last Chance Gulch.

"When is Constance going to tell Charlie about her condition?"

"I'm not sure. I know she plans to tell him before our wedding. I guess we'll just wait and see." She tried to sound half-interested.

Not quite finished with the subject, Alex went on, "Married people ought not to have secrets from one another."

"She has very good reasons. She didn't want to delay our trip—my trip—out here to join you, and she certainly didn't want to stay behind in Chicago while her husband went west. She was quite brave, actually." She stopped, knowing she had said enough.

"Well, it's a rather odd situation," Alex allowed. Changing the subject, he said, "We'll go to the Methodist church tomorrow so that you can meet Reverend Fitzgerald. Now, about the honeymoon. Do you want to go to San Francisco?"

"Let's wait." Persis inhaled the sagebrush-scented air. "I want to do some settling in. We can get to know one another just as well here at home, can't we?"

Alex looked pleased. "We could take a trip later in the fall, if you like," he assured her, and brought his arm around her in the familiar, firm way she had grown to love.

Charlie Allen came to Butte City at the very time that Marcus Daly, the Irish mining boss, was looking for a site supervisor with a background in engineering. One afternoon in early August, Charlie waited in the second-story foyer of Daly's wood frame office building on the town's main thoroughfare, Broadway Street. It was beastly hot.

Charlie had expected to prefer the dry heat of the West to the humid, sweltering oppression of the Great Lakes region, but today he wasn't so sure. Sunlight poured in the window and lay in warped yellow squares on the floor.

Finally, Daly's office door opened.

"He's all yours," said the departing visitor, touching his shabby hat before clattering down the stairs.

Charlie entered the office, quickly noting the roll-top desk, the pipe in the ashtray, the engravings of famous horses pinned to the walls, and the long table cluttered with drawings, deeds, claims, and assay reports.

"Rest your saddle," Daly said, pointing to an armchair.

Charlie sat down and quickly launched into a narrative of his background and education. It all sounded good until he got to the point in his story where he had to tell the plain truth—that he had yet to work an actual diggings. Making this confession to the camp's most eminent manager was humiliating. He finished, determined not to wipe the perspiration from his forehead.

Daly tapped his pencil on the desk. "It's not just the experience I'm wanting, mind you," he said. "I want a fellow who understands the science of it all. I want level collar timbers and straight posts, and I want each shaft and stope built to sustain whatever digging comes after. I want a fellow who's not afraid to build a reduction works and tear it down two months later to build a better one."

He stopped and stood up, walking to the window. "It's plowing new ground we are, in more ways than one. I know the right fellow with the right education can estimate the ore in a piece o' property, and the value of it. And I know ciphering can help calculate the load a structure will have to bear to be safe. Safety's a big thing to me."

He paused, studying Charlie. "You know what they say back in Ireland about this Rocky Mountain inferno we're running over here?"

Charlie shook his head.

"They say the streets of Butte City are paved with Irish bones. And it's the truth they're peddlin', to some degree."

"I don't suppose this vocation will ever be completely free of danger, Mr. Daly," Charlie replied softly.

"Every day someone gets hurt somewhere in this camp. If not in one o' my operations, then in someone else's. I look after a lot of mother's sons. Hirin' good men with good ideas, men like yourself, will help shorten my trade with Finerty."

Seeing a blank look on Charlie's face, Daly said, "Finerty's the Irish undertaker."

Charlie gave a wry smile. He hoped Daly didn't expect him to effect a massive reduction in mining deaths and injuries. Other than that, all of the tasks Daly was laying out for him sounded as familiar as brushing his teeth. He knew he could do it. "Thank you, sir. I'd sure like to put my training to use."

"And you shall. But there's somethin' between us that we're going to set straight right off," said Daly, stroking his short beard.

"I'm sorry, sir, I'm not sure what you mean."

"I know you've been lookin' in the gold camps south of here. I heard about you. Word gets around." He winked. "It's silver we're mining here in Butte City, not gold. Gold's about played out. It's gettin' beyond those gold thoughts you've got to be now. Savvy?"

Charlie barely got out a slow nod when Daly slapped him on the back and said, "You're hired." His first assignment was to help supervise the construction of an enormous 60-stamp mill and the installation of new roasters and a revolving ore dryer. In addition, he would begin assessing the potential of Daly's undeveloped properties. It was a huge job, but Daly assured him there were plenty of job bosses on the team.

Charlie strode rapidly to the place he and Constance had bought on Idaho Street. The day Constance told him about the baby, he had left her at their temporary lodgings with a promise not to return until he had located "the best little cottage Butte City had to offer." The white frame house on Idaho, with its tall brick chimney and tidy porch, put a dent in their savings, but keeping his family out of the mire of Dublin Gulch was worth every cent.

Clomping up the steps, he flung open the door. Constance was standing alone in the front room.

"I'm hired!" he said. "He—Daly—wants me to work on some big doings—I mean really big—at the Alice Mine. That's his biggest holding. And there'll be more work after that."

Constance threw her arms around Charlie's sweaty neck. "That's wonderful!" Prosperity was coming, but better still, Charlie could start doing what he loved to do. Smiling, she withdrew her arms and tipped her head toward the kitchen. "We have company, Charlie."

Charlie turned around to see a gray-haired woman reaching for her hat. "I'm Ruby Cornish," she said. "I met your wife and sister in Sheridan. I'm a midwife."

"Oh, yes," said Charlie, shaking Ruby's hand. "I heard. It's a pleasure to meet you." He threw a piercing look at Constance. "Is something wrong?"

"Of course not! Ruby is on her way to Helena. She owns a bit of property there, and she wanted to see how I was."

Ruby stood up and began making her farewells. "I think everything will work out just fine," she said, "although I do agree Helena might be better for your lying-in." Her voice was mellifluous and soft, like water running over rocks.

"I'll stop in next month," she said, "Good day."

After dinner, Charlie went to a mining bosses' meeting. As he made his way down the hill through the puffs of yellowish smoke drifting up from the smelters and roasting pits, he saw that what little vegetation grew in the dooryards was fast withering. Butte City is a smoky damned place, he thought. But if things work out, within a year my family and I will have a fine place well away from the smell and the fumes.

* * *

The MacKinney wedding was held at Helena's eminent Methodist-Episcopal Church on Saturday, August 7. Columns of men and women stood on the curved walkway, and as Persis and Alex came out of the church, they were greeted with cheers from a small ocean of beaver hats and beribboned bonnets.

Their private wedding dinner was sumptuous: champagne, roast pheasant and duck, corn soufflé, pastries stuffed with mushrooms, and chocolate cake. Alex saw to it that her glass was never empty, refilling it even after she had taken only several sips. This artful technique, she noted, made it impossible for her to gauge how much she was drinking.

They revisited the idea of a honeymoon and agreed on a short jaunt to Yellowstone sometime in the fall. When they had finished their cake, Alex leaned back in his chair and swirled a snifter of brandy. Grinning, he pulled out a cigar and asked playfully, "Do you mind, my dear? It isn't every day that a man gets married."

"Go ahead," she said, feeling pleasantly light-headed. "Just be sure and blow the smoke in the other direction."

They began to make small talk, recalling the events of the day and laughing with relief now that it was behind them. Alex set his cigar in a crystal dish and reached under the table for Persis's hand. "I love you, Mrs. MacKinney."

"I love you too," she said, blushing and looking down as his fingers grasped hers. She felt awkward, but the champagne had made her body warm and relaxed. She knew the effect of her every movement on him. As she shifted her legs under the table, her stockings made a soft, sliding whisper.

"I want you," he said.

She felt a deep twinge, as if someone were wringing out her very core.

"It's funny," she said, feeling suddenly apprehensive, "before, when we were courting, we always knew what to do—I mean, those times when we . . . came close. Now that we are husband and wife, it's as if we don't know what to do."

He stood up and pulled her to her feet. Placing his right hand under her chin so that her jaw rested on his thumb and forefinger, he raised her face. "Believe me, darling, I know what to do." He kissed her softly, his full lips slipping over hers.

Every fiber of her yielded to him. He felt it, and she knew he felt it. He kissed her again, wrapping his arms around her and pushing his tongue well into her mouth. For a moment this repulsed her, but she gave herself over to the sensation, and soon her own tongue was expressively moving with his.

He pulled back and said, "Where did you learn to do that?"

She blushed violently. "I didn't. I mean, I just did it. Should I not have?"

He bent down, bringing his left arm low behind her to scoop her up and using his right to bring her shoulders and face close to him. "I like it. You're a natural, Persis Allen MacKinney. A touch of the vixen, perhaps, but just the woman for me."

He bore her effortlessly up the stairs, his tall boots clicking lightly on the steps. In the master bedroom, he placed her on the bed, and then sat down next to her and began removing his clothes.

Persis longed to put out the lamps on either side of the bed. She thought it odd that he left them lit, but she stared at him, transfixed. She had never seen him bare, not even his arms. He was barrel-chested and solid. What struck her most was how much strength was evident in his powerful limbs. He left on his under-britches and reached for her, raising her to her feet.

She could smell the citrus waft of Bay Rum as he came close. He began kissing her on the lips, the neck, and across her bosom, right through her clothing.

Dizzy, she fought a nipping fear. He suddenly seemed so big, so unlike her. A beast, really. She didn't know what she was doing, not at all. Kissing was one thing, but *this*. She was swimming in a lake of dark mystery.

But what man wouldn't seem like a beast, she thought, on the first night? Millions of women have done this and have felt the same mix of longing and fear. If there is pain, I can bear it.

His damp hands ran down her sides and over her buttocks. He grabbed her hips and forced her against his groin, bringing his mouth down on hers in a penetrating kiss.

Molding herself to him, Persis stopped thinking. Desire took over, making her fumble eagerly to undo her dark blue dinner dress, which fell in a rustling heap around her ankles. Alex deftly swept away her petticoats and lace pantaloons. She had unhooked the top inch or two of her corset when he stopped her.

"Wait. Let me look at you." He was breathing heavily. His eyes flickered quickly over her entire body. She colored deeply and her hands fluttered up to cover herself.

Laying her down, he tugged the corset aside, exposing her breasts. Before she knew what was happening, he was completely naked and was stripping away what was left of her undergarments. He rapidly moved on top of her. With one arm, he supported himself and with the other, he positioned himself carefully over her.

The many hours she had spent in the Allen horse barn had given her an adequate knowledge of what was about to happen. All of that animal power and urgency came flooding back to her; he was her chosen one, and she was his. It was time, and there was no turning back.

As he rocked gently into her, there was a rending pain. Then, as he filled her, she ached to feel him more deeply. Immodest as it seemed to begin moving rhythmically against him, she did. She was sweating herself, like the mare, but she no longer cared. They writhed wildly, reaching the height of tension and the cataclysmic release.

He covered her mouth with his in a long, sweet kiss. Euphoria settled on her, and Alex slid to her side, staring at her intently with his topaz-brown eyes. She was awash in the discovery of physical intimacy, and found it more powerful than she had ever imagined. Mesmerized by this new vulnerability, she studied his face and found gratitude there, as if he had won something he had not expected.

"Are you all right?" he asked, stroking her hair.

"Very much so," she whispered.

He pulled her close, placed her head on his shoulder, stretched his leg over her thighs, and fell asleep.

* * *

The initial strangeness of married life lapsed into a predictable rhythm that began to make a certain blended sense. The furnishing of the house, a significant task, allowed Persis to impress Alex with her creativity. In the evening, while she pored over the Bloomingdale's catalog, he teased her about rearranging what he had already done. At first, Persis looked up with concern, but as time went on she could tell he was glad of her efforts and liked nearly everything she did.

A silent, implicit acknowledgement of one another's vanity gradually made its way into the relationship. The two saw certain aspects of pride in each other, and not only tolerated these bits of hubris but felt enhanced, greater because of the power they wielded as a pair.

Persis only found cause for anxiety when Alex left town on business. By the end of August, he had already taken three short trips—first to meet with surveyors about a Utah and Northern grading contract, then to meet with Sidney Dillon in Salt Lake City, and a third time to meet with Conrad Kohrs in Deer Lodge about some of Sam Hauser's cattle interests. Persis observed with admiration and some amusement how he costumed himself for each of these outings. He was either the companionable working man's advocate, the polished railroad executive, or the gentleman rancher.

After each tender good-bye, Persis settled in, dismissing her feelings of loneliness and concentrating on what needed to be done around the house. She took advantage of this time to go out and dig in the flower beds, saving her husband the vexation of seeing her thus engaged. This was the only domestic pursuit of hers that displeased him.

"We've got Donny, for heaven's sake, Persis," he had said a few weeks before. "If you think a woman's touch is needed, take one of the female help out there and direct her." He shook his head. Then, a moment later, "I had forgotten how much your mother enjoyed that pastime. Do you really like it?"

Persis looked down at her hands. "Yes, I do. It's relaxing, even fulfilling. I find so much pleasure in watching things grow."

She smiled and added, almost to herself, "My mother used to say, 'Women do a lot of heaven's work on earth.'"

He looked up at her from the papers on his desk. "How can I possibly argue with that? Perhaps I'll get used to it."

Charlie and Constance came up from Butte City at the beginning of

September. Alex seemed to be up to something, Persis noted. She could tell he was planning some kind of surprise, but he was coy and silent when she pressed him, so she left off.

The second night of Constance and Charlie's stay, Alex invited a number of his male friends in for cards. Persis had met several of these men and looked forward to having Charlie and Constance entertained. While this particular group of Alex's intimate friends was not numbered among Helena's elite, they were educated, respectable merchants and businessmen. Persis wondered if she could ever grow to like Jack Hascombe and Baron Coleman. Alex had let it slip one evening that Jack had written a jesting, scolding letter to him on the subject of his recent marriage. "He's just sulking," said Alex. "Thinks we won't have any jolly times anymore."

Persis didn't hold out a great deal of hope for a friendship with Jack. She had no reason to dislike Baron Coleman, at least none that she could name; she just didn't care for the way he looked at her.

One by one they arrived: Jack and Baron, Robert Hancock, Arthur "Artie" McGruder, and Anton Schulz. Persis became fond of Artie right away; he was a sensitive fellow who didn't quite fit in with the others. A tolerant butt for their jokes, he lent a dose of reason to their card-party discussions. He was interested in Persis's collection of books, and when she found him to be an admirer of Dickens and Keats, their friendship was confirmed.

This evening, which was made up of much laughter and story-telling, Anton Schulz told a gruesome tale about the wolfing trade near Fort Benton. A wolfer, while skinning a week's worth of poisoned wolves, was set upon by a skinned wolf he had of course believed dead.

It was a ghastly image, one that Persis could neither believe nor banish from her head.

Constance gave her a queasy look.

"How could such a thing happen?" asked Charlie.

"The wolf must have been merely unconscious," said Anton. "I know it's a true story; I heard about it from Avery Burke. He knows the fellow it happened to."

At the sound of the name, "Avery Burke," Persis's interest ratcheted up a notch.

"How's Burke doing these days?" asked Rob Hancock. "He's probably got twice as many steers as old Con Kohrs by now."

A chuckle ran around the room. Kohrs, the most well-established cattleman in the Territory, had more cattle than all the other ranchers combined. "Not quite," said Alex. "But he's doing all right, that's certain. I was just out that way last week, visiting Kohrs on Sam Hauser's behalf. I stopped in at Avery's place. It looks fine."

Persis had not heard about this visit.

"He's got a new log house," continued Alex. "Big place with a veranda and so forth. Must have twelve rooms. Quite the line shack."

The men laughed.

"He's right serious about cattle," said Jack Hascombe. "That's what it takes. Don't think I could do it," he opined, adjusting the diamond stickpin in his linen stock.

"A wise decision, Jack. You might get dirty," said Artie, making everyone laugh again.

"Burke said there's some great hunting over on Flint Creek," said Alex, "a day's ride from his place. What do you say we form a party and join him out there in a month or so?"

Persis took a sip of port, which had become her favorite drink. I probably want to go out and see Avery's place as much as anyone else in this room, she thought. She had told Alex about meeting Avery on the train and had related a little of the dinner party. Alex found the tale interesting but, to her relief, inconsequential.

Still, she avoided looking at Constance, who knew far more than Alex about her brief acquaintance with Avery.

The conversation turned to hunting and rifles, with the men in general agreement that they ought to accept Avery's invitation. The last week in October was pinpointed as the date for their trip.

At the prospect of Alex being gone again, Persis absently twisted her handkerchief. She felt the beginnings of a headache and wished the party would break up.

Alex came to stand next to her, then turned to face the guests. "I have an announcement to make," he said.

Everyone's eyes moved swiftly to Persis in a collective appraisal of her figure. She was mortified.

Oblivious to the implication of his overture, Alex went on, "There has been some suggestion in recent weeks that I might demonstrate the advantage of the MacKinney Freight line over that of Gilmer and Salisbury by staging an overland race."

The men's faces lit up and Persis breathed a silent sigh of relief as their attention left her.

"Splendid idea!" cried Jack Hascombe. "A race between the Territory's two leading transfer agents! Why has no one thought of this before?"

Alex grinned. "This spectacle will take place two weeks from tomorrow. We'll start at Clancy and finish our course at the south end of Helena. I hasten to advise you," he said with a wink, "the Gilmer and Salisbury people weren't too thrilled with the idea – principally, of course, because they know I'm going to win. But I issued the challenge in public, so what could the old gents say?"

The excited conversation that followed revolved mainly around Alex being the most colorful and worthwhile companion west of the Mississippi. At the end of the evening, Persis walked their guests to the door, joining Alex in a round of good-byes. Later, she had a few minutes alone with Constance.

"When will I see you again?" Constance asked. She held her hand to the small of her back. By now, her condition was obvious.

Persis bit her lip. "Soon, I hope. Surely before Christmas, when you will come to stay for your confinement."

"I hope so," said Constance. "I miss you. Good-bye, my dearest friend."

The only good thing about Alex's absences, Persis decided, was his homecoming. She loved the light she saw in his eyes as he came up the stairs to greet her, his boots dusty from the ride and his hair disheveled by the wind. She forgot every lonely hour when he grinned hello and caught her in his arms.

As the weather changed and the leaves began to yellow, his days in town began to outnumber his travelling days. They accepted invitations from prominent families like the Powers, the Hausers, and the Kesslers. These were usually formal dinner parties, stiff affairs that didn't offer Persis much of a chance to get to know the wives.

Of Alex's intimate friends, only Rob Hancock was married. Hoping she and Abby Hancock might become friends, Persis listened to Abby's helpful hints on everything from window-washing solutions to the best rags to use in braiding rugs. Sooner or later, Persis reasoned, a topic of real interest will have to arise.

In early October, Alex's friends convened at 610 Gilbert to review the glorious victory Alex had won over Gilmer and Salisbury. That night, Persis had a mild sore throat and knew she would be retiring early. Like most of Helena, she had watched the last quarter-mile of the race, a pounding, hazardous demonstration of skill and showmanship. She enjoyed walking away with the victor, but on reflection she felt the contest was divisive and vain. It exacerbated the rivalry between the two prominent companies and made her feel separate from a part of the community she had hoped to know and befriend.

* * *

At sunrise on October 28, the MacKinney kitchen sounded like a cavalry camp. Tromping about in heavy boots, the men milled around the stove and the maple table, stuffing their mouths with Grace's biscuits and chokecherry jelly.

Alex rapped a spoon on the coffeepot to get everyone's attention. "Yesterday," he said, "I received a letter from Avery. I'll hit the high points for you." He withdrew the letter from his pocket.

"'Regretfully, I will not be able to join you. There is a serious situation on the Sun River range, where rustlers have become a problem with every herd within a 200-mile radius. Cattlemen across the Territory are convening to form a campaign to stop the thieves.'"

The letter insisted that the hunters come ahead, advising them their quarters had been made ready and that his *segundo,* a man named Miles Grayson, would be their guide through the Deer Lodge and Flint Creek wilderness.

Leaning against the counter and the kitchen table with their steaming cups of coffee, the men sympathetically acknowledged the rising threat of the rustlers.

"It's a pity he is not coming," said Alex, "but he says we'll do fine with this Grayson fellow." He read the last sentence. "'I'll have to enjoy my hunting later on, when I'm more likely to freeze to death.'"

Persis smiled slightly. That sounded so much like Avery.

After making a thorough mess of the library by cleaning and comparing their rifles and revolvers, the men put on their coats and made for the door. It was cold. Not bitterly so, but the encircling mountains were scarved in low, feathery clouds and there was a biting mist in the air.

As Nora and Grace cleared away the dishes, Persis went out into the graveled driveway behind the house to watch the men work on their horses and loads. In addition to the saddle horses, there were several packhorses loaded with bedrolls, foodstuffs, and ammunition. One horse, she noted, had been designated entirely for liquor. Seeing its panniers stuffed with straw and bottles, Persis was dumbfounded, but Artie quietly told her this was standard practice, even among more "conservative" hunting parties.

She pulled her cloak tighter and watched wistfully as the animated party made ready. The men in their heavy woolens, the low sky threatening snow, the bridles jingling as the horses shook their heads—it all filled her with a sense of adventure and longing she had not felt since she set out on her trip west six months ago. Oh, for my wonderful Astarte and a pair of riding pants, she thought with a secret smile.

Finally they mounted and began filing out of the driveway. Alex led the way, his horse dancing with eagerness. He turned and waved, and several of the others called out, "Good-bye, Mrs. MacKinney!"

Jack Hascombe yelled back, "We'll come back with enough stories to regale you for the entire winter!"

Persis went back inside. She knew it would be a hard-drinking, unshaven weekend for them, although Alex had confided in her that Artie was going to try not to drink on this trip. He had apparently been off the bottle, Alex said, for over a week.

It came to Persis just then that if Artie quit drinking and retained his status in their group, perhaps Alex could do the same. It also occurred to her, in the cold light of this autumn morning, that she herself had been drinking more liquor than ever before. She frequently joined Alex in a five o'clock cocktail or glass of wine with dinner, and often took a nightcap of port or sherry. She had not expected married life to evolve this way. Their world was full of parties and gaiety, however, and she had to admit she didn't see how frontier society could be managed without spirits. Drinks reliably propelled each late afternoon and evening toward the social frolic that had become a part of her life with Alex: the late-night card games, masquerade benefits for the Volunteer Fire Company or the hospital, and the midnight dinners after Sawtelle's Theater.

She had begun to see, too, that she more adroitly executed the arts of the bedroom when she'd had something to drink. No, she decided, challenging this thought. It is not that I am more adroit, it is that I am more willing. Still, I am not sure what pleases Alex more—a virtuous wife or a coquette who charms among the pillows. I guess most wives endeavor to be something of both.

She watched the cortege of riders and packhorses trot down the hill until their oilcloth slickers faded into the gray morning. For them, the next few days would be filled with rough but happy companionship:

the casual, essential tasks of building campfires and plotting their assault on the ungulate wildlife of the Pintlar Range. At the end of each day, they would raise their tin cups in a toast to the hunter of greatest consequence.

And for me? Well, she thought, giving her head a little shake, there are those pictures that need to be hung in the guest rooms. Nora can help me with that. And the four-poster would be much improved with the addition of a dust ruffle. No question, there's plenty to do. Turning away from the window, she vowed to keep as busy as she possibly could for the next six days.

*   *   *

A frenzy of domestic activity absorbed her, but as Thursday and Friday ticked away and she fell into bed bone-tired each night, she had to admit that her zealous program of household improvement was not fueled by a simple desire to beautify her home and enhance her married life.

No, she thought as she lay awake late Friday night, the plain truth is, I resent being left behind. Of course I don't think they would have taken me, and I wouldn't have wanted to go, for heaven's sake. But this loneliness is becoming a bit of a theme, isn't it?

The next morning, as she stared at the road, empty except for a lone, snuffling pig that had wandered in from the edge of town, the thought of several more days of housework, or even forcing her attention into a novel, settled on her like a shroud.

The pig, nosing under a pile of leaves in the gutter, made her think of the Butte mining camp, where, Constance had written, "one is likely to see livestock of all description roaming the streets." She watched the animal absently, feeling increasingly sullen about having absolutely nothing of significance to do except sit and imagine Alex and his merry little band disporting themselves.

Butte City came again to mind and with it, like a spark from a fire, the idea of visiting Constance. Butte City is sixty or seventy miles away, she thought; a full day's carriage ride. But I'm up to that. Still, the thought of going alone; I am not sure!

She mused over possible companions. Nora and Grace were her only choices, really, since the women she had met over the course of the past three months were all part of Alex's established social circle and would undoubtedly find the proposal appalling.

Grace? No; she should stay here and mind the house. Nora. Yes, Nora it would be.

She pulled the tasseled brocade strip near the door and heard Nora's quick step on the oak floor. Her slender form and pale, freckled face appeared.

"Nora, please get Grace and come here. I have just had an idea with which I must acquaint the two of you."

The two women listened as Persis quickly explained her decision to visit her brother and sister-in-law. She quickly saw in Grace's expression something she did not want to consider—a maternal view on the impropriety of this spur-of-the-moment idea and the obvious questions it raised about the safety of the master's new wife.

"Don't be looking at me in that motherly way, Grace. I've a mother of my own back in New York State. She's just as Irish and as proper as you are, and she raised me right. And I'm no child. I'll be twenty-four in January. This is nothing more than a short trip to visit family. Besides, Nora will have the chance to see her people as well. This house will be as quiet as a mausoleum, Grace. You'll enjoy it."

"I didn't say a word, Missus Persis." Grace looked at the top bookshelf.

"You don't have to." Persis leaned forward excitedly, splaying her hands on the table. "Be happy for me! This is the first time—will be the first time—I have seen them in six weeks. They're my *family*. Get along with you, now," she said officiously, masking the mischief she was feeling. "Put together a few things, Nora, then please come upstairs and help me. Grace, please send Donny downtown to get two seats on the next Gilmer coach."

"It's a wild place Butte City is, ma'am," said Grace. "Be careful." In a softer voice, she added, "Mr. Alex will be asking for you, if he gets back afore you. You've never seen it, ma'am, but he's a handful when he's upset."

"They aren't coming home until Monday or Tuesday. I'll be back by Sunday night at the very latest. Don't worry."

Now that she had decided to go, each obstacle, real or imagined, only increased her determination. Neatly putting aside the issue of

Alex's possible displeasure, she went upstairs to pack. Within an hour, she and Nora were rumbling down the damp, hard-packed highway on the southbound stage. As they passed a group of riders near Unionville, she shrank into her seat, looking surreptitiously out the window.

Nora suppressed a smile.

"And what, pray tell, is so funny?" Persis demanded.

"If you'll forgive me, Missus MacKinney, it's a pleasure findin' that you're a high-spirited woman. My Aunt Kathleen is like that. Says you won't find adventure by stirrin' a hole in your gravy."

Persis smiled at this odd wisdom and adjusted her cloak around her. The only other time she had seen this road was on the drive north from the Utah and Northern terminus, in the blistering heat of July. Now, at the end of October, there was a penetrating chill in the air.

The pine-covered foothills of the Rockies were all around, here and there encrusted with outcroppings of granite. Close at hand, the evergreens were distinguishable as lodgepole pine and Douglas fir, but as the low hills shouldered up into mountains, the trees became a uniform, green-black carpet rumpling into gentle folds, ascending toward the peaks. Thunderbolt Mountain was already dusted with snow.

Several hours later, as they entered the outskirts of Butte City, the road got muddier. The traffic increased and freight wagons were everywhere. It was nearing dusk and many workers were on their way home, slogging through the ankle-deep mire.

As the stage lurched along, Persis looked continuously out the window. Butte City did weave a kind of spell, she realized. People talked about it with a mixture of disdain and affectionate loyalty, but to behold it for one's self was startling. How such a rough and squalid place could maintain its position as the economic focus of Montana Territory was difficult to comprehend. Yet there was something about the place; something seductive. Every person she saw, from the lowest of immigrants picking his way across the puddling ruts to the posturing, well-heeled merchant stepping down from a bespattered black carriage, had an aura of intention. The air was charged with energy, like a theater, and every person had a role to play.

The miners coming off shift dominated the scene, speaking foreign languages and slapping one another on the back as they headed eagerly into the saloons that far outnumbered every other commercial establishment. The pale sky had darkened, but still it did not match the sooty faces of the miners.

"I suspect things start to calm down as the night goes on," Persis observed. It was more a question than a statement.

"Oh no, Missus. It's always like this. All day and all night."

"All night? When do people sleep?" She wondered how all of this was settling with Constance.

"It's the mines. It's workin' round the clock these fellows are. There's always someone comin' home with an empty dinner pail and another on his way up the hill with a full one. And they do spend a good bit o' time in the saloons and dance halls. The miners came first, then the ladies came to look after 'em, that's what Kathleen says."

Persis stared out at the ceaseless roil of humanity. To the right was a lively dance hall. The brightly-lit, smoky interior was packed with men and gaily-dressed women. Near the door stood a young woman with well-rouged lips and cheeks. Her dark blue cloak was thrown back, exposing white shoulders. One beringed hand lay across her bosom, hinting to passers-by of the sensations available for a price.

The young woman passed from view. A skinny boy lit oil lamps along a gaming house façade, and a cluster of Chinese men stood directly in front of the door, chattering loudly. They scattered like bowling pins as a human projectile hurtled out the door, slamming directly into the side of the coach.

Persis screamed and reached for the door-latch, convinced that the man's skull had been cracked. Her eyes widened and she called a sharp "Halt!" to the driver. The stage rolled on.

Nora reached for the latch and re-fastened it, then timidly looked at Persis. "Merciful Jesus, ma'am, don't get out."

"I had no intention of getting out! That man—he must have been killed, or nearly killed." She craned her neck to look out the small window at the rear of the coach. The man was picking himself up out of the mud.

"He's alive," she concluded, shaking her head.

At the stage depot, they cornered a heavy-set Italian man who had a buggy for hire. It was dark now, and the two of them were tensely focused on reaching Charlie's house at 201 Idaho Street. Persis let Nora direct the driver, and away they went. As the buggy left the heart of town and bumped along the soupy streets, the lights died down, but a buzz of activity was everywhere. Nora was right; Butte City was not a quiet place.

The driver easily found the house. The mere sight of its windows glowing yellow-orange in the dark filled Persis with pleasure. It was a quaint but roomy frame structure, a fine representation of Butte's aspiring middle class.

Nora waited until the front door opened and Constance appeared, then waved good-bye, calling, "We'll be back in the morning."

Constance had her hands wadded into her apron, caught in the middle of dish-washing. "Percy! My God, is everything all right? Where's Alex?"

Persis bustled in, pulled the door closed behind her, and explained in a quick, offhand way that she had come only for the night, while Alex was away on a hunting trip.

"Your house is wonderful!" she exclaimed, tossing aside her wrap.

Constance closed her slack jaw, fumbled her hands out of the apron, and embraced her friend.

Persis took everything in: the fading scents of the dinner hour, the whistling teakettle in the kitchen, and the mining books liberally strewn across the long table that served as Charlie's desk. The house hummed with the rhythms of genuine life.

"I was just making some tea. Charlie's working late at the assay office."

"The assay office is open?"

"They'd be fools to close, Percy. I rather think they're open twenty-four hours a day. Come into the kitchen."

The teacups were filled, but so much time was spent talking that the women repeatedly had to set their cups on the stove to warm the contents. No matter; catching up with one another was the refreshment each of them wanted most.

Adjourning to the front room, Persis went to the pot-bellied stove, stirred the embers, and added kindling.

"Seeing you stir the fire reminds me that this is All Hallow's Eve," said Constance.

"It is, isn't it? October 31 . . . time to think of lost loved ones. We ought to climb the hill and light a bonfire. Mother and Father always did; they loved the old country ways. Well, in Butte City, I guess a bonfire would be a bit redundant."

They both laughed. The town was peppered with huge fires at all hours of the day or night, all year long, as the mining wagons dumped ore and lumber into the roasting pits.

"Yes, there are bonfires aplenty," said Constance, standing near the window.

Suddenly Persis sat bolt upright.

"What's the matter?" asked Constance, seeing an odd, almost stricken look on Persis's face.

"Constance! No, it can't be. Get me a calendar. No, I'll get it. Stay where you are. Where is it?"

Before Constance could answer, Persis had found a calendar on the desk. She was silent for a few moments, but her lips and fingers were moving. She looked up, her eyes wide. "Constance! I . . . I think I'm with child!"

"What? Are you sure?"

"Of course I'm not." She fluttered her hands. "I mean, of course I'm not sure. How should I know, really? But my flux was due over a week ago. It's never late. At least it hasn't been since I was a schoolgirl."

"How have you been feeling these last few weeks?"

"I felt sick this morning, but I thought it was because of that cream soup last night. We should have thrown it out." Wide-eyed, she stared at Constance. "Don't say anything to Charlie. I want to be further along before anyone knows."

"I understand."

Well into the night, even after Charlie had stumbled in, dog-tired, and climbed the stairs to bed, the two women talked and laughed. In keeping with the ancient All Hallows custom, they set out a glass of wine for the faithful departed.

As the fire burned low in the stove, Persis lay her head back on the sofa and looked drowsily at her friend. The firelight played over Constance's rose-colored dress, casting long shadows across her rounded belly and the hand that lay at its crest.

"Right or wrong, Constance, I feel closer to you than I think I could ever feel to Alex," Persis said softly.

She turned her face toward the window and looked out at the indigo sky. "I love him passionately," she said, "and I'm devoted to him, but I am beginning to feel that he may never share his deepest self with me. Oh, perhaps he might, but I really don't think so. It's just not the sort of man he is. I am trying not to take it personally, but I long for the spiritual communion I have always had with you. I guess I am trying to say that I miss you."

"I miss you too," said Constance, her voice tight. After a moment, she added, "I wonder, Percy, if perhaps we choose our mates because they have something to teach us."

"Not because we can't keep our hands off them?" Persis said with a giggle.

"Well, we both know there's some of that. That's why we are both in this—condition. Anyway, Persis, I need you as much as you need me. You are an enormous spark of joy in my life. It has been rather . . . isolating here."

She laid her hand on Persis's wrist for a moment. "You mustn't think I am unhappy with Charlie. I adore him. It's just that Helena sounds so refined and glamorous, so far removed from where I am. You must have noticed on the drive in that this place is rustic in the extreme."

Persis compressed her lips and nodded.

"Carrying a child has put me in touch with my mortality, Persis. You'll feel it too. That's what makes a mother different from a woman who has borne no children. You come preciously close to death for the sake of your second self."

"I want to see you more than I have these last two months," said Persis. "I think Alex will understand." As she uttered those words there was a silent caveat in her heart: He must understand.

"Let's promise one another that we'll do better at sharing our fears as well as our dreams," said Constance, holding out her hand.

Persis placed her hand in Constance's palm and said, "I promise."

When Persis crawled into bed, she was grateful for the hot bricks they had placed between the sheets an hour before. She looked out the frost-laced window at the moon and wondered just exactly what it was that she and Alex were teaching one another. Could he ever learn to place more trust in her?

As she snuggled into the fragrant tick, which was filled with the sweet-smelling hay Constance called "pasture feathers," her thoughts swirled with intense curiosity around the tiny creature taking shape within her. Her heart was full of a new eagerness to get home. Home to 610 Gilbert and to the father of her child.

10

Good weather favored the stagecoach ride back to Helena, bringing Persis and Nora home earlier than they had hoped. Just minutes
after they entered the kitchen, however, Persis heard the crunch of
gravel in the driveway. Through the window, she saw Alex and two of
his friends trotting up.

Her valise stood in the center of the kitchen floor. Before she could
remove her cloak, Alex bounded up the stairs from the mudroom. He
looked dirty, unkempt, and glad to be home. But as he looked Persis
quickly up and down and saw her traveling bag on the floor, his face
darkened.

"What has happened? Is everything all right?"

"Of course it is, darling. I . . . I went to visit my brother and Constance for a day, that's all."

They heard the sound of the other men's boots on the gravel, coming toward the house.

"Take your cloak and hat off and take your bag upstairs," Alex said
firmly. "I don't want them to know you have been gone."

She scurried up the back stairs with her valise. I'll come back down
appearing as though I had never left, she reasoned, and listen to the
stories that he and the other men will tell. By the time they leave, he
will feel less shocked about my trip, and I'll pay him an especial
amount of attention. She ran to her dressing table and touched up her
hair, dabbed fresh rouge on her lips and went to the front stairs to de-
scend with the restrained eagerness a wife would normally display
when her husband had been gone nearly a week.

The men—Artie MacGruder, Anton Schulz, Baron Coleman, and Alex—had gone into the library for a glass of brandy. Taking a private roll call, Persis saw that the only ones missing were the married ones, who must have gone home to their families.

Persis stood in the doorway, a book in her hand.

"Come in," said Alex. A little too calmly, she thought.

She went in, smiling brilliantly at them all. "So, the great hunters are back from the bosky wilderness!" She went immediately to Alex, embraced him warmly, and said, "Welcome home, dear."

He responded by placing his arm around her waist for a moment and allowing her to kiss him. His mind was clearly on his guests.

She turned to them and said. "No accidents? Everyone is well?" Then she realized with chagrin that all four of them—including Artie—had been drinking for quite some time.

"Aside from minor perils such as grizzly bears and highwaymen, we've had a very mild experience, Mrs. MacKinney," said Baron, rolling the ash of his cigar into a crystal dish.

Despite her efforts to like Baron, he remained her least favorite of Alex's friends. She smiled benignly. "Well," she said, surveying the group, "surely you aren't too weary to tell me of your adventures?"

With this small urging, the men recounted that they had overpowered a gang of thieves near Unionville, setting the ruffians on a dead run back toward Helena.

"And then," said Anton Schulz, "a grizzly bear invaded our camp night before last! Fortunately, we were using one of Burke's old line shacks, and the bear did not attempt to enter the cabin. Alex winged the brute," he said. "Through the window, mind you, but then he wanted to go out after him!"

Persis turned sharply and looked at Alex, who returned her gaze with a boyish half-smile.

"'Twas after a bit of a card game and a little whiskey, y'know," interposed Schulz, "enough to embolden any man. But we wouldn't let him go out. What a fuss he raised! He wanted that bear. Said he wanted to bring it home and put its great shaggy hide on this very floor."

Hardly in a position to remonstrate, Persis responded with a simple, "I am very glad you are all home."

The men regaled themselves for another half-hour with Rob Hancock's fall into the creek and Artie MacGruder's habit of forgetting his bid at cards. When they finally took their leave, Persis readied herself for the inquisition she knew was coming. She was not afraid. She knew she could calm Alex's fears. She was lit from within with the knowledge of the child they were bringing into the world.

The door had scarcely closed on the last of the men when Alex, swirling the brandy in his glass, said, "So you went to Butte City."

"I was so lonesome after you left, Alex. It just isn't the same here without you. After two days I began to feel so bored, and I started thinking about dear Charlie and Constance. Their baby's due in less than two months, you know." She came around behind him and leaned over the couch, placing her arms around his neck.

"I can't believe you went to Butte City, Persis. This is amazing to me."

She circled around the couch and sat next to him, touching his arm. "I am so glad to see you," she said. "I missed you!"

He continued looking at the drink in his hand. Persis saw the dark stubble on his cheek ripple slightly as he shifted his jaw. When he raised his eyes to hers, they were dark. He was far more angry than she had thought he would be.

"I'm going out to help Donny dress out the deer," he said curtly, and left the room.

Persis sat in the library for another hour, getting up once or twice to examine her reflection in the glass. She looked especially well this evening, and told herself it was only a matter of time before Alex would realize her trip was nothing to be concerned about.

She picked up her yarn, remembering how much he enjoyed seeing her do needlework. Strange, she thought, how the sight of me stitching on a piece of fabric is so intensely appealing to him.

The clock on the mantel struck quarter past ten when she heard Alex's step on the floor of the hall. He came into the room, poured himself another glass of brandy, and went up the stairs without a word.

His coldness went through her like the blade of a knife. I most certainly do not deserve this, she thought, swallowing thickly, for simply having taken a trip to visit my brother and his wife. This is unfair.

She rose to go upstairs, then hesitated. Should she leave him alone?

Some squabbles fester a while but are best left alone and cauterized by time. She paced. No, she couldn't behave as if nothing was wrong. Filled with the desire to resolve the situation, she stuffed her needle-work into the tambour table and went up the stairs.

He was taking a bath, so she sat down with a book to wait. When he finally came out, he ignored her and began preparing for bed, as if she were no more than a piece of furniture.

Still fully dressed, she began to feel foolish. After all, it was late. She undressed quickly in the adjacent room. When she came back in, the lights were out and Alex was in bed.

She climbed in beside him and reached over to him, finding his back to her. "Sweetheart," she said softly, "I don't want to go to sleep with this coldness between us." She gently touched his back with a slow caress.

He rolled over suddenly, sat up, and lit the lamp. His jaw was firmly set and his features showed no trace of softening.

"You've handled this situation very badly, Persis."

"It was a spur-of-the-moment thing, Alex! I was completely safe. I didn't go alone. I took Nora. I've traveled alone, I mean, with a female companion before."

"Is that all you care about? Defending yourself?"

"No, please, I don't mean to sound that way. What is it? Tell me. I *want* to understand."

"You ought to know. I shouldn't have to tell you these things, damn it." He flung back the bed covers, stood up, and started pacing. "You may be a lot of things, my dear, but stupid is not one of them."

Persis wracked her brain. Of course I am not stupid, she thought. She sat in silence for several moments, feverishly tracing the events of the last few days, looking for the word or deed that had so sorely compounded her offense.

"Is it . . . are you concerned . . ." she stumbled over her words. "Is it a case of impropriety? I mean, do you think it was so very improper?"

"I see," he said. "You still want to defend what you did. There is no point in discussing it."

He came over to her side of the bed and stood there, glaring at her. She noticed that he was curling and uncurling his fingers. Tension emanated from him, oppressing her and filling the room.

"Alex, it really was harmless. I only wanted to see Constance. We have a special sisterly love, and I have missed her."

He grabbed her by the upper arms and brought her roughly to her feet. "Can you imagine any other woman in this town doing this to her husband?" He was shouting, his face inches away from hers. "*Can you?*" he repeated. He shook her violently until her head wobbled on her neck, then shoved her back onto the bed in disgust.

Stunned, her mouth hanging open, Persis feebly tried to collect her thoughts. Any other woman? Another woman going to visit a friend? Her stomach lurched with a wave of nausea. What form of idiocy has come over me that prevents me from seeing Alex's point? Oh, dear God, I simply don't understand. I don't know whether to say yes or no.

"Do you think Abby Hancock bounded onto the first stage as soon as she knew Rob was gone? And what about Catherine Drexel, or Louise Kessler? I'll guarantee none of them went running off as soon as their husbands rode out of town," he sputtered. "A woman—a *wife*— belongs at home, not diverting herself in a filth-ridden mining camp."

Persis wanted to point out that all these women had small children at home, but she held her tongue.

"But you," Alex went on, pointing his finger at her, "you couldn't wait until I left so you could run off and be with someone else. How do you think that makes me feel? For God's sake, I'm your husband!"

At last! Persis nearly gasped with relief. He is drawing back the curtain and letting me see. He takes this trip as a personal affront, a betrayal.

She quickly turned this discovery over and over in her mind, each time gaining a clearer idea of how Alex viewed their marriage. She felt a bizarre range of things, all the way from terror to pity.

"Why couldn't you have included me, Persis? I like to visit Butte City. The two of us could have taken this trip together, as a couple."

Her mind sifted through a hundred words, seeking the most palliative response. "I . . . I would like to visit them with you. They would like it too." At the same time she knew that having Alex accompany her on a visit to Constance would preclude any real intimacy with her bosom friend.

"What you did was a very selfish thing, Persis." His voice began rising again. "I repeat, you handled this very badly. Very badly indeed."

He mustn't get any more upset, Persis realized. Shaking, suppressing the bile rising in her throat, she forced herself near him, then reached up and put her arms around his neck.

Pressing her face into his chest, she whispered, "I am so sorry. It won't happen again."

He was completely unresponsive. The only movement she sensed was a slight back and forth motion as he weaved from the effects of the alcohol.

"Come to bed, won't you?" she asked as tenderly as she could. "I have missed you. Besides, it's midnight. Tomorrow is Monday."

"I just can't understand this," he said, shaking his head in disbelief. "I thought you were different. . . ." his voice trailed off.

She took his hand and he, docile at last, allowed her to lead him to the bed. He was still sullen, apparently unwilling to touch her. In bed, she took his arm and placed it around her shoulder and molded her body to his.

"I love you," she said.

For the first time that night, he took hold of her with something other than anger. It was not, however, a pleasant embrace. "Don't make a fool out of me, Persis," he said finally, in a strained, almost menacing tone.

Persis was silenced by the emotional power she felt in both the embrace and the admonition. There had been such anger in him just now, but there had also been a rare display of vulnerability. This last was oddly gratifying. It's a beginning, she decided. We've a long way to go in getting to know one another, but he has let me see inside him. It has at last begun!

*   *   *

The cool light of the November morning poured through the lace draperies, making faint patterns on the breakfast table.

Persis, applying her most cheerful manner, saw the old Alex beginning to reappear. She wanted to tell him about the baby as soon as possible.

When Grace finally left them alone, he busied himself with fried eggs and sausage.

"I have some wonderful news," she said, adding quickly, before he could make any sarcastic observations, "I am not positive, but I believe we are going to have a baby."

His eyes suddenly warmed to their lively gold-brown color. His brows raised and his lips parted, he set his fork down on the plate with a barely discernible clink.

Persis felt her heart soar.

"A baby?" He reached for her hand. "Do you know? I mean, when will you know, for certain?"

"In a few weeks," she whispered, holding his hand in both of hers. At last, she thought, we are together again, in every sense of the word, and in an entirely new way as well!

Alex left the house in such a euphoric state that he forgot his hat, even though snowflakes were falling from the chalky sky.

* * *

That afternoon, in the small sitting room off the library she had commandeered for her very own use, Persis began a letter to Constance. She wrote of snowflakes, of the comfort of the special little writing room Alex had given her, and of the curious sensation of expecting a child.

The natural flow of her thoughts was to tell Constance how upset Alex had been about her trip. But, she reasoned, if I tell Constance that Alex was angry, she will think he wants to stand in the way of our friendship. And if I tell her he was upset enough to handle me roughly, she will certainly think ill of him.

Suddenly thrown back into the events of last night, her hands trembled. And all the time my heart was full of the tenderest desire to make things right! He didn't care; he was determined to be angry. When he shook me, I felt my teeth rattle in my skull. And he shouted at me. No one has ever shouted at me. He shook his finger at me and accused me of being selfish.

The letter fell into her lap. Her eyes welled with tears that went splashing down her bodice, barely missing the vellum stationery.

"I'll just have to prove to him that he's wrong about me," she whispered to herself, fishing her handkerchief out of her pocket. "I'm none of those things. I am loving and kind and devoted. Eventually he will feel more at ease with my social habits. Perhaps if I had a female companion here in Helena. If I consult him on this, he will surely see the sense of my having companionship, especially now that I'm to be a mother."

And some things, she decided, are meant to stay between husband and wife. With new determination, she put Constance's portion of the truth into an envelope and put it on the hall table with the outgoing post.

*   *   *

Two days later, Alex came home from the office in a buoyant mood. As soon as he saw her, he slipped his right arm around her waist and grabbed her left hand in his, spinning her around the front hallway in a waltz.

"Good afternoon, Alex," she said, laughing.

"How soon can you be packed for a trip back east?"

"What?" she gasped. "Where are you—are we—going?"

"New York City, my dear. But maybe you don't want to go," he said, a naughty smile playing about the corners of his mouth.

"Of course I do," she cried out. It would be an adventure, and for that reason alone it was appealing. "Is it business?"

"Yes and no. Sam Hauser and Sidney Dillon want me to represent them at a meeting of several of the Utah and Northern principals. Hauser's off to San Francisco, and Dillon is tied up with a real estate problem. They've asked me to go to New York for them."

Alex uttered these words matter-of-factly, but Persis detected pride.

"That's wonderful!" she said, "They clearly place a great deal of trust in you. But I have known that all along." After a few minutes, she asked, "I'll be able to see my mother, won't I?"

"Well, I think we could work that in, my dear. She needs to know that she's about to become a grandmother again, doesn't she? And won't you need some things for the baby?"

Persis kissed him fervently. With time, she thought, the memories of last week will fade entirely away.

Suddenly she remembered how close Constance was to the end of her pregnancy. "When will we be coming back?" she asked lightly.

"By Thanksgiving," he said. "Which reminds me. You asked if I would keep you abreast of our social plans, so I must tell you that we are invited to Thanksgiving dinner at Avery Burke's outfit, the Double Diamond. You heard us talking about it. Quite the spread. We may just go there from the Butte mining camp on our return."

Later that evening, Persis carefully framed a question. "Darling, since you will have me all to yourself for three entire weeks, I am hoping you won't mind if we have Constance come and spend a fortnight with us when it's her time."

Alex took a sip of whiskey and said, "As a matter of fact, Persis, I've outguessed you on this one. I knew you'd want to do that, and I knew Constance would want you with her. The baby is due before Christmas, isn't it?"

Persis nodded, eyeing him carefully.

"I am planning to have them come back with us. We'll all go to Avery's for Thanksgiving and then come to Helena. Besides, the best doctor in the Territory lives right here in Helena. His name is Ben Lyons. So, what do you think about all that, my errant little wife?" He shuffled some papers on the table, then looked up at her with a trace of a smile.

"You've thought of everything," she murmured. "It seems impossible that all of this could transpire in the next month and a half. It sounds wonderful, Alex, I don't know what to say. Thank you. Thank you so very much."

He rose and leaned over her, kissing her hair and letting his hand slip down her spine. It stirred her, that touch of his, like nothing else could. She cocked her head and looked up at him, wondering if he wanted her as much as she wanted him.

"I'll be back. I've got a card game at Anton's. Wait up for me, won't you?"

She nodded and watched him walk down the hallway toward the back door. He had anticipated more than she ever thought he could. It was like him and yet unlike him. Then the reserved, enigmatic smile he had when he told her of his detailed plans. Was it a witness to his new peace of mind or a smile of conquest?

As soon as she heard the back door close, she pulled a sheet of paper out of her desk drawer and began a list. The prospect of a trip was exciting, yes, but what swelled into her mind right now was the stark knowledge that as soon as they returned to 610 Gilbert, Constance's lying-in would nearly be upon her. Dear God, just let everything go well, she thought, absently drumming her quill on the blotter.

Three days later, they were on the Utah and Northern, headed for Ogden, Utah, where they would board the Union Pacific for points East. Staring out the window at the Rockies, Persis couldn't see their summits. The clouds hung low and thick, and there was a darkness to the canyons and passes she had never seen before. With their majestic striae of dark granite and ermine-white snow, the mountains awed her. Cloaked in the mystery of coming winter, they beckoned her to stay. "Wherever you go, you will dream of us," they whispered. "You belong here now; you belong to this land of rock and sage and sky."

A gust buffeted the window and she felt its cold caress on her cheek. Yes! Yes, it's true, she thought, nodding an answer to the nipping wind and the rugged landscape that had become far more than mere weather and geography to her. Montana Territory had made its way into her soul.

She silently mouthed the words: I have never felt as close to God as I do here. The towering, wet granite, the silhouette of a soaring hawk against the pale ceiling of snow-laden clouds, the dense pines blanketing the high slopes . . . even the last, brittle box elder leaves quivering tremulously over the creek . . . I love it all, more passionately than I ever thought I could. No matter what, I will always come back.

* * *

Persis had to buy another trunk in New York City to transport her purchases back to the Territory. In addition to lace-trimmed maternity smocks, she bought skirts of heavy silk or worsted wool, christening gowns, pillowcases, undershirts, and two dozen phials of home remedies.

The Goulds insisted that she visit their favorite French clothier, where she spent even more money on items that would suit her once she regained her figure: high-heeled boots, evening slippers, an amber-hued evening gown, Parisian chemises and petticoats, gifts for Constance, and finally, a pair of purple stockings, which were all the rage in New York.

When she boarded the westbound train in late November, she was dead tired from all the socializing, the opera, and the dinners at Delmonico's. She wanted to hear Grace and Nora bickering in their thick brogue, and to see the look of joy on Constance's face when she opened her gifts.

En route, Alex spent a good deal of time in the gaming car. Persis felt sick all day, not just in the mornings. The only thing that seemed to help was to eat. She began to feel heavy and self-absorbed, fussing about small things that normally would not have bothered her.

One evening when Alex had promised to be back in their compartment by eight o'clock, he did not appear until almost midnight. By the time he arrived, Persis had been asleep for two hours. Between her eyelashes, she stole a look at her watch while he was washing his face. Speechless with resentment, she pretended to be asleep.

In the morning, she woke early but could not bring herself to look at him. Finally, as they were getting dressed, she said, "Alex, I do not know what you mean by saying you will join me at eight o'clock and then not appearing until midnight. For all I knew you were shot in a brawl or fell off the train."

Alex looked up with surprise, but gradually the corners of his mouth turned slightly downward.

At that moment, Persis realized she was learning very well just how to read her husband. In fact, even before the firm line formed along his jaw, dread poured into her. Yes, she thought, I have seen that look twice before. First on the night prior to our marriage when he shared his misgivings about my "obsession" with Constance, and again after my unsanctioned trip to Butte City.

"Alex," she began cautiously, "can you please pause for a moment and try to look at this from my point of view? I felt hurt. I imagined you having fun with your friends and not even giving me a thought."

"Does the idea of me enjoying myself disturb you?" He counted out his change and tossed it onto the shelf.

"Of course not. It's just that I need you, Alex. And I feel frightened about a lot of things. When you say you will be with me at a certain hour, I tend to pin my hopes and my comfort on that hour."

He exhaled, toying with his collar. "It didn't occur to you to ask what might have detained me, did it?"

Taken aback, Persis replied, "No, I am sorry to say it did not."

"It just so happens I ran into none other than Ralph Masters, Vice

President of the entire Union Pacific Railroad. He's Sidney Dillon's principal lieutenant. By happy coincidence, he was in the company of a Beaverhead Valley man whose land I am considering for a timber purchase. I suppose I could have said to these gentlemen, in the middle of our card game, 'Please excuse me so that I may go and tell my wife I will be late.'"

Persis was thinking, yes, you could have. But she knew that for Alex, such an act may have been impossible. Once in the company of his friends and business associates, nothing mattered but the company and the moment.

She stared at the bedding, trying to overcome the pall of dejection settling on her. She was beginning to believe that, despite the important position she seemed to occupy in his life, Alex could be a selfish and unreasonable man.

Tense expectation hung in the air between them. As the seconds passed, she wondered if he was waiting for her to apologize. I most certainly will not, she vowed.

At breakfast, Alex looked at her with the trace of a smile on his face and asked, "Now, are you going to be my sweet wife?"

There it was, that familiar, cajoling tone. Looking at him across the table, she suddenly comprehended his masterful ability to manage their marital discourse to his advantage. Whenever there was a conflict, Alex structured their communication so that she would emerge as the transgressor. It was a tactic at which he was extraordinarily adept.

This epiphany rendered her speechless. The balance of power between them, she realized, was irrevocably skewed. Staring down at her tea, she watched the sunlight dance on the silver table service. She raised her face and looked him in the eye. The skin around the corners of his eyes was crinkling and there was a ghost of a playful smile on his lips. It was as though he knew exactly what she was thinking.

She tried to pull an invisible shade across her face, something, anything, to keep him from reading her, but it didn't work.

He leaned back. The reflected light shone in his brown eyes, giving them a warm, liquid look. She hated herself for feeling what she next felt, but she couldn't help it. She smiled back.

"Oh, you mustn't smile at me!" he said, gently mocking her.

She compressed her lips tightly for a moment and then said, "You are the most maddening person I have ever met."

"Well, my dear, I may be maddening, but I am not totally unreasonable. I promise that the next time I am detained, I will make every effort to let you know the nature of my detention."

"That's all I wanted, Alex. Just to hear that." She put her hand out on the table, palm up. He took it, then released it.

She suddenly felt his hand on her knee, beneath the table. He hoisted the hem of her skirt, then her petticoat, and lifted her leg onto his lap, where he could caress her ankle and calf unobserved.

"Alex!" she whispered, trying to pull her leg away.

"I'll let you go if you promise not to eat too much. I want to take you back to our little room for some exercise," he said huskily, still grinning at her.

In their post-breakfast lovemaking, everything else slipped away, and the two of them quickly found the highly-charged language of sensation and belonging.

Each time the axe struck the wood, Avery listened for the right sound. If the pitch was too high, it meant he had split the log unevenly. Too low, and he had done even worse, perhaps only flaying off a shingle. The proper sound was a satisfying crack, almost a pop.

As he wiped his brow with his sleeve, he smelled the damp wool of his jacket and the acrid scent of cottonwood leaves fluttering by. One discriminating look at the woodpile—a good thirty feet long and four feet high—told him the Double Diamond had a fine start on a winter's supply of firewood. Another one just like it lay around the corner on the north side of the barn. But he knew both stacks needed to get another two feet taller before Christmas. Even now, a few lonely flakes danced on the gusty air.

"Half your wood and half your hay, you should have come Candlemas Day." He repeated the old rhyme, slinging the axe out in swift, true strokes, watching the logs open and fall in two, often as perfectly matched as the halves of an elk's hoof.

In a week, he'd see Persis Allen again. Persis MacKinney, he reminded himself, and don't you forget it. He heard news of her now and then, for even though the Territory was a vast area, the citizenry was scant, and someone like Persis set tongues wagging.

What he had heard was consistent and predictable: "Seen Alex MacKinney's bride? She's a looker. Always knew he'd find a good one. Pleasant, too." And then the inevitable, "Hope she holds up all right. Territory's hell on women."

Good-looking and pleasant she was, indeed, he thought. But life goes on. A young schoolteacher he had met in Bozeman last month had turned his head. Given enough time, he expected he might stop thinking about Persis. Yes, he figured Emma could probably help that along quite a bit.

Avery leaned on his axe, breathing hard, and looked down into the broad pasture south of the ranch house. Pete was there, just as he was every day, absorbed in talking to another of his green-broke horses.

"Come on and get it, 'fore I throw it out," called Sparky from the kitchen window.

Pete looked up. Avery grinned, glad that Pete had heard the call. Avery moved his right fist as if using a fork. Pete nodded, pulled off his hat and waved it, revealing the scarf he always wore bound over his right ear during cold weather.

The sight of that scarf made Avery wish for the hundredth time that he could have prevented the accident on the Platte River eight years ago. He had felt the snag in the water; his own paint's front hoof had struck it. But just as he tried to warn Pete, the cattle took a fool notion to climb a vertical cliff. Of course, the wall of mud gave way and buried a dozen head or more.

In the pouring rain and the bawling melee, Pete had plowed into the river to help. His faithful black horse faltered about halfway across, even before the place where Avery thought the snag lay.

The horrific sight of Pete's face as his horse began to lose its draft was all it took to set Avery in motion. He remembered nearly flying off his own horse when a slippery-looking bit of plaid flannel billowed past.

Somehow, with no footing of his own and only one free arm, he had dragged his brother nearly to shore. With every passing second, though, it seemed the river would claim them both.

Then, as if descending from heaven, a dark, oval ring appeared in the sky just above him. A tidy lasso drifted right down across Pete's body and settled there. Much later, Avery would learn that it was their tough old trail boss, Fox McCourt, who threw the lariat that saved them that fateful morning.

And it was McCourt's spring wagon that hauled the Burke brothers into Casper. Avery remembered that bumping, interminable ride, but most of all he remembered staring at Pete's bluish face and the lock of hair that lay plastered like a raven's wing across his forehead, wondering how in God's name he'd tell his mother if Pete died.

But Pete woke up two days later.

"Where's my horse?" he had said, while everyone in the hospital room stared, slack-jawed with shock and joy.

The fact that Pete had lost the hearing in his right ear seemed a miniscule price to pay for getting another chance at life, Avery told himself as he tipped the axe against the woodpile and walked toward the corral.

"What's cooking?" Pete asked, pulling off his gloves as he came through the barnyard. "Smells good."

"Chicken stew, I think. Mrs. Kohrs brought over some plum jam," said Avery.

"We'd die if it weren't for the neighbor women," Pete said loudly.

"I heard that, you skunk." Sparky scowled at them from the doorway. "You fools are lucky to have me as yer wifey-dear. A couple of ineligible bachelors stranded up on the Clark Fork!"

"He's got a point, Pete," said Avery.

Twenty minutes later, over the remains of dinner, Pete eyed his brother across the table.

"What's on your mind?" asked Avery, getting up for the coffeepot.

"I wager," said Pete, leaning back in his chair, "you've got a secret reason for going over to Bozeman twice in the past month. Next thing you know I'll come in from the rain and find doilies all over the front room."

Lolling his head back and looking at the cook, Pete added, "Sparky, your days as wifey-dear might be numbered. Want my hanky?"

Sparky ran a kitchen knife across his stubbled chin with a rasping sound. "I don't need no whetstone," he said menacingly.

"At least I don't stand out in the sagebrush spoonin' with my horse," said Avery. "You can help chop wood this afternoon, by the way. We've got a big bunch of people coming next week."

* * *

Persis watched Avery's face as the words settled on him. He looked at her, his face registering surprise and concern.

"A baby," he said. "Persis, that is wonderful. Congratulations to both you and Alex." His eyes dropped quickly over her figure. "Not soon, obviously," he said.

"Not until May," Persis said. "A long way off, and yet a short time too."

It was the night before Thanksgiving, cold and still. Persis stood alone with Avery on the back porch of his log ranch house. Inside, past the kitchen, on the other side of the house, the Double Diamond's guests were busy at cards and listening to Miles Grayson on the fiddle. The lively strains drifted through the house, just audible to Avery and Persis as they looked out at the dimensionless sky. The air was rich with sage, pine, and crisp wood smoke.

"Tomorrow is Thanksgiving already," said Persis, changing the subject. "And Christmas is just around the corner. How do you celebrate Christmas here?"

"We eat," Avery said simply.

"I can just imagine," she said with a laugh, "if what I saw in the larder is any indication. It's a wonder you aren't all more—well, portly."

"We have gifts too, mind you," Avery went on. "Nothing too elaborate. Maybe a new pair of spurs, or boots if we're really lucky. That usually only happens if someone's got a sweetheart with a bit of a bank account. Christmas Dinner is really the highlight for us cowboys."

Persis was silent. The tune of the fiddle died away under the soft rush of the wind in the pines. She looked past the nearby trees to the meadow, where a few horses stood, intent on a pile of hay.

"Do you—I mean, is there. . . ." she began, then swallowed quickly and began again, "Is there a special woman in your life, Avery?"

He looked down at the plank flooring and edged a bit of bark off the porch with the toe of his boot. "Lately there is. Over Bozeman way. I've only just met her. Her name is Emma Fenton."

Persis was glad he told her the name. A lot of men would make a woman pry that bit of information loose with a stick. Avery's directness had a curious effect on her. It continually caught her off guard, yet at the same time it put her completely at ease.

"Emma," she said. "That was my grandmother's name, back East."

Avery looked at her, then quickly away. "As I said, I've only just met her. Her family has a sawmill in the Gallatin Valley, and she's teaching school."

"A teacher," murmured Persis. "That's good. You need someone of intellect." She stopped, raising her hand to her mouth. "Oh, I am sorry! I can't presume to know what you need. I'm only saying what I imagine to be true. Forgive me."

"There is nothing to forgive. I think you understand a lot of things, Persis. You've got a good mind. I knew it within five minutes of meeting you. For better or worse, I will always expect more from you than from most people."

Persis was glad for the twilight and the cold air that kept him from seeing her reddened cheeks.

"Now it's my turn to be sorry," Avery said. "I probably said more than I should have."

"It's all right. I think we understand one another."

He picked at the porch rail a moment and said, "I hope you are finding life in the Territory to be all you expected."

It took Persis longer to respond than she would have wished. "I am. Alex is a fascinating man, and I am full of gratitude nearly every day for all that I have and enjoy." After all, she thought, I am not an unhappy woman.

"That's good," Avery said simply. "I can see Alex is doing well, and will be able to provide for you and the baby just fine."

He changed his position slightly, craning his neck to look at something beyond her, in the pasture.

"What is it?" asked Persis.

"Look, over there, above the trees. Can you see it?"

There, above the black fringe of pines brushing the night sky, hung the strangest vision she had ever seen. It looked like some vast, diaphanous drapery, first opalescent green, then shimmering into pink and deep rose, like a fire.

"The aurora borealis," she said with awe. "That's what it is, isn't it?"

Avery nodded. "This is only the second time this fall I've seen it," he said. "This is a real treat."

"It's beautiful," said Persis. "Let's get the others!"

Hurrying back to the large, well-lit room, she went to the table where Alex sat with his card-playing friends. As she approached, she hung politely back, waiting for a lull in their conversation.

Grinning, Alex looked up, his cigar between his teeth. "What is it, my dear?"

"I know you all get very intent on your cards," Persis said, "but if you could tear yourselves away, there is a spectacular display of the aurora borealis above the hills beyond the pasture."

"No kidding?" said Artie MacGruder, lowering his cards. "I'm rather fond of the northern lights."

Alex looked up at her and winked. "We'll be there shortly. I'm about to double the family fortune."

"In a pig's eye," shot Jack Hascombe.

Persis helped Constance out of her chair and flung a striped Hudson's Bay blanket around her. Within several minutes, the entire congregation of guests followed, assembling in the chilly darkness between the house and the pasture.

Persis and Alex stood next to Constance and Charlie, while the other men gathered with Avery, Pete, and several of the over-wintering cowboys a few feet away. Quiet conversation, now and then punctuated by a bit of laughter, floated out across the meadow.

Persis was filled with nature's vibrating spirit. Years later she would remember this evening with surprising clarity. She was, as she told Avery, full of gratitude for everything. Now, as she stood in the cold, dark air with her treasured Territorial family gathered around her, tears came to her eyes as gratitude turned to awe. Heaven has come down to earth for all of us tonight, she thought. Joy enveloped her, and she savored the fleeting taste of pure happiness.

* * *

The party roamed around the Ranch the next morning, gingerly testing the ice on the Clark Fork and inspecting every corner of the enormous new barn.

Strolling back to the rambling log house, they stopped to watch Pete work an appaloosa in the broad, flat pasture across the lane. He doesn't look anything like Avery, Persis noted, except a little bit about the nose and mouth.

Avery called his name loudly, and as Pete angled his head to hear, his dark hair poked out from beneath a woolen hood. He trotted up, guiding the nervous horse toward the small cluster of guests.

Persis removed her glove and slowly extended her hand. The appaloosa's dark nostrils opened wide as he sucked in the scent of her skin, daring to come close.

Pete looked at Persis and smiled a shy greeting.

Persis smiled back. Alex noticed this fleeting exchange, she realized, and slowly withdrew her hand.

A moment later, she saw something far more noteworthy. Pete glanced often at Nora, who stood alone near the back of the group, her red curls blowing softly around her face as she looked toward the snow-dusted mountains.

* * *

That afternoon, extra tables went up in the large front room as pitchy logs crackled on the hearth. Avery blessed the meal, and the guests fell upon the feast of roast wild turkey, fried trout, potatoes, tinned vegetables, and apple and pumpkin pie. Much of the conversation focused on the cattle industry and the rustling problem.

"The epidemic seems to have started on the eastern edge of the Territory, near Miles City," said Avery. "Now, herds all over the Territory are being ruthlessly decimated."

"Did you catch any of them last month?" inquired Anton Schulz, "When you was up on the Sun?"

Avery nodded. "Could you send those potatoes down here, Pete?"

The dish was quickly passed, but no one spoke.

At last, Artie observed, "Rustlers generally meet with a very unhappy end, but they know full well it awaits them."

Avery nodded again. "A poor choice of livelihood. Say, Charlie, those electric lights at the Alice mineshaft look pretty smart. A bunch of us rode over to Butte City last week and spent the evening just so we could see the hoisting works all lit up. Looks like a Christmas tree."

Charlie grinned. "The only trouble is, now the boys don't know whether it's night shift or day shift."

Everyone laughed, and Anton shot out, "That's just because they're Irish and have day-old scones for brains."

"Well, we won't discuss what lies between a German's ears," replied Charlie. "After all, it's Thanksgiving and we must be civil."

"Anyway, Avery," Charlie continued, "It is quite amazing to see. Mr.

Daly—and all the other citizens, of course—they're quite proud to have the old mining camp as the Territory's first electrified city. Helena's next," he added, nudging his sister.

"Alex," began Avery, "what's the latest on the rail plans? I hear Butte City is probably going to be the ultimate terminus, not Helena as so many have hoped."

Alex affirmed this, explaining that the mining around Butte City had far outstripped the diggings at Helena, making it the wiser choice. "We're hoping to get there by next fall, but you know how that goes."

"That makes it a little difficult for you," said Avery, "Being on the road between Helena and Butte City and points south, I mean."

Alex nodded, raising his glass. "Very perceptive. Ranchers and railroad men may have their differences, Avery, but we share the misfortune of having to spend a fair amount of time away from home. Although I don't mind travel, it has lost a bit of its appeal for me. In fact, I have been thinking about investing in a new block being built in Butte City, and may design an apartment into the building. I'm the kind of fellow who must always have one too many irons in the fire."

Her fork halfway to her mouth, Persis stared at Alex.

"I see," said Anton. "A sort of vacation home in the south."

The table roared with laughter.

Persis put down her fork. As Alex patted her hand, she bit her lip.

"Don't worry, dear," he said, "it's a ways off. We've got plenty of time to talk about it."

Later, Alex explained to her how he had conceived the plan on the train to Cheyenne last summer, but their newlywed life had been so busy he had not had time to think about it, let alone mention it to her.

"Avery's comment reawakened the idea," he said. "What do you think?"

"Well, I suppose it makes relative sense," Persis replied, realizing that the arrangement would bring her closer to Constance and Charlie for at least part of the year. She began warming to the notion, but was careful not to seem excessively interested.

"Having a place in Butte City," Alex was saying, "will put me in closer touch with Will Clark and other important folks in the mining camp."

Persis smiled and nodded. She had heard of William Clark, one of the crown princes of the mining trade. Beyond this, she knew little about the man, except that he was emerging as a rival to Charlie's boss, the popular Marcus Daly.

* * *

On the morning of December 15th, Angus Blaylock drove a MacKinney Freighters spring wagon into the driveway behind 610 Gilbert Street. By the time Persis had thrown on a cloak and descended the back steps, he was unloading his cargo—a fresh and fragrant Douglas fir.

"Halloo the MacKinney house," he said loudly, his ruddy cheeks puffing out as he lifted the tree and stood it up for Persis to see, "and Merry Christmas! This will give you one less thing to do during this busy season. I hope you like it. They've got them lined up against the storefronts downtown. Makes the place look near civilized."

"It's glorious, Angus. You are so thoughtful. I know exactly where I want it."

"That doesn't surprise me, ma'am. Have you a large bucket?"

Grace and Nora followed closely as Angus carried it to the front room, then judged its straightness as he set it in a bucket weighted with stones.

"Constance will be here in a week," Persis reminded the two women as they all stood on the rear steps and waved good-bye to Angus. "She can either help decorate the tree or sit and rest while we do it."

The day leaned toward evening, and by four-thirty it was nearly dark. Persis stood next to the aromatic tree and looked out the window down the hill toward town. She could see the last, rosy light of the sun to the left, silhouetting a dark lace of branches against the sky.

Alex came home and the evening unfolded just as she had hoped. As she lay in bed curled up next to him, she looked at the window on her side of the room and saw delicate frames of frost growing toward the center of each pane. The next day was a Saturday, when Alex insisted on her staying in bed late with him in the morning. He would stage a mild pout if she got up too soon or seemed overly eager to begin her day. Reveling in the knowledge of her growing importance to him, she felt gratitude well up from deep inside her. She pulled the quilted satin around her chin and sank into sleep.

* * *

Constance came December 20th. "Charlie couldn't wait any longer," she told Persis. "I think he's flat out nervous."

Persis watched with amusement as her brother deposited Constance in the front room, then turned right around and went back to Butte City to wrap up pre-holiday construction at the Alice.

"He wants the child to be born here," Constance said. "You should have heard him. 'We can't have the babe draw roasting smoke for his first breath,' he said." She laughed and hugged Persis. "Oh, Percy, it is good to be here. Merry Christmas!"

That evening, they sat in Persis's reading room with their toes resting on the fender of the little stove. Constance stood up and went toward the door on another of her trips to make water, then stopped stiffly and winced.

"What is it?" asked Persis sharply.

"Nothing," said Constance. "It's not the baby. Ruby said it's a nerve that runs down the back of my leg. It's passing now." She made her way out into the hall.

When she returned and had settled back into her striped chair, she put her feet up on the fender and said, "While you were in New York, a woman died of childbed fever just a few houses from us."

Persis's mouth went dry. The idea of losing Constance was beyond comprehension. "I—I can't imagine a woman not thinking about it."

"I'll be glad when Ruby finishes up with her work down in Sheridan and sends word that she is back in Helena," said Constance wearily. "She told me the house she bought here in Helena is on Warren Street, but I don't really know where that is."

"Warren Street? I think I know the neighborhood. It's near the cemetery."

"Yes. Ruby said it's just a little stone house," said Constance. "She bought it from Josephine Airey, the one who runs the Coliseum Dance Hall here in Helena. Chicago Joe, they call her."

"Yes, I've heard of Joe," Persis said, remembering a conversation with Abby Hancock and several other women over a hand of whist. All the women at that card game had deplored the illicit comings-and-goings of the Tenderloin District.

"Ruby could stay here," Persis said. "I mean, when the time comes."

"You have only to invite her, Percy. It's your house."

"Well, I shall, then." She didn't want to think about Alex, but he hovered on the edge of her every decision. He had told her a couple of weeks ago that he wanted her own lying-in attended by the well-known Dr. Lyons.

"You were right about Ruby," said Constance. "She *was* a lady of the evening, a long time ago."

"She told you?" Persis felt a twinge of envy over the intimacy that had obviously sprung up between Constance and the midwife.

"It was years ago, when they had the first strike at Bannack." She shifted heavily in her chair. "You know, I think our impression of these women as immoral or wanton is a shallow one. The vast majority do it because they have to. Most of them want to be like Ruby, or like Butte's own Magda Navroski – they've both gotten out and have started respectable lives."

Persis knitted her brow. She knew Constance had a point, but at the same time, she didn't like making excuses for fallen women. When she thought of women who lived loosely, she thought of Bess Daltry, and she could not remove the rancor from her heart.

* * *

The morning of December 21 dawned cold. The light gray sky spoke one word: snow. By noon the flakes began to fall, and by three o'clock there were four inches on the ground.

Persis stood at the window, absently combing the drapery fringe with her fingers. This would surely mean a delay in Ruby's arrival. Sheridan was over eighty miles away, making it a two-day trip under the best conditions.

"Calm yourself," said Alex. "That baby isn't coming until Christmas. Besides, even if it came early, you've got Grace. No doubt she's helped with a few births."

The next morning, Constance did not come down for breakfast on time. The mantel clock in the dining room said seventeen minutes past seven.

Persis wanted to bolt up the stairs but checked herself. Alex was right; everything would be fine whether Ruby came or not.

Half-past seven came and went. If Constance *was* in labor, she reasoned, it would be best that Alex know it before he left for the bank. He could get a message to the doctor. She excused herself, walked out of Alex's sight, then dashed up the stairs.

Constance was sitting on the edge of the bed, still in her night shift.

"How are you?"

"I think today might be the day after all, Percy," smiled Constance. "I woke up at a quarter to five and the pains have been coming stronger ever since, keeping me awake."

"You should have awakened me!"

"It has only been two hours."

"I'm going downstairs to tell Alex before he leaves. He'll get a message to the doctor."

Dr. Lyons came mid-morning, but genially told the household that it was still too early for him to be of any useful service. Persis thought he seemed preoccupied, a state of mind which was confirmed a moment later when he added, "There are several patients coming into the hospital from Hamilton. A logging accident."

"I'll be back about 4:00 p.m.," he said, as he picked up his hat.

Through the window, Persis watched him climb into his buggy, his black frock coat whipping in the wind. She left Constance alone for a short time and tried to read, but when she finished a couple of pages, she had no idea what she had just read. She sent Donny on the first of what would be many trips to the telegraph office to inquire after any word from Charlie or Ruby. I'd rather have one Ruby than five Charlies at this point, she thought.

When Alex came home that afternoon, the snow was coming thicker than ever. Exhausted from managing the horse and buggy on the impassable streets, he got into dry clothing and settled in the library.

Upstairs, Constance paced the length of the guestroom, pausing to rest on the bed for five or ten minutes at a time.

"Ruby told me to stand up as long as I could," she told Persis. "If the babe must come down out of the womb, then indeed it makes sense to be standing rather than ly—" she stared at Persis.

"What? Are you all right?"

"I . . ." she stepped gingerly to the side and lifted the hem of her shift. There was a puddle of water on the floor.

Persis stared, thinking at first that Constance had accidentally made water. No, she realized, it's the baby's bag of waters.

"Persis," said Constance stiffly, "this means the baby is coming sooner than we thought."

"Well, we know that, now, don't we?" Persis said matter-of-factly. She grabbed a towel from the stack on the bureau and glanced at the clock. Four thirty-five. Where is that damned doctor, she thought, mopping up the floor. And why hasn't Ruby even telegraphed? She stole a look at Constance's face. There was a furrow of pain between her brows.

She excused herself to go and get another jug of water, walking slowly out of the room and closing the door with a gentle click. As soon as she was out of sight, she reached down, swept up her skirts and tore down the stairs.

"Where is that doctor!" she demanded of Nora, who jumped up and pushed her auburn hair back from her face. "And where's Grace?"

"She went to the telegraph office, Miss," said Nora. "And Donny is with some folks down the hill, helping them with an overturned wagon."

"Didn't Dr. Lyons say he'd be back by four? Someone else can take care of those loggers for an hour, for heaven's sake. It's after five, and it's dark! Oh, where is Ruby?" she wailed softly.

The back door opened and Persis spun around, hoping to see Dr. Lyon's bearded face and dark suit. It was Grace.

"I've a telegram from Mistress Ruby. Here 'tis," she said, briskly removing her gloves and rubbing her palms together. "Bitter it is abroad tonight. My blood is snow-broth!"

But Persis was not listening. Her eyes devoured the flimsy message: "Came as far as Butte. Gilmer and Salisbury cancelled all stages till further notice. Will find wagon or horse for hire. Ruby."

Persis's hand rose to her forehead and her heart sank. Then she remembered Constance, alone upstairs. "Fill this jug with boiled water," she said, pushing it towards Nora. "If it must be, Grace and I will deliver the child."

Alex strode into the kitchen and picked up Ruby's message. "Where's the doctor?" he asked as his eyes scanned the note.

The wind gusted in as Donny opened the back door, his clothes crusted with snow. "Missy Persis," he began, "the doctor, he sent man up from hospital to say he come late."

"Alex," Persis said calmly. "There were some accident victims at the hospital, I believe. But the birth is imminent. Grace and I are going up to—assist Constance."

Alex blanched. Persis studied his face and realized this was the first time she had ever seen such an expression on his face. For once, he was entirely out of his element.

"Alex," she said evenly, "after Donny warms up, please send him out again after the doctor. Once Dr. Lyons knows how urgent things are, he will come."

Alex nodded, averting his eyes. "Well," he said with a forced chuckle, "I'll be in the library if you need me."

As Persis watched Alex's figure recede through the hallway and disappear into the library, a thin column of smoke rose within her, like paper catching fire. He wouldn't, or couldn't, be of any help. Here was something that Alex MacKinney, with all his charm, money, and influence, could do nothing about.

She lifted her chin and looked up the stairs. A year ago, she would have been frightened, but something was sweeping through her like a hot white wind. She was not afraid. She knew that there was no person alive, except perhaps Anne-Marie in Chicago, who could care for Constance and her child with more vigilance and love than she herself.

She turned to see Grace at her elbow with the jug of boiled water. As they ascended the stairs together, Persis said a rapid prayer.

Constance was lying down. Persis sank down and looked into the pale face. "What is happening?"

"It hurts so. I don't think I can walk anymore," Constance caught her breath. Her hands flew down to the sides of her abdomen.

Persis watched with amazement as the round outline of Constance's belly rose up in a ridge beneath the thin fabric of her gown, the way a wave reaches a crest before it flattens on the shore.

"It's hard labor, Miss Persis," came Grace's soft voice, "but I don't think she is ready yet. You'll know when the time comes."

Persis stared at Grace and thanked God that she was there. They settled into their respective chairs, watching the bed and the oil lamp's play of light and shadow on the walls. Persis looked at Grace and knew from the way her hands were clasped that the older woman was praying.

She leaned over and touched Constance's face, pushing back the strands of white-gold hair stuck to her pale forehead and cheeks. The next contraction made her moan and thrash from side to side.

She bowed her own head, pleading for protection and guidance. "Illuminate this room with divine light, and all within, please," she murmured.

The sound of Donny's voice coming from downstairs made them both jump. In an instant, Grace was on her way down to gather the news.

Persis tiptoed to the door and leaned out into the hallway when she heard Grace's soft footfalls coming back up the stairs.

"He has been to the hospital, Miss, and Dr. Lyons says he's coming. Within an hour, is what he said."

An hour? Persis could hardly stand it. Striving to remain calm, she pulled the door closed behind her. "We have laudanum, don't we?"

Grace nodded. "I was just about to suggest it myself. We don't want to give her too much, but we can give her a little. It's quite customary."

"Go, then." Persis stared out the window. The snow was nine or ten inches deep on the granite sill just outside. Beyond, she saw nothing but two fuzzy rectangles of yellow light where the carriage house windows lay beyond the billowing, snow-laden air. Her hands were cold. She was angry—angry at the doctor, angry at Ruby for not coming sooner, and angry at God for sending such a storm.

She gave Constance a moderate dose of laudanum. The contractions still came, but she was not as anguished, and her face was less contorted.

Male voices drifted up from downstairs. She stepped to the door and heard the plangent sound of Doctor Lyons' voice.

"At last!" she cried, but at the same time felt a sense of alarm. A man? What does he know of all this? She banished this thought and opened the door. Dr. Lyons stood outside, his hand raised, prepared to knock.

Entering quickly, he set down his bag and checked Constance's pulse. He questioned them as to the pattern of the labor and, detecting that Constance had been given laudanum, asked when they had administered it. "Please wait outside for a moment," he said. "I will examine the patient."

Reluctantly, Persis withdrew, with Grace following. Persis left the door slightly ajar, for reasons she would not pause to contemplate. As they stood in the dark-paneled hallway, she strained her ears and heard the faint rustle of sheets, then a long period of silence. She stared down at the landing and out the large cut glass window where the stairs turned from west to east. Again she saw the yellow shapes of Donny's windows through the white, roiling storm, but now they were faint patches that nearly disappeared in the wake of each curling, driving gust.

Dr. Lyons appeared in the doorway and motioned to Persis. "There is some cause for concern, I am afraid. The child is not in the proper position for delivery. If there is no noticeable change within the next hour, I will bring in my special instruments from the carriage."

"Instruments? Of what do you speak, Dr. Lyons?"

"Obstetrical forceps," he said, looking directly at her.

Persis's fear was palpable.

"Please don't be frightened," he continued. "You are from the East,

I believe. Surely you have heard of this method of handling difficult deliveries."

Overwhelmed with concern for Constance and raging inwardly at her own lack of knowledge, Persis hesitated. She looked at Grace, who stood silent and deferential. She had heard of the forceps, but it seemed to her that the tales of childbed success from the use of forceps were matched by an equal number of unhappy stories. She remembered a child in Mill Creek whose eye had been damaged. Then another memory came to her, this one of a prominent woman in Dunkirk who praised the instruments and gave them all the credit for the safe delivery of her healthy daughter.

Dr. Lyons studied her face. "I assure you, Mrs. MacKinney, that the forceps have earned a place as standard tools in the delivery of babies, and have often spared the life of both mother and child." He bowed slightly. "I will join your husband below, and will return to examine your sister-in-law at half-past nine."

"All right," murmured Persis.

She looked through the bedroom door at Constance, who was lying on her side, pale and fretful. Her unintelligible mumbling was broken by an occasional sharp question. Some of them seemed to make sense; most did not. Grace and Persis moved silently back into the room and closed the door.

Constance's shift was drawn up over her knees. Realizing the doctor had probed Constance's private parts, seeking the form of the child, Persis felt her cheeks redden. She hastily pulled Constance's gown back down around her ankles.

At last it was Grace who spoke. "My mother—" she stopped, uncertainty choking off her words.

"What?" Persis knew Grace came from a large family, and that family-attended home births were the standard among Butte City's Irish. "Is there something we could do, Grace?"

"My mother, God rest her soul, I watched her once, when I was a girl . . . she rubbed the belly of my oldest sister, and somehow turned the babe inside her."

"Could we do it . . . I mean, could you?"

"I've done it, yes."

"Well, then, what happened? Did it work?"

"It was two years ago, down in Dublin Gulch. Sure, the babe was born aright. And the mother's fine today. But Mrs. MacKinney, you've got to know that it was the good Lord above that turned that baby, not me. I could never say 'twas me that brought that babe along."

"Well, it won't hurt, Grace. Of that we are certain. You do it, and I shall watch. If you get tired, I will take up where you leave off."

"Ring for Nora," said Grace quickly. "When she comes, tell her to fetch the mineral oil. And tell her to come up the back stair, and to hide the bottle in her skirts if she sees anyone. Devil take us," she said, jabbing a hair pin into the thick coil at the back of her head, "but it's time for a bit o' womanly interference."

Persis asked no questions and did as Grace bade her. Soon the older woman was at work on Constance's swollen belly, using just enough oil to keep her hands from chafing Constance's skin. Persis watched intently but kept one eye on the door, which she had locked after Nora delivered the oil.

Grace began muttering to herself and Persis leaned closer. "Faith, women have been birthing babies for thousands of years! Ever since the menfolk got involved there's been a lot more mothers makin' St. Peter's acquaintance."

"At least," Persis began, "people understand more than they used to about the spread of germs. It took the Europeans to figure it out, but thank God the knowledge has come to the States."

"With respect, Mistress, we aren't in the States."

Persis looked at Grace sharply, then away. The older woman was right. To call Montana Territory part of the United States was both technically incorrect and a huge overstatement. But, she reasoned inwardly, if I know about septic infection, then Dr. Lyons does as well. Damn those forceps; they frighten me more than anything.

Persis began to see a change in Constance. She seemed more lucid. "Constance, can you hear me?"

Constance turned her face toward Persis and murmured, "Yes . . . Oh, Percy!" Another contraction washed over her. As it ebbed, Constance licked her lips and said, "What about the baby? Is the baby coming? Is it all right?"

"Constance," she said firmly, "the baby is not in the right position.

Grace and I are going to massage your belly to see if we can turn the child. I am not going to give you any more laudanum, at least not for a while. Can you stand the pain?"

"Yes. What . . . what will we do if the massage doesn't work? Ruby told me sometimes it doesn't."

Persis wished her friend had not posed this intelligent question, but at the same time she knew having Constance alert was preferable to having her adrift on an opiated sea.

"I don't know," she responded with complete honesty. "The doctor is downstairs. He is coming back up in—" she glanced at the clock— "twenty minutes. He will examine you again, and we will just have to wait and see what he says." She swallowed and added, "He knows more about this than I do."

"The doctor is here?" Constance looked confused.

"Yes. He examined you, but you were feeling the laudanum deeply then."

"I—I feel like pushing the baby out," Constance groaned.

Persis turned to Grace. "What does it mean? Should she push?"

"I think the babe may have moved a wee bit, but not enough. Tell her not to push. Tell her to think about something else. Give her something to think about."

Persis scrambled onto the bed and put her face down on the pillow. "Constance. Constance, it's a good sign that you want to push. But you mustn't just yet. Think of something else. Think about—" her mind flew over dozens of images. "Daffodils! Think of how they fluttered in a yellow wave around Grandmere's house in Dunkirk! I brought some of her bulbs with me. They're in the root cellar. We'll plant them when the ground thaws."

"Daff—" began Constance, but her belly tightened up again and a groan edged into her breath. She clutched at the pillowcase and glared angrily at Persis. "Let me push!"

Persis heard the click of a heel on the stairs. Grace heard it too, and quickly wiped the oil from Constance's belly and pulled the gown into place. Persis dashed to unlock the door and opened it as calmly as possible. Dr. Lyons entered with a polite nod of his head. "Well, Mrs. MacKinney, how is the patient?" Under his arm he carried a long black leather satchel.

Persis gestured half-heartedly toward the bed. "It appears that the baby is coming," she said as diffidently as she could.

Dr. Lyons looked at Persis, one of his eyebrows arching up.

Grace excused herself to get more hot water. Just then Constance let out a long, throaty moan.

Persis watched Dr. Lyons' fingers tap the side of his satchel as he looked down on Constance's sweaty face. Placing the satchel at the foot of the bed, Lyons turned to Persis and said, "If you will excuse me, I must help your sister-in-law. We can't wait any longer."

"Who are you?" came Constance's voice, suddenly strong. "Where's Ruby?"

Lyons placed a fatherly hand on her arm and said, "I am a doctor here in Helena. Everything is going to be all right." He turned back to Persis and said, "She needs more laudanum. Why haven't you given it to her?"

"It appeared that she was less in need of the opiate, Dr. Lyons, during the last hour. We felt it best if we could communicate with her."

"I see. Please excuse us," he said, and ushered Persis gently out the door.

Grace, carrying a basin and ewer, met Persis in the hallway. They perched on two stiff side chairs and waited. After an interminable period of time, Persis looked at her pocket watch and saw with disbelief that only twenty minutes had passed. She reached for the doorknob, then snatched her fingers away.

She dropped her head into her hands. "Oh, Grace, I am so worried. Pray with me, won't you?" Persis laid her cold hand in the soft palm of the older woman. In low tones, she babbled a disjointed prayer, tears tumbling down her cheeks. When she released Grace's hands and opened her eyes, she knew she couldn't wait any longer. She tapped lightly on the door. No response. She turned the knob, pushed the door open officiously, and went in.

It was no wonder Dr. Lyons had not come to the door. He was perched on the lower end of the bed and had a baby's head in his hands. Within seconds, the rest of the baby's body slid out of Constance. Persis was dumbstruck.

Mesmerized, she looked from the doctor to the tiny baby and up to Constance's sweet, relieved face. She glanced at the side of the bed, where the black satchel lay unopened.

"A boy! And as beautiful a one as the saints ever looked upon!" cried Grace.

Thank God! But was the baby even alive? After such a long labor . . . perhaps the trauma had been too much. Then there was a gurgle, and another gurgle, followed by a lusty wail. Grace was in the middle of everything now, taking the baby from Dr. Lyon's wet hands and wrapping the squalling form in a clean towel.

Constance raised her head. "I did it, Percy."

"Indeed you did. God love you, my friend."

A smile spread across Constance's wet, weary face. "Winston. Winston Charles Allen," she whispered, and took the baby in her arms.

*   *   *

Two days later Persis rose and hurried down the hall in her dressing gown to Constance's room. She wanted to get there and back to bed before Alex fully awoke. Although she had seen very little of him the last few days, he had been unusually tolerant. She was grateful to him, and wanted to crawl back in bed with him as soon as she looked in on mother and child.

Charlie and Ruby had arrived in the night, bone-tired from their journey up the snow-shrouded Butte-Helena road.

"Winston Charles, eh?" Charlie had whispered to Persis. "Why not 'Charles Winston?'" He winked.

In the half-light of dawn, Persis gathered her robe around her and reached stealthily for the latch on Constance's door. Surprised, she found it slightly open. The room was filled with the silver-white light peculiar to winter mornings.

Something was wrong. Charlie was sitting next to the bed. He looked up, his face pained. "She's feverish, Percy." He stared hard at his sister. They both knew what it meant.

"Infection . . ." Persis dumbly mouthed the word. Dread flowed over her like an ice-cold draft. "Cold cloths," she said mechanically. She spun around in the door frame and floated like a wraith toward the stairs. As she passed the archway leading to the master bedroom,

Alex's dark form appeared. She glanced at him, distracted, and opened her mouth to speak.

Alex cut her off. "You just can't do it, can you?" he said acidly. "You can't lie in bed with your own husband, even on Christmas Eve morning. Even when all of Helena has ground to a halt under the snow. You've got more important things to do." He fastened an iron grip on her arm.

Furious, Persis tried to wrench herself free. "It's Constance!"

"When has it ever been anything but Constance!" he challenged her. "Persis, I have been a very patient man, but you have pushed this too far." He stepped backward into the doorway of their room, dragging her with him.

"Stop it!" she screamed a whisper at him. "Stop! It's the fever! God in Heaven, Alex, don't keep me from my errand! Constance has childbed fever!"

He dropped her arm, still glowering. "She is probably fine."

Persis stood still, breathing hard. She hated herself for waiting to hear him say it was all right for her to go, but she waited nonetheless.

"Go, then," he said sullenly. "Post me a letter one of these days and let me know when you're ready to be my wife again." He stalked away.

Persis stared a moment at his broad shoulders. She shook her head slightly, unable to comprehend this riddle of a man and his consuming needs. I don't have time to try to understand, she decided, and left in haste.

Dr. Lyons came but had no encouraging counsel. No chemist's powders were effective against childbed fever, he gravely informed her. He instructed Persis to force liquids into the patient and to keep her as cool as possible without inducing a chill. Persis followed this advice to the letter and wove in Ruby's tisanes and herbal lotions.

Grace helped Ruby find a young woman from the Tenderloin District who was nursing a three-month old infant. She and her baby would stay in the carriage house, while Donny was given temporary lodgings across the street with the Kessler's servants.

Persis flinched at the mention of the wet-nurse's neighborhood, but asked only one question. "Is she healthy?" Grace replied in the affirmative, and that was all she needed to hear. "Pay her well," she said simply.

Leaving little Winston in the care of Grace and Nora, she stringently avoided Alex, staying with Charlie at Constance's bedside.

They watched as Constance's little, upturned nose took in whiffs of air, and saw her chest rise and fall beneath the blanket. Her fair hair, which Ruby had sponged clean, was curling around her face.

Charlie made observations about her movements, her thirst, and her obscure comments. In his dark visage and hunched shoulders, Persis saw the toll of powerlessness.

When Alex looked in on them, a spark of hope shot through Persis. She needed to feel his compassion, to detect in him a genuine concern for someone other than himself.

The constant sight of Ruby's hazel and silver-streaked head bending over the bed became burned onto Persis's optic nerve.

Once, in the hall, Persis took Ruby's hands in her own and choked out the words, "I am so glad you are here!" Tears spilled down the front of the dress she had been wearing for days.

A mist formed in Ruby's eyes, but she quickly picked up a lamp and went back in. Gently rolling up the sleeve of Constance's muslin shift, Ruby inspected the skin. Persis looked on, and saw what Ruby was studying . . . small, purplish spots. Constance's eyelids had a peculiar translucent look, as though her skin was becoming thinner. Persis looked closer and realized that there were several bruise-like spots on her jaw and one along the side of her nose.

Turning to Persis and Charlie, Ruby motioned them into the hall. "As the doctor said, it's an infection of the blood, commonly known as asepsis. There is perhaps the slightest chance that she may recover, but not as a result of any efforts we make."

Later that night, as Charlie slept in the chair, Persis knelt alone by the window and stared out into the night. The shadowy room was thick with the hot, fetid smell of fever, but outside, stars were scattered across the cold, black firmament. Persis had seen barns buckle beneath the snow dumped by Lake Erie blizzards, but this Montana Territory storm was different. Everything was crippled, silent, and numb. The brittle stillness changed only when a plume of sparkling crystals rolled off the cornice of the carriage house.

"Persis, you and Charlie—" a ragged whisper came from the bed.

Persis flew from the window to Constance. "Yes, darling. I am here. Charlie is here."

"You and Charlie and Winston . . . you are together?" She exhaled, her strength depleted.

"Yes, yes. We are. You rest."

Constance gave the slightest nod, then settled back into her vapid state. Taking little backward steps, Persis returned to her vigil at the window, looking at her friend every minute or two, watching the satin quilt rise and fall.

She herself was nearly delirious. Had that exchange really happened or had it been a waking dream? No matter. On this darkest of all nights, she was thankful for any connection, real or imagined.

Outside, the wind blew and the snow danced. The forces of nature are merciless in their disregard for me and my own, she thought, shuddering. The air seeped in with a little whistle from beneath the sash. With it came a thin whisper from the frozen past. It was Anne-Marie's voice. "I know you will look after one another," it breathed.

Harrowed to the core, Persis shook her head and squeezed her eyes shut. I *have* lost my mind. The wind rose again, muttering against the panes, and the voice came again. "It is a remarkable thing, this love that grows between women."

"Good God," Persis whispered aloud. But she was filled with wonder. In that silent mystery that was a woman's way, could Anne-Marie know what was happening two thousand miles away? Her heart raced and she glanced back at Constance. Had she heard her mother's voice?

But Constance lay quiet, her breath barely audible.

"Let her live, let her live!" Persis prayed. The weight of it all dragged her to her knees. Clutching at the cold windowsill, she cried softly, "Think of those who need her! Of Anne-Marie! Of little Winston, of Charlie and . . . of me! How will I ever be whole again if she is taken?"

Disbelief crept over her, hardening like mother-of-pearl. She remembered the child inside her and bitterly wished it away. She hated the silent injunction that she go on living. There was no reason large enough or sacred enough to warrant that! As a vast numbness swirled up around her, she plunged into the dark, inchoate heart of it and stayed.

* * *

Persis woke when the sun struck the hallway couch that had become her bed. The sky was a pale, luminous blue and the snow on the windowsill glinted gold. Shoving the quilt aside and forgetting her slippers, she ran into Constance's room.

Charlie knelt by the bed. Persis fumbled beneath the coverlet and found Constance's fingers, now cool, and clutched them in her own. Constance opened her eyes and looked around. Her eyelids flickered and her gaze lingered on Charlie.

The silence of the room was broken by a long, wheezing exhale. The blue eyes lost their last trace of luster as sunlight poured in, forming a pool of gold around the lifeless form of Constance Eugenie Parment Allen.

Months later, Persis would look back on that Christmas season and not remember where one day ended and another began. It was one continuous dark night, except the vivid sunlit morning of Constance's death on December 27. Even the days and weeks that followed escaped recall for the rest of her life. She was forced to rely on others' accounts, for she had none of her own.

Silent and hollow, Charlie rode toward Butte City the morning of New Year's Eve, leaving his son with the MacKinneys. Neither he nor his sister tried to lift the weight of grief from one another. Constance's death had sent every member of the household into a centrifuge that whirled in icy silence and exploded, releasing them each into their own lonely orbits.

Persis moved doggedly from one task to another, mechanically managing the baby's care and making sure the wet-nurse was fed. When Alex tried to speak to her, she smiled and appeared attentive, then looked past him into the air. When he put his arm around her in the way that had always charmed her, her arms hung limp at her sides, or worse, her ribs went into spasms, meaning she was going to cry again.

Since it was the fashion for well-to-do couples to have separate rooms to which they might retire after becoming accustomed to one another, the second floor at 610 Gilbert had been designed accordingly. Alex was shocked, however, when Persis began using her own room after Christmas.

He watched her climb the stairs at night, knowing she was going to *her* room, not the room they used to share. Our marriage is only five months old, he thought, and it has come to this! Even in death, he fretted, Constance has more of Persis's heart than I do. He spent another night alone before the fire, rubbing his forehead, trying to make sense of what was happening.

Both Charlie and the baby were friction points, but Alex struggled to be courteous. "Perhaps I'll grow accustomed to the little chap," he muttered to himself one morning on his way out the door.

Maybe it was because Persis and their unborn child seemed nearly lost to him, maybe it was because Winston's cradle sat almost in his path when he came through the kitchen every night, but little by little, he began looking forward to seeing the boy tucked in near the wood box by the stove. Grace and Nora exchanged surprised looks when Alex took five or ten minutes before dinner to lean over the child and talk to him, dangling a calico puppy or silver bell.

Soon, however, he was finding the billiard room at Chicago Joe's Coliseum to be an appealing, familiar haven. By mid-January, he had fallen into a pattern of lunching daily at the Last Chance Coffee House next to the bank and visiting the Coliseum after four-thirty. He would take a few drinks, enjoy some laughs and a game of cards or billiards, then go home, only to return later in the evening, after an hour of dining in silence with his nearly catatonic wife. What a sham, he thought bitterly.

Artie, Anton, Rob, and Jack frequently met him at the Coliseum. One evening, Alex sat quietly a few feet away from the billiard table while Jack and Anton argued over the legality of a shot. Swirling a glass of bourbon, Alex was deep in thought. Might Persis somehow intend, through her ceaseless work, to cast forth their unborn child? Forced to admit he had lost complete control of his household and his wife, he was terrified in a way he could not explain to anyone. It was a deep, stealing fear that plucked cruelly at the raw fibers of his vision of himself.

Persis had been a dream come true to him; it had been love at first sight. Nine-tenths of his personal effort and his resources for the last eighteen months had been directed at welcoming her and setting the two of them up securely on the Territorial frontier. Now, where was she? Where were the attentiveness and the soft-spoken virtues that made her so remarkably suited to him? Where were his dreams of their life together?

He took a hearty swallow and looked past the billiard table into the smoky darkness of the wide dance floor, where several men were enjoying the company of Chicago Joe's girls. Most of the girls were common in appearance and carried a few pounds of excess weight, but out of the corner of his eye he saw a young blond lingering close to the draperies framing the wide doorway. She was looking at him. He turned away.

The evening passed in the same manner as the other January nights. The group adjourned to Anton's elegant rooms near the Assay Office for a few rounds of cards. As Alex poured himself another drink from the array of bottles on Anton's sideboard, he felt something building inside him.

Surely she must know the depth of the pain she inflicts on me by ignoring me this way, he thought. He stared down at the tawny liquid in his glass and squeezed, wanting to shatter the tumbler with his bare hands. If she doesn't do something to acknowledge me, to demonstrate that she cares for me, within the next twenty-four hours, then . . .

Humiliated, he saw her moving like a drudge from room to room, doing the housework that Nora and Grace had been hired to do. He slid into an incoherent rage, feeling nothing but pain and the desperate insistence that his wife come to her senses.

* * *

At a quarter to twelve, after ringing Donny's bell and turning his horse over to him, Alex stumbled through the back door into the mudroom.

Persis heard noise in the kitchen, but her thoughts were far away. She was standing in the library, staring at the veined patterns in the marble mantel. The voice of the stage driver in Sheridan came drifting back to her: "These ladies think we're takin' 'em to the marble farm," he had said.

The marble farm. Well, Pie Eye, one of the ladies has completed the journey, God rest her soul. The other one is still here. For now. Her distracted thoughts floated like feathers around her as she waited for a blessed hint of fatigue to prompt her up the stairs and to bed.

A hand came down on her shoulder. She turned stiffly to face Alex and knew instantly he was drunk.

It seemed to her that she watched the scene that followed from a perspective outside her own body. Alex glowered at her. Normally, she observed, she would have been afraid. She faced him with no more than apathy, yet something inside her told her to disguise it.

There was a malevolent energy coming from him, sharp enough to penetrate the cotton-wool that covered her senses. "You're my wife," he said thickly. "It's time you remembered that."

She stared at him but no words came to her lips; none even came to her mind. Something made her lift her arm and turn her palm up. Slowly, she extended her hand to him.

Seconds passed as she held it out steadily. Alex swayed and stared down into her open palm. Then he covered her hand with his own and clumsily drew her to him.

As his lips covered hers in a rough, hungry kiss, she felt his trembling hands begin to move in rapid, stroking movements up and down her torso. She surrendered, knowing that the sooner she satisfied him, the sooner she could re-enter her familiar melancholia.

Alex's hand came up to the back of her neck and spun her around so that her back was to him. He kissed the nape of her neck, using his teeth, nipping, making her flinch.

Her sleeping soul began to wake, gripped by a visceral memory. She suddenly wanted pleasure, carnal gratification, more intensely than she had ever wanted it.

I don't care if he's drunk, she thought. Her hands flew to her fichu and brooch, and within seconds they were discarded and covered by her jacket, blouse and skirt. She turned and faced him. He sank to his knees and began kissing her thighs. She lowered her body to the Turkish rug and gave herself up to his rough caresses.

Neither of them got up to close the heavy paneled doors. Persis's fervor was so overwhelming that she was aware only of his hands touching her, his lips on hers, and the cramping ache inside her.

The next day, she recalled the scene of their union only as a dim vignette, as if she had been Nora gazing in for a shocked moment before hurrying away.

But Alex remembered. His attentiveness and physical closeness the next day were a consternation to her, but she realized how long it had been since they had touched. She could see that for Alex, last night had been a rekindling of their love, a sign that life might someday return to its old rhythms.

She struggled to put herself into a similar attitude, hoping for both their sakes that she was convincing.

* * *

Charlie trudged down the long slope from the Alice hoisting works. It was twilight on a bitter January evening, and though shifts had changed three hours before, the saloons were still lively with piano music and laughter. Passing the Vienna Brewery, he looked at the thermometer mounted next to the door. Seventeen degrees below zero. He quickened his step and came up close behind a group of miners. Veering to skirt them, he overheard some fragments of their conversation which made him hang back a bit to avoid notice.

"Ah, yer alus' getting hang-dog when yer in yer cups, Clancy," said the slender man in the middle. "Who says silver's playin' out? Yer still butterin' yer bread with a silver knife, ain't ye?"

Clancy was silent, but the man on the right spoke up loudly. "What's the o'clock? Due fer 'nother Sean-O, I am. Damn me, if it ain't cold enough to put hell outa business."

Charlie himself had just had a couple of Sean O'Farrells, a shot of whiskey with a beer chaser. It was the favorite drink of all Butte City.

The two men ignored their inebriated partner. Clancy kept his eyes on the ground and his shoulders hunched up about his neck. "It's the divil's work tryin' to follow that silver now, we all know it. It's older than ye both I am, and I don' want to go back to livin' hand to mouth. These is fast-changin' times. A man's got to be ready."

"Old Marcus Daly's a good man. He'll look after us."

"And sure he is a good sort, but it's makin' a mistake ye are, Goggins, if ye think he can care fer ye when the silver's slipped through all our fingers."

Charlie moved his scarf away from his ears.

"You know, there's talk o' minin' copper. Just copper and nothin' else," said Clancy, eyeing his partner.

"Daly's a silver man. What good's copper, anyway?"

"Let's be stoppin'," said the drunk. "Here's the Centerville Hotel. I'm due."

"Go on wi' ye. It's makin' a blaze in my own stove I'm thinkin' of now," said Clancy. "And it's damn soused y'are if y'aren't thinkin' the same."

Their conversation fell off. A sleigh moved briskly past, its runners making a violin-like whine on the whitened street.

Goggins cast a glance over his shoulder and saw Charlie. "Evenin'," he said with a nod.

"Evenin'," responded Charlie, who took his cue and crossed over to the other side of the street, where the Buffalo hoisting works loomed in the darkness.

It unnerved him to realize that he knew almost as little as the miners about Daly's plans for the future. Everywhere throughout Butte— for that was what the great bulk of the miners were beginning to call Butte City—there were rumors about silver tapering off and the increasing "nuisance" of copper. Charlie had seen plenty of it already— bits of enargite and bornite, compounds that signaled large copper deposits below.

Shoving his gloved hands into his pockets, he walked on briskly. As soon as he turned the corner onto Idaho Street, he saw the dark windows of his house and winced. No light might mean no fire in the stove. Ruby Cornish had found him a housekeeper, a portly Austrian woman he knew only as Mrs. Schumann. She lived a half-block away and did his washing and ironing and came every afternoon at five to bring dinner and to light a fire in the woodstove. He looked enviously up at the smoke rising from his neighbor's chimney and knew it would be a good two hours before he could call his kitchen even passably warm.

Turning the key in the lock, he pushed open the door and felt a warm rush of air on his face.

"The old gal was here, after all," he murmured. Feeling his way through the darkness, he struck a match, lit the table lamp, and pulled the linen cloth off the crock. Roast pork and potatoes.

He stirred the fire back to life, stuck his feet up on a chair directly in front of the stove, and ate dinner. The soft crackling of the fire and the orange glow between the black plates of cast iron mesmerized him, and his long day caught up with him. Leaning back, his eyes fell on a crystal pitcher on a shelf above the china cupboard. A wedding gift, he remembered. One of Constance's favorites.

The feeling he unconsciously fought all day, every day, surged into him. His throat stiffened and his chest was rent with pain.

"I miss you!" he burst out, flinging his head forward into his hands. His sobs tore the still air. "I miss everything about you. I feel like you're still here, hiding from me. I smell you!"

His rough hands raked through his hair as he looked wildly about, his face wet with tears. "You must be somewhere! You—your spirit— didn't just evaporate. You can hear me! Answer me, Constance, for God's sake, answer me!"

He stopped, covering his face with his callused hands. How much anguish must a man feel before his Creator takes pity on him? What constitutes genuine suffering, if not this? His anger welled up all over again. He was enraged, disgusted with himself and with God.

The pain began to shift, giving way to a familiar, gnawing ache. He sat back, breathing deeply, trying to get rid of it. Whenever he went to bed with it, he woke with it. He concentrated on his breath. Gradually, the tension began to subside.

Bed, he thought, suddenly exhausted. I'll read in bed a while to shut down the workings of my mind. And after that, there'll be nothing left to do except put out the light.

*　*　*

From a pitiful diggings of 65 feet, Marcus Daly's crew had brought the Anaconda up to the 120-foot standards of the middling claims. It still lacked the depth and prominence of the Alice or the Colusa, Charlie reflected, but it had come a long way since the days of its original hand windlass. Charlie knew Daly well by now, but still hesitated to put any pointed questions to him on the sensitive subject of "silver versus copper." As he shaved one morning over a steaming basin, it occurred to him that he might get a little information out of his friend, Dan O'Neill, another of Daly's shift bosses.

But before he could track down O'Neill, he had to put in a quick appearance at the Anaconda office. As he drew near the gaping mouth of the mine, a clot of eight or ten miners were speaking in low tones, a strange thing in itself, as miners were not the quiet sort.

He walked past as if nothing were out of the ordinary. "Mornin'," he said.

"Mornin', boss," returned a few voices from the group, but not a single pair of eyes came up to meet his.

That settled it; he needed to talk to Dan. After checking a few assay reports and lumber orders, he buttoned up his Mackinaw and turned back down the hill. When he was scarcely a block from O'Neill's apartment, he saw his friend coming toward him, huffing in the crisp, smoky air.

O'Neill clapped a strong arm around him. "Have you heard?"

"What's going on?"

"Callahan says they're going to shut down the Anaconda. I heard something last week about silver prices dropping, but we hear that all the time. Even if the other outfits are worried, the Anaconda is such a healthy producer. You can't shake a stick at 60 percent silver. I can't believe Daly would do this."

"Well," Charlie said, "it's not good news, you just said it yourself, Dan. There's been a lot of talk about silver playing out. And if the prices are dropping, Daly's got people he must answer to."

They hunched their shoulders and shifted from one foot to the other, as animated by the topic as they were by the near-zero cold. "I know the copper doesn't mean much to the workers," Dan said. "They see it as low value, no glamour. But things could take a new turn. Remember, the Utah and Northern rails are coming."

"Yeah, well, so's Christ," muttered Charlie. He wasn't worried at having to lay off the pickers, the muckers, and the millmen. Many could get hired on at the Lexington or Travona. Some might even cross the line and work for Daly's arch-rival, Will Clark, although that was hard to imagine.

The more he considered the situation, the more Charlie felt a kind of relief. Everyone *had* been wondering what would happen when the silver ran out, but no one ever dared talk about it. He recalled with a twinge that Daly had tried to sell his interest in the Anaconda last summer. Hell, Marcus could be turning into the same kind of mine owner as Ben Haggin or George Hearst—the long-distance kind. If Daly sold, he might go back to California. But why would he spend so much money and time on the Anaconda if he didn't plan to stay? He cautiously shared some of these thoughts with Dan as the two of them walked up the hill.

"Dammit," said Dan, "even the big fellows go broke sometimes."

The payroll officer looked up from his books as the two men entered the Anaconda office. "Just in time, boys," he said. "The old gent himself is coming at nine o'clock."

Charlie drew a chair up to the stove. Dan dished out two battered enamel cups of oily black coffee. Through the window, they could see a few of the miners still clumped near the hoisting works, while others headed down the hill. Daly's buggy pulled up and the silver-haired owner swung nimbly down from the seat to greet the workers, shaking hands all around. After a few moments, he touched his hat, leaving them behind to stamp their feet on the frozen, gravel-strewn earth.

Charlie pushed open the door to greet him.

"Faith, it's a cold one! Too cold to swap stories with my friends out there."

Charlie felt the bitter breath of January swirl in as Daly quickly entered the room. When they had adjourned to the privacy of Charlie's tiny office, Daly removed his heavy coat. "Good morning, boys," he said quietly.

"Mornin'," came the replies.

"I'm thinkin' you could use a bit of this," Dan O'Neill said, pouring a cup of coffee and handing it to Daly.

"Thanks, Dan. Well, you're both waiting to hear what's going on, and I'm not going to keep you in suspense. It's just this. We've got to shut her down. Silver prices are dropping and the freight costs are raising the devil with the bank account. I think you'll hear similar news from other claims within the next few days."

"The Walker Brothers don't want in. It's other fish they're frying now." He stopped, drumming his fingers on the side of his cup. "Now," he resumed, "this next bit is to go no further than the walls of this room, or I'll have my sweet Maggie put a curse on you all. The truth is, I'm near broke. I have no buyer and the cost of hauling ore to the terminus has about dragged me under the turf. Those freighters are a greedy bunch, but they have to make a living just like the rest of us. These last six months, we've near roasted our privates off with all our smelting, and we've got precious little to show for it."

Daly moved slowly to the window, looking out on the men, who stared unabashedly back. "I'd put my eyes on sticks for those fellows, and for all their brothers down below in the dark. I've sat in many a place the likes of where they're sitting now, with nothing but an oil lamp by which to eat my noontime bread and boiled egg."

"I'm going to San Francisco," Daly said quietly. "I want you to just go about your lives as if the Anaconda is closed indefinitely."

"But silver prices go up and down all the time," protested Dan. "Isn't there somehow—"

"In many ways, you're right, Dan. We just treated 8,000 tons of silver at the Dexter. But you know what? We've all been thinkin' gold-and-silver, gold-and-silver, ever since we came to this scaldin' perch o' the devil." He looked at them hard. "Tell me I'm wrong."

Charlie and Dan were silent, but Daly's eyes glittered with passion. "All that silver we just clawed out of the Dexter had even more copper in it than silver, you hear me? Within a year, copper production is going to top a million dollars, you boys mark my words. And I know three East Coast firms paying top dollar for copper from England. So," he said, touching the table with his fingertip, "I'm going to see George Hearst. He owes me a favor."

Charlie, who was staring at the spot where Daly's finger met the tabletop, started thinking out loud. "Those manufacturers back East would rather buy American copper shipped by rail instead of by sea on Her Majesty's barges. And think of all the copper folks will be needing for the new electric lights."

Daly winked at him, but Charlie wasn't looking. "Charlie Allen, what is it you're thinkin' on so deep now?"

Charlie held both hands out, palms up. "Might not be a bad idea to get our hands on a few more of these claims. If there's copper glance down there, who knows where it'll apex."

Daly grinned and slapped him on the back.

"It's readin' my mind you are." But his face clouded. "Dan O'Neill and Charles Allen, you're to seal your lips tighter than the ancient barrows of Galway, you hear me? The value of all the claims around here has dropped substantially, and I want prices to stay down." He clapped his hat on his head, already in a hurry to get to San Francisco. "Wish me luck, and a red hot nail on the tongue that flaps, you hear?"

"Yes, sir." came the unified reply.

That evening, by the light of the brass table lamp, Charlie dove into his assaying books and shaft diagrams. He re-read everything he could find about copper, studying the descriptions of copper glance and its signs. He'd seen chalcopyrite, a primary ore, near the surface at several locations throughout Butte—the Alice, the Anaconda, the Neversweat, and at a smaller mine called the Angel. He pulled out a leather-bound case of flat drawers and found a slab of cardboard with various copper ores glued into small squares. He pored over these until his eyes burned. Finally, shaking the rosy gleam of copper from his thoughts, he stumbled wearily up the stairs.

Nearing the top, he stopped. From nowhere, into his mind speared the bright visage of an infant boy. "Winston," he whispered into the darkness. Taking slow steps, he weaved from fatigue. "Winston," he repeated, this time nearly choking out the name.

This wasn't the first time his son had stolen into his mind, confronting him in a way he never thought an infant could. All the other times, he had cached the child away in a sacred place, a kind of crystalline chamber in his mind, full of channels impossible to navigate: a place at once mysterious and safe.

He swallowed hard. Then, from somewhere in his gut there surged a thing that felt like courage. He leaned against the wall, feeling strength infuse his arms, his legs, even his lungs. For the first time, he resisted the familiar, cold undertow of guilt and anger, and considered what it might feel like to someday provide for a little boy he hardly knew. He grabbed at the energy rising within him and held it fast.

Yes, he would wash away his sins, real or imagined, just as Constance would expect him to. In the vast darkness, a taper had been lit. She had done it for him, God bless her.

His feet made light scuffing sounds as he continued his way along the dim hall, and an unbidden smile crept across his face. She would tell me I lit that candle myself, he mused. No, my darling Constance, not entirely. The pain may fade, but the love never does. You help me still.

14

Persis sat alone in her writing room, looking out the window at the wooded slope that curved up behind the house, where the trees appeared to be covered with a soft green fuzz. Her eyes traveled down the hill to the meadow that ran into crusty brown earth near some new construction.

Her hand lay on her belly, in a pregnant woman's unconscious way, and as she felt the rolling movement of a tiny heel, she realized that it was spring. Lime-green buds were bursting on the chokecherry trees and on the amber spears of the willows.

Incredulous, she thought hard about what month it was. April. A fine rain was falling, freckling the windowpanes. "Mountain weather," she said aloud. She had heard the phrase somewhere, but where? Then she recollected the tone and meter of the voice. Avery Burke. Last fall, at the Double Diamond, when mist shrouded the mountains and fell on the ranch the morning after Thanksgiving.

Pictures of that morning fanned out before her. Alex stood near her, his arm around her waist. Constance was there, big-bellied and rosy, alive and breathing. And there was Charlie, preoccupied over his coffee.

She smiled. Even then, he was thinking of the promises scribbled all over the rutted face of Butte City.

Gathering up her skirt, she went to her desk for a calendar. April 29, 1881. My God, April is almost over. She had cloudy recollections of several events—a party here and there, a sleigh ride with the Hancocks on a snowy day. At the beginning of March, James Garfield had assumed the Presidency back in the States; she remembered that. And she had been to Easter services at the Methodist Episcopal Church. Ruby's visits she remembered well. The midwife had come to Helena every month, and the two of them sat and talked over tea in the kitchen.

And Alex. Persis had tried vainly to explain to him that what happened to her when Constance died was involuntary. Looking at her with a creased brow, striving not to be angry, he endeavored to understand, but he clearly did not. How could he? She was walking the shadowy byways of the netherworld, clutching Constance's spirit-fingers in her own, uncertain whether she would ever return.

As the days grew longer and brighter, somehow the rational world and her wandering soul began to knit, forming at first the consciousness of a wound and finally, the beginnings of a scar.

Now she spent her morning energy on Winston, getting acquainted with his infant ways, counting his fingers and toes, doing whatever it took to make him smile, and watching his fair eyelashes rest against his cheeks as he slipped into the blessed peace of baby sleep.

She often walked to the MacKinney Freight office, not to see Alex, who was seldom there, but rather to see the animals and Angus Blaylock, who was in a way a huge, quiet beast himself. After a greeting and an inquiry about her health, he would give her a bit of news about one of the draft horses or the mules, then leave her alone. This respectful detachment endeared him to her. The damp springtime smell of the barn and the acrid scent of the animals were aromatic and healing.

Charlie had only come to Helena once, for Constance's burial.

"He's become quite the will o' the wisp, hasn't he?" Alex would say, fishing for reasons to explain Charlie's complete severance from his family and his son. In a gesture that touched Persis deeply, Alex reached over and covered her hand with his. "Don't worry. I'm actually taking a shine to the little tyke. God knows this house needs more men."

* * *

"You've got about four weeks left, I think," said Ruby, gently spanning and pressing on Persis's belly with her long fingers. "I'll begin stopping in every Wednesday, if that suits you," she said in her businesslike and yet gentle voice.

As they sipped their tea in the kitchen, Persis reached across the table and touched Ruby's arm. "I have no way of proving that Constance contracted sepsis through Dr. Lyons," she said tightly, "but any fool can see he failed to cleanse himself after leaving the hospital. That was the night they did the amputation on the logger from Hamilton. He was raging with gangrene. We both know Lyons must have done the surgery. I sometimes wonder if I hate him."

"It was ignorance," said Ruby simply. "It doesn't absolve him, but someday it may make it easier for you to forgive him."

"No, Ruby. Ignorance? Dr. Lyons is an intelligent, learned man. Every doctor on this continent knows the antiseptic principle by now. You told me that yourself."

Ruby shook her head and rubbed her brow. "I only wish there was something we could have done. But sepsis runs its course, despite us all." She sighed heavily and lifted her teacup. "What does Alex think of your choice in this?"

Persis smoothed the creases in her sleeve. "He knows how I feel," she said at length.

This is not the same girl who fainted on the street in front of the Hotel last year, Ruby thought. Wiser, yes, but there's something else that has happened.

"You know I'll help you," she said. "I'm in Helena for the entire summer."

Persis, rousing herself from dark memories, embraced Ruby. "Thank you."

Putting on her worn black hat, the midwife took her leave.

Persis eased herself back into her chair and looked into the basket where Winston slept. At last, she realized, I can look at those curling locks of blond hair without feeling a stab of loss. Instead, I gather something more precious than I ever imagined.

She fell to thinking of Charlie, and decided to take a bold step. She would have Nora deliver a letter to him in person, inviting him to come to Helena.

*   *   *

"He said he'd come," Nora cried out as soon as she set foot in the kitchen.

Persis drilled her. "When? How is he? Is he eating?"

"He said, 'when the baby comes.' He looks well, Miss. Thin, but it's a fine looking man he is, our Mister Charlie." She threw a defensive look at Grace, who appeared intent on a jelly stain in the tablecloth.

Persis savored this happy news, which soon blended with her excitement over the coming birth. Her thoughts swirled around the mid-June delivery date Ruby had calculated.

She rang Nora for her bath. "Would you like the window open, Miss?" asked Nora. "It's a lovely morning."

"Yes, Nora, that sounds wonderful." Persis was sitting on the edge of the four-poster bed in her private room, to which she had returned as her pregnancy advanced. She knew her nightly risings kept Alex awake, and it was easier on both of them to sleep separately.

"I think I'd like to go downtown this morning, Nora. And if I don't tire, perhaps even visit Ruby—you know, over on Warren Street past the cemetery. Will you drive me?"

Nora's face brightened. "Oh yes, Miss, you know how I love to go abroad of a morning, especially over near the Gulch. It's so interesting down there."

Persis smiled. Nora was right. In a single block one could pass a gaggle of Czech laundresses, a couple of their Chinese male rivals, an Italian barber leaning against his doorframe, and a German butcher shooing away the threshold-sniffing dogs. The Gulch was the social epicenter of Helena.

The bedroom window opened easily and the June breeze poured in. A mourning dove cooed from the spruce tree near her window. Stretching languidly, Persis traced the pattern of Battenberg lace around her pillowcase. "I don't know how I managed to end up with such wonderful help as you and Grace," she said.

"Oh, Miss, we're happy here," Nora called out from the bedroom closet. "You know, Mrs. Fisk has been talking to the other mistresses, sayin' that it's only $30 a month any domestic should be makin'. If we was to say that you and Mr. MacKinney give us $40 a month, it would cause a riot, to be sure."

"Well, Elizabeth Fisk is a woman of conviction," Persis said diplomatically. "But your positions are secure here, as are your wages. Perhaps Mr. MacKinney doesn't say it, but you are appreciated. Having consistent help is good for everyone, especially little Winston. I'd like to have him grow up with you both, if it works out that way."

"I don't see why not," said Grace, coming into the room with a bundle of towels. "It's not an easy thing to grow up in this rough country."

"As for me," said Nora, flashing her gray-blue eyes and tossing her red hair, "I like livin' in a place where the men outnumber the women. It's much better than havin' it the other way."

Grace gave her a stern look and continued, "Well, Nora's romantic pursuits aside, you can rest easier than some folks, Mrs. MacKinney," continued Grace, "because we've both got family here. I mean, either here or in the mining camp. Everyone's taken to callin' it simply 'Butte,' these days. And Nora's got those two brothers there—and of course her eminently quotable Aunt Kathleen."

* * *

Rosemary Adair MacKinney was born June 21, 1881, on the night of the summer solstice. Ruby made much of the baby's hour of advent. "There couldn't be a more auspicious birth," she said. "The entire world is paying homage to nature and the flourishing life of summer."

Forever engraved on Persis's mind was the luminous sky that evening, touched with the opal fingers of the low sun, when little Rose made her appearance. She remembered, too, that the solstice was a special time for her own mother, who had remarked on it every year as far back as Persis could remember.

When no one was looking, Persis would raise her wrist to her forehead, checking for signs of childbed fever. By the morning of the fourth day, both she and Ruby had each come to a private and grateful acknowledgement that the danger was past.

Charlie kept his promise and arrived on the fifth day. Persis observed her brother, unselfconscious and at times even delightfully silly, spending time with his son. She kept a respectful, casual distance.

When Charlie wasn't paying attention to Winston, he was standing over Rosemary's cradle. Both he and Alex were falling under Rosemary's spell.

"What am I to do?" Persis asked Alex playfully one morning. "You've found a girlfriend, and she's a beauty."

He looked up from the cradle, raising his eyebrows, and then smiled. "She'll give you competition for a while, but you'll be trimmed up soon." He turned back to the baby.

*   *   *

Marcus and Maggie Daly returned to Butte at the end of June. Daly called another private meeting of his lieutenants at the General Office near the dark mouth of the Anaconda. Straining to suppress his exuberance, he told them of the results of his journey to San Francisco.

"My friend George," began Daly, "Hearst, that is—for those of you who haven't heard of him—wants in on the Anaconda diggings. And it's a big piece he's wanting, too. Not only that, but two other fine and well-heeled fellows, Lloyd Tevis and James Haggin, are in now too. We'll expand this office, and at the same time we're going to widen the main shaft from one compartment to three. Men, lumber, pickers, blasters. Charlie, you're to get working on that right quick. Lots of muckers too, to move the diggings."

Within a week, construction on the three-compartment shaft had begun. After they reached 220 feet, Charlie began checking the walls of the shaft. As he dropped to the deepest wells of the dig and saw the lanterns bobbing below, he wished the men could apply themselves more assiduously. But the sweat on their brows, their grimy forearms, and the stale, humid air passing from one set of lungs to another were a testament to their exertion.

Daly himself was in the habit of going down twice a day. One morning in July, they found themselves in the cage together. "Very little gas," Charlie noted. "Makes for a safe mine. Look here," he said, pointing to a long gash of greenish rock. "Chalocopyrite. There's plenty of it between 150 and 250. You know what that means."

"Plenty of traces of silver, too," said Daly. "We can't produce the volume of copper just yet to justify abandoning silver."

Charlie set his jaw in frustration and made his way back to the cage. Might as well just mine dirt, he thought, kicking the woven wire. Halfway home, he changed course. "Where's Dan," he muttered. "I could do with a Sean O. Or five."

Ten minutes later, he found Dan in an equally surly mood, trudging down the hill toward town.

"Let's hit the Vienna," said Charlie. "They're doing a big business. It's Friday night. They've got oysters."

"Fine. I'm ready," Dan snapped.

"It's a blessed fine mood you're in, me boy," Charlie said, mocking Dan's brogue.

Dan grunted and kept walking. In silence, the two of them descended the scrabbly hill into Walkerville. Then Dan blurted out, "You want to know what's chafin' me? Women. I wish this town was nothing but men."

Charlie kept his eyes on the slaggy dirt.

After a few shots of Kentucky bourbon and as many bottles of Schneider lager, the two stumbled across the street for dinner at the Walkerville Cafe. Dan leered as their buxom hostess set plates of venison steak and boiled potatoes in front of them. Toward midnight, Charlie got Dan safely back to his place on Park Street, then picked his own way home through the dark, sulfurous night, ignoring the prostitutes wandering up from Galena Street.

*　*　*

Charlie woke with a pounding headache. After doctoring himself with a breakfast of eggs and bacon at the Franklin Boarding House, he walked up the hill to the Anaconda. The new shaft and its detritus formed another sad rent in the hillside. Tall, dark hoisting works stood everywhere, like propped skeletons over plundered graves.

As he descended the shaft, Charlie heard a ruckus below. Saturday morning hangovers and short tempers, he ruminated, and I'm as bad off as any of them. As he passed the 250 mark, the sound of the voices became clearer. There were no churlish tones after all. He thought he heard a muffled voice crying, "Stringer!"

He broke out in a sweat as the cables creaked, lowering him slowly down.

"Looks like graveyard clay," came one voice.

"Riley's pig knows stringer's the mither o' copper," snapped another.

Charlie bounded from the cage before it hit bottom. There, on the lowest part of the wall, was the unmistakable gray-green frieze he'd dreamed about—a narrow seam of copper ore. Grinning broadly, he grabbed a pick and tapped off a piece.

"This is it, boys," he said, shaking with excitement. "Keep at her. Pick her out good. Where are the blasters? This is only the beginning."

"Here's mud in your eye, Marcus Daly!" shouted John Barry, an older man from County Cork. The men guffawed and elation suffused the thick, moist air.

"He'll be proud of you all," said Charlie. "Nice work. I'll tell O'Neill to beef up the mucker team."

He rolled the piece of stringer over and over in his sweaty palms. It was all he could do not to start hacking away at the wall himself. I've got to tell Daly, he realized, forcing himself back into the cage.

Climbing in and starting his ascent, he called down, "You won't get champagne, but God knows you deserve it. I'll buy you all a round of the next best thing at the Vienna."

"We ain't no frogs, Charles Allen. We'll take naught but good brown ale," one of them shouted, loudly seconded by the others.

At the top, the sun was breaking through the white clouds. Charlie rolled the ore over again in the daylight, studying its color and density. It was beautiful, washed in a rich jade color and peppered with rusty red. Deep within were tiny chambers lined with minute dark green crystals.

In his haste to get to Marcus's house, he almost rattled past Daly's own buggy coming up the hill. Charlie waved his hands in the air and shouted, "We've hit stringer!"

Daly slapped the reins against the horse's rump and drew his buggy close to Charlie's. He raised his hands and Charlie tossed the long-buried ore into the summer sunlight. Glittering, it rolled through the air and fell into the old miner's seasoned hands. With one quick look, the Irishman took in every bit of its geologic promise. He raised his eyes to Charlie's, and both of them grinned broadly.

"This is the richest hill on earth!" shouted Daly. "Mark my words!"

After four o'clock that afternoon, the entire Anaconda day shift packed the Vienna Brewery. Daly bought a round for them all and left a big credit with the owners, who pledged to provide for the next two shifts.

Two weeks later, at 340 feet, the seam widened into fingers of solid, steel-colored rock, the crest of an enormous formation of copper glance. The mine was now yielding up a double bounty. It was more than the men could get their minds around. With a silver-plated present and the rosy aura of a copper future, they had the world by the tail, and they were just beginning to know it.

* * *

"Lizzie Fisk is having some women over tomorrow evening for discussion," Persis ventured to Alex on a Sunday afternoon in early August. "I think I'll attend," she added lightly.

"What's the purpose of the meeting?"

"Oh, the usual civic concerns. Hospital linens and lap-robes and that sort of thing. The library, too."

"Well, go then," he said, shaking out the newspaper and refocusing. "I hope it's what you expect."

I hope it's far more, Persis thought. Aloud she said, "What do you mean?"

"Well, Lizzie Fisk has the reputation of being something of a bluestocking. I wouldn't want you to adopt any . . . odd notions. This talk about Helena's articles of incorporation and women voting and that kind of prattle."

Hearing the word "bluestocking" fueled her desire to go. As she continued her reading, the only sound was the distant clatter of pots and pans in the kitchen.

Although Alex had returned his attention to the newspaper, it suddenly came down on his lap. "You know, Persis, I suppose it is a good thing that this came up." He rose and went to the liquor cabinet.

Persis withered. He was taking that tone with her that she had come to dread. Now he's going to have a drink on top of it, she thought. If I hadn't brought up the subject, he wouldn't be doing this.

He turned and faced her, drink in hand. "It's fine to be community minded, but I must say I would be far more sympathetic if you were to display a greater spirit of domesticity in our home." His face was strained and his topaz eyes were averted.

Persis looked at him and murmured, "Spirit of dom—" She swallowed. "Why, Alex, I am very much taken up with the affairs of our home. What do you mean?"

Alex sighed heavily. "Must I spell everything out for you? Surely you see a contrast between yourself and women like Alma Bradley and Priscilla Wilkes? Just the other evening, Mrs. Gordon, whom you mentioned earlier, showed us a sample of crochet work she is doing for their dining room table. It's a fine accomplishment and it says a great deal about her commitment to her home. Men admire that sort of thing, Persis. Surely you know that."

Before a stupefied Persis, Alex waxed passionate on the subject, citing examples of the other wives' accomplishments. "I find these traits particularly attractive in a woman," he said, raising his hands in an entreating gesture which, a year ago, Persis would have found engaging. "They carry such a message of . . . home comfort."

At first, Persis attempted to defend herself. "But Alex, the menu for today's dinner was one that I myself developed from family recipes. I made the sauce for the roast, didn't I?"

"Did you?" he said, sitting down again and picking up the newspaper. "Well, yes, I now recall that you did." He looked up at her and smiled. "Come and sit beside me, darling. You do understand me, don't you? I'm not some kind of ogre."

Persis went to the couch. He took her hand in his and began, "I can't help it, Persis. I like to see a woman employed in cooking and sewing." He tapped his fingers against the back of her hand, thinking. "It feels like love to me," he said slowly. "Like I am being taken care of, like my world is all in place."

"It makes you feel secure," Persis said.

"Secure?" He let out a little sniff. "Well, yes, I suppose you could put it that way."

A torpid smile passed over her face. "I think I understand you, Alex."

"Well, then, at any rate," he said briskly, "you can then imagine my alarm at the prospect of you pursuing any unbecoming activities. Strikes at the very foundation of how I see our life together."

Persis nodded slowly, staring at the hearth-screen.

"There, there. It's not like I am chaining you to the kitchen stove, is it? You have an enormous amount of freedom." He jumped up, infused with his typical verve, and announced, "I've gotten a bottle of truly fine port. Let's share a nip, shall we?"

Persis nodded again, smiling up at him. I need it, she thought.

* * *

The meeting at Lizzie Fisk's was much less interesting than she had hoped. The best discovery of the evening was that Alma Bradley was far from the domestic seraph Alex had described. Alma did remarkable handiwork, this much was true. But she had an incisive, forward mind and, together with her attorney husband, did an enormous amount of reading. Persis liked her immediately and made plans to see her again under any circumstance she might contrive.

Entering the kitchen at 610 Gilbert, she was dazzled by the electric lights Alex had just had installed. Nora and Grace were both in the kitchen making baby clothes.

Nora announced, "Mr. MacKinney's not home, Mum. He left for Parker's shortly after you did. Said he didn't want to sit home alone." There was a timid inflection in that last phrase, evidence that Nora sensed Alex's disapproval of Persis's sortie.

Seized by an impulse of freedom and rebellion, Persis said gaily, "Would you ladies like to join me in a glass of port? Just because we've got Mr. Edison's lights doesn't mean you've got to work all night. Grace, as you would say, why don't we all 'take a little sit-down'?"

The two servants exchanged cautious looks as Persis headed for the liquor cabinet in the library. She returned with the everyday glasses from the cupboard and poured each of them a couple ounces of dark, ruby-toned liquid.

Once Nora and Grace relaxed, the three of them marveled over the electric lights, trying to decide if they were really a change for the better or if they might hold some unanticipated threat to the eyesight of the human race.

Persis's mind drifted to Alex. "How those men can amuse themselves for hours on end over cards," she said absently, her chin in her hand. "I've played whist, but it's not that fascinating."

"It's the money, I've always thought," said Grace simply. "The fear o' losin' it and the thrill of beatin' their mates. They win just often enough to keep up their excitement."

"I've played poker before," said Nora casually.

"Where are the cards?" said Persis.

"It's jokin' y'are, Miss Percy," said Nora.

"Why, no! Let's just have a quick go at it. We'll play for matchsticks. Nora, you must tell me all, for I don't know a thing."

"Nor do I," said Grace. "Not one blessed thing."

The three women hunched like crones over the table, sipping their port and guiltily stumbling through a hand of five-card stud. Now and then, if they heard a noise on the street or in the carriage house, Nora would whisper a commanding, "Shush now! What's that?" But it was nothing, and their hilarity returned.

Persis was completely bewildered by the terminology and the values assigned to the combinations of cards. After twenty minutes, she gave up.

"Well, we shall try that again sometime," she concluded. "Not a word to Master MacKinney, now." The vision of a wrathful Alex gave her an inward shudder.

"Crows fly in and out of me skull should I say a word," said Grace solemnly.

"And mine as well," Nora added.

When Persis left the kitchen, they were still in high spirits. The bright, whitened glow of electric light was everywhere. Persis wasn't sure she liked it. How it was made possible by the cloth-covered copper cables snaking everywhere through the walls of the house, she had no idea. Something in her yearned for the old, soft yellow flame of an oil lamp or even a candle. Like Avery's kerosene lanterns, she remembered. It'll be years before the lights come to his beloved Double Diamond.

Alone in the library, she poured another dose of port. Feeling the texture of crystal beneath her fingers, she savored the dark peace of the evening with each sip. Chances are Alex will be in good spirits when he gets home, she thought, and I won't hear much about my outing. Even if he never comes to understand that women form important friendships in community, he will see that I am improving the town that he had a hand in establishing. He can't help but grow proud.

Alex broadened the scope of the liquor cabinet, adding claret, cognac, and whatever he could freight in. The bottles arrived, nested in wood shavings in curious foreign crates, intact from their thundering ride over the mountains. One evening over a cognac, he conceived the idea for a dinner party, for which Persis immediately began to plan. The guest list included the Hausers. Even though Alex grumbled frequently about Sam Hauser and his projects, Persis knew Sam was a lynchpin in many of Alex's own pursuits.

On the grocery trip, Nora was at the reins of the runabout. As they drew up to Highland Meat Market, Persis spied a petite and yet robust-looking woman, fashionably dressed, heading for the stationer's. She had dark, carefully coifed hair and an ample but stately figure. I ought to know who she is, thought Persis, but I don't.

"Sure if it isn't Joe herself," Nora remarked under her breath.

"Joe?"

Nora looked sideways at her. "Chicago Joe. The one what's got the bawdy house, mum."

Seized by the desire to meet this woman and feel her notoriety first hand, Persis's mind raced. "Stop and tie up here, Nora," she ordered suddenly. "We need some magazines. I forgot all about it 'til just now."

Nora reined the horse in and Persis stepped agilely down from the buggy. Joe was heading for Rosencrans and Klaue, a well-stocked stationer. Persis was closer and reached the door in just a few steps. As she grasped the brass doorknob and went in, she held the door for Joe. Joe's gloved hand rested on the door a moment next to her own.

They exchanged looks and Persis smiled brightly, saying, "Good morning."

"Lovely day," replied Joe, moving into the store with a sense of purpose.

Inside, Persis busied herself with children's magazines and the latest issue of *Harper's Weekly*. Joe, who went directly to the toiletries, placed several bars of milled French soap into her basket and momentarily studied the section entitled, "Eau de Toilette." Persis did not look directly at the woman, but saw peripherally that Joe took at least five bottles of perfume from the shelf.

"What's become of the White Heliotrope, Ben?" she asked the clerk.

"It's there, ain't it, Joe? I know we've got it. Just got a new carton from Colgate's last Friday. Let me look in back."

Persis approached the counter with her magazines. Looking at Joe, she smiled again. "We haven't met. My name is Persis MacKinney."

"How do you do, Mrs. MacKinney. The wife of Alexander?"

Persis nodded.

"I'm Josephine Airey." She extended a hand. "Just call me Joe."

Persis ventured, "You like the White Heliotrope? I had an aunt who favored that scent."

"Oh, this isn't for me. Can't stand the stuff. This is for—a friend."

The clerk emerged from the back of the store with a small crate. "Eureka," he said with a grin.

"Put in four tins of Riz face powder, too," ordered Joe in a brisk but pleasant tone. "What do I owe you, Ben?"

"Let's see. Riz, that's gone up . . . forty five cents each, plus six bars of French soap at fifteen cents each . . . and six bottles of perfume plus the heliotrope . . . that'll be five dollars and sixty cents."

Joe paid for the toiletries and turned to Persis. "It was nice to meet you, Mrs. MacKinney. Perhaps we will meet again. Helena is a small town."

As Persis made her way back, a caravan of huge, ox-drawn freight wagons was rumbling down the street. A bullwhacker's whip snapped overhead, making her jump. Nearing the buggy, she saw Nora engaged in conversation with someone on horseback. It was Avery Burke.

Leaning on the pommel of his saddle, he looked at complete ease. His high cheekbones were tanned, and there was a red silk neckerchief knotted loosely at his throat. His hat was pushed back slightly, and he was sporting the odd half-smile that always made Persis smile too.

They shook hands warmly. He asked about her new baby, and wondered if Winston was still with them.

"Rose is fine. She's a very healthy child. She'll be two months old this Sunday. She has no hair, though. Just a dab of peach fuzz! Winston will be a year old in December."

Avery nodded. "Glad to hear Charlie's getting beyond his loss a bit now. And you as well."

She nodded, looking him in the eye and feeling a rush of gratitude for his simple, steadfast friendship.

"Who was that imperial-looking woman that left Rosencrans' right before you?" he asked.

"That's Josephine Airey. She runs the Coliseum." Feeling Nora's sidelong look, she added simply, "She was very pleasant."

"So that's Chicago Joe," Avery said dryly.

Nora piped up irreverently, "Don't most men know her?"

"Nora." Persis shot her a look, then shook her head apologetically. Avery smiled.

"I didn't mean . . . well, I'm sorry, Mr. Burke. Sometimes a bit o' foolishness slips out the corner of my mouth."

"No offense taken, Nora. Well, ladies, I am in town for the stockgrowers' meeting. We're trying to talk the growers from the east half of the Territory into joining forces with us. Here comes Pete. I'm sure he'll give me the devil for keeping him waiting."

Pete didn't look annoyed, Persis thought. In fact, quite the contrary. "Mornin', Mrs. MacKinney," he said, smiling. A lock of dark hair slanted across his forehead beneath the brim of his hat.

"Please call me Persis." She shook his hand.

Pete turned toward the runabout and asked, "What about you, Miss? May I call you by your Christian name? Nora, isn't it?"

Persis was looking at Pete, but out of the corner of her eye, she saw Avery turn his head and stare at his brother.

Nora was even more surprised. "Saints! Sure you can, Mr. Burke. I mean . . ."

"Pete," came the reply. "Call me Pete." The dark lock of hair lifted in the light breeze as he reached forward and took Nora's fingers in his own for a moment and then released them.

Persis and Avery looked dumbly at one another. He's as surprised as I am, she thought. We both look like jackanapes. She felt a smile sneak over her lips and turned abruptly away, stroking the muzzle of Avery's strawberry roan, staring at the horse's long whiskers and feeling his hot breath puff against her hands.

"Well," said Nora, whose cheeks were far more pink than usual. "Well."

Avery came to her rescue. "As I was saying, the cattle industry's just getting too big for us to be divided like this. Miles and Sparky are over at Vawter's Grocery, loading up on provisions. Most of our boys are up on the Sun River with the cattle. Someone's got to do a little politicking, and I guess I'm elected."

"You will do a fine job," said Persis. "How is everything out at your place? It seems like years since I was there. It must be glorious now, in the prime of summer."

"It's looking real good. I'm on the range so much in the summer that I feel I don't even live there. I miss it . . . the sound of the wind in the cottonwoods along the creek, or a cool evening in the rocker on the front porch. Come fall, once the roundup and shipping is over, it'll be a relief to find a roof over my head instead of a tarpaulin."

Their eyes met again. How, Persis thought, can a man make me so comfortable and self-conscious at the same time? A smile stole over his face as he watched her fidget. Yes, it almost seemed as if he wanted it that way.

"There's a horseshoe pit and an outdoor barbecue now, too," Pete added with pride, looking at Nora.

"The height of ranching elegance," said Persis.

"When are you and the small fry going to pay us another call?" Avery asked.

"Oh, don't tempt me!" Persis laughed. "You know very well that Rose is too small just yet. Winston would be fine, but guess who'd be chasing after him all day?"

"Bring Nora. Alex could go fishing. Can't beat August fishing along the Clark Fork. You just might find it to be more relaxing than you think. Raid my library. I've got quite a few new volumes. You like Thackeray. You told me so. Sit on the porch. Drink lemonade. Pete's been schooling a new mare, dapple gray, and she's plumb gentle."

"I—we'll try," Persis answered.

"You've got an open invitation. And you too, Nora. Mrs. MacKinney needs you."

"Oh, and it's lucky we are to have her, Grace and me," Nora chirped.

Avery touched his hat. "I'm off to some smoke-filled room. God bless you and yours."

"Stop and see Alex at the bank if you can," Persis called after him. "He'd love to see you. And make that fishing proposal."

Pete lifted his hat with more ceremony than usual, taking a last look at Nora, then maneuvered his horse into a graceful trot alongside his brother.

For several blocks, Nora was quiet. Persis finally ventured, "I think you have an admirer."

Nora laughed. "I remember him from last fall. He's nice. Don't you think he's nice?"

"Yes, I do."

Then, as if tucking Pete away in some safe place in her mind, Nora asked about Josephine Airey. "What is she like? I've known a few of those . . . ladies in Butte. Not well, mind you," she added prudently. "But this here Joe, well, she's a bit different."

"Wherever there's a frontier, Nora, there are going to be people who cater to the needs of its pioneers, for better or worse." Lord, listen to me, Persis thought.

* * *

For the third time, Alex asked to look at the menu. Persis retrieved it from Grace, who raised her brows.

In the library, Alex studied it for a few minutes, pushed it aside, and then drummed his fingers on the desk. "I've been thinking about running for office," he announced, coming over to sit beside her. "Nothing too lofty, at first. I want to start out as humbly as I can, perhaps as a county representative to the Territorial Legislature." He squeezed her hand. "I'll need your support."

Persis affected her most amiable smile. As popular and engaging as

Alex was, she had never perceived him as a statesman. He's a parvenu, she thought guiltily. An upstart. But perhaps the real opportunity here, she reasoned, is a means of helping him grow.

The day of the party arrived. In the morning, as Alex employed Donny to rearrange the lawn furniture and lay out a croquet pattern, Grace fastened a sleeve button and observed, "Mr. Alex is surprising us all. Nervous as a bug in a skillet."

"He wants very much to impress the Hausers," was all Persis said. She wished her crocheted tablecloth was finished.

Fortunately, the Hausers had just returned from a trip to upstate New York, so she found plenty to talk about with Ellen and even Sam. She was delighted at his interest in her thoughts on the railroad and on Marcus Daly's Anaconda Mine. She was more than able to hold her own regarding current events in the mining camp.

As they were discussing the partisan nature of the press in Butte, Alex approached and listened in. She could tell her grasp of political issues in Butte surprised him. Relaxed by the Bordeaux, she warmed to her subject.

"It makes so much sense to start intensively mining copper," she said, "especially with the advent of electricity."

Ellen Hauser missed her point. "What do you mean, my dear?"

Sam put in, "Mrs. MacKinney is absolutely right. You see, copper is an ideal electrical conductor. Daly's going to become a rich man." He paused. "You have a keen sense of the issues, Mrs. MacKinney."

"I—Alex and I—take the Butte newspaper. And my brother works for Mr. Daly."

"Even an arm's length relationship with Marcus doesn't make a person well-versed. I appreciate your perspicacity."

Persis beamed with confidence and delight.

The meal was a triumph, although it seemed to Persis that Sam Hauser teased Alex a good deal. When the subject of Scotland came up, Hauser quoted Samuel Johnson, saying, "Much may be made of a Scotsman . . . if he be caught young!"

As the laughter subsided, Alex countered graciously, raising his glass. "Much may be made of any man, if he has good friends."

"Here, here!" came the voices from around the table, glasses clinking.

When the company had departed, and the house was still except for the distant rattle of domestic chores, Alex took Persis firmly by the hand and led her up the stairs. He stopped in the middle of the bedroom and left her standing there while he strode back to the door and closed it.

What happened next was one of the most astonishing experiences of Persis's life. Alex bade her stand still while he removed her blue silk dress and petticoats, then her corset cover and pantaloons. He stopped several times to kiss her hard on the mouth. She smelled and tasted the heavy, fuming scent of alcohol. He unstrung the upper front laces of her corset. She was quivering, but for some inexplicable, maddening reason, she responded. As she felt her core churn with desire, she also felt a seed of self-loathing, sown long ago, germinate and begin to thrive.

Leaving her in her corset and garters, he lifted her to the bed and proceeded to make love to her with a more lustful passion than ever before. Her underclothes were an impediment, but he seemed to want it that way. The entire scene felt theatrical and peculiar; still, she took immense pleasure in how much he needed her.

Drained by ardent lovemaking and yielding gratefully to the sedation of the Bordeaux, she fell asleep. Drifting into a dream, she went to Alma's house and was surprised to find Ruby there. The two of them were planting something—flowers or herbs—in Alma's garden just beyond the kitchen gate. She felt a presence behind her and wheeled around, convinced that Alex had followed her. There was nothing there, except the wide street leading down into Last Chance Gulch. She felt the presence again, this time like a hand on her shoulder.

"Persis!" came the insistent voice. He *had* followed her. Why didn't Ruby and Alma warn her?

"Persis! Wake up!" It came to her that she was in bed, and that Alex's hand was indeed on her shoulder. "Wake up."

Annoyed and tired, she looked at the clock and saw that she had been asleep a scant forty minutes. What awakened him after so long an evening and such exhaustive lovemaking? Swallowing her resentment, she responded, "What is it?"

He didn't say anything. She waited a moment and asked again, "Alex?"

Still no response. Persis closed her eyes with anguish and her throat tightened. His mood had taken that dark turn, and now it must run its course. She could no sooner stop it than she could a locomotive.

He lay very still. She moved to rise and light a candle, but as she shifted to leave the bed, Alex's arm hinged out and gripped her like a vise.

"Where are you going?"

Persis swallowed. "I'm getting a match to light the candle."

He released her and she lit the thick white candle on the bedside table. "What's wrong, Alex?" She saw the line of his jaw.

"You're quite pleased with yourself, aren't you?"

Persis sat still, rapidly examining this comment. He resents something I did or didn't do. Her hands grew cold. What has triggered his anger? Did I display too much knowledge of over-grazing, or of mining? She felt certain this was it, but she dared not say so, in the event that Alex was thinking of something else.

She carefully said, "You seem upset."

He gave a derisive laugh.

"Alex, what is it? I can't help you if you won't talk." An edge of exasperation flickered in her voice and she regretted it instantly.

"Persis," he said, glaring at her in the candlelight, "You may be a lot of things, but you aren't stupid."

Persis winced at this old remonstrance. "If I have done something to upset you, Alex, please tell me what it is, and I won't do it again. I thought . . . you were happy . . . the way we made love tonight. . . . I don't understand. I thought you were pleased with the way the evening went. We've been getting along so well these past months . . . what's wrong?"

Alex flung back the covers, exposing them both. He was naked, and Persis realized that she was still in her corset and garters. The window was open, and the draft of night air on her skin made her shiver. She saw her dressing gown, folded neatly at the foot of the bed. Bless you, Nora, she thought as she reached to put it on. Alex got out of bed and stood staring at her.

Here it comes, she thought, wrapping the muslin awkwardly around her. She felt almost cavalier about whatever might be in store for her. Every one of her limbs ached from the household effort she had expended for three days straight. Let him scream at me, she reasoned. The sooner he does, the sooner I can go to sleep. She knew her silence was pushing him toward rage, but she had also learned that her words never helped. There was nothing to be done; the steam engine would come ahead.

"Persis, do I have to draw you a picture?"

She did not reply. It was unpleasant to look at him. She was rocketing through this altercation with a new sense of apathy, but for some powerful reason, she couldn't bring herself to humor Alex. What difference would it make?

"God damn you, Persis," he swore, and lunged at her. With mighty strength he lifted her bodily from the bed and sputtered, "Listen to me!"

She was terrified. She looked at him, square in the eye, and said, "I am listening, Alex."

They were embarked on the inexorable excursion of his fury. "You handled things very badly! Do you know what I am talking about?" His fingers dug into her shoulders.

"I . . . I am wondering if it was the fact that I discussed politics with Mr. Hauser," she ventured helplessly.

He glowered at her. "You see, you aren't stupid. Perhaps you haven't noticed that I've been having some difficulty with the illustrious Mr. Hauser lately. That bastard thinks he can run my life."

Why, then, thought Persis, did we have him to dinner? She sank into confusion. "I thought . . . well, yes, Alex, I have sensed some dissatisfaction. But I thought I might be able to sort of . . . compensate."

"Compensate? Is that what you were doing? I never knew you to be so outspoken. His wife certainly won't like you much after this! I'll be polite and say you were a . . . coquette! She'll soon see you for what you truly are—a pathetic woman who needs to upstage her husband."

Persis's brow furrowed. What is behind these senseless accusations?

He began ridiculing her opinions about mining and copper, about cattle and grazing, and about open range and fences. He ridiculed her for having opinions at all, and for having the conceit to think they mattered to his business associates. White spittle formed at the corners of his mouth.

To Persis, the scene became steadily more histrionic. Her spirit of contrition slipped away like sand. Why am I tolerating this absurd behavior?

As Alex shouted on and on, she began thinking of her little writing room and the soft, green velvet couch. She could sleep there, under the satin quilt, and the two of them could talk in the morning.

She got up from the bed and faced him squarely. "We'll talk about this in the morning. We've both had too much to drink. I'll sleep downstairs tonight." She turned and started for the door.

There was a loud ripping of fabric and she felt herself lifted, formed into a ball, and sent sailing through the air. She landed with the full force of her body weight on the back of her neck against the massive walnut headboard of their bed. Her right knee flew up into her face, jamming against her cheekbone.

Nearly senseless, she was aware that Alex was deriding her, but she couldn't string his words together. She struggled slowly into a sitting position, teetering on the edge of the bed, unable to speak or even think. She was dimly aware of only one thing . . . that she was in danger and needed to get away. But not now. He'll hurt me if I try to go now. When he is done, and goes to sleep, I'll leave. But what about the children?

As the shock of physical impact began to ebb, her mind cleared as her spirit retreated deep inside. Random thoughts bounced through her head. This is living death, she thought. I am a shapeless being. I can't leave. I can't take the children. Surely he'll see how wrong he has been. Maybe he won't. I hate him with a passion I never thought possible. She longed for her writing room, but she pictured him splintering the French doors to get at her.

Alex raged on. "All you did tonight was damage my position in this community. Hauser already thinks I'm a *bon vivant*. And you call yourself my wife!"

She wondered how she could be thinking about the varying shades of ivory in the drapes.

"Persis! Persis, you heartless bitch! Are you even listening?"

She nodded, quailing.

"Do I have to describe to you the meaning of the word 'wife?' Do I?" he demanded.

Persis wondered if the servants could hear. "No, Alex. I am very sorry." She fumbled for the shreds of her dressing gown. As she looked down, she felt him looking too.

"You are so cold to me!" His voice was bitterly sad. "God in heaven, I wanted a companion. I needed you so!"

This was a summons. It went through her like a dagger made of ice. He's calling me to come to him, to touch him and bring him back to bed. Nauseated with dread, she rose shakily to her feet and moved slowly toward him.

"I am sorry, Alex. I see that I was insensitive to you. Why don't you come to bed? We are both tired." Ruled by the most primal sense of self-preservation, she willed her hand past a wall of hate and revulsion to touch his arm.

"I've . . . torn your wrapper," he mumbled. "I'll buy you a new one. I'll buy you a hundred of them, Persis, if you will only learn to support me." The message of his rage was always the same: Betray me and you will live to regret it beyond your wildest imaginings.

She trembled in front of him as he lifted the ragged muslin back up to her shoulders. He paused, resting his hand on her arm as the shapeless gown slipped to her waist. She felt exposed, more vulnerable than she could stand, and flinched. His hand went again to her shoulder, then descended to the crevice of the loosened corset, and slipped in to touch her breast. His lips were on her neck, her collarbone.

He wants to . . . he wants to take me again, she thought incredulously. How can this be? How can he think such a thing?

"Make love to me, my wife," he murmured as he kissed her neck. Love, she thought. I'll give him what he thinks is love. Brutalized and drained of hope, she unbound her spirit and let it go, out the window into the velvet August night. Go and wait with the mourning doves, she thought; my body must stay here.

Her arms went up around Alex's neck and she surrendered. It will be over soon, she thought, and then he will stop touching me, at least for a while.

16

Before they went down to breakfast, Alex told her he was willing to try for a better marriage if she was. Persis assented numbly and then, fearful that her lack of enthusiasm might offend, she forced a spirited, "Yes, of course I am."

He took her arm, this time very gently, as they walked down the stairs. Her stomach churned. *I am a parcel, a piece of livestock. I am owned and controlled.*

A newspaper article from last week's *Helena Herald* flashed across her mind. *Man arrested for wife-beating in Butte. The unfortunate women's head was swollen and two ribs were broken by the villain's blows . . .* Alex is no different, she thought. He is breaking the law. But he didn't actually beat me. Or did he?

Her mind swam. *What can I possibly do? No one would believe me. Alex is the toast of the town. Of the region! Could I tell Alma?*

Then she remembered the Butte man's sentence: a fine of one hundred dollars and three month's imprisonment in the county jail. *A hundred dollars. Alex gives me twice that each month to spend on groceries and trifles. And after three months in jail he would be more furious than anyone could imagine. And I can't tell Alma. I can't imagine telling anyone.*

I strive to do everything right, but he is unceasingly jealous and possessive. I once found his jealousy charming—it told me he valued me and wanted me all for himself. This is something else altogether. What is happening? Have I some aspect that calls forth this hateful thing?

As they sat at breakfast, she strove to be compliant and pleasant, but she was aware of every mouthful of food he took. She waited, with each tiny shift of the clock hands, for him to leave.

Finally, she sat alone. A yellow warbler darted past the dining room window and perched on a tree limb. She watched his tiny beak move as he sang, then let her eyes drift to a flock of sheep on the side hill, then up to the sky, where the clouds mounded high and white.

When she looked at the clock, an hour had passed. Grace and Nora had avoided the dining room, leaving the dishes where they sat. Perhaps they know, she thought with a heavy sigh. Then she realized with dread, *he'll be back in eight hours.* I wish he'd never come back. Maybe something will happen to him. Maybe he and his friends will have another one of those foolish horse races, and he'll fall and break his neck.

A huge bouquet of flowers came mid-morning. The note enclosed read, "I will try if you will—Alex." As she arranged them, she felt a tear slip down her cheek. How ironic, she thought. Here I am in my little mansion on the hill, overlooking the pitiful Gulch where women from tawdry walks of life weather storms like this every week. And I had the vanity to think I was separate from them!

Her throat tightened and she ran quickly upstairs. Perhaps I should leave him—perhaps that would be best for us all! As wounded as I am, it is clear that I cause him heart-wrenching pain. Some marriages are simply not meant to be. Just think of the comfort and gratitude we might both feel if I could spare him this agony.

Filled with new grief and fear, she slumped on the bed and sobbed. "I can't leave!" she cried aloud. "I love him! I waited my whole life for him. As angry as he is, he knows how devoted I am. It wouldn't be fair to leave now. I'm made of stronger stuff than that, and so is he. We've only been married a year; these things take time. Surely we aren't the only couple who fights."

In the afternoon, a parcel arrived. She knew what it was. When Nora brought it to her, she sat with it on her lap for several minutes before reluctantly plucking apart the paper and twine. The dressing gown was expensive dove-gray sateen with ecru lace.

Sitting with the wrapping paper at her feet, the gown lying across her lap, she fingered the lace. Clearly, she and her husband must not be trying hard enough to understand one another.

It occurred to her that if she could provide Alex with enough opportunities to gain greater confidence in himself, then he would be more at ease in their marriage. *If I retaliate without mercy to the darkness that ensnares my husband, then don't I also enter that darkness? There must be a way to lay at least some of his fears to rest. Compassion. I must reach inside to find new resources of compassion.*

She had a fleeting, visceral sense that her personal dignity had slipped a notch. *I won't permit my marriage to sink to this level of degradation,* she vowed. *It must be possible to make life between us flow more smoothly. I simply need to pay more attention.*

She sensed someone near and looked up to see Nora in the hall.

"Excuse me, Miss. Is't all right you are?"

"Oh, yes, Nora. I'm fine. I was just thinking. Isn't this a beautiful thing my husband sent me?" As she spoke, she thought of the torn muslin gown stuffed in the bottom bureau drawer. She would have to dispose of it somehow, so that Grace or Nora wouldn't find it. She stood up and held the new one up to herself in front of the looking-glass, turning from side to side and acting as gay as possible.

Nora smiled and complimented her, then picked up her feather duster and walked toward the kitchen.

As Persis looked at her image in the mirror, she brushed away a smudge of dust on her face. Stepping closer, she brushed more vigorously, then realized it wasn't dust at all. There was a semi-circle of purple beneath her right eye.

* * *

When Alex came home that evening, he was as tender as Persis had ever known him. She had applied a combination of petroleum jelly and powder to her upper cheek, skillfully hiding her black eye. Although he had no idea of the injury, it was plain that he was regretful. It perplexed her, though, that in his stiff comments, he did not take more responsibility. It seemed important to him that they share equally in the blame for what had happened. She felt *he* was responsible, yet here he was with the boyish cajoling that always had a mollifying effect.

It was such a relief to see him smile! He spared neither compliment nor solicitous gesture in his efforts to win back her alienated heart.

Little by little she gave in, influenced both by his ardent amiability and by her passionate desire to have their marriage return to the pleasant, companionable level that meant so much to them both. She longed to bring him into the light, to shed on him an abundance of pure, selfless love, creating in him the self-confidence he so desperately needed.

More and more over the last few months, she reminded herself, she had felt him preciously close to the level of security she yearned to instill in him. He had been responding well; the dinner party was a tragic fluke.

"What would you say," he was asking her, "to a trip down to that smoky mining camp your brother calls home? We could take the children. He'd like to see his son, of course. Although, I am so used to the little fellow, I sometimes think of him as ours. At any rate, what do you think of the idea?"

Persis let out a little gasp. He was being utterly delightful. "Alex, you know perfectly well I would love to do that!"

"Then it's settled. We'll leave Thursday morning."

On the short trip to Butte, Alex told her that he had been invited to visit William Clark's elaborate stables. Clark was holding a horse sale, with buyers and sellers coming in from all over the Territory. Persis hadn't seen a decent horse in months.

"I think I ought to buy a thoroughbred," Alex said expansively as they drove up to Butte's Northwestern Hotel.

"Let's leave Nora and the children for just an hour," Alex whispered in her ear. "I have a surprise for you."

She looked at him and smiled. "Alex, what have you been up to?"

Helping her into the hired buggy, he said, "You'll see, Percy."

He never calls me that, she thought. It sounded odd coming from him, but she sat back in the padded seat, enjoying the easy conversation between them.

"I'm glad we are staying at the Northwestern," she said. "It's exciting to stand near the hotel and know that I'm on the very spot where the new rails will be laid. You must be so proud and so full of anticipation," she said, slipping her arm through his. "We can even stay here for the big celebration, can't we?"

"Certainly," was all he said. His eyes were bright, focused on the long, straight stretch of Main Street leading up the hill. Turning right on Park Street, Alex stopped the team in front of a new red brick and sandstone building directly across the street from the Continental Hotel. Two men on a scaffold high above them were glazing the third-story windows. Two more walked past Persis carrying a large oak bureau. They turned sharply and ascended the front steps.

"As you were saying, Persis, we should definitely be here in Butte to welcome the little wheelbarrow line, as my critics are fond of calling the Utah and Northern. But would you rather stay at the Northwestern, or would you rather stay here?" He made a sweeping gesture with his right hand and offered her his arm.

Persis's head swiveled around to look at his face. "This—this isn't the place you—"

"It most certainly is," he answered. A curl of chestnut hair fell over his forehead as he pulled her close. "I want so much for us to be happy, Persis. Think of what this can mean to us. Homes in both Helena and Butte. You being able to see Charlie far more often. Winston can get to know his *other* papa."

Persis couldn't hold back the tears. They tumbled down her cheeks and onto Alex's hand as he clutched her fingers close to his chest.

"I feel so much hope, Alex. It feels so good to be here, to have such a future to share with you. I too hope the very best for us." Wiping her eyes, she buried her face in his shoulder.

"Now, now, let's not have a scene," he remonstrated gently.

They heard a voice from across the street. "Mr. and Mrs. MacKinney!"

Persis turned and saw a handsome woman step onto the sidewalk from the long stone steps of the Continental. The figure was distinctive, stirring an old memory. God in heaven, she thought, it can't be. Or can it? Her question was answered in a heartbeat, because the stylish woman was fast approaching.

"Well, if it isn't Bess Daltry," said Alex, lifting his hat.

"It's wonderful to see you!" came Bess's response. "I'm here for Clark's horse show. I thought you lived in Helena."

"We do," said Persis, determined to be open and pleasant. "We are in Butte for the same reasons you are."

"You're looking well," said Alex. "So you took pity on all of us who've had nothing but wild mustangs to ride. How many did you bring?"

"Eleven. One of them—a wonderful little bay mare—is off her feed, but I think it's just the stress of travel."

"I heard a rumor about Birchwood a few weeks ago," said Alex. "Is it true that the jockey who won the Kentucky Derby—McLaughlin, I think his name is—trained at your place?"

Bess smiled warmly. "That rumor is very much true." Her violet eyes flashed with pride. "Too bad he wasn't riding one of mine." She waved a sheaf of papers, fanning herself. Persis realized the papers were a list of the horses she'd be presenting at the sale.

Persis gestured to the papers. "Is that—"

"My stock manifest. Would you like one?" she handed Persis a sheet. As Bess moved close, she looked searchingly at Persis. They held one another's gaze for a second or two, then Bess looked away and smiled at Alex.

"It's good to see you both," she said cordially. "Until this afternoon, then. Alex, you'll have to catch me up on how the express business is coming along."

Persis watched Bess skip quickly back across the street to her waiting landau, the bustle of her pale-green suit bouncing as she went. But Alex was tugging at Persis's hand, eager to show her the new townhouse.

The place was spectacular. Not as elegant as their home in Helena, but fresh and modern. Each of its three stories had tall banks of broad, south-facing windows, which meant they didn't have to look at the smoking hill and the black, groaning hoisting works.

The fireplace, trimmed with irregular pieces of sandstone, was especially appealing. Approaching the mantel, Persis caught sight of herself in the mirror and suppressed a gasp. The tears and the embrace with Alex had completely wiped away her makeup. A dark demi-lune of purple was clearly visible below her eye. There was no question that Bess had seen it.

"I'll be back in just a moment, Alex," she blurted out. "The withdrawing room, you know," she called back over her shoulder. She was quite certain he had not seen. A few minutes later, freshly made-up, she returned and finished their hasty tour.

Alex hurried her out to the carriage. "The sale starts in twenty minutes," he said, slapping the reins.

After retrieving Charlie, they went directly to Clark's place. Both Alex and Persis were eager to see the horses, but Marcus Daly was in the beverage tent, waving insistently for Charlie to join him. Laying a hand on Persis's arm, Charlie said, "I'll catch up with you later."

Well-dressed stock tenders were everywhere, mounds of green hay were visible in the lofts, grain buckets overflowed outside each stall, and the aroma of tanned leather and saddle soap wafted through the air. The place reeked of luxury and refined horsemanship.

Alex paused to look at one of the Daltry horses, a black thoroughbred. Turning to Persis, he asked, "Well, your father was quite the horseman. What do you think he would have said about this fellow?"

Persis judiciously supplied a scrap of her knowledge. "High withers are often the sign of a fast horse, Father used to say. And this black is splendidly muscled." She let the observation hang in the air.

"Yes. Yes, indeed," Alex responded, looking down at the breeder's sheet at the statistics and price. "Miss Daltry is asking a mere five hundred dollars."

Persis wandered to the next stall, where stood a little honey-colored bay with black legs, mane and tail. The manger was full of untouched hay.

This must be the horse Bess was talking about, Persis thought, her heart melting. I shouldn't even look at her; I'll think of nothing else but those dark, sensitive eyes for days.

Arabian. She couldn't see the tail, but the delicate face, the flaring nostrils, and the slender legs were a good indication. She looked at the breeder's sheet. "Birchwood's Sutherland Skye, out of Terrestre, bloodlines traceable to the Godolphin Stables of England." That confirmed it. The Godolphin's Arabian connections were legendary.

Sensing someone at her elbow, Persis assumed it was Alex. She murmured, "This little girl is part Arabian."

"I am impressed," came Bess's alto voice.

Persis turned and gave an awkward smile to the dark-haired woman. "I—I think Alex likes the black next door."

"Let's go and see just how much he likes him, shall we?"

Alex was busy, however, talking with Will Clark. It was not a conversation to interrupt, Persis quickly discerned.

"I think I will go and get a glass of lemonade," she said. "Maybe Alex will be finished in a little while. Would you care to join me? Or perhaps you need to tend to business."

"I'd be honored," said Bess.

Seated at a small table in one of the tents, they chatted about Butte, the railroad, and Alex's freight business. "I know he enjoys horses," Persis said. "But I simply love them."

Bess smiled. "I know. My mother died when I was quite young, and Father raised me along with the horses. Our neighbors joked about it. They said I probably ate bran mash and had a stall with my name over the door."

Persis laughed. "My father was quite the horseman too. He died from a fall, when I was fifteen."

"I am so sorry. My father just died last year. I know how difficult grief can be."

Persis's mind flashed to Constance. The blue eyes across the table seemed suddenly familiar, sending a little spasm through her chest. "It is hard. But we find a way to live with it."

"May I call you Persis?" Bess asked, suddenly earnest.

Persis nodded.

"Thank you." She leaned forward slightly. "You—you know that Alex and I are friends . . . from before, don't you?"

"Yes," Persis said, her heart beating faster. What was Bess about?

"First of all, I want to tell you that I have no lingering attachment to Alex. I know you may not care a whit, but I wanted to say so in case it bothered you in any way. But that is not the crux of what I want to say." She looked toward Alex, then back at Persis. "I haven't much time," she said, her white teeth catching at her full lower lip. Her hands fisted and then opened, then fisted again.

"Are you all right?" Persis asked, reaching out but not quite touching Bess's arm.

"Well," Bess said with an odd smile, "I am now."

"Now?" Persis responded quizzically.

Bess stared into her eyes.

Persis felt a slow, heavy wave moving over her.

"I am now," repeated Bess. "But there was a time when I was not all right. A time when I was in danger. Persis, do you know what I am saying?"

Persis's eyes were riveted on Bess. Her heart was thumping. She wanted to get up and run back into the stable, run anywhere, but something bolted her to the spot. "Do you mean . . . that in Alex's company you were . . . you were not safe?"

Bess barely nodded, never taking her eyes off Persis.

The wave continued moving through Persis, at once boiling and icy, reddening her neck, then her cheeks. Bess had not only seen her black eye but knew, at least in a way, the intimate details of how she acquired it. Persis was flustered, aware only of a hot need for Bess to believe that Alex was capable of growing beyond the problems that plagued him.

"Alex worries about things," she said obliquely, fussing with the strings on her handbag.

"I have met many a man who did not like to see a woman put other interests above him. And it makes a bit of sense, but—"

"It will all work out," Persis interrupted. "I don't know you very well, Bess, and I admit when I first met you I did consider you . . . a threat. I don't now. Please believe me. What I mean to say is, even though I don't know you well, I know you are a strong woman. I am a strong woman too. My point is, I believe it is within Alex's and my ability as a married couple to surmount any obstacle placed before us."

Bess cast her eyes down. "I would have expected nothing less of you. I pray you won't resent me for this. If you take anything away with you—besides a horse or two," she laughed gently, "will you please take with you my highest regard and wishes for your future happiness? I hope I have done nothing to stain the quality of our new acquaintance."

"Everything is fine between us, Bess. And I am glad you spoke what was in your heart."

"May I write to you, now and then?" she asked. "Don't worry, my letters will be circumspect. I'll bore you with news of my horses and their accomplishments."

"Of course. We can write to one another," Persis said, picking up a couple of the pencils that were scattered everywhere. The women quickly exchanged addresses written on scraps of cast-off price sheets. "We have a place in Butte now, too," she added. "But I don't know the address just yet."

Bess's eyes moved from Persis to the crowd outside the tent. "Ah, here he comes."

As the three of them walked back to the stable to discuss business, Persis's senses were painfully heightened. She and Bess were now in league with one another in a way she never could have imagined. Alex, she thought, probably assumed Bess's shame over past episodes of violence would prevent her from saying anything to anyone, least of all his wife.

Despite all of this, she vowed, there is no doubt in my mind that Alex and I will find our way through this difficulty. I obviously mean far more to Alex than she ever did. She is kind, bless her, but she doesn't realize how great my influence is, or my love.

In the stock barn, the sweet smell of hay mingled with the sharp tang of horses. Persis was drawn back to the melancholy bay.

"Skye," she whispered. Dipping into the grain bucket, she lifted a small amount through the window, slowly reaching toward the horse. "Skye," she said again. The bay nickered so softly it was almost a whimper. "Come here, darling," Persis coaxed. The straw rustled beneath the horse's hooves as she took a shuffling step toward Persis. Her graceful neck stretched out and she placed a silky muzzle in Persis's palm. Her lips twitched, nibbling up a few bits of grain.

"She likes you," Alex said from behind. He and Bess were watching her.

"How long have you been there?" she asked, smiling back at the two of them.

"Only a moment," he said, "but long enough for Bess to make me an interesting deal. She told me she'd sell me the black on one condition, that being that I accept this little half-breed as a gift to you."

"Oh, Alex, I have fallen in love with her. Can we really take both of them?"

Bess nodded, laughing. "I'm certainly not shipping any animals back to Saint Louis! Please, take her with my compliments. She's gentle, but she's got spirit too." Bess winked at Persis.

That evening, over dinner with Charlie at the Silver Salver, the subject turned to the MacKinney's new townhouse on Park Street.

"I've been watching that place go up all summer," Charlie said. "It will be grand having you and the children nearby," he began. "I can't thank you enough for . . . providing for Winston." His voice faltered and then picked up strength as he fixed Alex with a penetrating look. "I think it is best for now, but it won't always be that way."

For once, a moment passed before Alex found his tongue. "Well, a toast! Here's to the Allens and the MacKinneys, and all the joint ventures in between!"

* * *

The following evening, Alex took longer than usual with his toilette. He was in high spirits, having been invited to play cards with Clark's newly formed Silver Bow Club, the elite group that rotated its gaming through prestigious homes in Butte. Persis complimented him on his jacket and waistcoat, smiling brightly as he strolled out the door.

Between eight and nine o'clock, she and Nora and Grace did their best at another amateur hand of poker.

When they were done, Grace nodded approvingly at Persis. "It's progress you're makin', Mistress."

"Sure, and soon she'll be wanting to play with silver dollars instead of matches," added Nora.

Persis replied gaily, "I think I may be able to tell a good hand from a bad, but that, my friends, is all. The Butte Barons are still safe."

* * *

September came to the Double Diamond and with it, fall roundup. The clatter of enamelware in the washtub, the drone of voices around the campfire, and the bursts of raucous laughter were welcome sounds to Avery.

The second night out, jokes and stories rollicked around the fire, each tale spawning a taller one as sporadic guffaws drifted into the purple twilight. Finally, one by one, each cowboy rolled himself up in his blanket and Avery found himself a lonely spoke in a wheel of snoring companions.

He made his bed on a grassy patch out in the open and lay down. Rolling up the edge of his *sougain,* he let his body sink heavily into the matted grass. Searching the dark peaks of the Sapphire Mountains, he let his eyes move upward. The sky was a deepening blue sparked with white, and the air smelled of hoof-ground sage, juniper, and dying coals.

My prosperity is something I guess I deserve, at least a little bit, he thought. I have worked hard, and I've got good men working hard for me too. But this place; it's got more magic than I ever thought I would know.

While the fire dwindled into an orange heap and the dark heavens expanded with stars, Avery settled into a deep and dreamless sleep.

* * *

The Double Diamond crew arrived in Cheyenne in a sportive mood, and wasted no time in getting the cattle securely penned into the stockyards. The next stop would be the bathhouse, then it was on to Main Street.

As Avery sipped a lager at the Bon Ton, he heard a man laughing on the boardwalk, telling a story about a horse. He couldn't tell for certain, but he thought the name of the horse in the story was Pug. Within a few minutes, a tall, rangy man accompanied by several friends entered the Bon Ton and Avery saw his face. It was Deke Wakefield. Their eyes met and Deke winked.

"If it ain't them Burke brothers," he said, coming over to slap both Avery and Pete on the shoulder. "I heard you brought down twelve hundred. Not too shabby for a couple of coyotes." He motioned to the waitress. "Give these fellows another one of whatever they're drinking. And one for me."

"How about you? The XIT is as big as they come. What did you run?" asked Avery.

"Two thousand, give or take. We got here day before yesterday."

"I thought you got an outfit of your own," said Pete.

"I did, but the XIT pays so good I can't turn 'em down. They think I'm some kind o' good wrangler."

"Well, you must be pretty good," said Pete, swirling the foam down on his beer. "I heard you roped a filly and tied the knot."

Deke smiled crookedly. "Yessir, I did."

"Where'd you ever find a woman in eastern Montana? They're scarce as clean socks in a bunkhouse."

"She's a widow. From Fort Benton. Real pretty, too."

"Heard that too," said Pete.

"Her name's Beatrice," Deke went on. "Bea. Sweet as honey and tough as jerky."

Avery chuckled. "Bring her to a Stockgrowers' meeting sometime. We'd all like to meet the woman that hobbled you for good."

"What about you fellows?" Deke asked. "You been doin' any parlor-sittin'?"

Pete smiled. "Avery's got a lady friend over in Bozeman. I—I might have one, but she doesn't know it yet."

Deke chuckled. "When's this sage hen of yours supposed to find out she's got a coyote on her trail?"

Avery put in, "I think she might have a few suspicions, despite what Pete says."

"Mind where you're goin' with the fair sex," said Deke with a grin. "You remember Bill Pokarney? He married a nice gal from Oklahoma. He says things would have been just fine if'n her mother-in-law didn't live half a mile away. Guess she sleeps with a six-shooter. I bought him a beer and told him, 'Bill, the only thing I can recommend is to just drown your sorrows.' He says, 'Hell, Deke, that ain't gonna work. The old girl can swim.'"

The men burst into laughter. Avery looked at Pete and shook his head, smiling. As gangly, unshaven, and crude as Deke was, you couldn't help but like him.

He pushed aside his beer and began thinking about the clean sheets that awaited him at the Inter-Ocean Hotel. His thoughts ran back along the trail, first to Bozeman and the fair-haired Emma Fenton, then further west to Persis MacKinney. Why the Almighty keeps lacing her path back into mine is a mystery to me, he mused.

* * *

By the last week of October, everyone at 610 Gilbert was preparing for a household exodus to Butte. They would leave November 5 and be gone "two or three months," Alex had said.

Persis was exhausted at the thought, even though it meant being closer to Charlie. Alex's political posturing and meaningless cocktail parties were wearing on her. Residence in Butte only meant more of the same. To keep up a mien of graciousness, she relied on her favorite wines and cordials.

She would miss her long talks with Alma and Ruby, but at least Grace and Nora were coming. The three-story townhouse was full of steep stairways, and they'd all need to keep a close eye on the children. She would miss Angus too, and her frequent walks to the barn. Angus had shown a genuine interest when she told him about Skye, who waited for her in Butte.

Thankfully, Alex was away just now, overseeing a lumber purchase in Hamilton. After supervising Grace and Nora as they cleaned the icebox and pantry, she set them to work spreading dust-sheets over the furniture. By the time she had finished packing four large trunks, it was dusk. She mustered what remained of her energy and set out for Ruby's house to say good-bye.

Fallen leaves scuttled along the damp, hard-packed streets as she drove the little runabout past the cemetery to Ruby's low stone house. Inside, a cheerful fire crackled on the small hearth. Ruby looked like a mystic in her green silk shawl and long black skirt.

"Are you well, Persis?" Ruby asked. It was more an assessment than greeting.

Persis had long ago learned that, in conversations with Ruby, a perfunctory response would not do. The wind moaned in the chimney and rattled the dogwood branches against the windowpanes.

"I am not sure."

"Something is awry in you. Something deep," said Ruby. "I saw it in you last spring. And it wasn't only your grief for Constance, God rest her soul."

"Marriage—" began Persis, "Ruby, you have never been married, so this may sound foreign. But marriage is not . . . what I expected. Oh, I am so tired." Tears welled up and she raised her hands to her face.

"You mustn't think I don't love Alex," she said, digging for her handkerchief. "I am devoted to him. But he doesn't trust me. I am so confused. He trusts me with household decisions and with money and those sorts of things—but he suspects me of betrayal. Not that I would make him a cuckold, no, but he thinks my actions are somehow intended to hurt him."

Persis sighed heavily as she focused on the oppressive ocean of her feelings. "I'm sorry to say it, but I believe that suspicion seldom, if ever, leaves him."

Ruby stepped to the stove and removed the grumbling kettle. "Your soul needs tending, Persis." She poured steaming water into a stoneware pitcher, over a bag of sweet-smelling herbs.

"Some people," she went on, "have wounds so deep that another person cannot heal them. I can't tinker with your spirit. But what you are telling me tonight gives me great hope." She trained her steel-gray eyes on Persis. "I believe you are just beginning to learn to heal yourself. As for your ability to heal Alex . . ." She lowered her eyes.

"But Ruby! I *can* help him. I feel him inching his way toward wholeness. If he doesn't get better, what does that leave for me? Life with a man who has a terrifying temper, who wants to make something of me that I will never be? Who cannot accept me having friendships with anyone, not even women? You can't mean what you are saying." Persis put her fingers to her temples, angrily looking away.

"Women have enormous power to heal, Persis. I am not taking one ounce of that away from you. But it is easy for us to be seduced by the notion that our power is greater than it is. Hear me, Persis, when I say this. All your indulgence and giving will not help Alex. If you remember anything of this conversation, remember this: keeping your true self from him will only retard his growth and without a doubt cause more injury to you."

Persis stared into her teacup, vacillating between the horror of permanent bondage to a violent Alex and an imperious faith in her ability to change the man she loved.

"Sometimes," she began in a halting voice, "sometimes I think of his reckless behavior—the way he rides, or drives a wagon, and I imagine him being killed." She shook her head, struggling to understand her own mind. "The bad times are few, Ruby," she added quickly. "Much of the time everything is just fine between us. You should see his face when we ride together in the hills."

Ruby sat in respectful silence. "God is love," she said finally. "We both know that. You are well-guided in your desire to be a loving woman, and you must continue as you see fit. But I believe Alex will continue to mistrust you. And I believe you may find yourself wanting to spend time away from him."

Persis stared at Ruby. The thing she spoke of was already happening. She had begun looking forward to Alex's trips and his evenings out. Just today she had heaved a grateful sigh of relief that he was gone.

Avoiding Ruby's eyes, she looked into her now-empty teacup and wished she had brought her flask of port. "I must go soon," she said weakly. "But there is one more thing."

Ruby raised her brows.

"I know the women—the women with rooms, on Clore Street—they avoid becoming pregnant, somehow. I want to know how they do it. I have two small children—and if I count Alex, I have three children." She laughed nervously, lacing and unlacing her fingers. "I can't face the idea of another pregnancy. Not now." She looked into Ruby's dark eyes. "Can you help me?"

"I have something many women use. It's a small sea sponge, but it must be soaked in a clear decoction before you use it, and it must always be cleaned with soap and water afterward. If not, it can become toxic."

As she explained the method, she led Persis to a tall cupboard, where she rummaged through a deep drawer that smelled of lavender and orris-root. She withdrew a sponge and placed it in a small bag of dark blue cloth, then turned to a shelf lined with corked bottles of potions and elixirs.

"Have you a flask?"

"Not with me," answered Persis.

"Choose one that you will not mistake for an imbibing flask, fill it with this, and keep it in your toilette-case. No one will know. Keep the sponge in the cotton bag when you are not using it. Here, I've wrapped the bottle in a bit of flannel to keep it from breaking on your way home."

Persis cradled the supplies in her hands. "It seems relatively simple."

"What did you think I was going to tell you? To spit three times in a frog's mouth?"

They both laughed. Then, laying a hand on Persis's arm, Ruby added, "You are somewhat safe for the time being, anyway, since you are still nursing little Rose, but do this as well."

Persis reached for her cloak. "Thank you for telling me what you think. I confess it is difficult to hear, but I will always count on your honesty."

"God *will* deliver you, Persis, if you tend to your soul. That is the best thing you can do for yourself, and believe it or not, the best thing you can do for Alex. For everyone."

* * *

Artie McGruder and Jack Hascombe rode to Butte with the MacKinneys. Not equal to their boisterous jesting, Persis sat quietly in the corner of the coach.

Finally, Alex turned to her. "Are you well, my dear?"

"Just a bit tired, is all," she said, smiling back at him.

"Well, you can have as much time as you like to relax in Butte. And you'll be able to see your big brother, too." He chucked her under the chin.

The old spark of resentment flew off the flint of her soul, chipping hot and sharp. She unclenched her teeth and told herself, so what if he treats me like a child? It's far better than having him *behave* like one.

Alex and Jack joked about Sam Hauser, calling him "The Emperor." As Alex boasted about his position as bank vice president, Persis tried not to think about the liberties he took, coming in later in the morning than the other bank officers and taking too many holidays. In her estimation, Sam Hauser treated Alex well and paid him handsomely. Might Alex view the Butte townhouse as a means of drifting away from Sam and aligning himself more closely with Will Clark? Alex's carelessness bore an ominous message, but there was precious little she could do about it.

* * *

On her evenings alone, after nursing Rose and playing with Winston, she tried to read, but heard frequent sounds of revelry on the street below: a carriage rolling by, peals of lovers' laughter, or a collection of drunken miners singing *Molly Malone*. Behind it all was the incessant metronome thud of the stamps.

From her brother, Persis learned a little more about mining each week, and was stunned to hear that mines were won and lost at the faro tables, or traded for horses, dwellings, even rail passage back east. When Charlie came by on a Saturday morning and offered to take Persis and Alex on a tour of the Anaconda mine, Persis nearly leaped out of her breakfast chair. "How fascinating! Alex, let's go. We can still go riding this afternoon. We have plenty of time."

Alex lowered the morning paper and looked at the two of them. "You'll forgive me, Charlie. I have an appointment this morning to look at some rooms over the Hoffman Dining House. Potential office space. But Persis has many questions about mining. You two go on."

This scenario might be played back to me later on, Persis thought, but I'll take that chance. On the drive up the hill, she wanted to blurt out her concerns about Alex's temperament, but she knew that to Charlie—and to everyone else—Alex was never anything but pleasant and jocular.

As they boarded the Anaconda skip and began descending, she looked around, watching the dark, rocky walls rise quickly up. She wanted to reach out and touch them.

Charlie read her mind. "Settle down," he said, amused. "You can play in the dirt all you want when we get to the first adit."

"What's an adit?"

"Like a tunnel. Helps access different layers of ore."

The cage bumped to a stop and they stepped out into a long chamber, lit by oil lamps on one wall and dim electric lights on the other. The ringing of picks and hammers was everywhere, but above it all, she heard singing.

"Those are muckers," said Charlie, "the least skilled and the most easy-going of the workers." He showed her the tools of the miner's trade, a hammer called a single jack and a long bar of steel, about one-and-a-quarter inches in diameter, known as a drill.

"Once a blasting hole is drilled, we put in a stick of dynamite and a primer of fulminated mercury. The fuse is lit, and there you go. Ore. The muckers put it into the cars and it rolls along back to the hoist and goes up the left hand side."

He explained different kinds of passageways with odd names like "stopes" and "winzes," and told Persis a little about the different signs of copper and silver.

Back above ground, she shook out her skirts, thankful she had worn dark gray. Charlie drove her past the reduction works and handed her out of the buggy. Persis watched with fear and awe as huge pieces of rock were smashed by enormous hammers on a rotating shaft driven by a steam-powered flywheel. Charlie's voice could not be heard over the deafening din. He scribbled hastily on his notepaper, "The ore is broken down to concentrate the valuable material."

Persis nodded, her hands over her ears. Charlie pointed and she turned around to see a roasting pit the size of a city block. Even though it was a hundred yards away, she could feel the heat. Some men, their chests bare and glistening with sweat, were working the far edge of the pit, shoveling cooled ore into carts.

"It goes from here to the processing furnace, where silica and slag make this dull gray rock come out looking like copper. Then we ship the blocks overseas and lose most of our money," he concluded with a wry smile.

* * *

In December, Alex conceived the idea of an excursion to Homestake Pass for the purpose of finding a Christmas tree. "I'm inviting Cyrus Dern. I believe you met him on the train last summer. He owns a claim up near the Anaconda Mine."

"I remember him, Alex. A very nice man."

"And I'm inviting Artie. He's got a new girl. Pretty little thing, although I'm not sure about her background. She wears a split skirt when they go riding, for Christ's sake."

Persis smothered a smile and was instantly disposed to like Artie's new friend.

The excursion turned out well. Cyrus made apologies for his wife, saying that she generally preferred to stay at home. Artie's friend, Mabel Trask, was about Persis's age and was pleasant and intelligent. She was pretty, too, Persis quickly saw, with a tiny waist and an abundance of curly dark hair that wanted to escape from her tortoise-shell combs.

Back at Park Street, the women hurried to the fireplace to warm their hands and feet, while the three men put up the tree. Alex pulled out a deck of cards and motioned the men to sit around the oak table. Grace appeared with a tray of hot buttered rum cups, and soon host, hostess, and guests were caught up in a mood of holiday abandon.

"Why don't you girls pull your chairs up to the table," said Artie, "and we'll try us a hand of poker, just for fun?"

A grinning Alex endorsed the idea, pulling Persis's chair across the oak floor, making her throw her hands up and reach for his arm, laughing. "Here," he said, "I'll show you the basics of how to hold and play a hand."

Watching Grace's sturdy form recede down the hallway, Persis bit the inside of her cheek.

"Mabel and I play sometimes, don't we, girl?" Artie nudged his companion.

"For sure, we do," said Mabel. "But Artie doesn't like it at all when I win." She put her full lower lip into a pout.

"Well, it wouldn't be right for a girl to best her man at this sport too often. Hallowed ground, you know," said Artie.

"Nothing wrong with learning, I always say," said Cy Dern.

Within a half hour, Persis had picked up several new ideas. Her eyes darted around the table, watching faces, eyes, and mouths. She did miserably on purpose, but it amused her to think of pressing her newfound advantages in future kitchen games with Grace and Nora.

Finally, weary from the strain of feigned ignorance and too much rum, she sat back in her chair and gained a view of the sky. The low angle of the sun glanced off the frame buildings across the street, gilding them with the cold light peculiar to December. On the sprawling plain of south Butte, thin lines of smoke rose from the shacks and cottages of Dublin Gulch. In the distance, near Homestake Pass, over the hills where they had just been, a lone star glittered in a sky of palest blue.

A whirlwind of people she had known and loved came dancing into her head. She thought of her father, and then of Constance. Their faces rose and fell, like perfect snowflakes landing on a woolen sleeve and melting away. It isn't good to be without friends, she thought, casting a hopeful look at Mabel.

As Artie helped Mabel into her coat, Persis wondered if their paths might cross again. I don't know a single woman outside my home, she realized. Except Bess Daltry. And where did I put her address?

Later, as she and Alex climbed the stairs to bed, her thoughts drifted down the hall toward the children and she thought how wonderful it would be to sleep with them, to smell the warm scent of their little bodies, to feel the fluff of hair on their heads, and to feel their innocent nestling.

Beneath the layers of linen and wool on the master bed, Alex fell asleep with no interest in lovemaking. Persis was grateful. The mound of bedcovers heaped between her and her husband was a small matter compared to the wall that separated their spirits.

* * *

Christmas frivolity in Butte mounted to a fever pitch with the hysteria over the hastening reality of narrow-gauge rail service. Alex was gone a good deal, making arrangements for the proper locomotive to first arrive in Butte, scheduling dignitaries, parades, hotels, and parties. In addition, he was negotiating the sale of his Corinne freight office. Times were changing and his life was full.

Persis was as consumed with excitement as any Territorial resident, but often, while studying the symmetry of the Douglas fir that stood tall and fragrant in the parlor, a kind of catalepsy stole over her. Railroad, railroad, she reflected dully. We're about to lose another Christmas holiday. That's two in a row.

Charlie popped in frequently, talking excitedly about both the Alice and the Anaconda, speaking copper prophecies and impressing Nora and Grace with his knowledge. One such evening, he brought a bottle of rum and said to Grace, "It's such a fine cook you are, Miss Mitchell, can you make us up a batch of hot buttered rum?"

Grace blushed and reached without a word for the tin of brown sugar.

"I know we've got the electric lights," said Persis, "but let's put them out and light the candles anyway. It's Christmas, and Nora did such a nice job with the ribbons and juniper. Let's have a little of the Old Country tonight!"

The candles were lit and rum was poured into spicy, sweet hot water. The patchwork family settled into their chairs and listened while Charlie talked of mines, Daly, and the future of Butte's great hill. By now, everyone in the Territory had shortened the name of the mining camp to simply "Butte."

"You know," Charlie confided, "Marcus and his Maggie have asked me to go to mass with them the Sunday before Christmas. And I'm not even Catholic, really. Well, half of me is," he added quickly, looking at Grace and Nora.

"But you should hear him talk," Charlie went on, slapping his hand on the table. "He's ruminating on a more sophisticated smelter than we ever dreamed of. The design would carry the fumes aloft, to be borne away on the wind."

"Go on with you, Mr. Charlie," teased Nora. "Why would old Marc want to take away the roastin' piles? Such a lovely aroma they give our fair city." She clapped the lid on the teakettle. "Some days it's so thick that the pickpockets don't have to wait till nightfall. Makes a girl nervous."

"Growing more fierce all the time, it is," Grace muttered. "The cows' teeth are turnin' brown!"

Charlie gave them a reproachful look. "How often do cows smile? When you realize that this sulphurous cloud puts bread and butter on the tables of Butte, it's not so bad, now, is it?"

"Ah! Forgive us for speaking ill of mining. I could cut me tongue out," Nora intoned.

"Seriously, we know it's not good to have this pall of vapor hanging about," Persis ventured. "Miners' tuberculosis and lung ailments of all description are cropping up. Really, it can't go on."

Winston had fallen asleep with his favorite, tattered blanket on the rug in front of the stove, and Rose was blissfully dreaming in her basket.

"It's flying by these years will be," said Grace softly, tucking a wisp of gray hair back into her loosely coiled bun. "You don't see it so much in the mirror as you do in their wee faces."

Silence fell. Winston stirred in his sleep, yawned, and curled into a little ball.

"Another spot of drink, anyone?" Grace lifted the kettle from the stove, sending a few drops skittering across the hot metal.

"Not for me. It's getting home I ought to be," Charlie said in his best brogue. "Winston's happy here. And I am happy that you are all here. I don't like the idea of you all going back to Helena, though I know you must, sometime."

"We may stay on after Christmas," Persis answered. "Let's not worry about it now." She embraced him tightly. It was hard to see him go out into the cold night to his solitary little house.

"We'll be keeping the feast on Christmas Day," said Grace as Charlie headed toward the mudroom and the back door. "And you'll be coming for dinner."

Charlie smiled and nodded.

Persis remembered something. "Here, Charlie, I'll walk you to the edge of the drive," she said quickly, grabbing her fur-lined cloak.

"It's too cold, Percy."

"Nonsense," she said, taking his arm.

They went through the pantry into the crisp night. "Charlie," she said, affecting a lighthearted tone, "I need to correspond with that St. Louis woman, Miss Daltry. The thoroughbred breeder. It's a surprise for Alex. Could I have her send letters to me at your place?"

"Sure," Charlie shrugged.

"You can just leave them in the kitchen drawer where you keep the matches. It can be my little mailbox."

"You still have the key I gave you?" he asked, stuffing his hands into his pockets.

She nodded. "Thanks, Charlie."

The weather grew steadily colder, and on December 20, the day before the first Utah and Northern train was to arrive in Butte, the temperature plunged to eighteen below zero.

Alex was in a black mood. Persis was glad he'd be gone all day arranging the reception for fifty-some passengers. There was a time when his preoccupation would have bothered her, but not now. Ruby's prophecy steadily gained more credence.

Going out to shop, she found the city buzzing. Pine boughs or sleigh bells were nailed to every door. Customers lingered in the coffeehouses, the taverns, and the shops, talking about the railroad or finding any excuse not to resume their errands in the bitter cold.

At Warren's Dry Goods, she found high-button boots for both Grace and Nora, along with books and toys for the children. By the time she entered Dillinger's Hardware, her fingers were numb and her cheeks burned from the cold. As she carried several lamp chimneys to the counter, she realized she couldn't possibly make it back up the hill with all her packages.

Pondering this problem, she stared absently into the clot of shoppers standing around the potbellied stove. Her gaze came into sharp focus when she realized Mabel Trask was there, rubbing her hands together and leaning close to the chromed grille.

As soon as their eyes met, Mabel bustled toward her, grinning. "Good morning, Mrs. MacKinney, and Merry Christmas to you."

"A Merry Christmas to you too," said Persis. "Call me Persis, won't you? What a lovely cape," she added, noting that, while Mabel tended carefully to her appearance, she lacked the pretensions of the railroad and banking wives.

After Persis showed her the spoils of her shopping, Mabel said, "I hope you have a buggy."

"I've decided to leave them here and pick them up later. I have even more shopping to do. I guess I didn't plan very well."

"I have my buggy. May I help you take your things home?"

"I couldn't possibly inconvenience you."

"What kind of friend would I be if I didn't help you get your Christmas purchases home? The horse needs the exercise. We'll go slowly so as not to freeze the old fellow's lungs."

"It's too cold even to snow," said Persis, as the buggy bumped up the hill. "If there were some snow clouds, we'd at least have a promise of things warming up."

Mabel pulled up in front of the red brick townhouse. "I'll help you get everything in so no one will see Santa's hoard," she said, jumping down and not waiting for a reply.

When the pile of Christmas gifts were stacked on the hall table, Mabel extended her hand.

"Won't you stay for some tea?" asked Persis.

"Oh, I would love to, but to be perfectly truthful, I'm worried about my old horse, and won't relax 'til he's back in his stall at Valiton's. Next time—if I may be so bold as to assume I may be at your house again—I would like to meet your little girl, and your nephew."

"Of course!" Persis said.

Mabel turned the doorknob. "You know, Persis, here in Butte we have great fun with masquerade balls. There's one coming up in January. Maybe you and Alex could come with Artie and me."

Persis hesitated. But, of all the things Alex might object to, a party would certainly not be one of them. "I should think we could. It might be just the thing Alex needs after all this railroad hullabaloo. These masquerades—they're held at the Theater Comique on Main Street, aren't they?"

"Well, the ones at the Theater Comique—they call them 'Bal Masques'—are rather ribald. There are much more refined masquerades at McGuire's. I hope you decide to come. Merry Christmas!"

The glass rattled slightly in the door as she closed it behind her. I should have asked her where she lives, thought Persis. I could have sent her a Christmas package.

The next day dawned bitter cold. The Utah and Northern train was scheduled to arrive near midnight. Free pine-pitch torches were available on every corner, supplied by the U&N to ensure a mood of celebration. Poor Alex, thought Persis; he had been in charge of even that!

The saloons and hurdy-gurdy houses were teeming with young men in from the ranches or on holiday from railroad labor. Miners scheduled to work the late evening hours grumbled over their Sean O'Farrels. Overindulgence in alcohol was commonplace in Butte, but during the Christmas season, it was a passion.

At 10:30 that evening, Alex inspected the retinue of carriages and wagons lined up to receive the passengers, then he and Persis gathered with Rail Superintendent Thatcher and a dozen well-bundled nabobs at the depot office. Crowded against a window, Persis shivered and rubbed the fog-frosted glass. About two hundred citizens were grouped in clumps along the length of the new platform, their words and laughter marked by puffs of vapor. Bottles of beer or whiskey moved from one gloved hand to another as the crowd looked enviously at the musicians warming up inside the depot lobby. Persis felt a body squeeze in beside her. Mabel Trask's face peeped out from a fur-lined hood.

"Well, hello, Mabel! Are you here with Artie?" Persis looked around and saw Artie waving to her from across the room. "Isn't this exciting? The railroad is finally here."

"D'you think there'll be life after this?" Mabel asked dryly.

Persis laughed. Having paid so much obeisance to the icon of the Utah and Northern, she found Mabel's irreverence delightful. "Are you going to Thatcher's party tonight?" she asked.

They were interrupted by a roaring cheer.

"It's here, it's here," squealed Persis, jumping up and down and shaking Mabel by the shoulders. The band struck up *She'll Be Comin' Round the Mountain* and the depot office was emptied instantly as everyone swarmed onto the platform.

The two women pushed their way to the front of the throng. Amidst clouds of swirling, billowing steam, there appeared the shiniest little locomotive Persis had ever seen, dark green with brass trim. Its sides were frosted with gleaming white ice from the journey. It couldn't have looked more like a fairy tale engine, with three diminutive Pullman cars in tow.

Suddenly Alex was at her side, beaming. Proud and tender, Persis reached around his neck, pulling his ear close to her mouth. "Here's to the next ten years of watching you work your miracles!"

His eyes sparkling, he kissed her exuberantly. Then, in that old way that used to set her insides churning, he put his arm snugly around her waist. The speeches were short and within half an hour, the passengers and their baggage were hastily loaded into the carriages lining the street. The crowd dispersed, but no one went home; there were parties scheduled in every quarter of Butte.

"The constables will be busy tonight, I'll wager," said Thatcher as he assisted his wife into their buggy. "See you on Quartz Street," he added, and clapped Alex on the shoulder. "We did it, didn't we?"

Alex, still smiling broadly, nodded and ducked into his own shiny coach with Persis. Once they were inside, Persis studied his face. The smile sagged and his mouth puckered slightly. Persis knew that look. She shuddered to think of Alex having no fond obsession. After months—years, really—of what might be called purposeful mania, Alex was unlikely to make the upcoming career transition easily.

* * *

In the closing days of December, Alex took a stronger interest in the children, playing games and even reading their Christmas books to them, but his restlessness was obvious. Returning to Helena seemed the sensible thing, Persis thought, although it was impossible to imagine him going back to routine duties at the bank.

He readily agreed to Mabel's plan to attend the affair at McGuire's. Two nights before the masquerade ball, Alex announced that he was going out to the card room above the Arpeggio Tavern and wouldn't be home until late. Pleased at having the house to herself, Persis feigned disappointment but breathed a long sigh when he put on his long coat and stepped out the door. Although she didn't consciously analyze the inevitable outcome of his restlessness and tension, a deep aspect of her knew she was better off if he could have a companionable, even boisterous, evening of cards to let off some steam. As the clip-clop of his horse's hooves receded, the dark thought occurred to her that, for certain men, the release of tension could involve much more than male companionship. She swallowed thickly and shook the notion from her head.

After dinner, when she went to the kitchen to get a biscuit for Winston, she found Grace having supper alone.

"Why Grace, you are all by yourself! Where's Nora?" asked Persis.

Grace shook her head and swallowed a bite. "She's gone to mass."

"Tonight? I didn't know there was one on Thursdays."

"Sure there is. There's always a mass somewhere in Butte. Nothing wrong with it, but—"

Persis rummaged in the biscuit tin. "But what?"

"Faith, I'm as regular a Catholic as God ever lumped out o' the mud, but it's takin' things a bit literal our girl is."

"What do you mean?"

"Well, the legend goes that any unspoilt girl should take to bed without her supper on the Eve o' Saint Agnes. That's tonight, mind you. She's to lie still and look neither to one side nor the other. When sleep comes, she'll dream of her future husband."

Persis smiled and wiped the crumbs off the metal countertop. "Is that all? I think it's charming." She thought immediately of Pete Burke, of the way he looked so steadily at Nora that day on the street last summer, and of how he turned his head in order to hear the few words she was able to speak.

"But," continued the agitated Grace, "she goes 'round singing that old tune about the maiden, 'I'll have a tinker or a tailor, a fool or witty; don't let me die an old maid, but take me out of pity!' If she was smart she wouldn't go near a man. Balderdash and heartache, that's all they—" Grace stopped short and her hand flew to her mouth. "I'm sorry, Miss Percy. I meant no disrespect."

"It's all right, Grace. None taken. I'm going up to be with the children for a while."

Alex came home after midnight, reeking of smoke and liquor, and slept in his clothes. The next day he was morose, revealing in stiff tones that he had lost heavily.

Persis let the subject alone. She wondered about his work, about

the new logging operation in Hamilton and the livestock loans await-
ing his attention at the bank in Helena.

The next day was better. Both looking forward to the masquerade,
they dressed as pirates, he in a loose white shirt, belted tunic and high
boots, she in a lace blouse, short buttoned jacket, and calico skirt.
Masks in hand, they went to pick up Artie and Mabel.

Now I shall discover where Mabel lives, thought Persis. Alex directed the driver to the corner of Platinum and Montana Streets. As
they passed Galena Street, Persis furtively watched Alex glance to his
left, where the women stood with their long skirts caught up well
above the ankle, showing petticoats and patterned stockings. In the
mid-winter darkness, oil lamps with red globes hung from hitching
posts and small fires glowed orange in the street.

"Saturday night in Butte," Alex said with a grin, pinching her thigh.

Within a half block, the carriage stopped and Alex jumped out, returning a moment later with a laughing Artie and Mabel. As soon as
Persis got a good look at them, she knew the reason for their laughter. They too were dressed as pirates.

"McGuire's is about to be overrun by a legion of scurvy scoundrels!"
she cheered.

"Fresh from the high seas, carrying secrets of the briny deep," said
Artie in a raspy voice. "And what d'ye think I have for refreshment?
A bottle o' rum!" With this he drew the familiar silver flask from his
makeshift doublet and presented it to Persis. "Go ahead, mate! Can't
go to the Theater without your sea legs!"

Persis smiled at Artie, who had obviously abandoned his vow of
temperance. She took a mouthful. Rum was not her favorite, but she
held her breath and felt a warm sensation moving down her chest. As
the carriage rounded the corner onto Mercury Street, the flask came to
her again.

Mabel dug into her beaded bag. "Here, leave them to their poison.
This is rum too, but I've doctored it with honey and lemon." She
leaned forward with a conspiratorial smile.

As Persis reached for the sweetened rum, Artie gave her a friendly
wink. Something was affecting her, something she couldn't quite comprehend. Was it just the gaiety of the evening? Perhaps it was the
burning swallows of rum that had already reached her head—or was
it Mabel's dark eyes peering so earnestly into her own? The promise

of friendship she felt emanating from Mabel was as warm and compelling as the honeyed rum. Or was it just that she was being seduced by Butte, this strumpet of a city that feigned daylight propriety only to abandon all pretense at nightfall?

There was a low roaring in her ears. *It was all of these things.* This strange place, the likes of which she had never imagined she would see, these nightly activities and lurid scenes that two years ago would have shocked her eastern sensibilities, the increasing improbability of a happy marriage, and the peculiar promise of new alliances with exotic people. All these thoughts converged as her eyes came back to rest on Mabel's engaging smile.

Persis raised the flask. "To new friends," she said, and took a long swallow.

"Have you ever been to McGuire's?" Artie asked.

Persis shook her head. "We've done so much entertaining at home these last few months. It's nice to do something entirely new."

"Well," said Artie, "there won't be any big performances tonight—though they might have an act or two. Just good music, plenty to eat and drink, and lots of dancing. Masks on! We're here."

Inside, the air was thick with smoke, music, and laughter. Outlandish costumes were everywhere. A woman dressed as a bird in brilliant red feathers blocked their path. Miraculously, Alex found a table. Nearby were three men in sheets and turbans.

"Are you ghosts?" Mabel said with a laugh.

The closest twirled a false mustache and responded, "Why, we're lords of the desert, my little flower of Samarcand!"

"Is that you, Cyrus Dern?" said Persis, recognizing their friend. "What are you doing here?" She wondered about his wife. What was her name . . . Polly?

"I might well ask the same of you, Madame," he said. "We're having a bit of a good time."

Alex appeared with rum cocktails and the evening got underway. After the first set of music, a skit of ludicrous buffoonery, depicting a wedding between a miner and a lady who in the end turned out to be another miner, brought the laughing crowd close to tears. As the evening went on, Cyrus Dern and the other Arabs drew up to the pirates' table and formed a group.

"Let's go over to my place and have a card game," said Alex.

"It's only a few blocks away," urged Persis.

At Artie's direction, the pirates led the sheiks through a narrow alley, taking a short cut to Park Street. As the carriages lurched over the frozen ruts in a dark alley, Persis detected a strange, aromatic scent on the cold air. Peering out, she saw dim cracks of light behind closely shuttered windows just a few feet away. Two Chinese men leaned against a nearby doorway.

"On a half-reaped furrow, sound asleep, drowsed with the fume of poppies," said Artie.

Poppies. This must be one of Butte's infamous opium dens, Persis realized. She craned her neck to look back. "That's Keats, isn't it?"

Artie nodded.

At the townhouse, cold chicken was set out with plenty of bottled beer. Artie stirred new life into the fire and the group settled around the oak gaming table. As they began their wagers, Alex turned to Persis, grinning broadly. The light was dancing in his soft brown eyes. He pushed a stack of silver dollars toward her and leaned into her.

"Have a little fun," he said, thinking he was coaxing her into unfamiliar territory.

The frost of resentment Persis felt about his condescension melted away as the entire table, men and women alike, threw social convention aside and began to play.

After a few hands, Cyrus Dern slapped a piece of paper down on the table and sucked on his cigar.

"What's that?" Alex asked, lighting a cigar of his own.

"The deed to the Angel."

Artie snorted. "You're fixing to part with your claim? What happened to the big plans you had?"

Alex waved out his match and Persis saw him nudge Artie underneath the table. "Another beer, Artie?" he asked. Then, casually, "Still not panning out up there, Cy?"

"Not hardly. I finally got the hoist paid for, so I'm square with the timber men. Sold my cattle, too, so I'm not broke. Don't worry about me. But there's no trace of anything at the Angel except a pitiful trail of lead and a smattering of copper. Only about five percent. Hell, I don't want to talk about it. The Angel's on the table, and that's all you need to know. Deal," he ordered.

Mabel and Persis exchanged glances. Mabel's upswept hair was coming down at the temples. Persis wondered if she looked equally *deshabille*. Her clothes smelled deeply of smoke. She shifted in her chair and looked at the clock. Quarter to one. Being part of a high-stakes game was intriguing, but she wasn't sure she wanted to watch Cyrus Dern take what seemed to be a terrible risk.

Cy seemed cavalier and undeterred.

Persis peered through the dim light at the two cards in her hand and set aside the natural impulse to make the most of what she had been dealt. No pairs, no face cards, just an ace of hearts and a four of diamonds. I'll fold before I get myself in any hot water, she thought, yawning.

The sheiks turbans' had fallen from their heads and lay like shawls around their necks. Persis suddenly felt fatigued down to her bones.

The next three cards came to each player face up. Persis stared down at the three lying before her and could not believe her eyes. A two and three of clubs and a five of diamonds. She had a straight, which was probably enough to beat anyone else's hand. She felt the urge to lick her dry lips, but she sat mute and yawned again. Her heart was pounding. I mustn't win, she thought to herself. Having made this simple vow, she breathed a silent sigh of relief.

Alex looked at Cy and said, "Let's hope your hand keeps that deed right where it belongs—in your pocket." He gestured toward Cy and in doing so, disturbed a beer bottle on the table.

Persis rose slightly from her chair to snatch the wobbling bottle before it spilled. "The long evening seems not to have impaired your reflexes, my dear," said Alex.

Persis sat down, smiling. A flicker of apprehension ran through her chest as she wondered if she, during this spontaneous act, had revealed the cards in her hand to Alex. She leaned back in her chair, trying to control the pace of her breath. I'll fold at the first opportunity, she thought wildly.

One by one, the other players folded. When her turn came, Persis did likewise, quietly laying down her two secret cards. Finally there was no one left in the game but Alex and Cy.

Persis was certain Alex was bluffing. The glitter of victory was not present in his eyes. When the cards were displayed, her suspicions were confirmed. Alex's best cards were a pair of queens and an ace. Cy fanned out a pair of sixes and three jacks.

"Well," Alex barked out jovially, "All's well that ends well." He pushed back his chair, signaling the end of play. A nightcap, anyone?"

"Hold on a moment, please" said Cy, turning to Persis.

Persis froze. No, she thought. *Don't.* You mustn't. Let it be. *Let it be!*

"Forgive me, Mrs. MacKinney, but I think you have made a mistake," he said softly.

"Oh, surely not," Persis said feebly. "I—am sure I have not."

"Please forgive me, but when you reached across the table, I am afraid you inadvertently revealed the two cards in your hand to me. My eyes are always restless during poker. It's a long-established habit."

Everyone was quiet, watching. Persis glanced quickly at the mystified Alex. Like everyone else in the room, he continued to stare at Cy Dern and at his own speechless wife.

"May I?" Cy asked, reaching for the five cards lying in front of Persis.

Persis shrugged. "They are all low cards—nothing of value, I assure you."

"Your husband needs to give you a tutorial, my dear," said Cy, as he turned over the ace and the other four cards. "This is a very lovely little straight."

Persis felt Alex's eyes on her. She did nothing but stare at the cards. "A—a straight," she repeated. "That's what that is?"

"Absolutely. One of the finest hands of the evening. The Angel belongs to you." As he pushed the folded papers toward her across the oak tabletop, they made a soft scraping sound. The room fell completely silent.

Persis raised her hands as if to fend off the deed. "Surely, Cy, you wouldn't give away your mining claim in a game of cards!"

"The deed is done, Mrs. MacKinney, if you'll pardon the pun." He laughed shortly, "and the poor rhyme!"

He tucked the edge of the document beneath her hand. "You won it fair and square. Look at all these witnesses. Besides, it's extremely unwise to offend Lady Luck. It's yours to sell or to dynamite or to plant flowers on, whatever you like. Alex must be very proud of you."

He wadded the unraveled turban around his neck. "I'm stealing away into the night. Good night, everyone. I'm very tired, and Polly will be worried about me."

For once, Alex looked perplexed. "But Cy, sit down, let's have another go. Persis doesn't—we don't—want the mine." Then he burst out laughing. "What on earth is a woman going to do with a piece of real estate like that," he went on, "even if you don't want it? Not that I'm not grateful for your chivalrous gesture. And of course Persis is flattered. But really, sit down. You can win it back. Then, if you still don't want it, run an ad in the *Miner* or the *Helena Herald*. I know I could find you a buyer." He pushed a chair toward Cy.

Cy leaned over the table and stumped out his cigar in the pewter ashtray. "My relations with the Angel are extinguished, and I am well rid of her." He looked at Persis. "Let me know when you're ready to record the deed. Good night, my friends."

He picked up his hat and moved toward the door. The spell of the long evening was irrevocably broken. In unison, everyone stood up and began collecting coats and hats. Persis and Alex, unable to lighten the mood, were forced to simply walk their guests to the door. It was quarter after two.

"This will all be rectified in the morning, Persis," Alex said with a forced chuckle as he closed the front door. "We'll be hearing from Cy. There's no question."

As he guided her to the stairway, she made a feeble move of protest, intending to go and clean up the den. "Nora and Grace can get it in the morning," said Alex. "That's what I pay them for."

In the darkness of the den, the fire had dwindled to glowing coals. On the sideboard stood half-emptied bottles of beer and the remains of the late evening meal. Each player's final hand of cards lay on the smooth surface of the golden oak table, and at Persis's place lay the neatly folded deed.

*   *   *

Persis woke with a headache. "I feel awful," she murmured into her pillow in the early morning darkness. Alex brought her some bicarbonate of soda dissolved in a glass.

"You know I despise that stuff," she grimaced.

"Do you want to feel awful all day? This will help."

By evening she had recovered and even had a snifter of brandy after dinner. As she and Alex prepared for bed, Alex said offhandedly, "We'll need to stop and see Cy one of these days. We'll take care of that silly business about the mine."

"What?"

"The mine, Persis," he said. "We can drop the deed off sometime this week."

"Give it back to him?"

Alex looked up at her from the bench at the foot of their bed with an amused, patriarchal gaze. "You're deluding yourself, darling. You don't think that deed is really yours, do you?"

Chagrined and exceedingly cautious, Persis concealed the anger flaring deep within. "He seemed quite serious about it. He seemed to genuinely want someone else to have it."

"He was drunk," Alex said flatly.

Persis fiercely smothered a derisive giggle. Nothing in this town would belong to anyone if transactions were declared void for want of sobriety. She held back, fighting the smile that threatened to appear on her lips.

"Yes, he was," she said. "We all were."

"Precisely my point. We'll take care of this nonsense before the week is out."

She wanted to blurt out that she had won it fair and square, but something—either courage or vigilance, or both—stopped her.

Alex turned out the lights and reached for her, taking her, as he always did, with an air of complete entitlement.

That he desired her was a physical incantation. She hated his touch but hated herself even more for being slavishly charmed by his passion for her. In spite of the discord that simmered between them, they still came together full of powerful yearning. Time and space would disappear as they lost and then found themselves again in one another. How she could be so viscerally aroused by him was beyond her comprehension, but it happened again and again, with mortifying predictability.

When it was over, she lay in the dark, listening to his light snore. I want the Angel, she said firmly to herself. I don't know how I can keep it, with Alex taking this position of authority. As far as I can tell, the transaction was quite legal, flawlessly typical of a thousand other similar deals. Besides, *I have the deed.*

The deed! Where is it? She had not seen it since late last night, when it lay at her place, barely visible by the dying light of the fire. Her heart raced. She didn't know why, but she knew she wanted that claim more than anything in the world.

She turned her silent, focused attention to the snoring Alex. Would he have hidden it from her? No, she reasoned; he wouldn't have thought it was important enough to hide. There was a silver tray in the den where, on mornings-after, Grace and Nora dutifully heaped money, notes, and other card-game detritus. She knew she could get out of bed without waking Alex; she had done it often enough. Slipping out noiselessly, she stole toward the door, avoiding the places in the floor that she knew to creak. Thankfully, the door was not latched. All she had to do was open it enough to pass through.

She looked and listened, pulling the door. God, keep those hinges quiet. All was silent, and still Alex snored. Once out, emboldened by the cool air of the hallway on her face and throat, her cotton gown floating behind her, she ran silently down the stairs and tiptoed through the parlor hall to the den. She struck a match and peered in the dirction of the buffet. The tray was there, and sure enough, there lay the folded ivory sheaf with its curled edges. She picked it up, awash in a new dilemma.

If I hide it, he will know I have hidden it. It will be an affront. Her hands and feet grew cold as she pondered her choices. I could leave it here and act as though it means nothing to me. But he'll take it, the moment he thinks of it, the moment he remembers. Then it will be gone forever, back to Cy or God knows where.

She stood there in the dark, her cold fingers tight on the deed. She thought of Alex sleeping upstairs, and knew what would happen if he awoke. Whatever I do, she thought, I must do it now. If I put it in the top drawer of the buffet, then it won't really be hidden, and anyone searching for it could find it instantly. But it will be out of sight and perhaps out of Alex's mind. Pulling open a drawer, she laid the folded paper on a stack of pressed linens. Closing it again, she raced back through the house.

When she got to the bedroom, Alex had shifted in the bed. Her heart pounded. If he wakes, I'll tell him I was looking in on the children—that I dreamed of them being ill, and had to get up to look at them. Satisfied, she crawled stealthily into bed and was soon reassured that she had no need of a story at all.

The next morning, after Alex had gone, the doorbell rang. Grace announced, "It's Mr. Dern, Miss Percy. I told him Mr. Alex wasn't in, but then he asked for you."

"Show him in, Grace."

Persis's heart sank. Cyrus had come to his senses. Well, so be it. It would be one thing to have Alex remand the deed to the Dern household, like a father returning stolen candy to the shop. It was quite another to be asked by the owner himself, who by now must have realized his folly.

It's his right, Persis thought as she braced herself.

"Good morning, Cy—what a pleasure. Alex is out, but may I offer you some coffee?"

"Good morning, Mrs. MacKinney. Coffee? Well, I'm only here for a moment, but yes, I will have a cup."

Grace, with her usual telepathy, was there already, setting the coffee before them. Persis pointed to an easy chair. "Sit down, Cy, here by the fire. January has been better than December, but I'm sure you're cold."

He perched on the edge of an upholstered chair. "I've come to talk to you about what happened the other night, Mrs. MacKinney."

"You mean the deed, don't you?"

"Yes."

"I know we all had a great deal of fun that evening, and a great deal to drink as well."

"You must have thought me very rash to gamble the Angel that way."

"Oh, no, Mr. Dern, I mean, Cy. I assure you, I can't judge you or any-one else. I am a newcomer to card games and know very little about things that are commonplace to you and my husband." She paused. "Are you regretful of your actions?"

Cy set his cup down and looked at Persis for what seemed like an eternity. "I haven't come to ask for the deed back," he said finally.

She had been holding her breath and now let it go, restricting it to a thin, inaudible exhale. Why, then, had he come?

"I don't mean to offend, but I am sick to death of Butte. Sick of try-ing to make a go of it, sick of breathing this foul air. And my Polly ab-solutely hates it here. We're going back to her family's farm in Penn-sylvania. Her father isn't well, which is sad, but it's an opportunity for us. I could have sold the Angel, you're right. And made a modest amount, perhaps. But no one knows what's down there, and they haven't found any appreciable amounts of copper—only enough to pay the bills. I've ordered new cables, but other than that, my outlay is—well, not significant."

He took a sip of coffee and asked, "Does Alex think I'm crazy?"

Persis hesitated. "To be honest, he did doubt your actions a bit. Does he know how you feel about the mine, and about the farm back East?"

"I don't talk to anyone here about these things. The residents of this boomtown don't like to have anyone express negative thoughts about it. Surely you've noticed that."

"Indeed."

"Butte *is* remarkable, perhaps mostly for its strangeness. I thought for a while it would be a marvelous place for an adventure and the making of one's fortune. But I want my children to grow up knowing what a maple tree is, and what it's like to hear the tadpoles chirp in the spring. Silly. But my wife feels the same way."

Persis smiled, knowing exactly what he meant, but she also knew that something separated her from people like the Derns. Her pas-sion for the Territory had taken a deep and fearless hold on her. She was as rooted here as the granite peaks of the Rockies; nothing would change that.

Cy continued, "So, I do not want the deed back. You won it fair and square. There is no arguing the point. I wouldn't think this sort of transaction would shock anyone—especially Alex—too much. Mining claims and cattle herds are frequent casualties in the gaming halls."

He sipped his coffee and stared into the fire. "I don't know Alex extremely well," he said at length, "and this may seem presumptuous, but I suspect that he—that some men might be a little troubled by such an acquisition on the part of a wife." Casting his eyes down for a moment, he added, "If that has caused him any concern, I hope he gets over it. You can, of course, give him the mine, or sell it, or do whatever you like."

"Well," Persis said thoughtfully, "I must first confess that I am glad you don't want it back." She smiled and raised her brows.

There was a curious spark in his eyes. "Tell me, Mrs. MacKinney, what do you have in mind?"

Persis dared to trust him. "As you may know," she began, "my brother Charlie is a mining engineer for Marcus Daly."

Seeing Dern flinch, she quickly said, "I won't be giving the mine away. I mention my brother's experience in order to tell you how much I have already learned and how fascinated I am to have the opportunity to learn more. I intend to work it," she said, with an air of self-confidence that surprised even her. "But would you keep this just between us, Cy?" she asked, with an earnest softness to her voice. "I think my brother and I can bring a lot of good out of the Angel, and make Alex—and perhaps even you—proud someday," she added. "You have given my entire family a gift."

Dern smiled. "You know, in coming here today, I had a flight of fancy about the best possible fate for the Angel. It is as if you read my thoughts. I'm drafting a letter this afternoon to Alex to confirm everything. Truly, I could not be more pleased. But I do need the deed back—just for a day or two—so I can have it properly recorded."

Persis stiffened.

"I am completely sincere. You can drop it off yourself at Wheeler and Schreiner, the attorneys on Main."

"Please be assured, I don't doubt you."

He studied her anxious eyes for a moment and ventured, "Is it Alex?"

Persis nodded slowly, trying not to reveal too much.

"Well, I will not tell him of your . . . shall we say, ambitions. I'll just tell him I want you and your family to keep the Angel. You'll sort it out. Good fortune is good fortune."

She smiled and said simply, "Thank you."

He took a last sip and picked up his hat. "Now that we have rail service to Corinne, Polly is more eager than ever to leave this—fair city."

They both laughed. Even on a sparkling winter day, Butte was anything but fair.

"I hope we see you before you go," said Persis, taking Dern's hand for a moment. "Give my regards to Mrs. Dern—Polly. I will write to you. That way, perhaps you'll still feel a sense of participation in our glorious and shabby little mining frontier."

Standing alone in the parlor, Persis was wildly excited. The menu for next week's dinner party seemed ridiculously irrelevant.

The first thing I have to do is tell Charlie. Nora had just returned from the grocery, so the buggy was ready and waiting. Wrapping her cloak around her, Persis took a bundle of cinnamon rolls for her brother and headed for the door, then stopped short as she laid her hand on the knob.

The deed. She went to the card room and found it lying just as she had left it, in the drawer that smelled of bay leaves and linen.

I'll show it to Charlie, she calculated, *so he will believe me, then I'll take it to the attorneys. Then it will be out of my hands.* She was trespassing on Alex's thin veneer of tolerance, but she went ahead. If it came up, she would tell Alex she only did as Cy asked. And Cy's forthcoming letter would reinforce what she did. He would affirm his wishes for Persis "and her family" to have the Angel. *Then Alex can think whatever he likes, but I will be the legal owner.*

The air was crisp and the sun was warm. At the intersection of Main and Copper, the staid brick and frame houses of uptown gave way to the scattered, disrespectful settlements grouped on the hill. Cabins and shanties were clustered in warrens all over the uneven landscape. As the wheels thudded from one rime-crusted rut to another, her hat fell back, baring her gold hair to the sun, the clouds of sulphurous steam, and the cold January air.

She began to feel a new sense of investment in the Territory. It felt solid and good, like a place she could be as a person, even a businesswoman.

Charlie was in the Anaconda office, a bastion of respectability in the otherwise rag-tag fabric of "the hill." Sitting on a wooden stool next to the tiny stove, Persis told him the story of the card game and of this morning's events. When she was finished, she placed the deed to the Angel on the desk in front of her incredulous brother. He studied the paper and looked up at his sister with knitted brows. They sat for a moment, their gazes welded together. In the front room, the miners laughed at a joke, while outside, the stamp mills kept beating.

"Sister," Charlie began, "I know you're excited, but this could blow up in your face."

Persis looked at him steadily and said, "It's not going to. You're going to help me."

"Am I? What makes you think I want a fool's errand like this? Perhaps for the enormous financial risk? Or for the likelihood of falling from favor with my influential brother-in-law?"

Persis had never considered the possibility that Charlie wouldn't leap at this opportunity. Her grip on the stool tightened. "Do you mean to tell me, Charlie Allen, that you would let this slip through your fingers? I'm offering you a mine, for heaven's sake. It's not just some worn-out claim that no one wants. The hoisting works is brand new. There are cables coming in from Chicago. They're paid for. This is a mine, Charlie, and you know as well as I do all a person has to do on this hill is dig deep enough to find paydirt." She paused. "Charlie, you mentioned this very mine to me last summer when you and Marcus were just starting to come down with 'copper fever'!"

Charlie's expression was softening. She knew she had a chance if she seized it now. "Obviously I can't do this alone," she said, leaning onto the desk and bringing her face close to his. "I want you to help me. You know what needs to be done. And don't think I'm going to shove all the work off onto you. I want to learn."

Charlie dropped his head into his hands. "Percy, it's a great opportunity, I know that. And I think we could probably make it work. But do you realize what's involved? Do you realize the sum of money we'd have to borrow? I'm just an engineer. And you – your status is derived from Alex, let's face it." He picked up a pencil and tapped it on the desk. "What on earth makes you think Alex would permit you to do this?"

"What about Daly?" Persis asked, ignoring the issue of Alex and focusing on the problem of financing. "Couldn't we borrow from Marcus? He can be a gruff old soul but he has a good heart. He thinks the world of you, Charlie."

"If I were a hundred percent Irish I might have a chance," he said, glowering. "Don't ask me to do this, Percy. You don't understand."

Subdued, she bit her lip. "Maybe I don't. But if I can get the money, Charlie, will you do it?"

"Even if you are able to wrangle some banker or businessman into giving you the money—and you'd have to ask for ten thousand to even give us a fair chance—what if we dig for a year and come up with nothing but bloody knuckles and sweat? What are you going to do about *our* ten thousand dollar debt?"

"Maybe Alex would cover it," Persis said weakly.

"You're pipe dreaming now, sister." Charlie tossed the pencil down.

Determination rose in her anew. "If I can get the money, and you do some looking around and testing at the mine, and if you think there might be a fair chance of making a profit off the Angel, *then* will you do it?"

"You know I could lie to you. Even if I found copper glance or even bornite over there, I could tell you it's a bad hole, just to save myself the perspiration and grief."

"If this pans out, Charlie, you can be a partner. I am standing here with your dream in the palm of my hand and you're balking. No, Charlie, you won't lie to me. You know you're going to find something over there at the Angel, and that's what's scaring you, isn't it?"

The defiance disappeared from Charlie's face. He studied her soberly for a moment and inhaled sharply. "If you can get the money, and I find some good indications over there at the Angel, we're in business. But, what about—"

"I'll worry about the money and about Alex," she said brashly. "You just sharpen your pencil and use all that schooling to figure out what's next." She rounded the desk and kissed him on the cheek. "It feels right, Charlie."

"There's something else you need to know," he said balefully.

Persis was putting on her gloves but stopped short at this last remark. "What do you mean?"

"I hate that name. I refuse to run a mine called 'The Angel.'"

"Anything you say, Mr. Engineer. We'll find something to suit your taste."

Driving back toward the heart of Butte and the three-story townhouse, Persis was jubilant. She checked herself, trying to be cautious. One step at a time, she told herself firmly, and the next step is Wheeler and Schreiner. She turned the horse and snapped the reins firmly. Her mind raced ahead of the light carriage as it gathered speed and bounced along the frozen road.

*   *   *

As January spun to a close, Alex passionately resumed his night life. Persis realized he intended to maintain his position at Hauser's First National Bank of Helena but also to ally himself with Will Clark and his support of the new Northern Pacific Railroad coming in from the east. It seemed an exhausting proposition. Which, Persis wondered, of his diverse ventures would be the one that truly sustained their family in the years ahead?

Chewing on a cigar, he told Persis that Sam Hauser would stand behind him all the way. She had no choice but to believe him. But she also knew he was spending more and more time currying favor with Will Clark. It was amazing how deftly he shifted his loyalties and managed others' perceptions.

"Sam wants me back in Helena, by the way," he added, twirling the cigar ash into the ceramic ashtray. He looked as he always did when confronted—annoyed, yet aroused.

"Are we moving back, then?" asked Persis. The Angel glowed in the shadowy background of her consciousness. She couldn't imagine going back to knitting parties at the Fisks'.

"No," came Alex's flat response. "Not yet. I think there is plenty yet to be done here in Butte. I can get the bank involved in making sure the new Northern Pacific has all the support it needs. And we can surely keep nudging the Utah and Northern toward Helena."

Persis recalled that somewhere in the whirling, smoky string of holiday evenings, a credible figure had said with finality that the Utah and Northern would not go to Helena and that the Northern Pacific instead would be Helena's first railroad, but she held her tongue.

Alex began packing in a random fashion, leaving Persis to her domestic duties. "There's no sense in you and the children coming yet," he said. "I have a feeling I'll be back soon. They're talking about a lot of things, a Butte branch, the consolidation of mining claims, the NP, and still the UN spur to Helena. I need to learn the old goat's game plan."

Persis left him to his lists and took his discarded copy of The *Miner* into the kitchen.

"It's a lucky man he is," said Grace quietly.

Persis looked up from the paper. She knew Grace felt Alex was fortunate to have a good position with Hauser. She bit her lip and turned her gaze back to the editorial page.

She heard Winston's babble on the landing as Nora led him down the last short flight of stairs. With rapid thudding, he plowed into the kitchen and flung himself against her knees. "Mama," he blurted, gazing up at her with Constance's blazing blue eyes. As she tousled his hair, her dark mood left her.

"Wawa," he said.

"Oh, no! He wants to play in the water again! He'll be drenched," said Persis.

"What harm is there in't?" said Grace, filling a blue enamel basin with warm water from the stove. She dug in the kitchen drawers for spoons and cups, and soon Winston was disporting himself with abandon.

Alex appeared in the door, staring. "What is he doing? This room is a mess."

"Well, darling, it's only water. He loves it so. Grace, Alex's coffee cup is empty."

As Grace hastened to fill his coffee cup, Alex compressed his lips in distaste and strode back to the study. Tension hung in the air behind him.

Persis frowned, knowing it pained him to see them being gay on the eve of his departure. She still hoped that with her help, these things would someday cease to trouble him. But that night he drank a good deal, and found fault with Persis's attitude. As he began the familiar tirade, she wished she didn't know him so well.

The dreaded, familiar refrain soon came: "You have handled this very badly." She knew if she sat numbly, as she wanted to do, he would become angrier still, so she made gentle protests, telling him earnestly that she loved him and wanted the best for him.

She shuddered as he poured himself another drink. He set it down with a hard "clink" on the glass top of the lamp table and glared at her with raised eyebrows. How many times had she been harrowed by that lordly look of expectation? She had to do something.

Impelled by raw fear, she began lightly stroking his hand, gradually moving up his arm. As she unfastened his collar, his head fell back.

He sighed heavily. "I just want to be taken care of, Persis. Is that too much to ask?" He looked at her with moist, unfocused eyes. To her relief and repulsion, he took her hand and planted it below his belt buckle, holding it there, smiling. Then, lifting her in the air, he flung her over his shoulder and staggered up the stairs, his shoulder grinding painfully against her hipbone.

In bed, she endured his ill-mannered passion, confused to distraction by the arousal she still felt under this degradation. When it was over, she flowed away like water into her hard-won safety. Soon he slept, and she was at liberty to cry.

*   *   *

Two days before he was scheduled to head north, the subject of the Angel came up. Alex asked for the deed and Persis, feigning indifference, casually pointed it out on his desktop. She knew Cy Dern had finally written to Alex confirming the transfer of ownership.

"The man's decision is asinine," he said. He surveyed the stiff leaves of the revised deed, then made an authoritative display of squaring it with a pile of papers on his desk. "Well, someday I might get to tinkering with it," he said with a sigh. "Charlie would help me, I am sure."

Persis bent over her crewelwork. Her heart pounded as she sat quietly, stitching in steady, even strokes. With every careful aim of the needle, she thought of her sharp-minded friend Alma in Helena, and wished she could tell her everything. Someday, she promised herself. But for now, every fiber of her was concentrated on appearing as Alex longed to see her—elegant, refined, and quietly engaged in the feminine arts.

As the evening passed, there was little conversation between them. She noticed with gratitude that Alex had only one glass of whiskey. The grandfather clock ticked heavily in the hall as the rumble of the stamp mills rolled down from The Hill. By nine o'clock, she had sunk into a state of anxiety and wistfulness about the gulf between them. She looked at her husband.

As he ran his hands through his bronze-streaked hair, she studied his profile. She marveled at how touched she could be, time and time again, by the noble look of him. Once more, she was overcome with a sense of his unfathomed potential.

"Alex . . . since you have known me . . ." she began.

He turned and looked at her, raising his eyebrows with a quizzical look.

She looked into the topaz eyes that sparkled with what Constance so aptly called *joie de vivre.* "Since you have known me," she repeated, "have you ever felt that you have been more inclined toward self-examination?" Knowing he would look askance at such a question, she hastened on. "What I mean is, because of our association, have you been at all drawn to considering the deeper meanings of our life together, or of your own life?"

"I know you mean well, Persis, but piety isn't the answer for everyone," he said, not unkindly, and looked at her evenly.

"Piety?" she repeated. "Is that what you think I mean?"

He looked puzzled for a moment, then frowned. "Well . . . yes, frankly. What else could a person call it?"

Persis chose her words carefully. "Piety, to me, means religious devotion. A sort of connection to what is sacred. Piety can even mean being overzealous. What I mean is different. I am not explaining myself very well."

He gave a little laugh and took the last sip of his drink.

"The best word I can think of is—inwardness. You know, an analysis of one's—of our actions and what moves us to—" she was about to say "behave as we do," but rephrased it. "To make choices." She saw him studying her and knew she was moving onto dangerous ground.

"Call it what you will, my dear," he said at last. "We are not all cut from the same bolt of cloth. You know that as well as I. Remember when we were first married and you wanted me to read your kind of books? And then you tried reading mine? Eventually you gave up, and it was good that you did. You have your books and I have mine. And that has worked quite well, hasn't it? Men and women are different."

He picked up his papers and looked at them. "I hope you are not trying to tell me that you have reached a point in our marriage where you are finding fault with me."

"On the contrary, Alex," she said. She knew she had to be firm, or he would run amok with his misinterpretations. "I love you enough to want to create the surroundings that will allow you to become everything you are capable of becoming."

"That's very dear of you, Persis. That means a lot to me. Rest assured I am quite comfortable with who I am and with all my pursuits." He reached over and patted her hand. "I love you too."

Persis smiled and let her eyes drift downward. She might as well whistle in the wind.

*   *   *

The following morning, Persis carried Rose down to the kitchen. As she approached, she heard Grace talking in uncharacteristic low tones. She paused, holding the sleepy Rose.

"If I wasn't afeard for the Missus and the babes," Grace muttered, "I'd put a hundred murderin' curses on that horse's ass of a man. Cock of the midden indeed! Devil take him, I say. His kind is better off— well, never mind."

It was quiet for a moment, then came Nora's unusually hesitant voice. "Grace, how—how does a girl know—I mean, if a girl contemplates tyin' the knot with a fellow she thinks is grand, how does she know what she's gettin' herself into?"

"She doesn't," Grace said. "It's as simple as that. Could be a decent life of honest effort with a good man, or she could dance a lifetime jig with Beelzebub himself. Peer or plowboy, it makes not a whit o' difference. Lean on the saints, Nora. That's all I can say."

As Persis stole back up the stairs and put Rose in her cradle, she heard the jingle of the harness on the street. Alex was back from his errands and would want her full attention for his departure.

An hour later, as he made ready to leave, he stood in the open doorway, staring into her eyes. She met his gaze fully. The February wind gusted in and the carpets rose along the hallway floor. He was in his frock coat and hat, but she, in her lightweight worsted dress, suppressed a shiver and disguised her wish that he would just go and close the door.

At last he left, and she turned to view a house that held the promise of peace and spontaneous laughter. A surge of gratitude welled up within her and she whispered heavenward, "Thank you."

* * *

Charlie stopped in the next afternoon and sat with her in front of the second-floor fireplace.

"I have a new name for the mine," she said.

"And what might that be? Some Greek goddess, I suppose."

"No, don't worry. I want to name it the Porphyry," she said.

"You're naming it after a street? How—pedestrian."

She laughed. "Good grief, it's not the street I was thinking of. I like the look of porphyry crystals. And the word rolls off the tongue. Don't you like it?"

"I suppose it's all right. It *is* a geological term." He nodded. "I can live with it. Anything's better than 'the Angel.'"

* * *

On Wednesday, the temperature rose into the forties. She took the buggy out to buy baby clothes for Rose, who would soon be seven months old. Alex had given her the household allowance for both February and March. Feeling rich and self-indulgent, she placed several diminutive dresses, sweaters, and jackets on the shop counter, then walked toward the familiar territory of the ladies' dress department.

Her step slowed. She fingered a dress or two, but stared vacantly down the aisle toward the door. I can't save much from what Alex gives me, she thought; after all, I need to keep the household going. But I can save a little. I'm now able to fit into all my old clothes and have no need for new things, except perhaps a riding skirt. Even in clothes that are old by my standards, she thought, I'm still the most fashionable woman in Butte.

Piling her goods into the buggy, her confidence grew. With these new things for the children and with the spoils of Christmas, they could get along for quite some time.

I can keep the extra money at Charlie's house, in the match drawer. I need to look there for a letter anyway, she reflected, feeling a stir in her breast at the thought of something from Bess.

Slapping the reins lightly, she called out, "Get along, Grayling. First to Charlie's, and then home."

At Charlie's, with fifteen dollars in her hand, she went directly to the kitchen. When she pulled opened the drawer, there, on top of the Montgomery Ward catalog, lay a gray-blue envelope addressed in elegant script to "Mrs. Persis MacKinney, in care of Mr. Charles Allen, 201 Idaho Street, Butte City, Montana Territory."

Her heart thumped as she sat down next to the stove, which still held traces of warmth from Charlie's morning fire. It was strange to eagerly tear open an envelope from a woman she once nearly hated, but her eyes settled into Bess's handwriting like a starving woman at a feast.

It began with a few pleasantries, but like Bess, it soon went to the quick:

> . . . forgive me for being bold enough to speak of my past relations with the man who is now your husband. As much as I would like to respond in kind to the letter you sent me, and tell you about the new foal that was born this morning and who now teeters on knobby legs next to his sweet mama, I cannot. I am compelled instead to speak to the heart of the matter that concerns us both. Please know that I completely forgive you if you should find yourself wanting to reject my counsel. After all, Alex married you, not me.
>
> When I look back on the time I spent in Alex's company, the most humiliating part of it all wasn't the bruises or the insults, or the time he broke the crystal vase that had been my mother's (if you remember, I never knew my mother), or the time he whipped one of my horses. Nor was it the time I found he had betrayed me with a common whore. The hardest part, Persis, was my flailing, precipitous fall into reason, when I first entertained the possibility that I, with all my charm, wealth, and position, was not enough to gentle the wild Alexander MacKinney. I am a vain woman, loath to admit that in this endeavor, I failed. But I most certainly did fail.
>
> Even as I write, an aspect of me still fears his reprisal. It whispers, "What if he finds this letter?" Thanks to the grace of God, I can tuck

those worries safely into my past. Alex can't hurt me anymore, and it's not because we are separated by 1,500 miles, or because he has fallen in love with you. It's because I have changed. I cannot tell you the joy and the beauty of the change I have undergone. I at last came to understand that I couldn't, shouldn't protect him anymore, and that others ought to know the sad nature of our relations.

I am free. Not just free of pain, shame, and fear, but free to taste everything I always thought life promised me, free not to look over my shoulder, free to follow my own heart. I wish this for you, in whatever manner it might happen. I wish you God's grace, and I remain your affectionate friend, Bess

Quaking, Persis set the letter down on the table. What am I doing here, she upbraided herself, sitting in my little hiding place, reading calumnious information about the man to whom I am married? The man with whom I swore to build a life of happiness!

She stared at the fifteen dollars in her lap. What has become of my dreams? If I listen to Bess, they will be dashed. How dare she say these brazen things! Alex's face, the face with the warm, brown eyes so full of laughter and charm, filled her mind.

The only sound was a soft, puffing noise as a charred log shifted among the ashes in the stove.

Then the tears came, gushing without warning, spilling over her coat and onto her lap. Wrapping her arms around herself, she rocked back and forth, opening her mouth wide as a breathless sob rose from her core, making no sound at all. The tears kept coming as she babbled out a prayer in confused, broken sentences. She didn't know what she said, or how long she went on.

Every time she raised her head and looked at the letter and the money, she wanted to die. Every time she thought of Rose and Winston, she clung to life. Finally, with red eyes and an aching head, she felt something between exhaustion and peace.

"I don't know what to do," she said quietly, looking at the ceiling, as if divine words of guidance might be painted there. "But I can do what I must. I can stand up and go home." She took another look at the money and the letter, grabbed both, and stuffed them into the drawer, sliding the heavy catalog over the top of them.

Back at the townhouse, she looked at the narrow table in the hall for the morning's post. By eerie coincidence, there lay a telegram from Alex. He would stay in Helena for another two weeks.

As she leaned against the newel-post, the hand holding his message dangled at her side. She needed time. Just now, she cared for nothing except to see things continue as they were—familiar, and for the most part, comprehensible.

Mabel leaned back into the ribbon-striped sofa cushions. There was a merry twinkle in her eye. "There's another Bal Masque this Friday night," she said, reaching out for Persis's hand. "We could disguise ourselves so that no one would ever know. What do you say?"

"Oh, Mabel, it would be great fun, but can you imagine what would happen if somehow, someone recognized either of us? Artie knows you're a madcap and loves you for it. But Alex—" she stopped. Her eyes met Mabel's. "You—you just don't know," she said.

Mabel's countenance changed "Persis," she said tentatively, "I must confess—"

"What?"

"There have been times I have wondered if Alex—hurts you."

Stroking the lace table runner, Persis lowered her eyes. "He's a good man, Mabel. Someday he'll have a stronger sense of himself, and little things won't upset him so."

"Persis, *does* he hurt you?"

Persis looked up, stunned. Tears came from nowhere, maddeningly, blurring the edges of her vision. "He—he has never struck me outright," she whispered hoarsely. She recoiled at the sound of her own words. She wasn't lying, but it felt like she was. She thought about various events. The black eye, of course; but there was the bloody gash on her forearm from being raked along the carriage trim last spring, the bruised thigh from being flung against the breakfront in the dining room, and the cluster of uprooted locks she found trailing down the back of her dressing gown after he yanked her hair as she tried to get away.

Mabel drew a deep breath. "What difference does it make how a man punishes a woman? You don't seem like the kind of woman who would allow this to happen to you."

"Allow it!" Persis lifted her chin and stared. "I have no choice, Mabel. Think of the hundreds—the thousands of women who live out their lives under worse conditions than mine."

Mabel was silent, picking at a tassel on the sofa pillow. "I'm sorry," she said at length. "I know you have very good reasons for being with Alex. I guess I've lived in this town so long, I've seen everything. A lot of women stay and get beaten, but just as many obtain a legal divorce. It may not be that way back East, but it happens every day in Butte. And up in Helena."

"But not to . . ."

Mabel finished the sentence for her. "Not to people like you? Well, that may often be true. But your reasons are as good as Tess Sullivan's, the lady who left her brute of a husband last month. He liked to beat her with a poker."

Seeing Persis's disdainful look, she added, "Violence is violence. Nothing justifies it and no one deserves it, whether it's delivered by a sooty poker or by a hand wearing diamonds." She straightened the sofa cushion and said, "Now, about the Bal Masque . . . I have a feeling you've probably forgotten what freedom feels like."

Persis wavered. Alex could not survive without her complete loyalty. The idea was unthinkable. Yet something inside her felt wildly eager to go to the Bal Masque and let the chips fall where they may. A part of her loathed a part of him.

And there was something else. Although it was humiliating to share the tarnished side of the celebrated McKinney marriage, she felt a new and brilliant liberty. She was filled with fresh conviction that yes, perhaps another sisterly woman, in this case Mabel, ought to know her dark secret.

"I don't know," she said finally.

Mabel made a motion as if to leave.

"Don't go." She reached out. "Not yet. If—if I were to say yes, could you obtain the costumes?" Though she could scarcely believe she was entertaining the idea, she had crossed some kind of boundary, and the exhilaration was potent.

"I already have something in mind," said Mabel slyly.

"Nothing risqué!"

"Oh, no, quite the contrary."

"No one must know, do you hear?"

"You have my word."

* * *

Lying gratefully alone in bed, Persis knew her life was changing, but didn't know if it was for better or worse. I've set something in motion by accepting Mabel's invitation, she realized. But if Mabel hadn't come along with her little plot, I would have found another way to rebel. That's what this feels like—rebellion.

She didn't care what she did, as long as she defied Alex. "This could be self-destructive," she murmured aloud in the dark. "What am I about?"

* * *

A February Chinook swept down the eastern side of the Rockies and melted two months' worth of snow and ice, making the city streets nearly impassible. Nonetheless, social life picked up and the street denizens came out of hibernation.

Persis rose to the thrill of upcoming adventure. When she did succumb to moments of sober reflection, they were hasty, yielding only a trace of uncertainty. By Friday she had decided to leap into the void and tumble to her fate, be it progress or doom.

With the aid of Wednesday's issue of The *Miner,* she developed a story to tell Grace and Nora: she would be attending a lecture at the library on the Monroe Doctrine.

Everything fell precisely into place. Arrayed in a sedate gown of brown wool with ecru lace, she put on a voluminous hooded cloak and, at eight o'clock Friday evening, climbed with self-possession into the buggy and drove out of the alley behind Park Street.

The intimate bustle that ensued at Mabel's made their costuming a protracted, hilarious affair. Out of breath from laughing, she looked in the mirror. This is quite out of character for me, she thought, and would shock all the wives of Alex's friends. The notion was even more delicious than the food Mabel had laid out—smoked oysters, crackers, apples, cheddar, and port.

The costumes could not have been better—they were to be Saracens. Long, loose robes and striped Bedouin-style headdresses provided ample coverage for their slight figures. Persis stifled fits of laughter as Mabel smeared carbolic salve over both their jawbones, then plastered ground coffee liberally over this base. The bearded effect was remarkable.

Persis leaned back, her costume complete. Mabel filled her glass again. The garnet liquid shone brilliant in the soft lamplight. Suddenly overcome with gratitude for Mabel's friendship, Persis reached out and held her friend's hand.

"We love men, but they are so seldom with us. Women—that's a different story. I am grateful for you, Mabel."

Mabel colored faintly. "You are a remarkable person," she said simply. "For some reason I expect great things from you—with or without Alex. I am lucky to know you."

*   *   *

"Let's leave the buggy a good block or two away, on Thornton," Persis said as she managed the horse through the muddy streets. "No one will see it there. And I don't want to stay later than midnight."

Mabel smiled and nodded.

Persis snapped the reins at the laboring horse. The two women talked and laughed in low voices until they reached Thornton Street. With their conveyance stowed in a dark alley, they made their way to the front door, handed their money silently to the Theater Comique ticket-taker, and went in.

Persis had fanciful ideas about what the Bal Masques were like, but nothing could have prepared her for what lay inside the doors of the Theater Comique. Dozens of men sat in the foyer around tables spread with cards, money, and whiskey bottles. The air smelled of liquor, leather, smoke, cologne, and sweat. Hurdy-gurdy girls waited on the tables and flirted with the gamblers who, unlike most of the revelers inside, had money.

Persis looked beyond, into the notorious pandemonium known as the Bal Masque. The dance hall was a dimly-lit, cavernous room, thick with tobacco smoke.

Someone passed behind her, jostling and wedging her into a circle of men observing a poker game. Mabel, moving in an arc around the poker table, tugged at her robe. "This way," she whispered.

They passed unnoticed into the raucous, heady commotion of the ballroom. At the far end was a stage where the entertainment was taking place, with honky-tonk music, whistling, and shouting.

The swirling mass of laughing, jesting, drinking merriment was a fairy tale in motion. Persis's disguise enabled her to stare, and stare she did. The port she had consumed made her blink in stupefied awe, not just at the tinsel and rouge, but at the novel joy of being anonymous and unencumbered.

About half of the revelers were in their everyday clothes. Probably miners and Butte's numberless ranks of hired help, she reasoned. Spying Jimmy Barsness, who worked at the dry goods store, she reached a heavily-gloved hand up to her mask to make sure he couldn't possibly tell who she was. But Jimmy had seen her looking at him.

"Hey there, it's the sheik of Araby!" he jeered. "You can afford to buy me a beer, can't you?" and he reached roughly for her upper arm. Snatching it away before he could encircle his fingers around an arm too slender for any sheik, she darted into the crowd after Mabel.

They silently forded the current of people until they came to a small open space near the wall. A long, ornately carved bar stretched down to the left, with patrons lining it three-deep. They were closer to the stage now and could see that the performance had something to do with the California Gold Rush. No one seemed to be paying attention, and if there was a plot, it went uncomprehended by the vast majority of the audience. The floor was slippery with spilled beer and expectorated tobacco juice. As Persis's robe dragged through a slick spot, the thought of the countless unnamed substances on the floor made her dizzy. She wished she had not had so much to drink.

Quelling her repulsion, she soon overheard bits of conversation. A man behind her laughed and said to his companion, "That waitress up front, working the game tables. Name's Gert. I'd like to put her on my spit and give her a turn!"

Just as they reached the end of the bar, a woman in an off-the-shoulder dress decked with blue feathers and beads leaned over and emitted a watery stream of vomit. The man next to her was dressed in the stiff, dark woolens of the mining trade.

"Penny, for Christ's sake!" he cried out. "I shoulda seen that comin'." He bent to hoist the woman over his shoulder. "Give me a hand, will ye, buster?" He called out to Persis over the din.

Persis stood stock-still. "Well, give 'er a shove," he commanded. "On the bum. Don't pay no never mind, she don't know yer doin' it."

Persis swallowed, placed her hands under the protruding rump, and boosted it up. The woman reeked of cheap perfume.

"Much obliged," the man muttered and walked away, his partner's beribboned head flopping before him and her legs dangling behind.

"I can't believe this place," she whispered. "I don't know if we really ought to stay here." She looked over her shoulder and saw Mabel's dusky eyes—they almost looked Arabian—begin to crinkle at the corners.

"You think this is amusing, don't you?" said Persis. "Seeing me so aghast?" Persis felt a smile stealing across her own face and quickly looked away.

"Look at me," teased Mabel.

"No!" Persis smothered a giggle. "If we start laughing, it's all over. Stop it."

Mabel's eyes glittered mischievously.

"Is this . . . is this what they call 'social intercourse'?" Persis quipped. They both burst out laughing.

"Ugh, my hands smell like French lilac," said Persis.

"Pity we can't take off our costumes to drink," said Mabel. "I wouldn't mind a bit more."

Someone bumped Persis, making her reel slightly. "I think I've had quite enough."

Mabel held her arm, steadying her.

"This," said Persis, "this is wonderful. I feel free."

"It is rather remarkable, isn't it?"

"My life—" began Persis.

"What about your life?"

"My life—is a corset," said Persis, letting out a peal of laughter and then slapping her glove over her mouth. She bent from the waist, letting go of all her concerns and laughing until tears came to her eyes.

"But is it whalebone or steel?" asked Mabel, giggling.

"Oh, definitely steel. But of course those steely stays are encased in the loveliest white satin."

"Only the best for Persis MacKinney," said Mabel.

Persis's smile faded as the irony sank in.

"Let's watch everything for a few minutes, shall we?" Mabel suggested lightly.

"Heaven only knows if we'll ever—if I'll ever—get to do anything like this again. As a woman who lives a corset-life, I envy you your split riding skirt," Persis joked.

Two miners were talking loudly over the riotous noise, and Persis could not avoid picking up the thread of the conversation.

"That's not what I heard, Mitch. I heard that Clark called Daly's partner a nigger. You know, that dark-skinned rich fellow, from San Francisco. Hagman or whatever the man's name is."

"Haggin?"

"The very same. Well, you see, our leader Daly had invited Clark to a kind of a shindig, and Clark says he won't come, not wanting to be seen with the likes o' some African fellow, meanin' Haggin. Only he didn't exactly say 'African fellow', if you see where I am going."

The one named Mitch whistled. "I bet old Marc Daly didn't take too kindly to that."

"Them two is headed for a train wreck, you wait and see," returned his friend. "Little sparks o' the devil's own fire come out o' Clark's eyes whene'er he sees Daly. Pretty soon the whole hill will be divvied up just twixt the two o' them."

"Ah," Mitch said, waving his hand. "What do we know? Two men never lit a simple campfire without disagreein'."

"Faith, don't you believe it. Clark is fast surroundin' himself with the lords o' the Territory. He's got that freighter, that MacKinney fellow, workin' with him now. You know, the one that won the wagon race against almighty Gilmer last year. They's birds of a feather. I've seen 'em, struttin' about in their white collars and rich adornins'."

Persis stiffened and was suddenly unable to think of anything but making sure Alex never found out about this evening. Her hands grew cold.

She was snatched from her private thoughts by a voice in her ear. It was Jimmy Barsness. "How 'bout a nip," he mumbled, looking hard into her eyes. "Awright, you don't have to buy me a shot," he rambled through swollen red lips. "But there are other things we could do."

Mabel was nowhere to be seen. Jimmy's hand closed on Persis's shoulder. "'Ain't no sheik's shoulder under this tent," he said. "Let's see if you're who I think you are."

Persis wrenched herself free from his drunken grasp, wriggling into the crowd. With a rush of relief, she spied Mabel talking to a dance-hall girl. Two steps and she had hold of Mabel's hand.

"We've got to get out of here. We're nearly discovered! It's that fool Jimmy Barsness—he's after me!"

Jimmy was craning his neck to keep Persis in sight as he lurched toward her.

"Come on!" insisted Persis.

The two of them slipped away through the milling crowd. They saw the glimmer of lights in the casino near the front door. As they neared the exit, something made her look back at one of the poker players—an angle of brow, a shadow beneath the brim of dark felt.

My God, she mouthed silently. It was Baron Coleman. She turned away slowly, her heart thumping. Gently, she pushed Mabel toward the door.

The grizzled stock clerk was still visible, hollering after them. Lord above, just get us out of here, she prayed silently. In less than a minute they were out the door in the cold March air.

"Quick, this way!" said Mabel.

They ran across the street and ducked into a narrow passageway.

"Will this take us to Thornton?"

"Yes," said Mabel, "but we've got to pass through a house to get there. It's all right. I know who lives here."

Behind them, Barsness emerged and stumbled onto the street. Two boldly-dressed street women were standing on the corner just north of the Theater Comique, eager for the attention of late-night patrons. Within minutes, Jimmy lumbered off with a new companion.

Weak-kneed, Persis stood in the dim passageway. Mabel took a few steps into the darkness and gave three short knocks on a door Persis couldn't even see. There was no answer. "We can go back the other way," said Persis. "Jimmy's gone. But we'd have to walk by the Theater again."

Just then the lock turned with a clink and the door creaked open.

Mabel whispered firmly, "Good evening. It's Mabel. I used to come with the Captain."

"Missee Mabel? We no see you for long time. You want to come in?" asked the middle-aged, plump Chinese woman. "You have a friend? Same girl? I forget her name."

"No, no." Mabel laughed softly. "I have a friend with me, but it's not the same one. We just want to walk through the house—to the kitchen and then to the alley. Is it all right?"

"Yes, all right. You smokee tonight?"

"No—no thank you, I don't think so, Mrs. Lo." Mabel glanced at Persis and bit her lip. "Come on," she said, motioning toward the half-opened door.

"Is this place what I think it is?" Persis demanded.

"Don't get on your high horse now, Persis MacKi—" Mabel inhaled abruptly. "No one is going to hurt you. There's a hallway through this house that leads to the kitchen and there's a door from there right into the alley. From there it's only a half a block to the buggy."

Although the scene before her was profane, Persis longed for the words to tell Mabel the truth—that this bizarre house didn't so much horrify as fascinate her. From the partly open door, a sweet, musky fragrance wafted past them on a draught of stale air.

"It's all right," she said. "I'm sorry, Mabel. I'm fine. Really." She took Mabel's arm and practically led her into the smoky-sweet darkness.

Cheap tin oil lamps in the corners of the parlor emitted a feeble light. The cloying smell of opium smoke permeated the drapes and furnishings. As they walked past a small alcove, Persis saw an old Chinese man reclining on a tattered chaise. The flickering lamplight showed a carved pipe and a small blue box on the table. Persis, thinking he was asleep, stared. Then she realized that his eyes, although merely slits in his wizened face, were indeed open. He smiled.

Persis turned away.

"Come on," said Mabel.

A figure was coming toward them down the long hallway.

"'Zat you, Mabel girl? Where you been? You come back for smokee with me, yes?" came a giggling voice. Lamplight fell on the features of a round-faced blond dressed in only her corset and pantaloons. She slipped her arm through Mabel's, making progress impossible. "Been to the Bal Masque, I see. Aren't you a sight! Who's you're friend?"

"Her name's Clara," Mabel said quickly.

"Clara smokee?" the blond extended her arm slowly and put an unsteady fingertip on Persis's nose.

Persis was dumbstruck, suspended between the life she knew and the yawning abyss of strangeness. This arcane world, she realized, turns every single day and night while I sit in my drawing room a scant six blocks north.

"I—never have," she responded, in a monumental effort to arrest Mabel's brisk progress through the house. Moonlight poured through a window and Persis felt as if the cool, silver beams were lapping at her feet.

She felt more than saw her friend turn sharply to look at her. A vapor of restraint rose from Mabel.

"Yes," Persis said suddenly, deliberately. "I will smoke."

Inside her head, a moral voice shrilled out, "How can you sink to such depravity? Think of all the kind souls in your life, the people who loved and raised you—"

Mabel's voice broke in, ringing with authority. "Are you sure you want to do this?"

"Yes, I am. If you don't understand, Mabel, it's all right. But I do want to." She dug into her pocket and found three silver dollars.

The blond heard the silver clinking. Pushing wispy curls away from her cheek, she motioned to a worn leather chair. Horsehair stuffing sprang from its cracked surface.

Persis sat down, her thoughts smouldering. There is something else, she swore, something other than the life I have been living. If my life were a looking-glass, I would break it in a thousand pieces!

She turned her face toward the scantily-dressed woman, who was wiping a small dab of wet, blackish gum into the bowl of her pipe.

"Here," said the blond, smiling. "Jus' a little. It'll make you cough if'n you've never done it afore. Jus' breathe in, not too hard, jus' 'til you feel it in your throat."

As Mabel sat down in a threadbare brocade chair across the room, Persis parted the striped madras around her face. Taking the pipe, she awkwardly put its stem between her lips. It was oily and bitter. The blond struck a match and held it over the bowl, where it cast a warm light up over her pale features and floating strands of hair. Persis wondered how bizarre she herself must look with carbolic salve and coffee grounds smeared over her cheeks.

She looked into the woman's gray eyes and wide, dark pupils. Her nerve began to slip and she knew she needed to proceed with her business. She stared into the flame hovering over the bowl, compressed her lips around the stem, and drew. The smoke was full and aromatic in her mouth, then hot and abrasive in her throat.

"Stop," said the blond. "Hold your breath a moment if you can. Not too long. Then let it out slow-like. Try not to cough. Might hurt a bit if'n you do."

Persis did as she was told. A moment later, she allowed a thin stream of smoke to pass from her lips.

"Twice," said the blond, gently urging. "You always do it twice."

Persis obediently repeated the procedure and began to feel dizzy. "May I rest here for just a moment?" Without waiting for permission, she sank into the forgiving leather. "We'll be leaving soon."

Mrs. Lo and the blond walked away together, murmuring as the beaded curtain tinkled with their passing. Clearly, they knew she was no regular in these clandestine bowels of the city.

Persis knew it was time to leave, but before she could reason her way through this concern, she lost track of it and another thought drifted lazily into her head. She sat for a few moments and realized she didn't care, at least not now. Nothing mattered. Her mind wandered from idea to memory to place to countenance. She stopped occasionally to examine her fingers, which were laced loosely in her lap. No image stayed with her for longer than a few seconds.

After a time that seemed both short and long, Mabel came and took her arm gently. "Let's go," she whispered in a firm voice.

Clear-headed enough to get up, Persis sensed the wisdom of getting home and to bed.

Out in the alley, the cold night wind washed over her face and brought a recollection of their circumstances.

"The buggy," she murmured. "Oh Mabel, how I wish we would have walked. Managing the horse in these boggy streets! And we still have to go to your place so I can change my clothes."

"There it is. I'll drive."

Once in the buggy, they picked their way carefully toward Mabel's flat, straddling the ruts and avoiding black puddles of unknown depth. Only a trace of grogginess still clung to Persis. She felt gratefully relaxed.

At the corner of Dakota and Mercury Streets, the mud sucked loudly at the horse's hooves. Mabel worked the reins furiously to keep him out of the watery slough. The buggy lurched, and the two women leaned forward anxiously as the horse struggled to maintain his footing. The wheels stopped turning and they heard a distinct, popping crack from the right rear wheel. To their horror, they began sliding sideways.

The buggy glided into a long, narrow pool and jerked sharply as the downhill wheels sank into deep water. The horse was in trouble, thrashing and fighting against the harness.

Persis's mind was now completely clear. She jumped from her seat into the muck, made her way to the horse's head and began working feverishly at the harness rigging, talking in measured tones to the frightened animal. "It would be one thing to lose a buggy wheel, quite another to destroy such a beautiful animal as yourself, Grayling," she murmured. "It's all right, boy."

With cold, stiff fingers, she undid the brass harness buckles. As she made fumbling progress, she saw Mabel working the other side. Persis unclipped the reins from the bridle, and as the last piece of leather rigging fell away, she tugged gently at the horse's head. He stumbled a half-step forward, wild-eyed and grunting loudly, and struggled away from the useless buggy.

They made their way to the uphill side of the street, where Persis tore a long strip of cloth from her costume and tied the horse to a rail in front of a commercial building. Running her hands over his mud-spattered legs, she concluded he was sound. She looked up and saw the lettering painted over the door: Hank Snyder, Blacksmith.

"For a disaster, we planned things relatively well," she said to the white-robed dervish floundering toward her.

"How serendipitous," replied Mabel, laughing nervously.

"Two women in strange costumes, standing near a wrecked buggy, laughing in the middle of the night. How odd!" A male voice came out of the darkness.

Persis grasped Mabel's arm. The figure drew nearer, walking along several thick planks someone had put down for want of a sidewalk across the street. There was an arrogance to the stride, a careless swagger that Persis immediately disliked. Into the murky half-light of the forsaken side street, there crept an odious vapor of alarm. "Who is it?" whispered Mabel.

"I've no idea," was Persis's tense, barely audible response. But there was something about him. The man stopped a few yards away. What little light there was fell briefly across him. With a shiver, Persis saw that it was Baron Coleman.

"Do I know you ladies?" came the gravelly voice.

"Could be," Mabel shot back in a mocking tone. "But you'll not be getting any better acquainted with us this evening."

"Begging your pardon, miss. It is 'miss,' isn't it? No self-respecting husband would leave his wife alone on a dark street in this part of town with their outfit wrecked. That is, unless the ladies were accustomed to this sort of adventure."

Persis could see his white teeth in the darkness. He was smiling.

"We'll thank you to be on your way," she said, lowering her voice to a disguised pitch that sounded ridiculous to her. "We've only a short way to go, and prefer to go alone. It's not our buggy anyway," she added. "We passed it earlier."

Coleman leveled his gaze at her, shifted his eyes to the buggy, and back to her. Persis's skin crawled with the dread of discovery. *Alex knowing, his friends gossiping, the scandal and disgrace of it all.* It seemed the unctuous Coleman could see through the layers of muslin right down to her naked skin.

The moon, which had been under cover of the clouds, emerged. Coleman stood still, his hands shoved into his coat pockets, faintly jingling a few coins. "As you wish," he said at last. He shifted on the plank walk as if to take his leave, then added, "I do hope your husbands know where you are."

Mabel's elbow landed in Persis's ribs before she could respond. "I repeat," Mabel said, "our home is near. We are in no further need of your solicitous attention. Good night, sir."

Coleman retreated, his boots grinding softly on the uneven boards. Soon he was a small silhouette at the end of the street.

By now, Grayling was calm. Persis ran a hand up his shoulder and rested it on his withers. "We'll go now, old boy. All three of us need to go home." She turned to Mabel. "At least you haven't very far to go. Will you be all right?"

"Me? You're the one who's in worrisome straits. What are we going to do about the buggy? And you can't ride the old fellow in this muck. You'll have to walk. It's at least seven blocks. And your costume!"

"I still have my long cloak on beneath all this sheeting. I'll take off everything else and stuff it in a rubbish heap. There must be one in this alley," she said, pointing to her right. "If Grace is still awake, which is unlikely, she won't think it odd that I wear my cloak up to the bedroom. You can keep my brown dress for the time being, all right?"

Mabel bit her lip and nodded.

They resigned themselves to leave the buggy where it was. Mabel would come early in the morning and arrange with the blacksmith to clean and repair it. He probably wouldn't ask any questions, but if he did, she was to tell him that she borrowed it from the MacKinneys.

Persis would leave her own house before the help was awake— thank God it would be Sunday morning—and go out for a bareback ride on the dry hill streets. Later, if Grace or Nora were curious, she'd tell them that she had taken the buggy down to the blacksmith for work on the axle. She would come home leading Grayling and no one would know a thing.

It seemed an air-tight plan. In the alley, Mabel stood watch while Persis disrobed and jammed her costume into a pile of scrap lumber. I hope this load of lumber is destined for a roasting pile, thought Persis. Shivering in her underclothes and wool cloak, she embraced Mabel and kissed her. "It was glorious, Mabel. You'll never know what this evening meant to me."

Mabel held her close for a moment and whispered, "Saints preserve you!"

Persis felt a stab of isolation as she broke away and reached for

Grayling's bridle. For Mabel, a snug apartment with pillowed furniture and a fire in the grate beckoned warmly. For me, the only warm spots are the faces of two children tucked in bed.

She focused on picking the best path through the muddy streets. Although her fingers were ice cold, she knew it would be the worse for Grayling if he cooled down too quickly. In silent fellowship, the two of them plodded up the hill.

Alex returned and life went on as it had before. Nearly every day, she walked past his desk and looked for the familiar pages of the deed. Sometimes, when no one was near, she would finger its edges as if she were rubbing a touchstone. Might he undertake some kind of legal maneuver to transfer ownership of the mine to himself as the head of the household? She was convinced that the only reason he hadn't done so was that she feigned such convincing indifference to the property.

The intrigues heating up between the powerful sovereigns, Daly and Clark, were the talk of the town. Clark controlled the newspaper, so the wagging of tongues was the only way to get at the real meat of the local culture. Persis pumped as much gossip as she could out of her most lucrative sources, Grace and Nora.

Alex gave her a different but equally critical kind of information. He confided in her that he was developing a major contract with Will Clark for shaft timbers and smelter fuel.

One evening he came home in high spirits after a convivial evening of cards with Will Clark, Pat Largey, and A.J. Davis, and several other prominent chieftains. Sitting down next to Persis, he proudly produced a brick-sized silver ingot and set it on the coffee table. "Look what Will gave me," he said.

Persis inspected the ingot curiously. It was engraved "SBC." For Silver Bow Club, she realized. "It's charming," she said.

"I'll keep it on my desk. A paperweight. Look right here," he said, pointing to the lower edge. "It's stamped 'Original' because it was smelted at one of Clark's earliest holdings, the Original claim."

Alex adjusted the position of the ingot and leaned back. Flicking a bit of horsehair from his jacket, he raised his arms and locked them behind his head, admiring the gift.

"He must value your friendship a great deal," said Persis.

"I would venture to say so, yes. We get along quite well. And we have similar tastes. There aren't too many men in Butte—or in the Territory, for that matter—who have our sartorial flair."

Persis smiled benignly, remembering the crude conversation she had overheard at the Bal Masque.

Alex leaned forward again and tapped his pen against the ingot. "He's not overfond of Charlie's boss, you know."

Persis nodded. "Rumor has it that the battle lines are drawn between them."

"Why did your brother align himself with Daly when he came here? Charlie's only half Irish. I would think the fact that both he and Clark graduated from the Columbia School would have made him lean toward Will."

"I guess I just don't know," she replied simply. "As you say, Alex, everyone is different."

* * *

The warming wind blew signs of spring into the foothills around Homestake Pass. Even around Butte, shoots of green poked up, struggling for a roothold in the smudge-pot climate. Despite her attachment to the Porphyry and the encouraging assay reports she received whenever she could make contact with Charlie, spring made her long for her garden, for the clean air of Helena, and for Alma and Ruby. She even missed the quiet company of Angus and the stock barn.

Riding with Mabel one afternoon, the two of them found the furry blooms of the pasque flower, little half- eggshells of smoky lavender against the sere grass. The Douglas firs were laden with fresh snow, but it melted and slid to the ground with soft thumps as they rode through the pine-scented woods.

"Oh, Mabel, I love it here. I've always loved nature, but this place has gotten into my blood in a way I never could have imagined. Everyday my love for the Territory grows stronger."

"It's like heaven on earth, isn't it? Soon the shooting stars will be out," said Mabel.

"Shooting stars?"

"Don't tell me you haven't seen them! They're tiny flowers the color of cherries and they smell like cloves." She pulled her dark sorrel close to Skye and said, "Will you be going back to Helena soon?"

Persis slowed. "I have to say, I am worried about the children. The air is so foul here. But you could visit! We have plenty of room."

"Alex doesn't like me," Mabel said, brushing a burr from her thigh.

Persis watched, coveting her friend's simple split riding skirt.

"I don't take it too personally," Mabel went on. "However, he also thinks I divert your attention, and he doesn't appreciate that."

Persis nodded slowly. There was no point in denying it. "Mabel," she began.

"Hmm?"

"Despite all that . . . will you please keep being my friend?"

"Of course I will! And you—will you be mine?" The warm Chinook wind made her long, dark ringlets dance about her face.

Persis reached for Mabel's hand and held it tightly. Tears came to her eyes. Her future seemed so uncertain, but the same was true for Mabel. Artie had held to his vow of temperance this time and had gone back to Ohio. No one knew if he'd be coming back or not.

She brushed a tear from her cheek and released Mabel's hand. "If I am not here when the shooting stars are blooming," she said, "I will find some in Helena and think of you."

As they rode back to town, Mabel said, "You know what else?"

"What?"

"I have an extra split skirt. I know I am shorter than you are, but I think we are about the same girth and I'm sure it will fit you. The only trouble is, I don't know when you'll ever be able to wear it. Alex would die of humiliation."

Persis smiled broadly. "Maybe I will find a way."

* * *

The next afternoon, Alex came home early. Persis took one look at him and knew something was wrong. His jaw was tight and his eyes were dark brown augurs drilling into her.

"I need to speak with you. If it isn't too much trouble, will you join me upstairs?"

Like a condemned woman in a tumbrel, Persis trailed hopelessly behind him. *What if he knows that I was aware of the hoisting cables for the mine, or that Charlie had them installed?* She could hardly think of it. *He'll kill me. He isn't drunk this time, though,* she reasoned, *so it may not be as bad.*

Irrational ideas pattered quickly through her mind. *If I were to die,* she speculated, *how would my death be explained to my mother? Who would care for the children when it was all over? If only Charlie had more interest in women! At least there would be someplace for Winston and Rose to go.*

Alex closed the bedroom door firmly and came to her, grasping her shoulders and backing her up to the bed. Pushing her down firmly, he made it clear that she was going to have to give some kind of testimony. Stepping away, he put his hands on his hips and faced her squarely.

"I need to hear it from your own lips, Persis. I need to know that it isn't true. Or," he said, clenching and unclenching his fists, "that it is."

Persis swallowed thickly. "What—what have you heard?"

"Oh, yes, that's good. Make me tell it. Then you'll know how much I know and how much I don't." He ran both hands through his hair as he stalked from the dresser to the window. "You are a crafty one, aren't you?"

Yes, she thought, *I am crafty. But this horrid situation has made me that way.* She braced herself for another of Alex's pulverizing monologues.

"Well, you win," he said bitterly. "I have no choice, do I? I am to play the buffoon in our marriage relations, that has been made abundantly clear."

He raised a thick forefinger. "If you have any sense of decency, you will tell me the entire truth. If you even resemble the woman I once thought you were." He set his lips in a firm line. "I saw Baron Coleman at the Virginia Chop House. He asked me if the buggy was running all right. I told him it was fine, but I realized he was referring to a specific incident. He said, 'that was a nasty night for the Missus to be out.'"

Persis was horrified. How could Baron have figured everything out? The buggy had been covered with mud. Her mind darted over the fact that Alex hadn't mentioned the worst transgression of the evening—their outlandish costumes. All she could do was wade through this quagmire cautiously and let Alex reveal what he knew.

"I wasn't alone, Alex," she protested softly. "I was with Mabel—"

"Mabel! Artie has come to his senses and left that strumpet, Persis, when are you going to come to yours? I despise her. I wish she'd join Constance, wherever she is."

Who is this man, she wondered vaguely. Yet here he stands, wondering who *I* have become. How could our marriage have come to this?

"I forbid you to spend one more minute with her," he went on. "Not one more minute!"

"All right," Persis said, not caring whether she lied or told the truth.

"Where in God's name were you, anyway?" His hand thudded on the bed next to her.

Persis took a chance. He seemed genuinely not to know. Perhaps Baron was going to blackmail her at some point with the full story, but she couldn't worry about that now. "We went to a lecture on the Monroe Doctrine," she said calmly. "We did get the buggy stuck on the way home. But it is all fixed."

"I happen to know that the lecture concluded before ten o'clock. Baron said he saw you close to midnight."

"We went to the coffee house," she said evenly. Despite his rising anger, he didn't know everything.

He shouted at her, "What are you up to, for God's sake? Are you out on the streets of this filthy city looking for a paramour? You're probably lying to me even now! How much more clearly can you tell me that you don't care a whit about me or my needs? God in heaven, who have I married, what have I done?"

He grabbed an oil lamp on the dresser and flung it against the wall. The glass chimney shattered and oil spewed everywhere, staining the wallpaper and draperies. Taking Persis by the shoulders, he shook her violently and then pushed her roughly away.

Staggering to the bed, Persis hoped it was over.

He whirled and laid a hand on her arm. Reeling her in, he crumpled her arm up next to his chest so sharply that she cried out. His eyes only a few inches away from her own, he held her completely motionless in an iron grip.

"Don't provoke me, Persis," he snarled. "You have no idea what the word *regret* really means."

He shoved her to the floor with such force that her head snapped back and struck the hardwood.

She tried to rise up on one elbow but was too stunned. Harrowed, she lay there, conscious only of him towering over her. From this angle, his body looked thick and barrel-shaped. The finger he was shaking at her was blunt and fat. Dazed, she stared up at him, watching his lips move. Word fragments came through the cotton-wool of confusion: "Your sense of timing is impeccable . . . most important deal of my career . . . while you make a fool of me . . ."

Had Grace and Nora heard anything? She felt an odd desire for them to know.

"We aren't finished discussing this," he said. He turned on his heel and went out, leaving her on the floor.

*   *   *

It wasn't as bad as some of the other times, she thought, creeping around the room, lowering her head to the floor in order for the sunlight to reveal the tiny, glittering remains of the lamp chimney. If Winston comes in here barefoot, the poor thing! I don't think Alex knows much about that night, thank God in heaven and damn Baron Coleman to hell. The oil on the walls, now that will truly be hard to clean.

When she raised her hand to touch the back of her head, her fingers came away wet with blood. She reached back again and felt a twinge of pain as she traced over the spot. There was a piece of glass imbedded in her scalp.

Startled by a noise behind her, she whirled to a sitting position and faced the door.

It was Grace. "Hush, now, it's not one word I want to hear out o' your mouth," said Grace, bending down. "Empty the glass bits out o' your hand over here, by the baseboard. He's gone. Let me help you up. Here, the chair by the window. Not one word."

Grace moved quickly to the basin and wrung out a white cloth.

"Bend over a wee bit," she said. "There 'tis. Now hold still." A moment later the fragment was out, but the blood was coming stronger. "It'll clot up in a moment," she said. "Hold this cloth on there, tight-like."

Persis wanted to cry, but her eyes were dry as a stone. She watched Grace move efficiently around the room, whisking the glass into a dustpan and blotting the oil spots on the wall.

"God bless you, Grace," was all she could say, and even that came out with a querulous, choking sound.

Grace came back to look at her head. "Come to the kitchen after you've composed yourself, Mistress. We can clean your hair up right nicely, I know." She placed a hand on Persis's shoulder. Persis reached up quickly, without thinking, and clutched Grace's hand. She could not look at her. Now the tears came. She fumbled for the bloodstained cloth.

Grace stood near her a moment more and then said, "You are not alone, Mistress Percy." She walked to the door and turned. "Nora and I have known for a long time," she said simply, and then made her way down the stairs.

*   *   *

"I like your hair that way," Alex said as he poured more coffee into his cup.

Persis reached vapidly for her hair and felt the long curls lying against her collarbone. She was so numb that until that moment, she didn't recall how she had fixed it.

Two days had passed since the incident in the bedroom. Conciliation had begun. She knew the dance. He would lead, she would follow.

Her mind wandered about the room, idly remembering a morning like this last fall when he flew into a rage because his toast was too dark.

"I've been thinking," Alex was saying, "part of the problem in our marriage is our physical separation. In this, I suppose—I suppose I am somewhat to blame. One can't expect to find peace in the kingdom when the king is often absent."

The tinder began to smoke. It was so easy to recoil, to wither secretly away from him. The ugliness between us is so profound, she mused, I can no longer tell right from wrong. Then, from nowhere, a voice echoed in her head. *Keeping your truest self from him will more than likely retard his growth and will without a doubt cause more injury to you.* The voice was Ruby's, from last October's windy night.

Few things were certain, but it was clear to Persis that Alex grew more dependent on her every day. It was as if he were a huge, dark void into which she could throw every atom of herself for the next several centuries.

She shook off the incoherence that had sedated her for the past two days. I must make a bold move toward greater honesty, she vowed. I have no choice. Now is the time.

He was staring at her.

"I—I won't deny that it is quite different when you are not here," she began. "I have had to operate independently in many—household decisions." She paused, collecting a breath. "You know I came to Montana Territory out of love for you. We now have two lovely children. You have been so good to Winston. The ideal picture would be for us to be—together, as a family—"

Girding herself to tell him that the deteriorating reality of their marriage was far from this ideal vision, she put a tender smile on her face and reached out to clasp him lightly on the wrist. Now. Tell him the truth. *Say it.*

But the risk of angering him with the truth became graphically clear. He would shatter the china. He had thrown her against the breakfront once before. That scene, now well-rehearsed, would be played out again. Bile rose in her throat. Sick with fear, she shrank from her task. I can't, she thought wildly, I just can't. Her eyes filled with tears.

Alex picked up her fingers and kissed them. He was clearly taking her tears as a sign of sincerity, even contrition, which pained her near to madness.

How can we perceive this so differently! He is relaxed and almost pliant, she realized, like a man after the spasms of lovemaking. He makes tentative gestures of atonement, expecting me to be impressed and warmly receptive. The tears tumbled down her cheeks as she grieved the wreckage they both persisted in calling a marriage.

Alex pulled a handkerchief out of his pocket and handed it to her. As she gathered it up and touched her cheeks with the soft linen, she noticed that it smelled of white heliotrope.

In an unusually soft voice, Alex began, "Persis, I think if we were together, it might get both of us on the right track. Another baby could be the answer for us. Wouldn't you like that? I haven't always been . . . the model husband. If we were living under the same roof, you could help me . . . be better. All in all, I don't believe Butte is the place for us to raise our family. We belong in Helena, together."

Holding the scented linen to her face, Persis nodded blankly, unable to synthesize the sentimental proposals he was putting to her and the bewildering realization that his handkerchief smelled of another woman's perfume.

He went on to say that he would return to Helena the next morning and would expect her, the children, and the help to follow as soon as possible. "I can even come back down and escort you," he said kindly. "I will do so if you like. You need only telegraph."

Persis watched his mouth moving, but she was thinking of the deed to the Porphyry. She had managed to get a copy of it to Charlie, yes, but she desperately wanted Alex to leave his papers—and the original copy—behind.

When they made their morning farewells, her smile was brittle. How hard he tried today, she thought later. That was the generous, charming Alex I fell in love with. Traces of her old love for him swirled up thickly. She cared for him, yes! But enough to throw her life away? To waste all her years with a violent, misguided profligate?

When she was certain he was gone, she fled to her room and sprawled on the coverlet, sobbing. "What a rotten mess this all is! There are other women; I've known it forever. There were other women before and there are other women now. In a pathetic way I think they added to his appeal. He's a rogue; everyone told me so. I thought he was dashing and exciting. I told myself he'd give it all up for me."

She stopped. "My God, I sound like Bess Daltry!"

She beat on the bed with clenched fists, raging, until she could pound no more. She slept, awoke, and cried again. She rolled over on her back, and for a long while lay still, watching the spring sun make lengthening panels of light on the wall.

Getting up, she dipped a cloth in the ewer and cooled her reddened cheeks. She stared at herself in the glass.

"My life is a lie," she said to her reflection. "I can either continue to collude in this catastrophe or I can do something, anything, to begin changing it."

She ventured a tendril of hope that the Porphyry might be an avenue, however remote, to independence. As she stood there, she became more convinced that this—the daunting, seemingly insuperable journey toward monetary freedom, was a critical first step.

* * *

That afternoon, she felt composed enough to sit in the kitchen with Grace, Nora, and the children. The *Miner* lay on the table in front of her. Able to do little else, she picked it up, reading the news about new machinery at this or that mine, the opening of another badly needed boarding-house, the growing hue and cry for an additional doctor in town, and so on.

On the second page of the paper, toward the bottom, she saw an article with a tiny headline, MEADERVILLE WOMAN PETITIONS FOR DIVORCE. It was the same recurrent, sickening theme. The husband beat and berated her on a near-daily basis. Pregnant with their second child, she had been so brutalized that she miscarried.

What will I do, she pondered, if Alex becomes violent again? What's the matter with me—what I really mean is, *when* he becomes violent again. Each time it happens I look for a route of escape. So far none has presented itself. But that doesn't mean I won't someday find one. What if I ran? What, then, of the children? The consequences were unimaginable, yet the thought flickered like a candle flame in a dark corner of her mind.

While Grace and Nora packed for Helena, Persis went out on errands. As she pushed through the heavy oak and glass doors of the bank, she nearly bumped into Marcus Daly.

"Oh, excuse me!" she said. "Mr. Daly! How are you? Persis MacKinney, in case you have forgotten. I am Charlie Allen's sister."

"Good morning, fair lady. And tell me, how could I possibly have forgotten the likes o' you?" He touched his hat and turned his eyes back toward his path.

In the brief second she had in which to ponder the providential nature of this chance encounter, a thought crossed her mind with lightning speed and she told herself, this was meant to be.

"How are you?" She asked, falling into step beside him. "Lovely day!"

"A blessed day, sure," the Irishman returned. "How are the babes?"

"Very well, thank you." Her lips parted and she paused, lifting her hand as if to reach for his arm.

"Might there be somethin' on your mind?" he asked, slowing his step.

"Well, yes," she said quickly, her heart hammering in her chest. She scrambled for the right words. "I have an idea I'd like to discuss with you. At your convenience, of course."

"An idea." As they continued up Main Street, Persis easily kept pace with the short strides of the mining tycoon. "Might this have somethin' to do with the Emmetts?"

The Emmetts. Her thoughts raced. He meant the Irish-founded Robert Emmett Literary Association. "Oh, the book drive!" she exclaimed with sudden recognition.

"I thought so. You see, I've already spoken with Mrs. O'Shea about it, so it's taken care of."

"Oh, that's lovely. How kind of you to help. But Mr. Daly, this is something else entirely."

His brow furrowed and he eyed her with mild suspicion. "Somethin' else, is't now?"

"Well, yes. It's a business idea. An opportunity, really. It's not something we can really discuss right here. May I make an appointment? Just to tell you about it, and give you time to think it over?" She was astonished at her own audacity.

"Well, we're just about at my office right now. Come along inside, then."

She could scarcely believe what was happening. On this April morning, she was about to make an enormous business proposal, upon which hung the fates of nearly everyone she loved.

Daly ushered her into his office and got straight to the point. "And what is't I might be doing for you this mornin'?" he said with a tone that was both expedient and patient.

Persis told her story as succinctly as possible. Out of propriety, she mentioned her husband, but quickly moved to the topic of the strangely capricious and yet darkly serious night of the poker game in which the Angel had come into her possession. She was careful to detail the meeting with Cyrus Dern several days later and his affirmation that he was willingly parting with the mine. She couched the proposal as delicately as she could, but left no doubt as to her desire to find an investor.

She wove Charlie into the picture too, telling Daly that while she was keenly interested in mining, she wanted to turn the technical aspects of the mine over to her brother. "I trust his judgment," she said finally.

Daly listened to her attentively; after all, the tale was at once peculiarly fascinating and predictably typical of Butte. When she mentioned her faith in Charlie, he nodded.

Her hopes climbed as he rose and walked to the window.

Looking up the hill toward the pounding Anaconda, he asked, "And your husband. What does Mr. MacKinney say about all this?"

She lied. "He thinks it's wonderful. I intend to use my share of the earnings to start a fund for the children." This last was true.

Daly studied her face. He knew full well that MacKinney was becoming a regular consort of Will Clark, toward whom he felt an increasingly bitter antipathy. He scratched his head. Alexander MacKinney didn't seem like the sort of man who would want his wife undertaking a business venture.

"And Charles, why hasn't he mentioned this to me?"

"He has enormous respect for you, Mr. Daly. He would never want to tax your friendship. Even though he has looked at the claim and feels it has potential, he was very hesitant about bothering you. I hope you won't think less of me, but the promise of a possibly lucrative claim has overridden certain of my—sensibilities."

"Mackinney," he mused. "A Scot. There's not a great deal o' love lost between the Irish and the Scots, you know." He gave her a quick smile that almost concealed the seriousness of the remark.

"But," he continued, "if you're a sister to Charles Allen, you've not got Scot blood."

"As my father used to say," Persis responded carefully, remembering one of John Allen's deeply Irish phrases, "a black hen lays white eggs." It was oblique but it was the closest thing she had to a trump card.

Daly's face softened and the corners of his eyes crinkled with memories. "My own Gran used to say the same thing. I will help you," he said with a quiet, self-assured voice that sounded like the rumble of the stamp mills and carried as much portent and power.

"Here are my terms," he began. "I'll give you the ten thousand at seven percent interest. It's to be paid back within three years, and if the mine plays the way I think it will, I want twenty percent of the profits for another three years. After that, you're on your own."

Persis stood stock-still. "You—you will help? Charlie and me? You'll help us! Oh, that's wonderful! You won't be sorry. You won't be!" She restrained the impulse to jump up and down. Instead, she took a step toward him, reached out her hand, and shook his hand firmly, holding herself erect and doing her best to look every inch the sensible businesswoman.

She stood there a moment, looking at this man who had just opened the gateway to her future and wiped away the futility that shrouded her life. It was the greatest chance she had ever been given, and it had nothing to do with Alex.

"I'll draw up the papers," said Daly. "And one more condition. Aside from your good brother Charlie and the . . . esteemed Mr. MacKinney, not a word of this to anyone. It wouldn't be good for either one of us. I won't be bringin' this up, not anywhere. If anyone asks me, I'm going to tell them the deal was struck between your brother and me. Is't a deal we have, then?"

"Yes. I understand," said Persis. Little did he know how desperately she wanted the matter kept quiet.

"We'll set about proving her and go from there. Let us shake hands once more. This means the deal is struck, and on the terms as I've just stated."

He held out his hand. Persis took it again and held it firmly. "Thank you," she said. "You'll not be sorry." She walked out and prayed to God she was right.

* * *

Charlie came by to take them to the stage depot. "How is my little man," he said, scooping Winston up in his arms. "I will be in Helena next month, you know. You'd better play with me, Winston Charles Allen." As he raised the boy over his head, Winston giggled with joy.

Persis held out her hand. In it was a key to the townhouse.

"I don't know why I need this," he said.

"I don't either, but just take it," she answered.

A little more each time she saw him, Persis observed Charlie coming back from the darkness that had enveloped him for so long. He was more interested in Winston than ever, and was clearly affected by the boy's departure for Helena.

"Before you go," he said, taking her aside, "I should tell you, I've taken a closer look at the Porphyry. I went down nearly three hundred feet and I think there's an apex there. A real handsome vein. Minimal silver, though. It's looking like a copper mine. I won't be able to tell you anything more about it until we've sent a few good heaps to the reduction works. But overall, this makes me feel a hell of a lot better about your deal with Marcus."

He stopped and reached out to ruffle his son's hair once more. "You'll be seeing more of me, Percy," he winked at her.

"That would make us all very happy."

* * *

Charlie telegraphed his intentions to come for Rose's first birthday. Although her birthday actually fell on a Wednesday, Alex was planning a large party for the following Saturday night. The guest list was extensive, featuring builders, bankers, mine owners, and ranchers. He had invited Avery, but in yesterday's post there was a message that he was unable to join the festivities. In his note, Avery re-issued his invitation to the Double Diamond, chiding them for waiting so long to return.

Persis wanted to see him. To renew their friendship, yes, but also because she was curious about Emma Fenton and wondered to what stage the courtship had progressed.

Guest list dangling from her hand, she stared across the room and wondered what Emma was like. Tall or short, plump or slender, fair or dark? She must have a good mind, if she is teaching. I would wish nothing less for Avery. She felt a prickle of envy about the fact that Emma was a teacher, a profession that had once held a certain promise for her.

What am I thinking, she scolded herself. Each of them deserves all the happiness in the world.

The list also included prominent Butte businessmen such as Will Clark and A.J. Davis. Scanning the rest of the long column of names, Persis shuddered when she saw Baron Coleman's name written there. She prayed he would not come. Surely she would be held hostage by his knowledge of her actions that night in March. She hated the way he looked at her. His attentions were even more reprehensible because he took care not to notice her whenever Alex was present. Even then, she felt him stealing lubricious glances.

* * *

The small birthday party on Wednesday evening, June 21, was just as she would have wished it. The sun hung copper-gold on the mountainous horizon until well after nine o'clock. Charlie rolled on the lawn with Winston. Ruby, resplendent in a new dress custom-made for her by a Bohemian woman in the Gulch, held Rose close to her bosom for upwards of an hour, reluctantly surrendering her to the other guests.

Alma and John Bradley came too. Even Nora and Grace put on new dresses for the occasion. Nora looked especially pretty, with her thick red hair drawn back in a chignon and her fair coloring accented by the blue of her sprigged muslin dress. Rose romped on a satin comforter while Persis unwrapped her gifts. Late in the evening, when the children's temperaments finally demanded they be put to bed, she turned them over to Grace and Nora and rejoined the guests on the long porch outside the library doors.

Fireflies danced on the night air. From the edge of the lawn came the perfume of peonies and the sugary scent of cut grass. Persis sank onto a cushioned chaise, sighing a private thank-you to Rose for having a birthday at such a lovely time of year.

"You're coming Saturday night, aren't you?" Alex asked the Bradleys.

"We'll be there," said John. "We're not late-stayers, though. You'll have to rely on your other friends to keep you up all night."

"I start thinking about my pillow at nine-thirty every night," said Alma, raising her slender hands up to cover a yawn.

"And what about you, Charlie?" asked Alex.

"You mean when do I start thinking about my pillow?"

"Ha! You know what I mean. A little social life would do you good," said Alex.

"It would be great fun," said Charlie, "but I have a prior commitment. With the Dalys, in fact. You know how these things go."

"What's old Marcus up to?"

"They're having a reception. I believe James Haggin is in town. Somehow I've evolved into his official *aide-de-camp.*"

Persis smiled at Charlie's use of French. Constance lives on.

"I heard Marcus is looking to build a reduction works out west of Butte somewhere," Alex said, looking off into the warm darkness.

"Really?" Charlie said, waving away an insect and then smiling blandly at Alma and John. "Marcus has talked about a number of places to build. Something does need to be done. Everyone in Butte is getting nosebleeds from the smelting fumes. The poor children! I am glad to see Winston and Rose in a better climate. Well," he said, stretching his long legs out in front of him before standing up, "I must be off. I admit, Mrs. Bradley, I have begun thinking of my pillow."

As Persis and Alex closed the front door after the last guest, she wondered what manner of verbal joust had taken place between Charlie and Alex on the veranda.

In the morning, she rose with Alex, who had an early meeting downtown. When he was gone, she went to the kitchen. Nora seemed always of late to be wearing a smile. Another letter had come from Deer Lodge yesterday. Persis wondered if Nora was sending regular letters in response.

I am happy for her, she thought, but if their courtship progresses much further, I'll have to think about finding someone to replace her.

"I see you received a letter from Deer Lodge yesterday," she ventured.

Nora looked up, her eyes darting over Persis's face to glean every shred of meaning.

"Yes, Miss Percy."

Both of the hired women had fallen into the habit of calling her this.

"He's evidently quite smitten with you," Persis said.

Grace watched this exchange, saying nothing.

"He's a fine man, Miss. A girl could do far worse," Nora replied.

"I agree with you one hundred percent," Persis said. "Has there been any discussion of—"

"Marriage?"

"Well, I guess I would start with an engagement. That's what I meant. Has there been any discussion of that?"

"Well, it's a fine thing for me to hope, and it's not misplaced I think my hopes are, because he seems so—true. We had a lovely chat when he came back from the telegraph office that day, you know, last month in Butte." She smiled to herself. "He is a grand fellow, really. But no, as far as wedding talk goes, there has been naught o' that."

"You ought to at least consider that fellow what runs the new stationer's shop," Grace said. "He gives you a nod every time we see him at mass. He's a good Catholic with a fresh start here in Helena. Mark my words, if you end up on a ranch, you'll be old afore your time."

"Old, is't now?" Nora's color rose and her blue eyes flashed. "*Old?* That fellow, the stationer, Mr. Bowen or whatever his name is, he's older than Hayes' goat. Just walkin' to the altar with him would shrivel me. Like a prune, Grace, a prune!"

"Old goat or young goat, a girl who goes to market ought to look them all over, 'tis all," said Grace officiously, picking up a dishtowel and drying a tea cup. "Either way, I suppose you will have the means of settling well."

"Nora," Persis put in, "I just want you to know I wish you every happiness. It may be a little awkward at times, trying to conduct a romance when you are tied to a household such as ours. If you want some time off, you need only ask. I do, however, think it would be best if your outings could be chaperoned until such time as Mr. Burke—Pete—demonstrates his intentions a little more clearly. You'll let me know, won't you, if he asks you to go for a drive or something? We can arrange an escort. Perhaps Molly from the Powers' household. She's sensible and fun too."

She watched Nora, who nodded blankly. She has never been courted, so how could she know anything of this, Persis realized. "At any rate, Nora, if you would like such an arrangement, which I do recommend, will you let me know?"

Nora nodded again, this time with a slight smile. "Thank you, Miss," she said.

"You don't feel that I am interfering, do you?"

"No," came the quiet response, "I am thinking I sure don't. It's fortunate I am to have folks who care."

* * *

Finding a light shawl more than adequate and with parasol in hand, Persis left the house and walked briskly down the hill toward Last Chance Gulch. She had just enough time to stop off at the stock barn before meeting Charlie for lunch at the International.

The mourning doves cooed from the treetops and a meadowlark sat on a gatepost, warbling its summer song. We deserve these serenades after the dues we paid over the winter, she observed gratefully. As she neared the stock barn, she saw Angus shaking hay into the big mangers and spreading it with a pitchfork.

"Why, if it isn't Mrs. MacKinney," he said, opening the broad wooden gate. He pulled off his cap and let the sun shine on his bald head. "How goes it with you?"

"Just fine, Angus," she replied cheerfully. "Alex said you had been up to the Hamilton logging camp with him. How did it go?"

Angus looked at her with what seemed like a trace of surprise but went on quickly, "Good. Good. Lots of timber up there. Plenty of work."

"And the animals here? Is there anyone new?"

"Nae, the same auld folk. And everyone's all right, except for Buzzard. Still cribbing every chance he gets. Look at that fence. He's made a mess of it."

Persis smiled and shook her head. "The hay smells good," she said, walking past Angus to see her favorites, the Percherons.

"Aye, it does," he said, following her at a slight distance.

Inside the barn, Persis saw his breakfast sitting atop a scrap of gingham on a bench and realized she must have caught him just as he was about to sit down. She looked again at the meal he had laid out for himself—a roll and a bit of jerky, some dried apples and a mug of coffee. Angus was a large man, standing well over six feet tall. What lay on the bench was a poor substitute for a morning meal.

She stroked one of the draft horses and stole a casual glance at Angus. As he hung his pitchfork up and bent over to lift a saddle off the floor, she saw that the extra fabric of his trousers was bunched up around the waistline.

"I have interrupted your breakfast," she said quietly.

"I'm in nae hurry. Don't you mind."

"So," she asked, "truly, Angus, how are you?"

He shifted the saddle onto a sawbuck and paused. "Hale and hearty as e'er," he said.

"I think I ought to send some food down to you."

"Times is a bit lean," he said softly. "But I am not complaining."

"Lean?" Persis was baffled. "What are you saying?"

"It's only natural that, with Mr. MacKinney pushing harder on the logging, that this side of his business might require a little tightening here and there."

"Angus, what are you telling me? Have your wages been cut?"

"Well, at least I have the opportunity to go back up to the logging camp and earn a wee bit to make ends meet," he said. "It's nae like I am unfamiliar with the work. That's where he found me two years ago, you know. If it gets real bad I'll go doon to the blacksmith's and help out."

She cast a quick look around. No obvious signs of hunger, but the horses' coats were dull.

It seemed for a moment that the sunlight shimmered more brightly off the water in the trough, the flies buzzed in a strange, murmurous way, and the leaves of the cottonwoods rustled with portent. She felt her world shift half a degree. She remembered the day she first laid eyes on 610 Gilbert and her boldly naïve comment to Alex. *You seem to have spared no expense. I hope it has not put you in an uncomfortable position.* The flicker of annoyance that had passed over his features, melting quickly into an expression of indulgence. *Get that out of your head,* he had said.

Exactly in what state were Alex's affairs? How many card games had taken place since she last saw him? She had ignored Ruby's observation that rumors of his dissipation were rampant in the Gulch.

Despite the warm summer air and the stroking sun, she shivered. Looking down, she saw that she had withdrawn her handkerchief from her pocket and was twisting it into a rope. She stared at it, remembering the heliotrope-scented linen Alex had proffered on the eve of his departure from Butte. What will become of us all?

She turned slowly back to Angus. "Donny will bring you some dinner tonight," she said. Seeing him raise his broad hand to decline, she added firmly, "Not one word of protest."

"Very well," he said softly. "Thank 'ee."

Persis nodded, thinking that she ought to empty her pockets and give him a good portion of the grocery money. "I am leaving you fifteen dollars to get some more hay for the animals," she announced, "and a bit of grain, if you can. Will you please take care of it?"

"Thank 'ee," was all he said.

She picked up her parasol. Angus moved quickly to the gate to open it for her. Their eyes met.

"Everything will be all right," she said.

"Aye, it shall. God's hand is in it all," he replied, nodding.

She slipped out and went down the gently sloping path toward the heart of Helena. The Gulch wasn't quiet; the freight business with Butte was still very active. But today, it seemed that for every MacKinney wagon she saw, there were five Gilmer wagons. She wished she had not noticed.

She walked into the lobby of the International and asked the clerk to ring for Charlie Allen.

"He's in the dining room, ma'am," said the clerk. "Just over there, to your left."

"I enjoy Winston more and more, Percy," Charlie said as she sat down and arranged her skirts. "I hope someday to be able to provide a good home for him. I even think that in a year or so I may just hire a housekeeper. But then again, I don't want him growing up thinking that she is his mother. It's a difficult thing to arrange. You know how much I appreciate—"

"Don't even say it, Charlie." Then she said the same thing she had said to Angus. "Everything will be all right. Do you mind if we talk business for a few minutes?"

"Fine. I'll eat and you talk."

"That will do for a few minutes, I suppose, but I want your reaction to a few things." She caught the attention of the waiter and ordered a pot of tea.

Charlie swallowed a bite of biscuit. "Persis," he said in low tones, "sometimes I wonder if it isn't the wrong thing for us to be—creating a sort of family business, just you and me."

Having come from a discomfiting visit with Angus and sensing ominous change pile up like a thunderhead in the June sky, Persis did not welcome Charlie's reluctance. She steeled herself and prompted him. "What bothers you most?"

"There are a lot of things that go on, Percy. Things you know nothing about. Let me just say it's harder than you realize for me to move between my world and yours."

"Does this have something to do with the little comments you and Alex made to one another on the porch last night?"

Charlie rubbed his brow. "We don't really need to go into the details. What concerns me most is that you and I—well, our little clandestine operation is one thing. It is a worry. It's probably tops on your list of worries. But I have many, and they are bigger than the Porphyry, believe it or not. I can't—" He stopped and rubbed his forehead again.

"You can't what?"

"Do I have your word, Persis, that you will not tell Alex any of what I am about to say?"

Persis drew her head back slightly. It was usually she who scurried through the day arranging which information would be made available to her husband. She felt the bond between her and Charlie knit up more tightly. The fact that not everyone succumbed to Alex's hypnotic charm was terribly reassuring.

She looked at him and nodded slowly. "You have my word."

"Well, here it is: You have no idea how polarized things are becoming in Butte. Marcus spends more and more time in a complete huff about what he reads in the *Miner*. He's fit to be tied. He absolutely cannot stand the sight of Will Clark. I sometimes wonder, Percy, if Marcus wasn't partly motivated by his animosity toward Clark in his decision to finance the Porphyry."

"What on earth does that mean?" Persis asked incredulously. How could she, a relative ingenue only lately arrived in the Territory, be caught up in an economic and political feud?

"Even though things are booming out here, it's still a small world in which everyone knows everyone else's business. It's not like life back in the States, you know that. Even if we achieve statehood, things will still be provincial, at best, for a long time. At any rate, with everyone able to look in everyone else's back yard, well, Marcus is no fool. He knows Alex is in thick with Clark. He's scheming, Persis. Everyone's scheming. Marcus wants desperately to get the upper hand with Clark, and you can bet Clark spends just as much time cogitating on how to do exactly the same thing. Do you see what I am driving at? It wouldn't surprise me one bit to find—although we will probably never know—that Marcus partnered with you to get at Alex. Even a little coup like that would bind up his pride."

As Persis shook her head, he lifted his coffee cup. "I may be wrong, but I don't think so. The tension in Butte is as thick as the fumes. Thicker, really. You have no idea."

"Marcus is looking for a way to create his own empire that will be connected to Butte and yet separate," he continued. "Whatever gossip Alex heard about Marcus wanting to build a smelter out of town was true. But no one is supposed to know that. Do you see what is going on here? The fact that Alex had that information paints a very clear picture of how enmeshed he is becoming in this intrigue. I am surprised he said anything about it at all. But we all know that Alex is the consummate negotiator. I can't help thinking that he was fishing for information, and that he and Clark may be forming a little war council of sorts."

Persis mulled this over. It was obvious that Alex's attention was shifting away from his role at the bank and from the express business. Many of his recent decisions had not seemed exceptionally prudent, but what did she know of his business? She had taken only a few risks in life, while Alex prospered through gambling of all kinds.

Would he, would *they* be better off if he became Clark's lieutenant? She almost wished for the old days of the Utah and Northern construction and the familiar challenges of obtaining subsidies. At least their lives would have some measure of predictability.

These thoughts, whipped into a frenzy by the discovery of unwelcome change at the stock barn, flew at her like hornets. She poured her tea and stared at it.

"Now, don't you be worrying about all this. I probably shouldn't have told you," said Charlie, eyeing her.

Persis let out a sardonic laugh. While she had only a hazy grasp of Butte's political machinery and how it affected Charlie, she was even more in the dark concerning matters at stake in her own life. The irony was superb. Once she started laughing, she could not stop. She held her napkin to her lips as her sides quaked and her eyes watered.

"What is the matter with you?" Charlie said, looking furtively around.

"God in heaven," she said, her laughter subsiding. "We have our hands full, that's all I can say."

Then she felt a different kind of tears prick at the corners of her eyes. She picked up her spoon and tried to stir down both the tea leaves and the emotion welling up inside her.

"I won't say anything, Charlie," she said, her eyes still downcast. "I know Alex is enamored of Will Clark. I don't care for the man, but he and Alex are as thick as thieves. What you have told me is probably true. I suppose there are hundreds of people like us who are either going to be directly or indirectly affected by what happens between Daly and Clark over the next few years."

"I don't like Clark either," Charlie said. "He's extremely intelligent, but it's a shrewd kind of intelligence with none of Marcus's benevolence. I don't see that changing. I can't picture Will Clark sitting down on the edge of a board sidewalk and swapping stories with one of his poor Cornish muckers. Can you?"

"No, I can't."

"Marcus does that sort of thing everyday. He's a good man, Persis, and whatever happens, I am going to line up with him. You know that."

"Of course."

"I predict that one of the first things we are going to see happening is a second newspaper," Charlie said with a smile. "Then they can lob ink at one another by the barrel."

"Let's just hope we can avoid becoming cannon fodder," said Persis.

23

With more feeling than cognition, Persis knew it would not be long before she and Alex had some kind of ugly disagreement. As far as Rose's birthday party was concerned, he didn't really care about Helena's elite coming to pay their respects to his year-old daughter. He wanted an occasion, a venue where he might launch himself on a new tide.

The night the Bradleys and Ruby came for Rose's birthday, as Alex observed Charlie rolling unselfconsciously on the grass with Winston, Persis saw lines on his face that spoke of consternation and alienation. He lives a lonely life, she thought as she left the International Hotel and climbed the hill toward home, and so do I. Two people united in the closest bond with which God can bless them, yet separated by a chasm.

She would participate as much as possible in the planning for the party. She had already hired extra help for the evening—housemaids to walk through the crowd with canapés and pour wine into freshly-emptied goblets. She would dress up, and dress Rose up as well, and they would promenade as a proper mother-daughter vignette.

But one more secret had stolen into the widening space between her and her husband: she had quit drinking. Thursday afternoon, she set about making a port-colored concoction of strained lemonade and blackberry juice. This will be my new cordial, she vowed. Perhaps I will tell him after the party is over.

* * *

"Tell me the menu again," Alex asked her.

"Oysters, cucumbers in vinaigrette, smoked turkey and trout, cheddar cheese and farmer's cheese in French pastry, pickled watermelon rind, three different kinds of cakes, and date-filled cookies," Persis reported. She followed him as he checked the ice chest and made notes in his leather-bound book.

When he was finished, he took her hand. "Come with me." He led her into the library, where she sat down in the chair she used for needlework. "What are you wearing tomorrow night?" he asked, moving toward his desk.

"I—I was thinking either the pale blue taffeta, you know, the one with the indigo velvet, or the green silk."

"What about the one you got in New York? You know, before Rose was born. It's a sort of dark gold color, as I recall."

"Oh. Well, yes. It's rather dramatic," she said tentatively. "For the opera, if we went to Denver or San Francisco." It was a ball gown with a deep neckline, not something a young mother ought to wear at her daughter's first birthday party.

"You wore it to the Governor's ball last year, I believe. Yes, I remember you did," he said. "You know how much I like you in that dress."

"Well, of course, I shall wear it—if you think it wouldn't be too dark for a summer event," she appealed to his vigorous sense of fashion.

"Let me show you, darling, why I think that would be the best. Close your eyes."

Persis stared. What is he up to? He was looking at her with that familiar, playful smile moving about the corners of his mouth and the penetrating gaze that still, despite the strange alienation that permeated their relations, stepped up the frequency of her heartbeat. Smiling back, she slowly closed her eyes.

She heard a desk drawer open. He was such a mercurial man; it was incredibly difficult to know what he was about. He was coming across the room. She heard him set something down on the windowsill behind her. Then she sensed his hands and suddenly felt something pleasantly cool on her neck. Jewelry.

"Keep your eyes closed. I am just going to walk you over to the looking-glass." He held her and directed her steps.

Persis tried to get to the glass as quickly as possible. She tripped on the Turkish rug, but he caught her and positioned her before the glass. "All right, open your eyes."

She did, and saw around her neck a fabulous necklace encrusted with warm-hued topazes.

"Well? What do you think?"

"It's unbelievable! Surely you didn't find this in Helena."

"Never mind where I bought it. I bought it for you, and I want you to wear it tomorrow night. Do you like it?"

"How could any woman in her right mind not be thrilled with such a piece?" As she slipped her arms around his neck and stared into his eyes, thoughts of how easy it once had been between them flooded into her head and made a tiny furrow between her brows.

"What was that?" he asked, looking hurt.

"Oh, Alex! It is lovely and you are lovely to have done it. I just— want everything to be all right between us."

"It has been for some time now, hasn't it? I am trying to have faith. Do you have faith?"

"I do, Alex. It has been better this last while."

After their lovemaking, Persis lay in bed looking at the ceiling and listening to the wind in the spruce trees. There had been many tender moments in this bedroom, but it also held black memories of punishment and despair.

For so long, her fervent, positive spirit had overcome the darkness. Now the scales seemed to be tipping of their own accord, forcing her to look differently at her world. It was like watching the sun rise, yet wanting it to stay below the horizon. At least I am not under the influence of alcohol, she thought in the quiet dusk. Then how much more baffling this would be!

* * *

There were musicians on the porch, playing Schubert. Paper lanterns, emitting a mother-of-pearl light, were strung throughout the garden and along the lilac hedge. As the hours passed, the lanterns became tiny moons floating on the night air. Perfuming the house and porch were at least a dozen huge vases of flowers—peonies, irises, and tall blue spikes of delphinium.

Rose, who was tiring quickly, fretted in Persis's aching arms. She wanted to greet everyone at least once, even if only in a fleeting way, before the child grew too irritable. She tarried as long as she could in her conversation with Alma.

"It is so wonderful to be back here, Alma, I can't tell you," she said, kissing her friend's smooth cheek.

"I wonder who missed the other one most," said Alma. "There aren't many women in Helena I can really talk to. Let's start some kind of project so that we can reinstate our weekly visits."

"I would like that," Persis said. Rose batted the air between the two women, then began clutching at the new necklace.

"That is a fabulous necklace," Alma said. "New?"

"Yes. From Alex. It's important to him that I look as splendid as possible. Between the jewels and the gown, I feel rather overdone."

"You do look splendid, and Helena is grateful to you. What would we all do if we didn't have the MacKinneys to show us the true meaning of style?"

"I thank you for that compliment, but there are others here who take style even more seriously. Will Clark, for example," she said, nodding her head in the direction of the impeccably-dressed mining magnate, who was standing near the champagne table with Alex and Baron Coleman.

"Will and Alex," she added with a laugh, "seem to have an ongoing contest—a good natured one, I confess—to see who can sport the most elegant waistcoat and the heaviest cufflinks."

"I had heard that about Clark. I must say, he is an odd-looking man. So slight of build and such piercing, cold eyes. Not the type I would warm up to, really."

"I know what you mean," said Persis, glancing toward the men. Unfortunately, she did so just as Baron Coleman turned to look at her. She jerked her head away, then wished she had not been so obvious.

Alma saw the interaction. "And I am not certain I like that other fellow either," she said, "although he certainly appears warmly disposed toward you."

"You have no idea," Persis murmured, just loudly enough for Alma to hear. "He is a scoundrel."

"Yes, we need to take up something together," said Alma lightly.

"Perhaps you've been harboring a desire to do new seat covers for all ten of the dining room chairs?"

"How did you know?" Persis gave her a grateful smile.

Finally, Nora appeared and whisked Rose away, consoling her with a pastry.

Stretching her stiffened arms, Persis went first to the kitchen for a long drink of water and then to the ice-box for her bottled cordial. Passing a mirror on the way, she caught sight of herself. I do look good, she thought. The topaz necklace draped well around her neck and accented her collarbone, while the center stone pointed straight toward her bosom.

Back on the lawn with her faux cocktail in hand, she could tell by Alex's frequent, appraising looks that he was pleased. The two of them joined hands and made careful rounds of the entire assembly.

It was near midnight. If Alex had not spent so much on canapés and champagne, she thought, the crowd would have thinned by now. But Alex, holding a near-empty glass of whiskey, was feeling his oats. She began to feel the brittle strangeness of being the only sober member of an inebriated group. The jests grew lame and the guests' faces looked ruddy and swollen.

Returning to Alex's side, she whispered, "You continue to hold an enthralled court out here, but I really must go sit down inside. It's midnight and I am quite fatigued."

"I think I saw some people leaving," he whispered back.

He is at least close to the same mind as I am, she thought, entering the dark, oak-paneled hallway, which was lit only by a pair of candelabra on the post-table.

At the base of the staircase, a figure appeared out of the darkness.

"Good evening, Mrs. MacKinney," came a rasping, slow voice. "Or may I call you Persis?"

She froze.

"Oh, you are still here, Mr. Coleman?" she replied casually. "I see some of our guests are at last drifting down the hill toward their homes."

"I couldn't leave until I had one last moment of your pleasant company," said Baron. "Can't you call me Baron?"

His face and physical form were not unattractive, but Persis could not see him as anything but repulsive. His thick lips and cheeks were reddened from drink. His eyes were directed at her necklace and the gems that hung pendulously above the cleft between her breasts. She watched his gaze travel across her bosom and down the tight bodice.

"I hope you have enjoyed yourself," she said sarcastically. "Now, if you will excuse me."

Coleman raised his hand and stroked her bare upper arm, murmuring, "My dear—"

Recoiling, Persis spun away. Thank God, here was Alex coming in from the lawn, with a few of the late-stayers following him.

She ignored Baron as he slapped Alex on the back. After making weary goodbyes to the last handful of guests, she walked toward the stairs and asked Grace to tell Alex that she had retired.

Once she reached the halfway landing, she felt safe. She wanted to bathe away Baron's oily touch, but was far too tired. As she entered the bedroom, the memories that dwelled there rose like a cold luminescence over a churchyard. *Safe,* she thought. What does that mean?

* * *

On Monday, Alex announced his plans to travel back to Butte. "You mustn't worry, though. I'll only be gone two or three days," he said. "I'm finalizing some plans with Will."

Persis nodded blandly. A veil of secrecy lay over the plans Alex and Will Clark were forming. "It was so kind of him to come all the way to Helena for Rose's party," she said. "I was glad to finally meet him."

"Well, first I am off to a meeting with Paul Gilmer. I can't imagine what he wants. Perhaps another wagon race?" He barked out a short laugh, picked up his hat and strode down the hallway toward the back door.

* * *

Alex let his horse amble slowly south along the ridge above Last Chance Gulch, speculating about the meeting with Gilmer. They had been arch-rivals for years, masking friction beneath a veneer of goodwill. Both men knew their businesses would suffer if they openly maligned one another, so gentlemanly conduct prevailed.

His mood was one of mild excitement. He usually felt especially robust after giving a good party. Furthermore, while his career with Sam Hauser was nearing an end, things were going very well with Clark, and an easy transition appeared imminent.

Life at home is also going better, too, he reflected. Persis seemed to have calmed down a good deal. Getting her out of Butte was an absolute necessity. The place is the "perch of the devil," as they say. Colorful, yes, but far from a positive influence on a woman of Persis's upbringing. And I am glad to have her away from the wanton leverage of that scarlet Mabel Trask!

His fears about Persis's waywardness had risen to a panic after the report he received from Baron Coleman about the buggy. He remembered little of his confrontation with her in their bedroom at the townhouse, but he knew he had hurt her.

What she does not understand, he brooded, was how much she continually hurt *him* with her flagrantly discourteous behavior. The thought of it filled him with an engulfing black dread. She is a bright woman, yet she doesn't see how damaging her actions are to me, to us!

The idea of allowing Persis free rein to do as she saw fit, either in her associations or pursuits outside the home, was not something he could even consider. This would be morally wrong. He had waited many years to marry the right woman. The women in his past had not stood by him during difficult times, when his fortunes flagged and made him unable to keep them in baubles. He owed it to both himself and Persis not to let her naïve conceit and impulsiveness ruin their chances at happiness.

His mind darted back to their courtship. The thought of a future with the lovely Persis Allen, with him presiding magnanimously over their marriage, had been such a happy vision. He winced. How differently things had turned out!

Still, all was not lost. Persis clearly wanted to please him, and on this he based his ongoing faith. It was up to him to channel her energy. When she taunted him by doing things to threaten the stability of their family, it was really a means of exercising the guile so common to women. If only she wouldn't force me to discipline her, he thought, shaking his head with renewed anxiety. She truly leaves me no choice in those miserable situations. Although she has not, thank

God, betrayed me in the literal sense, her willfulness requires an increasingly firm hand.

The very idea of her abandoning him, not standing alongside him through life's straits and strictures, made him feel as though he were teetering on a dark, gaping void. He shifted his thoughts. Things are going better for us now, he averred. I know she is in earnest.

A plain-looking woman walked by, pushing a perambulator. Her husband is a lucky fellow, Alex thought, tipping his hat. Not that I want a homely wife! But certainly plainer in her ambitions. Perhaps there will be another child for Persis and me. I wonder if she could possibly have already conceived? God knows our relations have been frequent enough these last six or seven weeks.

At Clore Street, he shook himself, scattering his concerns into the atmosphere. Spurring the black into a trot, he turned east and dropped down the steep street toward the Gulch. As he passed Joe's Coliseum, he thought of the heavily draped alcoves alongside the ballroom floor where a man could conduct private business with Joe's above-average girls.

He smiled. The poor whores of Clore. Someday, he speculated, he would no longer need this kind of outlet. Yet many men continue this throughout their married lives, he observed. As long as I am discreet, then no difficulty or pain will come of belonging to this fraternity. When he spied another member of the Board of Trade at the Coliseum, he said nothing. It was as if the encounter had never happened. That was the way it was handled.

Alex came out of Gilmer and Salisbury's office twenty minutes later, laughing scornfully. Shaking with fury, he leaped effortlessly onto his horse.

"Who do those bastards think they are," he muttered, wheeling the animal around and digging his spurs roughly into its flanks. "It'll be a cold day in hell before I accept a deal like that." Clods of muddy earth flew up from the black's hooves, pelting the sidewalk and striking the glass door of the Gilmer and Salisbury Freight Office.

* * *

Avery swung his left leg up, crossed it over the saddle, and began to rub his knee. He was tired. Their modest trail ride from Flathead Lake to the Sun River range had been harder than usual because of the rain. June in Montana can be heaven or it can be a soggy kind of purgatory, he thought, and this June has definitely been the latter. He let go of the sore knee and rested his hands lightly on the pommel of his saddle.

He and his horse stood on a high ridge less than five miles from the small city of Deer Lodge. He could see the tall cottonwoods clumped around the community and the evening sunbeams splaying on the valley floor. He thought he could see the June hayfields west of the Clark Fork, but he wasn't sure.

Hearing Pete and Sparky coming up behind him, he settled back into the stirrups. They would get back to the Double Diamond in time for the Fourth of July. He knew Pete planned to visit Helena and Nora O'Brien. Avery liked seeing the expression on Pete's face when he returned from the Deer Lodge Post Office. And he himself didn't mind getting information about how Persis and her little family were doing.

At long last, he felt he had reached a kind of comfortable neutrality toward her. They were friends, he had concluded, good friends. He wondered if the MacKinneys would take him up on his invitation to come to the Double Diamond this summer.

As the horses clip-clopped wearily down the hill, his mind wandered east to the Gallatin Valley and to Emma Fenton. She was a fine woman, he reflected, thinking of her firm, slim waist, her fair hair, and blue-gray eyes. With a fine mind, too. A wave of loneliness surged up.

Natural enough, he thought. I'm close to thirty and I ought to be thinking along the lines that Pete is thinking. I'll telegraph Emma as soon as I get back to Deer Lodge. We need to talk about the future.

As he pulled his collar up against the evening breeze, Persis came back into his mind. Another time, another place—who knows what might have been.

*   *   *

Within two days of their return, Pete insisted Avery come out and look at the stakes he had driven into the ground in Yellow Rock Meadow. "This will be the kitchen, right here," said Pete, waving his arm wide. "And there'll be a window over there, a big one, so she can look out over the creek toward the mountains."

As they outlined the house with their steps, Avery smiled. Pete was clearly thinking about the layout from two points of view. If I had a daughter, he thought, that's the kind of husband I'd want for her.

"And look here," Pete was saying. "She will always be able to look out this side window here, or the windows of the front room, and see the big house, so she'll never feel lonely."

"You're pretty sure of her, Pete?" Avery asked.

"Well, I'm going to give her a ring as soon as I find one. That's pretty sure, isn't it?"

"You're pretty sure your affections are returned, is what I am saying."

Pete leaned over to push a stake more firmly into the ground, then looked up. "Well, if I'm not to her liking, I'll find out soon enough, won't I? But I think I am." He dusted his hands. "She always looks real happy when I show up. She has the prettiest smile I've ever seen."

* * *

"Nora? *Our* Nora?"

"Yes, Alex, our Nora. Nora O'Brien," Persis said, trying not to laugh.

"Pete Burke, at the Double Diamond?"

"The very same. She's going to the band concert with him tonight. I have given her the night off."

She remembered Thanksgiving at the Double Diamond and Alex's obvious suspicion that there was some kind of flirtation between herself and Pete. But Pete never had eyes for anyone but Nora.

Alex wiped carriage wax off his hands with a rag. "Well. That will mean we'll have to find someone new."

"It's all right. I have a list started. She'll be hard to replace, but we mustn't stand in her way."

"Well," Alex said again, "most of the Irish domestics I have met seem quite well-suited to a rustic lifestyle. She'll survive."

Persis looked around, hoping that Grace and Nora were out of earshot.

"I suppose," was all she said.

"What will this mean if we go to the Double Diamond in August?"

"Are we to go?" Persis asked, rummaging more deeply through her tambour.

"I have been thinking along those lines, yes. But we'll need Nora.

She wouldn't be larking off with him, would she, if we brought her along? I'd like to organize a fishing or shooting party."

"Oh, of course, that would be great fun," said Persis, "and you know as well as I that Nora's first sense of duty is to us. For now, at least."

As always, their social life was arranged primarily for Alex's entertainment. At least at the Double Diamond there would be the creek, the horses, and, she hoped, some conversation with Avery. Something to look forward to in a life that seemed increasingly desultory. For Alex, she noted, the fascination with their repetitious social activities continued.

It had been a difficult month for him, she knew. Gilmer and Salisbury had offered to buy MacKinney Freighters. He had come home in a rage, his horse lathered and wet. "Who do they think I am," he scoffed, "that I would just surrender the efforts of seven—no, it is nearly eight—years into their clumsy hands!"

Now it was mid-July. Alex had soothed his wounded pride with a new phaeton and was now talking about a visit to the Double Diamond. Peace prevailed, at least for now.

"Nora's heart is drifting away from us," said Persis, "but I think she'll be so thrilled to be at the Double Diamond—if we do go—that she will enjoy her duties more than usual. She may be animated, but she is steady."

"Well, I'll have to talk to the other fellows. They'll be over here tomorrow night, by the way. Don't trouble yourself. The usual fare will be fine."

Persis smiled. This moment is as good as any other, she thought, her heartbeat picking up.

"Alex," she said, committing herself, "I should like to stop drinking spirits for a while. For my health."

Once she had said it, a weight was lifted from her. What magic comes from honesty! Let this be a new beginning for me, she vowed, readying herself for his reaction.

He was pulling a slender book from the shelf, a motion that was always followed by pouring a drink. At her announcement, he stopped and turned stiffly around, a slow smile spreading over his face. He continued looking at her steadily, the smile growing broader. "Are you trying to tell me something?"

"Oh! Oh, no, Alex. I am afraid that is not the reason. At least," she added, as demurely as possible, "not at this time."

His smile faded. He removed the stopper from the crystal decanter. "I see," he said. "Let me understand you, then. You want to stop drinking alcohol for your health, you say?"

"Yes."

"Then when we are together of an evening, such as tonight, you will not be joining me in a drink."

"Not an alcoholic drink, no. That is my intention," she said evenly.

"Have it your way, then," he said simply, sitting down on the couch.

His coolness was no surprise. She set about unwinding a skein of yarn and began working it into the design of the chair covers.

Alex picked up his novel and began reading. He took large sips of his drink and within twenty minutes had poured himself another. Tension lay thick on the air. Finally, he set down his glass and said, "Let's go for a drive in the new phaeton."

They went two or three miles west of town, toward Fort Harrison. MacDonald Pass rose dark and rugged in the distance. They got out to walk along the creek, which was lined on either side with enormous, flat granite boulders that stood ten or fifteen feet above the water.

Alex slumped against a pillar of rock, avoiding her gaze.

"How are you, Alex?" she asked over the sound of the rushing water.

For the first time of the outing, he looked at her. "What does this mean, Persis?" he asked. "What do you mean to do?"

Persis felt a layer of cold air from the stream snake up around her ankles. "You are asking me what it means that I choose not to drink," she said.

He stared at her, his eyes dark and wounded.

"It is not something I am doing to hurt you. It is a choice I am making for my health, much as a person would commit to taking daily walks, or something of that nature."

"How could you have chosen this time to do something so divisive?" he asked. "Now, when my business is so full of change—and yet when things have been improving between the two of us. You just don't seem to be able to let things alone."

Persis took in each subtle muscular movement in his cheek, every bit of agitation in his hands. She didn't like being so near the edge of the rocks. What future could she possibly create with Alex that would not be constantly fraught with mortal fear?

She went to him. "I am still here, Alex. Please don't worry so."

Straightening up, he took her roughly in his arms, burying his face in her hair. "You mustn't do anything that will drive us apart," he said hoarsely. "The consequences of that—neither of us should contemplate."

Despite this threat, she kept her arms around him. She had always been willing to throw her beliefs over in the face of his opposition, but now, from somewhere, came the ability to forbear. "Everything is going to be all right," she said, increasing the firmness of her embrace and breathing evenly. They stood together in the dusk, with the glacial water rushing past them and the nighthawks reeling in the pale sky.

24

$\mathbb{C}$harlie came at the end of July. He was in high spirits, having just completed plans for a network of adits to follow an exceptionally rich drift of chalcocite, a copper ore, at the Anaconda. They would reach six hundred feet by next spring.

Pleased with the drawings, Marcus had sent him off to Helena to spend a few days with his son.

"Marcus told me to give you his regards," Charlie said.

"He is a dear," answered Persis. "I wish he wouldn't let Will Clark upset him so." She rocked Rose in the porch swing Angus had built, while Charlie rolled a ball back and forth in the grass with Winston.

"Is Clark really that much of a threat?" she asked. "It seems to me there is enough silver and copper in The Hill to keep them both happy, with a few slag piles left over for the small owners like us."

"The daggers are drawn, Persis. As we speak, Daly is in Missoula meeting with lumbermen and the Northern Pacific Railroad. They are forming a partnership to log the railroad's land grants."

After Nora came out to fetch Winston for his lunch, Charlie came up on the porch and sat down on the wicker sofa.

"Marcus knows that Clark is expanding his contracts and creating joint ventures with small logging companies like Alex's. Both Clark and Daly need all they can get, and between the two of them it appears they're going to gobble up the forests from here to Canada. You have no conception. It is utterly phenomenal."

Persis knew the volume of lumber was enormous. She had seen

the wagons rolling down from the North and had wondered how many of the raw, damp planks had come from Alex's operation in the Bitterroot.

Leaning forward, Charlie added, "And Persis, trust me. You don't know the half of it."

"I'm sure I don't. And who is going to supply me with at least one half, pray tell? Don't be evasive."

"Well, you know this recent talk about building a smelter? It's reaching a fever pitch. Clark openly referred to James Haggin as a 'foreign Turk who tells Marcus Daly what to do and when.' What affected Marcus even more was an article in the *Miner* implying that he himself was no more than a 'eunuch in a sultan's palace.'"

Persis winced. She wondered what kinds of conversations Alex had been privy to.

"Marcus's principal disadvantage," Charlie continued, "is not having a big enough smelting operation to manage the stuff coming out of the Anaconda and the St. Lawrence, not to mention all his other holdings. Marc's still sending his ore overseas, while Clark has two huge reduction works right in Butte."

"But I heard Marcus is doing a lot of smelting locally."

"Clearly not enough. The cost of sending ore to Wales is astronomical. When the stuff is finally refined and hits the market, Marc and his partners are seeing a very poor share of the profits."

"What you are saying is that our benefactor is going to build his own reduction works."

Charlie smiled. "Well, yes. But—"

"But what?"

"Marcus isn't just going to build a new reduction works. He's going to build a new city."

A wagon rolled past just as Charlie was speaking. Persis was certain the rumble of the wheels had made her misunderstand him.

"What?"

"I said, Marcus is going to build a new city. And if you breathe a word of this to anyone—"

"I swear I won't! A *city*? You say that as if he was going to build a new outhouse this Friday! What does this mean?"

"Every bit of greenery in Butte has perished. Cats are dying from licking the ammonia deposits off their whiskers. Then you throw in the fact that there's no room to build anything anymore because you'd have to build on your neighbor's claim."

"You don't have to convince me!" Persis slapped the cushions. "Go on."

Charlie took a deep breath. "You can't utter a word of this, especially not to Alex. Speaking of Alex, after we're done with this topic, I want to know when you plan to tell him about the Porphyry. We can't keep on like this." He looked at her intently.

"Well, go on. Then we'll talk about it." Persis's lips twisted in a brief moue of discontent.

"You can't have a reduction works without water," Charlie resumed, lowering his voice to a near-whisper. "There is a stream south of Deer Lodge called Warm Springs Creek. It's about twenty-five miles west of Butte. I've seen the plat maps. This is really going to happen."

"Has he bought the land?"

"He has just begun the process of selecting the right property and finding out who the owners are. Much of it is grazing country. Construction will probably begin in the spring."

Persis's mind traced the countryside west of Butte, thinking of the Double Diamond. With relief, she remembered that Warm Springs Creek was far to the south of the Burke brothers' ranch.

"But," she began, "what's to prevent this new city from becoming another Butte?"

"The smelter's chief feature will be a huge smokestack that will bear the fumes upward and release them so high that the westerly winds will disperse them. It's a proven design."

Fascinated, Persis listened as Charlie explained the details. She was especially glad to hear that a short railroad would run ore cars back and forth, which meant that the Porphyry could still ride on the coattails of Daly's prosperity.

When conversation finally reached a lull, she knew it was time to address the subject of Alex.

"Charlie, a little while ago here on this porch you said to me, 'you don't know the half of it.' Well, if you can possibly accept the fact that you don't know the half of my marriage—" Feeling her throat thicken, she looked away.

Charlie was silent. "I suppose I don't," he said at length. As Persis turned her face back to his, he saw the pain in her eyes. "Percy—"

He awkwardly began rolling Winston's ball across the sofa cushions, then looked up at her. "Is this something I should know about?"

"Someday I will tell you more. But let me try to address your concerns about the Porphyry, at least a little. I want very much to tell Alex. I know it would be the best thing for all of us. He is a . . . strict man, Charlie. He believes the scope of my activities should be quite small, completely confined to our home."

Charlie nodded, his eyes averted.

"I keep hoping he will begin to feel more comfortable with some of my interests. I make progress with him in small steps."

"And if you should make no progress with the topic of the Porphyry? What then?"

"I just don't know. If he finds out—I mean, when he finds out that it has been in operation most of this summer, he may insist that I sell it. Or turn it over to him in some legal fashion." She blinked as tears wetted the corners of her eyes.

"I think he is enough of a gentleman to see that you are compensated. I am sure he would give you the opportunity to retain an interest in it."

She bit her lower lip to stop its quivering. It was impossible for her to imagine relinquishing the Porphyry to anyone. It was equally impossible for her to imagine that Alex's reaction to this news would unfold in the calm, businesslike fashion she had just described to her brother.

Charlie, not quite satisfied, puffed out his cheeks and exhaled. "I must trust your judgment in this," he said.

Persis mustered a smile. "It is my goal to tell him before September." Suddenly she felt that telling Alex was not something she would be doing for him, it was something she would be doing for herself.

* * *

Two days remained before the MacKinney household's departure for the Double Diamond. Persis was laying out her clothes and trying not to think about the carriage-load of guests, all invited by Alex, who would arrive at the Ranch in their wake.

Fortunately, most of the cowboys were on the Sun River range, so Avery would be able to offer expanded accommodations in the bunkhouse. Alex's friends, a party of six, thought this would be great fun.

Persis chafed at the idea of a large group, believing that her family plus one domestic was enough of a troupe. She hinted to Alex that they ought not impose so heavily on Avery. He scoffed. "With events of this nature, it's always better to have as many as one can. It'll be far more memorable that way. You'll see. And it isn't as though the Burkes don't have the space."

He went on, "Just because your piety—excuse me—your health has dictated that you no longer drink with me doesn't mean that we all must jump on your wagon with you."

This silenced her. She went about her work that day, steeling herself and hoping that the temper of their stay might fall short of hedonic. Most distressing was the fact that Alex's guest list included Jack Hascombe, who regularly fueled Alex's fears about having a "perverse" wife, and the undesirable Baron Coleman. Persis schemed as to how she would repel the latter if there were any scenes similar to the one at Rose's birthday party.

It was hot. As she spread out and prepared to fold the proper clothing for the trip, she picked up a magazine and fanned herself. The first few days of August had been unbearable and there was no sign of cooler weather. Wading in the Clark Fork at the Double Diamond was a heavenly idea.

Still, I'll need a shawl for the evenings, she reminded herself. As she lifted one from her bureau, she saw Mabel's split skirt, which she kept concealed at the bottom of the deep drawer.

Alex will be off shooting for at least half of the time we are there, she thought. There is no question I shall have the opportunity to ride. Even Avery and Pete will be busy serving as guides, so I will be completely at liberty. And even if Alex saw me, it would be another bit of honesty. She twitched uneasily.

Honesty. As much as it appeals to me, is it worth it? By taking my abstinence so personally, he has made me pay for my recent honesty. All those innuendoes about me being cold and thinking only of myself; if he only knew the full range of my thoughts! She shook her head, lifted the skirt out of the drawer, and laid it in her trunk.

Picking up the magazine, she sat down and began fanning herself again. She was sleepy. Her thoughts ran eastward like water, shed from the Continental Divide across the plains of Oklahoma and Iowa, through the leafy, translucent forests of Ohio, and into the bucolic hills of western New York. She thought of Mill Creek trickling through the woods, widening into a clear pond about four feet deep just above the flat shale rock from which she once ruled the sylvan domain of her childhood.

She missed her mother, she realized. I want to see her! And I want to see Millie, and the garden.

But this train of thought ground to a halt. Do I? she thought soberly. Do I want to see them, or do I want to find the person I used to be?

A memory long untouched came floating past. It was that day she raced across Mill Creek flats in order to be admitted into Charlie's elite Pony Express Club. Those boys had been forced to let her join; after all, she made it in one minute, forty-one seconds. She rode home victorious, laughing in the rain.

But her father had come home early that day, and was putting away his buggy. Persis remembered the dark cloud that passed over his features when he saw her, her wet hair curling in the summer rain and her dark blouse and trousers clinging to her womanly form. She paid for that independent act by being shut up in her room for the summer.

She laid the magazine on her lap as a tear slid down her cheek. It is all so familiar, she thought, so confoundedly familiar! I couldn't wait to leave home and begin a new life with Alex, a life of freedom wherein I could create a life for myself as I saw fit, with the encouragement of my husband and family. Yet now I suffer more strictures than those imposed on an innocent thirteen-year-old girl by a suspicious and unsettled father.

The tears came profusely. "Damn you, John Allen!" she sobbed. "What kind of life did you fit me for? Why can't I find a way to change all of this? And damn *me* most of all."

* * *

Their first night at the Double Diamond, Sparky Skidmore and the new housekeeper, Mrs. Lindquist, prepared a country feast of roast beef and corn on the cob. Afterward, the men adjourned to the Big Room for cards. Avery, tanned and muscular from summer work, opened some windows, admitting a breeze from the west, and joined the men at the card table.

Persis slipped away to the children's room.

"Miss Percy," Nora said when Persis entered, "If it isn't a great inconvenience—"

Persis knew what was coming. She had already asked Avery if Mrs. Lindquist could mind the children tomorrow so that Nora could go for a drive with Pete. "Yes, Nora?"

"If I was to . . . I mean if Pete was to . . . if it's nice tomorrow, which I think 'twill be, do you think that Mr. Avery's domestic might mind the wee ones? Just for a bit, mind you. And if it's an inconvenience, then just never you mind."

"It would be fine, Nora. In fact, it is all taken care of. You can take much of tomorrow off, if you like. And we'll make sure you have a little more time off before the end of our five days here, all right?"

Nora flung her arms around Persis and kissed her cheek. "'Tis an angel y'are, Miss. God love you!"

Persis spent the next hour with the children, reading them stories and feeding them as many cookies as conscience would allow. Returning to the Big Room, she sat near the card game and learned that they had all agreed with the plan for tomorrow, a fishing excursion. Avery had the men's itinerary mapped out. Wednesday they would move cattle, if they chose, and on Thursday there would be shooting on the western fringe of the ranch.

Avery turned away from the table for a moment. "The dapple gray I told you about last summer is broke now," he said to Persis. "You're welcome to ride her at any time. She's yours while you're here."

"You are so very kind, Avery." She looked him in the eye, thanking him with her heart. "You know, my riding is much improved, thanks to a little Arabian mix Alex bought for me last year. Your dapple gray—what is her name?"

"No Name." Avery gave a half-smile. "We told you last summer, re-member, that you should be the one to name her. Pete started calling her No Name last fall and it stuck. Maybe you can change that."

Persis smiled back, but as she did, she saw two things. First, she saw Alex looking at Avery. She remembered that he didn't know about her running into Avery downtown. Then she saw Jack Hascombe's eyes dart toward Alex.

That Jack is a complete fool, she fumed. He and Baron Coleman will be the ruin of me yet. She wondered what words might pass, later that evening or the next day, between Jack and Alex about her friendship—if they were decent enough to call it that—with Avery.

To shine immediate light on her innocence, Persis asked Avery, "How is the Montana Stock Growers' Association doing? Since I saw you and Pete in Last Chance Gulch, I confess I have not seen much in the papers."

"We haven't come together as effectively as everyone had hoped," Avery said, shaking his head. "There is a strong stock organization in the North called the Shonkin, but our efforts here, which have gone on since '79, have been meager. The Territory is so large that the cattlemen in the eastern part feel a world apart from those of us in the west."

"Except when the eastern half runs bulls of inferior quality up on the Sun River," said Pete. "Then the two worlds get knitted together right quick."

The men laughed. Persis looked down at her book, glad to feel the conversation shift.

"Well, roundup is only a month away," said Avery. "With so many outfits together, we'll make progress."

Persis sat near the card players until twilight deepened the blue of the spruce trees outside the window. Setting aside the copy of *Vanity Fair* she had been quick to borrow from Avery's library, she rose and went down the long, wide hallway toward the kitchen, where the wind was coming through the screened door. With light fingers she let the door close softly behind her and headed down the grassy slope to the deer trail along the creek.

The trail, mottled with fading light, was pleasant and level, wide enough for her to walk along the creek for nearly a quarter-mile, listening to birdsong and the rush of water.

On her return trip, she saw that the large doors of the barn were open wide. The glow of a lantern was visible within. She entered and looked up into the high, raftered darkness. The lantern was suspended from an iron hook at the far end of the barn, its light barely reaching the area where she stood.

In the gathering darkness she made out horses' heads peering out of their stalls, some reaching out over their half-doors to see if she bore anything worthwhile. The sounds of shifting hooves and softly grinding teeth were broken now and then by the distant laughter of the men.

A movement of air, like a gentle gust of wind, blew against her with a rushing sound that rose overhead. Had someone run past her? She spun around. No one was there. Holding her breath, she listened. It was as if a spirit had nudged her. She heard the rushing sound again, high above. Tipping her head back, she saw a great horned owl, flapping his wings as he settled onto a high crossbeam. The shadows were deep, and she could not tell for certain, but it looked like one thickly tufted foot held a dead mouse.

The owl looked imperiously down at her. Persis smiled, then formed an "o" with her lips and uttered a feeble, "Whuh-hoo."

His yellow eyes glinted like lamps in the darkness. Then he stretched, spreading his huge wings outward and beating the still air. The vibrating air filled the barn, and one of the horses nickered.

"Who-hoo-hoo-hoo," came the characteristic four-part cry.

Persis was spellbound. Only once or twice, as children, had she and Charlie elicited a response from the owls that lived in the woods.

Having overextended himself socially, the owl turned his full focus on the lifeless rodent, ripping it to bits and swallowing it in less than a minute.

A noise from the other end of the barn caused him to lift off in haste. The great wings beat again, slowly, powerfully, as he dipped near Persis. Her hair fanned back in the churning air. She could have reached out and touched the feathered wing tips; then he was gone.

A trace of guilt over being out so long alone directed her toward the opposite doors and on to the lights of the house. As she came out of the north end of the barn, she looked cautiously around for the source of the noise that had stirred the owl from his perch, but there was no one there.

After breakfast on Wednesday, Alex suggested a morning ride. Persis gladly obliged, not even minding the sidesaddle.

Because her horse was nearly always a few paces behind his, she could watch him unobserved. There was something unusual about him today. It wasn't the ominous tension she had learned to detect in its tiniest manifestations. Thank God, she thought. There had been no violence since April. She flinched, wishing she hadn't made a mental note of the time frame. Whenever she did that, she felt more keenly the finite, tentative nature of peace.

This mood of his was something different. He seemed preoccupied. A flicker of jealousy passed through her as she wondered if he was thinking of another woman, perhaps some *demoiselle* in the Tenderloin. But no, she decided, that wasn't it. Alex had never been transparent when it came to other women, save for the incident with the heliotrope-scented handkerchief.

Alex slowed and looked back at her with a pleased smile. "Sidesaddle suits you well."

She smiled briefly, watching him apply unnecessary pressure to the reins when turning and slowing his horse. Observing his hands, she saw again, as she had last spring in Butte, how shapeless his thick fingers were. More and more frequently, she looked at him with a less than admiring appraisal of his physical person. He is not perfect, she noted, as I once chose to see him. He is more real to me, more human and corporeal, than before. This is good, she affirmed.

And yet she did not feel thoroughly that it was.

* * *

That evening, the men convened at cards. Addressing Baron Coleman, who had arrived that afternoon, Avery said, "It appears that the two architects of Butte's prosperity have become quite alienated from one another, if we can believe what we read in the paper."

"I should say so," Baron said with a grin, removing the cigarette from between his teeth. "They don't even go to the same parties anymore."

Persis saw Alex watching this exchange.

Avery continued, "And politics has entered the picture as well. Is there truth to the rumor that Clark will aim for a senate seat if the Territory becomes a state?"

"He's a political fellow," said Baron. "He'd be a good one to send East."

"Statehood is a few years off, I'm afraid," replied Avery.

"In the meantime," Anton Schulz put in, "it will be interesting to see who comes out on top of the slag heaps on The Hill."

"Avery," Alex said casually, "will our hunting excursion tomorrow take us west, toward the Pintlar Range?"

"That was Pete's and my suggestion," said Avery, "but we are at your disposal. Where would you like to go?"

"Oh, there's no question that the best shooting will be found to the west," Alex said, nodding. "I am in complete accord with your recommendation."

Rob Hancock turned to Persis and asked, "And what of Mrs. MacKinney? Shall you attend us as Diana, goddess of the hunt? There are plenty of folks to look after the children."

"Oh!" said Persis, surprised. "No thank you. I am looking forward to some peace and quiet tomorrow. Thank you just the same."

With the men in general agreement about the excursion, Alex seemed to relax. His mood, however, did not go unnoticed by his companions.

"What ails you tonight, Alex?" said Anton. "Shall we send for the doctor?"

Alex's eyes flashed. "Nothing at all."

"I can doctor him," Baron said loudly. "His problem is plain as day: a clear case of unconsumed whiskey!"

The others laughed as Baron jumped up and went to the sideboard where the bottles stood. Returning with a fresh drink for Alex, he sat down and said, "Well, girls, are we going to chew the fat or are we going to have a little game of cards?"

* * *

Persis woke early to find that Alex had already risen. There was a nip in the air. Even August mornings at these altitudes are chilly, she reminded herself, slipping into her wool wrapper.

The barnyard, clearly visible from the bedroom window, showed Sparky Skidmore was loading panniers with tinned fruit and buckets of cold chicken. Avery and Pete had already mounted their horses, with Alex and the others following suit. Soon they were splashing through the shallows of the Clark Fork, making their way into the broad western meadows.

"Good morning, Sparky," Persis said as she entered the kitchen. "They're off, I see."

Sparky nodded. "Woke you, did they? They're a darn sight quieter in the morning than they are of an evenin'. Not that I mind," he added quickly. "Here's the coffee pot. No, ma'am, not that I mind. We like to see our visitors have a good time. Sugar in your java?"

"Just a little, thank you," she said. "How far are they going? I mean, when shall we expect them?"

"Pete says five o'clock. Avery's comin' back early, though. He's got to go over to Con Kohrs' place today to help him with a project."

"He is only going part-way with the hunting party?"

"He said he'd see them over to the front of the Flint Creek Range. It's about four miles. I believe your husband has hunted over that way before."

Persis remembered very well that hunting trip Alex took, and her own fateful decision to travel to Butte. She picked up a buffalo robe from a stack near the front door. Wrapping the huge pelt around her, she sat down in a large armchair on the porch and watched the eastern horizon grow pink and gold with the coming sun.

I'll ride today, she decided. And I shall wear my split skirt. I would just as soon be on my way before Avery gets back.

She was delayed when Rose tumbled against a table leg at breakfast and bruised her forehead. Although No Name waited outside in the shade, saddled and packed with a light blanket and picnic lunch, Rose was inconsolable. More than an hour passed before the tears were all kissed away and she was ready to play with Nora.

At last, Persis greeted No Name in the corral. She had just placed her hand on the pommel, preparing to mount, when she heard splashing in the creek. Avery. She stood well to the left of her horse, hoping he would just nod and tip his hat and go on his way to the Kohrs' place up the road. But he came toward her.

"I'm glad I caught you," he said.

Persis smiled at him. "Hello," she said. "It's going to be another warm one, isn't it?"

"A split skirt. Is that what the fashionable elite of Helena are coming around to?" he said. His tanned cheeks crinkled into a grin as he pushed his hat back.

"Not exactly. I'm departing from convention, just for today. I didn't think anyone—"

"Anyone would be around? Well, for what it's worth, I think a split skirt is a fine idea. I don't know why the rest of your gender doesn't abandon that damn—excuse me—that fickle piece of equipment known as the sidesaddle. Have you ever thought about it from the horse's point of view? Having someone perched so unnaturally on his back?"

Persis laughed. "Well, No Name should be happy with me today."

"She's a good mount. You'll be fine. Long as I caught you, I wanted to tell you about a fine ride I know you'd enjoy. You know the deer trail that runs along the river?"

Persis nodded.

"Good. Well, you go upstream, sticking to the trail on the east side of the river. You'll come to log bridge that takes you to the other side. After about three miles, you'll just barely have crossed over onto Con Kohrs' land, but he won't mind at all. I know where all his boys will be today and believe me, they'll be far away from you. Don't worry. There's a fine picnic spot there and a clear, ponded place with a pebbly bottom. You'll know it when you see it. A big cottonwood and a Ponderosa pine both lean over the river there, from either side, almost touching one another."

Persis smiled. "You are so kind, Avery, to look after my comfort and diversion so well. You have done so much for us all. And we have never repaid you, really."

"If I can make a contribution to your happiness—and the happiness of those you love—then I am well paid," he said. Their eyes met and she felt the peculiar uneasiness that haunted her whenever she was with him. Something made her terribly glad she still felt it.

"You are very gracious," she said simply, casting her eyes down.

"Have a good ride. You needn't think about coming back until four o'clock or so. Don't worry about a thing. Except—"

Persis looked up at him, attentive. "Yes?"

That slow smile was there again, reluctant but irrepressible. "You might give some thought to a name for her."

Persis smiled back and pulled herself up into the saddle. "I will."

*　*　*

As Avery had promised, the trail was perfect, just wide enough for her and the horse. Deep grasses brushed softly at No Name's legs and a constant parade of wild pink roses perfumed the air. Here and there, purple stars of fall aster winked among the low-growing foliage.

The brilliant blue of the sky seemed almost unreal to her, as if some zealous artist had overstated the color. The cottonwood leaves rustled like waxy parchment and the wind soughed gently through deep stands of Douglas fir.

They crossed the narrow bridge, No Name's hooves clomping softly. On the other side, a nuthatch spiraled his way around the flaked trunk of a pine, passing from light to shadow and back again. A pair of magpies rasped overhead. Last year's needles lay on the trail, warmly aromatic. With No Name solid and steady beneath her, she settled into the experience of the glorious day.

The sun had moved to her left and she knew it was afternoon. She wondered if she could possibly have misunderstood Avery, because no sign of the picnic spot appeared.

Then, moving around the next bend in the river, she saw them. There were the two trees, leaning across the river, wanting to touch one another. The trail opened into a clearing, shielded on the west side by a large bluff of granite. Although the clearing was well-shaded, it was still beastly hot. The water, blue-green and cool, lapped against the bank. A series of huge, flat rocks, like elongated steps, led down to the river. Leafy saxifrage and moss grew from the cracks, and wild clematis hung like gossamer curtains from the shrubbery, trailing white flowers along the rocky shore. The place was rather like her girlhood hideaway on Mill Creek, but there was something more here—an almost supernatural peace.

Dismounting, she picketed No Name in a grassy spot. Finding a smooth place on the rocks, she stripped off everything except her bloomers and chemise. Wading slowly into the water, she found the bottom just as Avery said it would be, forgiving and pebbly. The moisture crept up the muslin of her chemise, cooling her hot skin. Finally she reached the deep part of the basin, where the cold water was up to her collarbones. She stopped, in order to keep her hair from being spoiled.

Standing there, the hot sun beating on her uncovered head and the cold water coursing gently around her body, she thought back to the pond of her childhood, and gathered back the time when she did not care so much about her looks, when it didn't matter to her what kind of effect she had on others, especially men. She had spirit back then. Back then, she thought. And what of now?

Taking a deep breath, she sank down. The water fizzed around her ears as it penetrated the braids at her temples. She stretched out her arms and legs, letting the water rush through the space between each finger and toe, staying under as long as she could, swimming in broad strokes out into the teal green depths. Suspended in that liquid world, she was insulated and free, rinsed of every care she had ever known.

Finally, she burst into the air, crying out with exhilaration and joy. She felt tears pricking at her eyes, and wondered what on earth could make her sad today, here, in this place. But it wasn't sadness at all; it was pure happiness. For now, in this hallowed time and space, she was filled with the sense that all was well, that peace reigned in every living thing and in all that had ever been and ever would be.

Scrambling out, she spread the calico quilt out on the warm granite and lay down. Within moments, she was warm enough to sit up and dig through her saddlebags for the chicken, corn muffins, and honey Sparky had wrapped for her. Leaning over, she dipped the battered enamel cup into the river. A water ouzel watched her timorously, bobbing up and down like a marionette. Smiling at him, she began to eat, savoring every bite. The water, cold and refreshing in her throat, tasted faintly of rust from the old cup.

By the time she was finished, her underclothes were nearly dry. I ought to get dressed, she mused lazily. But her eyelids were heavy and the blanket was soft. Pillowing her wet head on her boots, she flung a corner of the quilt over herself and dozed.

She woke suddenly, having slept more deeply than she intended. She sat up stiffly and looked to make sure No Name was still safely tied to the chokecherry tree. The horse was there, her head lowered and her eyes blinking.

Persis pulled her watch out of the pile of clothing. A quarter after three. Relieved, she leaned back against a sun-baked, sloping rock and surveyed the spot. She knew other people had been there, but it seemed unique and secret, like a present Avery had given only her.

Slowly, reluctantly, she gathered her things together. Something about the day had altered her, but she didn't know what it was, and the more she thought about it, the less clear it became.

On the ride home, she found a low spot in the trail and turned No Name down to the river to drink. As she sat there, listening to the sucking sounds of the grateful horse, she reached her hand up to touch her hair. Her braids were still wet. She wondered what would happen if Alex returned early and saw her in this costume and wet hair. As she imagined this scene, she felt detached and neutral, as if his opinion were of little consequence.

Odd, she thought, as she tugged gently at the reins and directed the horse back onto the trail. Quite odd, to think of him and feel so—what was the word? Serene. That was it, exactly.

When they crossed the bridge, she was dazzled by the beauty of the glittering sunlight on the water. A light breeze had come up, rippling the surface. A hatch of insects hovered over a slow spot, and as the branches of the nearby trees waved in the wind, darkness and light passed over the cloud of flies, making them brilliant motes one moment and sending them into blue shadows the next.

On the other side, she dismounted and looped the reins over a low branch. Returning on foot to the center of the bridge, she looked upstream from where she had just come. Gratitude welded her to the spot. She felt she could stand on the bridge for hours, just experiencing a sense of indebtedness to nature, to her Creator, and to gentle people like Avery. And Mabel and Alma and Ruby.

Just as she leaned on the rail and stared at the slow, dark spot, a trout leaped from it and snapped at a fly. She watched his supple, silver form breach the gelid waters and pass through a beam of light. The sun shone on the lithe body, revealing the pink stripe along its belly. Its tail, curving with the effort of rising, flung a stream of water droplets into the air.

The trout was gone in an instant, and the water droplets fell like a trail of diamonds. Persis was mesmerized. She continued staring at the spot where the fish had been. In the blurred background, purple harebells nodded over the dark water. At the deep center of the river, the current swirled the water into effervescent bubbles around ancient boulders encrusted with lichen and moss. Startling her, a kingfisher whirred past, winging his way up the river's midline. She looked around. The wind had come up and was rushing in the cottonwoods. It grew louder, until it roared in her ears. Light glinted on the dancing leaves. Their dark green surfaces alternated with their silvergreen undersides, forming a riotous mosaic, nature's fresco of life, death, and rebirth.

It was too beautiful. Her heart was so full of love and longing, so overcome with wonder that it hurt. She lay her fingers on her chest and felt it pounding with ecstasy. The rising wind moved the tops of the fir trees back and forth. The sound of it, like waves on the shore, was the steady, infinite respiration of the universe. She was seeing, hearing, and feeling the breath of eternity. Her hands flew to her temples. Everything converged on her. Heaven's grand equation filled her with music and she knew. *She knew.*

As much as the lavender harebells, as much as the breaching silver trout and the dancing leaves, she was part of it all. Through the water and the rocks below her, through the rough boards of the bridge, something surged into her, singing in her ears. Beauty penetrated her like a knife, spearing into the tender quick of her soul. She was connected, charged with the truthful current of life. She gasped with sharp recognition.

I have unconsciously worshipped this my entire life, she realized. Everything around me, all of Creation. Yet as many times as I have lain in the grass and wondered at the aspirations of a lark, or been dizzy with joy over the scent of my mother's roses, I never felt I was as beautiful as even the smallest blade of grass.

Tears streamed down her cheeks as her heart ached with the grief and joy of comprehension. "I am part of this, part of the mystery, the song, the grand design."

When she broke the surface of the water only hours before, she had left something behind. That something was the husk of her former self. She could almost see it, discarded and translucent, drifting quietly on the river bottom. Now that it had happened, she couldn't imagine having held onto that shell one more moment.

Life spun a long, shimmering silver thread out before her. She thought of the children. Here am I, she thought, at twenty-four years, my childhood only just now leaving me! But the children! If the next few years pass as quickly as the past three! Dear God, what have I been thinking? What has it all been about these last three years except me and my narrow, horrid vision? They can't possibly grow up this way, made party to the terrible crimes being enacted by Alex— *and by me.*

But I must tread carefully here, because I can only—I *must* only— take responsibility for what I have done. My own misdeeds, not his. Else I shall be back where I started.

She looked at No Name, then back at the river. Running to the water's edge, she dipped her hands in, then raised them to let the water drip over the horse's ears and silver forelock.

"Music. Your name is Music."

As they made their way along the final mile to home, Persis's joy dimmed, graying with confusion. Such a short time ago, she had felt pure happiness and understanding. She had been spirit-filled. Now, fear had come. It wasn't the same familiar fear of life with Alex; no, this was different. She was afraid, ignorant of how to perform the tasks that lay before her.

How can I rise to be more than I have been? God help me! But I do know this: I can be more of who I truly am with the children, and I can begin to courageously consider the next course of my life. I will cache this irrefutable truth as my own priceless capital, and I shall manage it well.

* * *

Anton, Rob, and Jack Hascombe rode into the Double Diamond with Pete at half-past five. Persis and Nora were on the veranda. Avery, who had returned from the neighbors' only minutes before, was leaning against the rail.

A white-tail deer lay stretched across the packhorse Pete was leading.

Scanning the grassy prairie just beyond the creek, Persis searched for Alex. She stepped down and walked toward Pete.

"Where are Alex and Baron?" she asked.

"They took a different route coming back," said Pete, unbuckling the cinch and lifting off the saddle. "Said they wanted to scout the south front of the Flint Range."

Persis saw the displeasure in Pete's downcast eyes. She didn't know much about the role of a guide, but it seemed that if a guided hunting party split up, with one contingent pursuing its own objectives, the escort would have every reason to be irritated. What would have caused Alex, a man normally so attuned to etiquette, to commit this breach of courtesy?

"They said not to look for them before seven o'clock." Pete looked past Persis. A smile lit his face when he saw Nora.

Stepping out of the way, Persis led Pete's palomino to the barn and began to rub him down.

"What do you think you're doing?" Pete said, coming up behind her with Nora's arm linked through his. "You're a guest."

Persis smiled at him. "Won't you let me do one small thing for you?"

"Do you really want to?"

"I do. Why don't you go get some lemonade or a bottle of beer?"

Persis rubbed the horse vigorously, animated by concern over her husband's strange behavior. Slicking the palomino's coat with a piece of flannel, she turned him into the small pasture across the lane. Then, obscured by the pines and aspens, she headed toward the river, walking slowly, snapping off a dry seed-head now and then and casting it aside.

She watched the water coursing around a mossy rock and felt truth weave itself into her again. When had life with Alex not been spiritually exhausting? She realized that the constant pressure of vigilance, carefully parsed statements, and meticulous timing had made her dead tired. In her pain and fatigue, she had become docile, allowing him to lead her in directions that suited his purpose. As his wife, she pondered, I cannot make myself less vulnerable to him, but I can do something about keeping my spirit safe.

And what of this wreck of a marriage? I associate the legal dissolution of marriage with the lower classes, with people who don't have enough sense to address their problems. I should at least talk to Alma, and maybe even her husband John, about it.

As committed as I am to honesty, it is not without risk, she thought, with a rueful little laugh. Come what may, though, I must find the courage to stop misleading Alex by providing him with a half-formed idea of who I am. I have been profoundly dishonest. I did it out of fear, but it was still wrong. I betrayed him, but far worse, I betrayed myself.

There were times, especially at first, when I viewed surrender and submission to him as a delicious privilege. I enjoyed the notion of him possessing me. But how unfit I am for the purpose to which Alex has ascribed me! And what made me assume responsibility for that purpose, if not my own grandiosity?

There is absolutely no question the violence will come again, she mused, staring at the blue-green of the sage-covered hills. It is in his very nature to be dissatisfied with me.

A puff of tan dust bloomed in the distance. Alex and Baron. She stared hard at the dust cloud. Perhaps I will someday forgive myself, as Bess has forgiven herself, for the vain notion that it was my exalted privilege to change Alexander MacKinney.

* * *

The horses were covered with sweat and dust. There was no deer on the pack horse Alex led. He shook his head, saying to Pete, "I don't know why we didn't stay on the North Fork with you all. That nice buck you got is proof enough that I ought to have had more sense."

Alex's comments were modulated with convincing sincerity. Just when Persis thought he was in danger of falling too heavily on his sword, he changed the subject.

"Pity Miles isn't here," he said. "We certainly enjoyed his fiddle-playing on that Thanksgiving visit."

Avery leaned forward, addressing all the guests from his spot on the porch. "There's a dance at the old stage station tomorrow night. Fiddles, banjos, food, the whole works. The Double Diamond is contributing a tub of punch."

"Could we put a mound of hay in one of the wagons and cover it with blankets for the children?" Persis asked.

"I was thinking the same thing," Avery said. "That way, everyone can go."

Later, as Alex walked with Persis down the hall to their room, he grasped her around the waist and did a quick waltz. Odd that a day of unproductive hunting would restore his insouciant charm, she thought.

"What better way to end this trip than with a barn dance? Yes, it has been a fine trip. A refreshing dose of life among the rustics!"

"The setting may be rustic," said Persis, "but the inhabitants do not lack refinement and courtesy."

Oblivious, Alex opened the bedroom door and ushered her in. "I suppose," he said. "Sunday morning," he began, his tone shifting, "we will be driving to Butte rather than Helena."

She felt him search her face for a reaction.

"We'll only stay at the townhouse for a week," he said, "ten days at the most. I have some business matters to finalize with Will. Then it will be back to Helena."

"I see," said Persis. "I can visit my brother. He'll be glad to see Winston, too. Shall we leave for Helena early the week of the twentieth, then?"

"Plan on it. That reminds me," he added, "this coming Thursday is the fifteenth. I need to give you the household funds." He pulled out his tan wallet and produced several bills, handing them to her. "There is a little extra in there," he added. "Why don't you buy yourself something special?" As he touched her chin in the avuncular way that had so often disturbed her, she felt as though she were watching a play.

"That's very kind of you, Alex," she said, wondering if he wanted her to be more effusive. Honesty, she was thinking. I shall not confront him about our finances, but neither will I pretend to be elated when I am not. This extra money will go into my little fund.

They did not make love that night, but Alex wanted her close. He enfolded her in his arms, releasing her only after he had fallen into a sound sleep.

26

"We've got some weather coming in," Avery said to his guests as they readied themselves for the ride to the old stage station. A light mist curtained the hills, and dark clouds followed close behind.

"Ah, that's nothing to worry about," said Anton. "Provided the roof doesn't leak."

"There's a fine long row of deep stalls on the north side," Avery said, addressing Persis and Nora, "where we can roll the wagons beneath a shed roof."

Persis was satisfied that the children would be snug and warm when it was time for them to bed down in the wagon. In a deep mound of green hay, she had made a nest for them and lined it with a buffalo robe and a couple of heavy blankets.

As they approached the old, barn-like building, they could hear the musicians tuning up inside. People were arriving from all directions, carrying baskets and bowls of pot-luck. Avery and Pete carried in three milk cans full of punch.

"Mind what you drink," Pete said to Nora. "It's an old family recipe. The can with the blue mark is saddle-broke, the one with the yellow mark is only halter-broke, and the one with the red mark is plumb wild. I stick to the yellow for the first couple of hours and then drop back to the blue."

Persis watched the two of them duck under the broad eaves of the gambrel-roofed building. Nora, dressed in a cornflower-blue cotton dress, slipped her arm lightly through the crook of Pete's elbow. She had already formed the habit of walking on Pete's left, in order to speak into his good ear.

Having converted the building to a town hall of sorts, the community had strung an electrical cord. There were bare bulbs running the length of the building on either side. A semi-circle of old-timers were clustered around a pot-bellied stove, smoking and sipping punch from tin cups.

Within seconds, the band commenced a lively rendition of "Golden Slippers." Four or five couples ran out onto the floor. Persis watched Avery make his way through the crowd, past the musicians on their crude platform, and pull up a chair with the old men around the stove. He's going to spend most of the evening there, she predicted, probably to avoid the single girls, who seemed to be everywhere. She wished she knew more about his plans with Emma Fenton, but she couldn't bring herself to ask.

Winston was disporting himself on the dance floor, experiencing no shortage of admirers, but Persis saw him rub his eyes. Looking down at Rose's beautiful face, the smooth, pink eyelids and the long sweep of fair lashes, she murmured, "I don't know how it is possible," she said to the sleeping child, "but tonight the two of you are more of a blessing to me than ever before."

Within a half-hour, with Nora's help, both children were settled in their hay nest. Re-entering the barn, Persis saw her husband in close conference with Baron and Jack. She watched Alex. One hand deftly managed his cigar and drink, while the other slapped Baron heartily on the back. As Persis looked at him, she saw several of the young women watching him too. Alex's personal magnetism is having its usual effect, she observed. She felt a twinge of jealousy, but nothing like the flaming ire of the past.

When Alex swung her out onto the dance floor again, he was clumsy. Claiming fatigue, she retreated to a bench, then went outdoors to check on the children. Lifting her skirts high above the wet grass, she saw that it was no longer raining, but steady rivulets were pouring off the eaves. In the shed, the children were sound asleep. She could hear Winston's breath coming in soft puffs.

A lantern appeared in the darkness, bobbing closer. It was Avery.

"'Evening,'" he said. "I thought I'd come out and check on all creatures great and small."

"Everything appears to be fine, at least in the human department," Persis said. As she walked a few steps toward him, he set the lantern on a stump near the fence.

"Thank you again for everything, Avery," she said, knowing this would probably be the only opportunity she had to privately express her gratitude. "My time on the river was more meaningful than you may ever know."

Avery nodded, saying nothing.

"It's hard for me to put into words, Avery. I love your part of the country. Being here has been a gift. It has filled me with a new readiness to take up my responsibilities. I hope I am making sense."

The patter of the drops on the roof and the slow, shifting creak of the leather harness were the only sounds in the damp darkness.

"That's how I feel when I come down out of the high country or back from the cattle range. It *is* a renewal of sorts. It provides me with a kind of patience and strength to meet the days ahead."

Persis looked at Avery and smiled. Their eyes met in the simple pleasure of mutual understanding. They stood quietly, savoring the comfortable silence.

He was her friend. Part of her yearned to tell him everything, about how she'd come home to herself somehow, and about the new promises she knew she'd never break. Instead, she was suddenly aware of the warm scent of him and the way his body seemed to fit against the post where he leaned.

"The Territory is such a young place and yet so much is changing," she began, taking an imperceptible step away. "Even this stage depot. This building is relatively young and yet it is already abandoned."

"Johnny Grant and Con Kohrs had a lot to do with this place being built," said Avery, "but it was no longer functioning when I came to the Territory. Maybe the use we're putting the place to this evening is the best of all, so let's not think of it as abandoned. Certain places are too special, the same way certain people are just too special." He raised his eyes to hers.

Persis felt her breath coming faster. For the sake of them both, she needed to turn the conversation, and turn it quickly. "It is hard to believe so much has happened in the Territory over the last twenty or so years," she said unevenly. "People like you are working hard to improve things for everyone."

Avery scraped his boot along the damp earth. "There have been a lot of improvements to the Territory, Persis, but I confess I wish some of them had happened differently."

Persis tilted her head and looked at him, biting her lip. Now his face was bent away from hers. She could see the angle of his cheekbone and the gray-gold glints of his hair in the lantern light.

Voices startled them both, making Persis jump. Out of the darkness, Nora and Pete appeared. "Look!" said Nora. "It's your brother and Miss Percy. Let's tell them! Pete, the lantern, now. Would you hold it up so's the mistress can see?"

Pete lifted the lantern so the soft light fell on Nora's outstretched hand. There, on her left ring finger, was a large, fiery opal encircled by tiny diamonds.

Persis looked at Nora's glowing face and smiled. "It suits you beautifully. Congratulations," she said warmly.

"I know it's a bit o' strangeness for you, Miss, on account of it means you won't have me underfoot much longer, but is't not happy y'are?"

Persis embraced Nora and shook Pete's hand. "I'm no expert, believe me—" she avoided Avery's gaze, "but it seems to me you are very well-matched. I am already trying to picture your children in my mind."

"Just picture the two of us in our house for a while yet, thank you very much!" said Pete with a laugh.

"It's on your own now you'll be dealin' with Grace—and everything," said Nora.

"That's not such a horrid fate," said Persis. "You will always be family as far as I am concerned, regardless of where our paths may take us."

"You'll be wanting someone else soon," Nora said. Concern showed in her round blue eyes as she searched Persis's face.

"Never you mind about that," said Persis quickly. "It will all be taken care of just fine. Now, if you will excuse me, I feel the air cooling down and I think we ought to gather in the rest of our party."

Turning to Avery, she asked, "Will you help me—how would you put it—round up the strays?"

Avery laughed and offered his arm. "Of course. But maybe I ought to get my lariat."

"'Tis a bullwhip you'll be needin' tonight," said Nora.

*   *   *

Within an hour the Double Diamond party was home and the guests had dispersed to their rooms and to the bunkhouse. The intoxicated Alex had gone to bed and Persis was alone on the porch, watching the night sky. All around her were the fresh scents left by the rain—the scrubbed sage, the dampened dust, and the green haystack across the lane.

A shadow passed. The owl! It curved on broad, speckled wings in a wide semicircle toward the barn. Persis didn't hesitate, running quickly through the wet grass. I just want to see him one more time, she thought, tiptoeing into the musty darkness of the barn. The flap of great wings moved the air in a wave of percussion through the rafters. She was about to call to him when she heard the sound of a match being struck.

"Avery," she called softly. "There's an owl!"

No sooner had the words escaped her lips than she knew it was not Avery. The dark figure advancing toward her lacked his height and build.

"Good evening, Mrs. MacKinney," came the husky voice of Baron Coleman. "Bidding farewell to the animals?"

"Yes, I am, thank you." She wanted the owl to swoop down and plant its talons in the scalp of this repulsive man.

Baron positioned himself between her and the door, reaching out with his left arm to lean against the wall.

"You're quite a bewitching creature yourself, Persis," he said. "If you can come here to pay your respects to the beasts, then I can come and pay mine to my favorite minx, can't I?"

"Please excuse me," Persis said, circling around him.

His right hand shot out and caught her upper arm. "There's just no giving you a moment's uneasiness, is there?" He laughed, low and sinister.

With one quick lunge, he pinned her arms to her sides and pushed her against the wall. Muscling his right arm around her, he brought her chest roughly to his, making sure her breasts were pressed hard against him, then grasped the thick knot of hair at the back of her head.

"Now, madame, at last we shall get acquainted." He brought his mouth down on hers, covering her lips and chin with saliva, then forced his tongue into her.

Assailed by the reek of alcohol and the musky scent of him, Persis wrenched her mouth away. The stubble on his chin raked across her lips.

As a scream rose in her throat and pierced the air, the owl left its perch. Had there only been her cry, she later thought, Baron would have continued unfazed, but the combined sound of her scream and the preternatural beating of descending wings startled her attacker. Baron whirled around.

Persis could hardly see. She felt him dragging her back into his hateful embrace, then there was a scuffling of feet on the sandy floor. Baron's arm was ripped away from her. She heard someone curse. Then came a dull crack and a loud, gagging gasp. She ran for the lantern and held it up, surveying the scene.

Baron lay on the floor, blood already oozing from a welt beneath his left eye. Over him stood the tall, angular form of Avery Burke.

"Leave my ranch at first light," Avery said between clenched jaws, then turned on his heel and stalked toward Persis.

"Are you all right?" he asked, taking the lantern from her and holding it up to look at her face. "What possessed Alex to drag that bas— scoundrel along?"

"It doesn't matter," she said. "Let's go."

* * *

Persis looked for Avery in the morning, but he was gone. There was a peculiar disarray in the kitchen. The water in the teakettle had cooled and the fire in the stove was nearly out. At first Persis attributed this to the fact that everyone was busy loading the carriages for their departure. But when she couldn't find Sparky or Pete anywhere, she realized something was wrong. Through the window, she saw Pete near the barn, waving his arms and shouting orders to the apprenticing wrangler. The boy was leading the horses for the MacKinney carriage.

Closing the screen door behind her, she called out, "Pete! What's going on? Is something wrong?"

"Fire," he yelled back. "The rain let up last night but there were lightning strikes between here and Echo Lake. See the smoke?" He pointed to the southwest, where a smudge of gray stained the morning sky.

"Avery has already gone?" Persis said, looking where Pete had pointed.

"Yes, and I'm leaving too, in about five minutes. It's a heck of a way to see you folks off. I've already said good-bye to Nora. In a couple months I won't have to do that anymore," he added with a smile.

"That soon? You've set a date?"

"October 7. You'll be there, won't you? It's at the Catholic Church. She insisted," Pete said with a grin. "Here in Deer Lodge."

"I dearly hope so. Good-bye," she said. "Go ahead and go. And give your brother our love. You both have been so kind. And Sparky too."

With one smooth movement, Pete hoisted himself into the saddle, touched his hat, and set off at a quick trot.

Persis walked to the carriage to look over the trunks and make sure everything was in order. Sparky had packed them a lunch, which Nora was tucking into a safe spot. "I hope it's not a bad fire," Persis said, feeling useless.

"The best thing we can do is be on our way," came Alex's voice from behind her. "These fellows know what they're doing. We'll get some news later on to see how they've fared."

Anton walked up. "Baron left this morning," he said.

"Already?" Alex turned sharply. "Why?"

Jack appeared alongside Anton. "It seems our Baron got duked," he quipped.

Alex smiled. "What do you mean?"

"I don't know. He had the beginnings of a real decent shiner. Maybe it happened at the dance. I sort of lost track of him for a while."

Persis turned back to her work as Alex and his friends walked toward the barn to bring out the second carriage. Putting Baron out of her mind, she looked at Nora's furrowed brow.

"Pete'll be all right, Nora. The fire can't have gotten so bad in just a few hours. And the rain that came beforehand will help keep it from spreading."

"Pray for no wind, that's what Pete said."

"If they know you are praying for them and thinking of them, I know it helps." As she helped Nora pack, Persis picked up her own sense of worry. "We'll both pray for them. I wish Emma Fenton knew, so that she could join in our prayers."

"Emma?" said Nora.

"Yes, you know, the woman from Bozeman. Avery's—" She stopped, not knowing how to refer to Emma. Was she a fiancée?

"Miss Percy—"

"Yes?" Persis replied, holding her hand over her eyes to shield them from the sun, which was now a glowing orange ball on the eastern horizon.

"You didn't know?"

"Know what?"

"She—Miss Fenton—she has refused him."

"What?" Persis was incredulous.

"She has refused him. She's to marry a teacher. A fellow from White Sulphur Springs. Pete told me, so I know 'tis true."

"How could she? He must go to her and try to convince her—" No, of course not. Avery would not try to convince anyone of anything, not even Emma Fenton.

"It's no use boilin' your cabbage twice," Nora said flatly. "It's her loss, that we can all see quite clear."

Persis was not listening. Her eyes were searching the hazy, dark green thatch of pines on the south end of the Flint range.

27

Several days later, in the den with Alex, Persis watched him move hastily through some paperwork in order to get ready for an evening with the illustrious Silver Bow Club. Earlier in the day, she had decided to tell him about the Porphyry. She breathed deeply with each mental practice of her presentation, exhaling raggedly as none of the words seemed right.

The easiest thing would be to continue postponing the admission, letting fate blow her about like a leaf in the wind. If she did, she would passively countenance her own destruction. As certain as Alex was to go into a rage about the Porphyry conspiracy, as he would surely term it, he was just as likely to rage about it when he found out by some other means.

She steeled herself. First she thought it would be best if she waited until after the card game, since he was usually in good spirits after rubbing elbows with Butte's aristocracy. But no, she decided, he may come home intoxicated, then I would have to go through another day of this. I will tell him before he goes out.

From his favorite seat in the den, he cast a disdainful look at her glass of iced tea, then swirled the ice in his own glass of brandy and took a swallow.

"It will be nice to see all your old associates again," she began.

"Yes, it will. What are your plans for the evening?" He was as restless as he had been at the Double Diamond.

"I may go for a brief ride, just over to Charlie's," she said. Her heart thumped wildly. "Alex—"

He stood up and went to the cupboard. "What is it? Not the trip to see your mother? We'll have to talk about that later. I have a great deal on my mind, so your timing is less than ideal. I have to leave shortly."

"I thought you didn't have to be there until half-past six," said Persis.

"I'm meeting Pat Largey and Mitchell Black at the Virginia Chop House at quarter to six, and I have to walk to Valiton's to get my horse."

"I wanted to talk to you—"

"Not now, Persis," he said, downing his fresh drink in two swallows.

Then he was gone. Persis was alone in the den, looking at the clock. Tomorrow, then, she sighed. I can't live this way anymore. I will throw myself on him if I must.

She went to finish unpacking. Earlier, she had taken several baskets of clothing and linen to Mrs. Pokarney, the Bohemian washer-woman. When sorting through her things, she paused when she saw the split skirt. She didn't want it to go to Mrs. Pokarney. The risk of Alex seeing it return with the rest of the laundry was too great. She stuffed it into the toy basket beneath the stairs. I'll wash it by hand, if necessary, she decided, and take it to Charlie's house to dry.

Later that evening, at Valiton's, she found Skye in a clean stall with fresh hay. Skye nickered a greeting, and Persis ran her hands over her legs, picked the snarls out of her tail, and looked at her mouth. "Yes, you are looking just fine, although you are getting fat. We'll go for a short one tonight, and then a longer ride tomorrow. Someday I will bring you to Helena, my sweet Skye." She adjusted the sidesaddle with annoyance.

She rode up the hill, trying to avoid the thick clouds of smoke and haze. When she turned west, the wind blew fresh air along Copper Street. She filled her lungs gratefully. Riding on the fringes of town for another half-hour, she turned back and moved at a leisurely walk along Idaho Street.

At Charlie's, she dismounted and brushed herself off. Running up the steps, she tapped on the door. She had a key, but she only used it when she knew Charlie was not home. She saw his face in the side-light and heard the click as he unlocked the door. It opened, but he was already on his way back into the kitchen.

Surprised, Persis said, "Are you all right?"

She followed him into the kitchen. "Charlie? Are you all right?"

He was digging in a tin box for something and suddenly dashed it to the floor. He turned to her, his eyes glittering with anger.

"How could you?" he seethed.

Persis stared at him open-mouthed.

"How in the name of heaven and hell could you have done such a thing?"

"Charlie," she said steadily, trying to maintain her composure. His accusing voice pitched her directly into the same state of intimidation she always felt under Alex's raking searchlights. It was too familiar. "Charlie, don't scream at me. If I have done something to upset you, the least you can do is tell me what it is."

Charlie picked up the tin box and threw it across the table to her. It skittered across the maple surface and tumbled onto a chair. Money spilled out and fluttered to the floor. "I want out, do you hear me? I want nothing to do with you and your damned mine. I can't believe it."

"Charlie, stop it! What has happened?"

He gripped the wire-bound stove damper and flipped it angrily back and forth, eyeing her nervously. "Don't tell me you don't know what I am talking about."

"If I do not know what you are talking about, I am damned well going to tell you I don't. What on earth is the matter?"

Charlie sighed, bringing his hand up to his face, closing his eyes. Deep lines formed between his brows. "You don't know about the land?"

"What land?"

"Oh God," said Charlie, sinking into the chair next to the stove. He sat there for a moment and then sighed heavily. Persis could tell he was trying, with some reluctance, to believe her.

"Last month," he said finally, "when I came to see you and we talked about Marcus and the new city. Do you remember all of that?"

"Well, yes, most of it." It had sounded fantastic, difficult to believe, but she knew it could happen if Marcus Daly set his mind to it. "Has something gone wrong?"

"I told you not to tell anyone, didn't I?" Charlie looked up at her.

"Well, yes, you did. And I didn't tell a soul."

He stared directly into her eyes and asked, in an iron voice, "You didn't tell Alex?"

Persis stared. What was going on? Her mind traced over that afternoon on the porch, over everything Charlie had said to her. Then she scanned the memory of the last few weeks, straining to be certain she had said nothing to even remotely hint at Daly's plans.

"I did not say anything, Charlie. As God is my witness, I did not!" She kicked the money out of the way, pulled a chair close to her brother, and sat down. "Now, will you please tell me what has happened?"

"The three landowners whose property comprised the site of the future city of Anaconda—well, it appears that your husband, the real-estate acquisition expert, has purchased those very tracts of land in a series of secret meetings."

"What? The land Marcus wants? Why on earth would Alex want that property? This makes no sense. You must be mistaken. Alex has his hands full right now."

"He wasn't buying it for himself, you dimwitted goose," Charlie snapped. "He bought it for Will Clark."

"Oh my God," said Persis, leaning back. She let her mind roam over the situation, trying to comprehend the full measure of Alex's involvement. She knew he was adept at manipulating circumstances to achieve his own ends, but this was an entirely new realm of treachery.

Feebly offering solutions, she asked, "Is there somewhere else Marcus can go? Some other piece of land that will suit his purpose?"

Charlie shook his head bleakly. "The Warm Springs land was perfect. He can't go east, because of the Great Divide. And to the west, there isn't anything even remotely well-suited for fifty or sixty miles."

"What's Clark going to do with that property?" she asked, her anger rising.

"Well, the latest bit of intelligence is that he paid about eighty thousand for it. He's bruiting about the notion that he'll sell it to Marcus Daly for four times that."

Persis shook her head. She couldn't believe the sinister level to which Butte's machinations were rising. Nor could she believe that Alex was in the very thick of it.

"Clark. That weasel-faced, prissy little bastard," said Charlie.

"I couldn't have put it better myself," Persis replied.

"Marcus is home crying in his beer right now, although not for long. Clark's got another thing coming if he thinks we're just going to roll over and play dead. If he wants two or three times what he paid for that land, Marcus and his partners will find a way, although they sure as hell won't welcome the hardship. Damn that Clark."

Persis was staring across the room. "I know when he did it," she said. "Alex, I mean. It all makes perfect sense. The day he supposedly went hunting but left the guide and the party. He went south. He acted so strangely in Deer Lodge. Now I understand."

"I must say, Charlie," she added in an icy tone, "I am quite offended that you think I would have blatantly betrayed your confidence. Even though I had no idea of Alex's potential for duplicity, I would never have told anyone. Don't go throwing boxes at me unless you know beyond a shadow of a doubt that I am guilty."

"Even if they're boxes of money?" Charlie said sheepishly.

Persis compressed her lips and looked at him sideways. "You know," she said, "I am going to tell Alex about the Porphyry. All hell will—"

"That's the third time you've cursed tonight, sister. What's come over you?"

"What has come over me? Well, I have taken a long, hard look at my shortcomings. And I know that the best way for me to improve myself is by being more honest. Charlie—you may find this hard to understand. You had such a beautiful marriage with Constance. But not all marriages are made of such stuff. Alex is a captivating, charismatic person. But there is irony in us all, and the irony in Alex is that he feels unwanted in a way that you cannot even fathom. This makes him afraid. He has a pervasive fear about me—about my thoughts, my actions, my intentions. He sees me as selfish and unloving, and as a result he feels a great need to teach me a wife's proper place."

She knew how Charlie would react to this information. Sure enough, he was shifting uncomfortably in his chair. After all, what man would want to hear these kinds of details about his sister's marriage? In addition, Persis speculated, he knows his influence can have no effect in such a private arena. This is my battle and we both know it.

"Anyway," she continued, "all hell *will* break loose when I tell him.

There is nothing you or I can do to mitigate that. But I may need you in another way." Her voice shook slightly as she looked directly into his eyes. "If that time comes, I will let you know."

The clock over the dry sink ticked heavily, in time with the ubiquitous sound of the stamps. "Are you all right?" Charlie asked at length, looking in her eyes.

"I am better than I have been for a long time," she said, but her heart was full of dread. "I've got to go. By this time tomorrow it will all be out in the open."

* * *

Persis lay in bed, reading. The August night had grown cool, so she had put on a thick muslin gown. The coverlet and quilt were gathered up around her and she had a steaming cup of tea on her bedside table. By eleven-thirty she was nearly finished with *Vanity Fair*.

When Alex came home, his feet scuffed heavily on the stair. That meant he was drunk. The doorknob to their room turned and the door opened wide, banging against the stop. He walked quickly to the bed, ripping away the satin quilt.

Persis swallowed, remembering her pledge to herself. "Alex—"

"Shut up. You—you're worse than a vixen. There is no name for the likes of you." He grabbed her left arm and jerked her out of bed. She literally flew through the air, landing on her feet immediately in front of him, struggling for balance.

"You've accomplished a great deal, you filthy bitch. Why don't you just take a knife and castrate me? You'd like that, wouldn't you? Seeing every bit of me bleed away. I have never known anyone as selfish and dishonest as you. A female mine-owner. How big is your bank account, you pathetic excuse for a woman? What else are you doing to capitalize on your talents? You might as well be a Mercury Street whore. You disgust me."

He let go of her arm and stared at her with glassy eyes. White flecks of dried spittle lay at the corners of his mouth. Persis darted for the door. In two quick steps he was there before her, slamming it hard. He grasped her by the throat and held her at arm's length. "Haven't you done enough?" His voice was a hiss. "You won't leave me. Not unless it's in a box."

She dangled like a rag doll, her feet barely touching the floor. She couldn't swallow or speak. Her mind raced over the possible outcomes of this confrontation. *If I live through this night, I'm going to see Alma. This marriage is a travesty.*

But if I don't live through this—I told Charlie I might need his help in the future, and he will know that meant help with the children. Nora will tell him. Grace will tell him. And Bess, and Ruby.

These thoughts flew like lightning through her mind as she stared at her husband. Her hands flew to his wrist as the pressure on her throat increased. The blood was slipping from her head. She tried to speak but her tongue was constricted against her palate. Only a slight gurgling sound came out of her mouth.

Finally he released her, but it was only to give vent to the full measure of his rage.

The next half-hour was something she never fully reconstructed in her mind. She did recall with dim pride that she had swung a heavy crystal vase and clipped him on the right brow bone. Yes, she had fought back. Was it an intelligent thing to do? Not at all, as her injuries later bore witness. Her efforts to remember any other details of the fray were of no use. What little she could recollect was many days later, and by then it didn't matter.

When the violence was over, her eyes were wide open, riveted on the ceiling. The room was dark and its objects obscure, but her eyes had long ago become accustomed to it. She could not have slept even if she had wanted to. Her left wrist throbbed with excruciating pain. She knew it was broken. The iron taste of the blood that had seeped continually into her mouth from her split lower lip was beginning to fade. She didn't think it was still bleeding, but she wondered if her mouth had become as used to the blood as her eyes had to the dark.

Nothing was clear to her, nothing except the fact that she must get away from him, now and forever. And she must take the children with her. She lay frozen, motionless. He had been snoring for over an hour. She was convinced he was in a deep sleep, yet she was paralyzed with fear. *A little longer,* she told herself. *I'll wait a little longer.* She listened to the clock ticking and began to count the seconds. *Fifteen more minutes,* she decided. *Then I will go.*

He shifted, rolling away from her. His breath came unevenly for several minutes. She lay as still as a corpse. Please God, please. Just let him sleep.

The snoring resumed, and the ticking of the clock came back into the foreground of her awareness. She wanted to touch her left wrist, to feel exactly where it was broken, but she did not dare.

She slid her left leg outward by tiny degrees and let it drop slowly to the floor. She followed with her right leg, until both her feet were down on the cool hardwood. Then, in tiny increments, she raised her head. Minutes passed before it was fully off her pillow. Then her shoulders followed, and finally, she was sitting up.

Still he snored. Tipping herself forward, her hips still on the bed, she leaned outward so slowly that it seemed she was not moving at all. She gradually put more and more weight on her feet until at last she was standing.

As she tiptoed to the door, she felt as though she was not touching the ground. She had the overpowering sensation that something was lifting her on great wings, bearing her silently away. Her hand was at last on the knob, which turned easily, and then she was out the door. She raced past the guest room, then the children's room, and up the narrow servants' stairway to Nora's room. Thank God it's at the back of the townhouse and not over our bedroom, she thought. Haste! Make haste!

She prayed Nora's door would not be locked. With a sigh of relief, she entered the room and stole quickly to the bedside. The same moon that had shone down on her at the Double Diamond was now illuminating Nora's serene face. She put her good hand over Nora's mouth. The blue eyes fluttered open as Nora tried to cry out.

"Nora!" Persis whispered. "It's Persis. You must be very quiet. Shhhh." She lifted her hand.

"Miss! What is it? Not a fire, devil take us all!"

"No, no, it's not a fire. Listen to me. After I leave your room, I want you to go back to sleep. I am going to take your boots. Alex has beaten me again and I am running away."

Nora sat bolt upright. "Yes, Miss Percy! You've got to go! He treats you so ill, there is nothing holy about your matrimony. He's got the devil in him, that man. Grace and I fear for his immortal soul—"

"Yes, yes," said Persis, "so do I, but right now my thoughts are for the children and myself. Listen to me. I want you to repeat what I am telling you so there will be no misunderstanding."

Nora nodded, her eyes riveted on Persis.

"I am dismissing you. You are to cease working for me and Mr. MacKinney. But you are to go to work for my brother Charlie until the end of September. Then you are free to begin your life with Pete Burke. Tomorrow morning I will be gone, but I know Alex will be coming after me even before daybreak. He'll leave you in charge of the children; I have no doubt about that. Nothing will stop him from pursuing me. Once he is gone, I want you to take the children to Charlie's house and stay there. Charlie will be expecting you. He'll know what to do next. Now tell me what I just told you."

After Nora repeated the instructions, Persis stood up, wincing from the pain in her forearm. Nora pointed to her boots beneath the window. Persis picked them up and returned briefly to the bed, kissing Nora on the top of her head.

"Don't . . ." Persis began. "Don't tell Pete. Not yet." She turned away. "I am so ashamed. For now, no one must know except those who already do."

"Go, and angels attend thee!"

As Persis flew down the stairs, the winged feeling returned. She stopped at her sitting room to fish some money out of a drawer, along with the key to Charlie's house. From there she went to the toy basket and carefully withdrew her split skirt. When a tiny bell on one of the toys jingled, she stiffened. Then she tore through the house as fast as she could. There was still no sound from above.

I have been guided to this moment, she thought. Everything is in order. I don't know if these are the wings of the owl carrying me through this black night or the wings of heavenly angels, but I am grateful. She slipped out the back door into the alley and ran, turning right onto Montana Street and then bearing west toward Charlie's house, her bare feet pounding on the dusty streets and the bloody muslin gown streaming out behind her.

* * *

Despite her protests, Charlie made her sit down in the kitchen while he rinsed her face and examined her wrist. Her hand was already swollen to twice its size, and the gash in her lip was deep. There was a contusion on the left side of her head, near the temple, that had begun to show bruising.

"It's a miracle he didn't knock your teeth out," spat Charlie.

"I have to leave, Charlie," she said, trying to concentrate. "I need a coat and money. I have a horse. I'm going to Valiton's to get Skye and then I am going to Helena."

She told him about Nora, and about the children. "I told you I would need you. It just happened sooner than I thought." Tears filled her eyes. "I am going to get a divorce. He'll kill me, Charlie."

"Of course you're going to get a divorce. But you've got one thing wrong—it's Alex who is going to end up dead. But Percy, even though you are a fine horsewoman, I can't imagine you riding to Helena all alone, tonight. Are you sure?"

"I absolutely have no choice. I need Ruby and Alma. They know how to help me. You can't come. I need you to keep the children away from Alex."

Charlie nodded grimly. He gave her a flannel shirt to wear with her riding skirt and a Hudson's Bay coat that fell below her hips. Fashioning a sling out of a flour sack, he bound her arm close to her body and stuffed all the money he could find into her pockets.

"That's quite a bit. Several hundred. God willing, you'll meet up with no one at all. I'll send you another bank draft from the Porphyry right away. The money is coming in. Not in buckets, but more than I thought. Copper is our game."

Persis wasn't listening. She was staring at the floor, her head hanging.

"Are you sure you can do this?" he asked again.

When she looked up at him, she seemed aged and childlike at the same time. A swirl of lost innocence darkened her green eyes. "You know more than you ever wanted to, don't you, Percy?" he asked, his voice shaking.

She just looked at him. There was simply nothing to say.

"I guess you must go," he said. Hesitating, he added, "But here. I think you ought to have a gun. He pulled open another drawer in the kitchen and pulled out a six-shooter. "I wish I had something a little daintier, but this is it."

Persis stared, fidgeting. She knew how to fire a gun, but the thought of any situation requiring this knowledge was more than she could comprehend.

"It can go in your saddle bag if you don't want it on your person." He looked her over and said, "I don't know where you would put it, anyway, so the saddlebag it is."

He opened the door and said, "I'll walk you to Valiton's and help you saddle that pony of yours. You can't do it alone."

Within a half hour, riding astride on a stolen saddle, Persis was on her way out of Butte, heading toward the northeast route of the Boulder Valley trail. Skye had an easy gait, but even so, Persis's head began to hurt in a peculiar way. She dimly recalled a blow on the left side, but for some reason her head ached more on the right. It didn't make sense. She looked at her watch beneath a street lamp and saw that it was quarter to two. I have a head start, she thought, but I mustn't rest. "We'll have to do the best we can, Skye," she said. She urged the bay horse into a trot and set out on the lonely road.

28

She wasn't worried about highwaymen. Alex's face flickered in and out of her mind. Just as worrisome to her, however, was the nipping fear that she stood a good chance of ruining Skye. Their pace would be strenuous and the road long. Forming a haphazard strategy, she loped Skye on the flat stretches, then restrained her to a walk up and down the inclines.

If her chaotic feelings had held their shape, she might have understood them. Every thought that arose fluxed before her mind's eye, changing like characters in a dream. Running her tongue over her lip, she flinched as she felt the puffed-up gash. At Charlie's, she could not bring herself to look in the glass. Now, under the gentle sweep of her tongue, her mouth seemed grotesque.

She hated Alex, yet she did not. She wanted him to have mercy enough to leave her alone, yet part of her wanted him to love her enough to follow her. She never wanted to see him again, yet she knew within a few days she would begin to wonder how he was. She knew the routine so well that it sickened her. The shock and disbelief last several days, then come grief and anguish, followed by sadness and longing. What would make this time different? She didn't know. She could only trust the lodestar that burned with new fire inside her.

Trees, brush, and rocks lay on either side of the road. Anyone could be lurking there. The silver disc of the moon was descending, meaning daylight was only a few hours away. She urged Skye into a gallop.

Clutching her throbbing arm close, her mind raced reluctantly backward to the townhouse on Park Street. Her spirit-self floated through the glass-paneled door into the front room and smelled the beeswax on the floors. She drifted through the den, past the bottles and the crystal, swirling herself around the deed on Alex's desk. She should have taken it, but she had not even thought of it. Her spirit undulated up the stairs and stopped outside the bedroom, peering in. Alex groggily reached his left arm out in bed to find her. His arm slapped the blankets spasmodically, seeking her form beneath the bedcovers. He sat up, then leaped to his feet and ran to the electric light-switch, throwing it with a loud snap. Light flooded the room.

His wavy, bronze hair was greasy and his face was shadowed with stubble. His torso shapeless as a wooden cask, he moved stiff-legged from one room to another. He went to her dressing room, and then to her vanity, calling her name, quietly at first, then louder. He flung open the doorway to the landing and stairs, calling out, convinced she was below. His feet thudded ponderously on the stairs. Within moments, he had raced back up and gone to the nursery, turning on the lights. Seeing the children, he breathed a sigh of relief, knowing she could not be gone. His anger rose again and he mounted the narrow stairway to Nora's room.

"Faith, Nora!" Persis said aloud, biting her lip and then wincing with pain. Skye's ears twitched.

The sage-scented wind she loved so well could not soothe her; the slamming pulse in her head had become unbearable. Although Skye's trot was a good pace, she could tolerate it no longer, and slowed the horse to a walk.

Whether her spirit-self had seen all these things happen in the Butte townhouse, or whether it was pure imagination, she would never know. My God, how could I have come to this? Her eyes filled and the wind whipped the tears into her hair.

She passed Cardwell, then Whitehall. Next would be the community of Boulder. She inhaled deeply, taking in the full measure of the night. The Big Dipper stood on end, spilling stardust on the horizon. The valley, named for the massive rocks scattered across its rolling meadows, seemed haunted. Huge and silent, the stone monoliths cast dark pools of shadow.

She heard something. Skye heard it too, and they both stiffened.

She could not tell if it was behind or ahead of her. Skulking into the sagebrush, they kept to the black places between the boulders. Hoof-beats, she realized, but also the rumble of wheels. Alex wouldn't slow himself down with a buggy or a wagon. Or would he? To her relief, she saw that the wagon was coming from the north. She sighed heavily as it rolled by.

If Alex is on his horse, she thought, he won't care if he rides the poor thing into the ground. He'd kill the animal in order to cover this road. She nudged Skye and picked up the pace.

They were following the river closely now, which bothered her, because its rushing sounds lessened her ability to detect noises on the road. A den of coyotes yipped in the deep woods to her left. As their cries faded and her focus returned to her body, she realized she was ill. When she touched the sides of her head, it hurt where he had struck her, but the opposite side hurt even more. She could recover no image of falling against anything and striking the right side of her head. The pain had increased to a riveting throb.

They had come to a landmark, a cairn of stones about ten miles south of Boulder. We're more than halfway, she thought groggily. A thick wave of nausea penetrated her core. Something was wrong, something besides the broken bone and the blood-crusted lip.

The night sky whirled overhead and the Big Dipper swayed from side to side. She slumped forward in the saddle, resting her spinning head on Skye's black mane. The horizon settled back into flatness for a moment, but then she vomited. With each retching spasm, she thought her head would burst. To get down and lie in the dirt, to put her cheek against a cold, smooth stone! But she knew that if she did dismount, she would never be able to climb back on.

If I make it to Helena, she thought, painfully wiping her mouth, it will only be out of plain fear of dying. Grasping clumsily at the reins, she nudged the horse's flanks and pushed her into a lope.

They passed Boulder, then the gold-mining town of Jefferson City. The stars were fading and a pale blue glow lay along the eastern horizon. Even though the terrain had become more visible, more familiar, she observed less and less of the landscape as she concentrated on the two tasks that mattered most: staying in the saddle and monitoring Skye's growing fatigue.

Where the rushing river had widened out into a lazy, broad pool the color of pewter, she slowed the horse, guiding her to the river to drink.

As Skye sucked wearily from the shallows, Persis saw an animal moving through the brush several yards away. Skye threw her head up and laid her ears back. There, weaving in and out of the rustling weeds, was a large coyote with tarnished gold fur. She and Skye both stared as he came out of the deep grass and into the open. Between his teeth was a rabbit, its legs flopping limply as he trotted across the road and plunged into the opposite field. Persis could not banish from her mind the image of tiny, innocent white feet hanging from the clenched jaws of a determined predator. With a surge of terror, she quickly turned her horse away from the river and rode on, her heart pounding.

As they neared the foothills surrounding Helena, Skye was wet and lathered. Persis felt the hot dampness through the saddle leather. She looked around, confused. This is Helena, isn't it? Where else could I be? Yes, there's Reeder's Alley. She struggled to remember the route to the stock barn.

Passing Gilbert Street, she thought of Grace. Grace! If you only knew. The refined MacKinneys have come to naught. How I need you! But first, I need Angus.

She leaned against Skye's drooping neck and peered ahead. It was still too early for much activity on the streets, thank God. As Skye picked her way along the old footpath to the stock barn, Persis prayed that no unusual circumstances would have called Angus away. If ever an animal needed Angus Blaylock, Skye did. "My sweet Skye," Persis mumbled.

There was the gate. Persis was so inwardly agitated that she was unable to move. Tears slid down her cheeks. Skye plodded forward, her sides heaving.

Persis forced herself to reach out for the bell cord, but her right arm was so tired and stiff that she could not raise it. Skye moved forward. Persis's fingers closed around the cord and pulled.

* * *

With an eye to the coming autumn, Angus found he could nearly double his pocket money by cutting deadfall, hauling it into the barnyard, and chopping wood for the restaurants and saloons in the Gulch. Though it was a cool morning, he was already perspiring. As he heaved another armload into his wagon, he thought he heard the bell at the gate. The team raised their heads and pricked their ears.

There, at the gate, was a strange sight. A small fellow in an over-sized coat was slumped over his lathered horse's neck. Was he drunk? A rough night, perhaps. Despite the haggard condition of the horse, it was an animal of quality, not a drunkard's nag. Walking quickly toward the gate, Angus noticed the rider's boots. "Saints," he whispered, "it's a woman."

"What joke is this?" he asked, releasing the catchwire and tugging at the broad gate. With both hands, he lifted the head of the rider and looked into the bruised and blood-crusted face.

"God in heaven!" he cried. "Mistress MacKinney! Who has done this to you?"

His mouth agape, he stared at her and slowly released her head as she made an effort to sit up. Persis opened her aching eyes. "Help," she mouthed.

"Aye, the doctor!" He was so alarmed that he stepped forward to help her and then back again, thinking to get the wagon and bring it to her. "We'll go now," he said.

Persis raised her left hand and laid it on his arm. "No. Ruby. The mid—"

"The midwife? 'Tis the doctor you ought to be seeing, Mistress."

"Ruby. But first we must hide . . . my horse." Persis licked her dry, blood-caked lips.

"Hide her? The fiend who hurt you is still coming on?"

As she looked at Angus's eyes, Bess Daltry's words poured like liquid into her mind: *Others ought to know.*

"Alex," she said simply. Although she could barely cough out the name, it was easier than she thought it would be. Gaining a taste of sweet freedom from her honesty, she attempted to smile.

Angus's face hardened. He shook his head vehemently. "Whoreson bastard! He'll nae find you nor your horse."

He darted a quick look around and led horse and rider toward the barn. "Stay, now," he said, as he ran to get an armful of saddle blankets. Striding toward the wagon, he reached out and with one broad sweep of his right hand, cleared out an entire row of kindling. He threw the blankets onto the floorboards and returned to Persis. Gathering her up, he carried her to the wagon and laid her down. She winced as her broken arm bumped against the chopped wood.

"I'm going to put a canvas on you, to hide you," he said. He shook out a tarp and unfurled it over her, then flinched at the sight of her motionless body draped in the dusty white cloth. "I'll be back. You lie still."

He took Skye into the barn and removed saddle, blanket, and bridle. Homer Gartner, the stock boy, lived a half block away. Putting a halter and a lead on Skye, Angus walked her rapidly to Homer's house and instructed him to walk the horse for a half hour, then bring her into the Gartner's barn and rub her down. He dug into his pocket and pulled out a silver dollar.

"There'll be more for you if you do just as I have said. Once she is in the barn, leave her there until I come for her. Savvy?"

Less than a minute later, Angus's wagon and its cargo were rumbling along Jackson Street toward the cemetery and the stone house of Ruby Cornish.

When no one answered the door at the low stone cottage, Angus looked around in despair. "It'll have to be the doctor, then," he said aloud, shaking his head and turning away. Taking one more glance around the property, he saw a figure walking in the cemetery. It was Ruby.

He ran to the line of stones and brambles that formed the east boundary of the graveyard, waving his arms frantically, gesturing for her to come.

She came directly toward him, veering only to climb over the stile. "What is it?" she asked, eyeing him cautiously. "Aren't you the fellow who works for—"

"Alex MacKinney," finished Angus. "That's right. But as of right now I don't work for him nae more. His wife is in the wagon. He did it."

Seeing the white canvas shroud, Ruby's blood ran cold. The sunlight danced on the chokecherry leaves and the cry of a pheasant raked across her ears. The world turned beneath her feet. It can't be, she thought. All her fears had come true.

She gasped, "She's not—"

"Dead?" Angus responded. "No, but near to. We've got to get her inside, then we've got to figure a way to hide her. He's coming after her."

"I have no doubt of that. That's his way. Bring her in."

Persis lay on Ruby's worn couch. Her head felt like two railroad spikes had been driven into each temple and her mouth had grown too dry to speak. As Ruby adjusted her body on the couch, Persis let out a guttural moan.

"Your arm?" Ruby asked.

Persis nodded feebly.

Turning to Angus, Ruby said, "I think she has a severe concussion and some broken bones. Pray it's no worse. Come back as soon as you can. I'll need your help to move her."

The decision whether or not to dose Persis with laudanum was a difficult one. Ruby knew that a blow to the head could make the patient slip into unconsciousness at any time, and too much laudanum would hasten that descent. Relying on instinct, she gave Persis a small dose of honeyed water and a carefully calculated amount of the drug.

Ruby's head swam, but she went about the task of salving the deeply cut mouth, stabilizing the broken bone, and applying arnica poultices to Persis's heavily bruised face and ribs. Protecting the patient in her present crisis was only part of her healing responsibility. Tomorrow brought new danger. It was time to acquaint the authorities with the situation.

Drat, she thought, I should have asked Angus to bring Sheriff Borland with him. Well, first the hiding place, then the Sheriff.

Where can I sequester her? She tapped her fingers on the table. "That's it," she said aloud. "I know where. And Alex would never look for her there. Tongues may wag when it's all over, but it's his good name that'll be ruined, not hers."

29

When Persis awoke, she had no idea where she was. Her head still hurt, but the terrible pounding was gone. Raising her right arm, she found it was snugly bound in a splint. As she inspected her surroundings, she saw a window and realized it was evening. An oil lamp burned on a washstand next to the bed.

A tremor passed over her. Had Alex found her? Could this be some confinement of his choosing? Straining, she heard low voices outside the door. Women's voices. The door creaked open and a distinguished-looking woman in a *crepe de chine* dress peered in. There was something familiar about her, but before Persis could get a good look at her, she retreated.

"She's awake," said the woman, whose voice was now audible from the hallway.

Dear God in heaven, thought Persis, her heart pounding. Don't let it be Alex. *Don't cast me back to hell.*

Into the room stepped Alma Bradley. Persis tried to speak, but her words were jumbled sobs.

"My dearest one," said Alma, hurrying to the bed. "Hush, hush. You are safe. You have never been safer. All is well. Hush now." She placed her hand on Persis's shoulder and left it.

Persis could do nothing but lie there and feel the tears streaming down her temples into her hair. "Alma," she murmured querulously.

Ruby was back. Alma lifted Persis's head as the midwife slipped spoonfuls of honey-laudanum tea into her mouth. "This is the last," said Ruby. "Tomorrow she will have to get along without it."

Persis realized she was being sedated. As she drifted off, she thought for a fleeting moment of her clandestine visit to the parlor of Mrs. Lo. *The night I was free,* she mused dreamily, and then slid into a heavy sleep.

* * *

"Don't give me any more laudanum," was the first thing Persis said.

Ruby smiled. "I always know my patients are getting better when they start telling me what to do."

Persis smiled back, but a stiff spot on her mouth stopped her. She ran her fingers over her face, feeling the scab on her lower lip, big as a two-penny piece.

"I must look divine. Who has been gazing on me in my—indisposition?"

"Oh, you've had a few visitors."

"How many is a few?" Persis asked quickly.

"Well, one of the first people I brought to see you was Sheriff Borland."

Persis said nothing. Glancing around the room, she asked, "What hotel is this?"

"You're at the Coliseum."

"I am *where*?" she cried. "Not Chicago Joe's?"

"The very same," said Ruby. "It was the only place I could be sure Alex wouldn't look. And I was right."

"A bordello." Persis said gingerly. "My life has taken some strange turns."

"Let's call it something pleasant. A sisterly sanctum, perhaps," said Ruby, looking impish.

"How long have I been here?"

"Three days."

"Have you—has anyone—seen Alex?"

"He came to my house the very morning you did, but you had already been safely dispatched to the Tenderloin, thanks to Angus."

Hearing Angus's name made her think of her horse. "How is Skye? Is she all right? She saved my life."

"You'll be able to examine her for yourself soon. She's been receiving the best care."

"And I have been receiving excellent care from you, my dear Ruby. Thank you."

Ruby smiled down at the linen she was folding.

Persis inhaled and then let out a long, slow breath. "What about the children? Is there any news of them?"

"Alma got a telegram from Charlie yesterday. He wanted you to know they are safe. He says it's a little crowded at his house now that he has a domestic and two children, but all is well."

"At last my brother will get a good breaking-in. Maybe he and I could go back east with them for a while," she said. "To see my mother."

"You've got time to make those decisions," said Ruby. "But today you are going to get up and do some walking, perhaps even have a real tub bath."

"The bath sounds better than the walk," said Persis.

She lay still, looking out the window. Although it was late August, the aspens were still a cool green, shimmering among a dark blanket of pines.

"Ruby . . ."

"Hmm?"

"How is he?"

"I presume you mean Alex."

Persis nodded.

"He seemed to be in good enough health when I saw him. He may or may not know that Sheriff Borland has seen you and has heard Angus's and my accounts. I would imagine the Sheriff has visited your house on Gilbert Street by now."

"Alex will not be able to tolerate the humiliation."

Ruby said nothing for a moment. "Persis, right now it may seem impossible for you to consider, but Alex may be far less sentient than you imagine. What I mean is, perhaps you apprehend the humiliating aspects of this situation more than he ever will."

This description fit. Persis stared at Ruby, not knowing what to say.

"I know Alex is not a demon," Ruby continued, "but I also know that nothing, nothing on God's green earth justifies what he did to you. What he has done to you for over two years."

Persis rolled her head to the side and looked at Ruby. "I know. I'm going to leave him. But it is so terribly sad."

"You will be all right. As for your attachment to Alex, there is an old saying in Cornwall. 'For what cannot be cured, patience is best.' Time unravels our difficulties. What concerns me most is how Alex may deal with all of this, and by that I mean, how he may deal with you."

* * *

Persis woke early the next morning, savoring the quiet. From outside on the street below came the sound of wagon wheels and then the melodic, chant-like call of the Chinese men who paced up and down the Gulch with their baskets of garden goods.

She studied the room. The floral wallpaper was a pattern of faded roses and fern-like scrolls. It must have been gaudy when it was new, she thought, but the faded effect was rather pleasant. The floor was clean, except for a few tiny feathers that had escaped the quilt. A bar of Castile soap on the washstand scented the air. The surroundings were, in short, nothing as sordid and dirty as she had imagined they might be.

The irony was staggering. As she pondered this room with so much—perhaps too much—history, she realized these four walls were her sanctuary. She was grateful, but at the same time she knew the ease and refuge were temporary. Soon I'll be on my own, she thought. Well, I already am. I'm as independent as the ghosts of the Tenderloin. What if I can't make ends meet? Will I end up like them? I am no Chicago Joe, that's certain. The woman has grace but she could eat a bucket of nails.

A light tap at the door sent a paroxysm of fear through her. Please, God, she thought, let it not be him! It can't be him! He *couldn't* have gotten past Joe and all her minions. Or could he?

"It's Joe," said a clear voice. "May I come in?"

"Yes, of course," Persis called out, sitting up in bed and shoving aside the thoughts she had just been having about the infamous madam.

"How are you?" asked Joe.

Persis found Joe's elegance and grooming remarkable. Despite her tough, shrewd reputation, she was feminine. Every hair was perfectly in place, her clothing was custom-tailored, and she wore just the right amount of fragrance.

"Thank you for letting me throw myself so suddenly on your hospitality," Persis said.

Joe studied her. "The world is sometimes a rough place. You look better. I understand you were up quite a bit yesterday."

"Yes, I am fine," Persis said. "I was thinking of leaving later today or tomorrow morning."

"And where will you go?"

"I have friends—Alma and John Bradley. I have yet to ask them, but I believe they will allow me to spend a little time with them. Until I—make some other arrangements."

"Let me know if that doesn't work out. There are alternatives," Joe said.

Persis nodded, unconvinced of the wisdom of placing her fate in Joe's hands, no matter how generous she was.

"I had a reason for waking you at this hour. Can you accept another visitor—a woman—just for a few minutes?"

Persis hesitated. Who would want to see her? Someone interceding on Alex's behalf? She hoped not. Somewhere in the dark fog that billowed inside her, she began to comprehend that she was not as much afraid of Alex physically harming her as she was of her own weakness in resisting his appeals. How many times, following a violent episode, had she fiercely vowed not to succumb to his blandishments, only to crumble beneath a shower of gifts, professions of love and aching need, and of course, the passionate reunions in bed! What would make this time any different? But she drew herself up, slid the blanket over her splint, and nodded.

An attractive but very thin, pale girl came in.

"Hello," said Persis, looking first at the girl and then at Joe.

"Persis, this is Marie Vladik," said Joe. "She is a working woman, like most of the company I keep. But Marie doesn't work here. She is an independent."

Persis forced a calm smile, but she was horrified. The girl couldn't be more than seventeen. In fact, she looked sixteen.

"How do you do?" she asked.

"I'm fine, Miss. I mean, Mrs. Mac—" her voice trailed off and her chin quivered.

"Marie has some intelligence to pass along to you," said Joe. "Marie, it's all right. Don't worry so. Now, out with it."

Wrapping her thin arms across her body, Marie began, "Like Joe said, I'm a working girl. I have a crib over on Bridge Street." She glanced at Joe, who nodded for her to continue.

"I was out—walking last night, and a smart-looking buggy pulls up. I was happy, because that usually means there's a gentleman inside who wants my company."

She stopped and began to sob. "I didn't know—he was your—husband, Mrs. MacKinney." She shot an agonized look at Joe. "Ma'am, are you sure this is right, that I tell her this?"

Joe looked at her with expressionless eyes. "Go on, Marie."

Persis's gaze was welded to Marie's wan face and watery eyes.

"Well, we was at my place. We had quite a bit to drink, Mr. MacKinney and I. The evening went—much as I expected, until later. He was smoking a cigar and I—" she stopped again, looking at Joe.

"I—in my drunkeness," she recommenced, "I gossiped about this and that in the Tenderloin, and I told him something I shouldn't ought to, that there was a poor soul hiding somewheres on Clore Street, on account of her being viciously beat by her husband. Well, Mr. MacKinney, he jumps out of the chair and yanks me off the bed."

Nausea crept into Persis's dry mouth. She could easily visualize Alex wringing the truth out of Marie. As she compressed her lips in distaste, her wound throbbed. "Are you all right?" she asked, scanning the girl's face and bare arms for bruises.

"I get roughed up a bit now and then. It's all right. But the fact is—the fact is I told him where you was."

Persis nodded. "It's all right. You had no choice. And I don't blame you for being—with him. You must believe me."

Marie nodded, staring at Persis. "I don't know if I'll ever get married," she began. "I don't think any woman deserves what Mr. MacKinney dished out to you. Any man can hit a woman. And they can dress it up in fine talk and excuses, but it's still the same evil thing." She stopped, blushing. "How I go on. I wish there was something I could do for you."

"Marie, you can help Mrs. MacKinney," Joe said. "You can run an important errand for her that will help her to safety." She pulled out the city directory and thumbed through it, jotting the Bradley's address on a slip of paper. "You can read, can't you?" she asked sharply.

"Oh yes, ma'am. I can read." Marie took the slip of paper and moved toward the door. "I'm to tell Mrs. Bradley to come after Mrs. MacKinney?"

"Exactly. Beg her to do so with the greatest dispatch."

Marie colored again. "I am sorry, Miss," she said, turning to Persis. "I know what brings about my foolish loose tongue. It's the drinking. Some of us are pure fishwives, and I guess I'm as bad as the next."

"Marie, I am thankful for your honesty. I know it took courage for you to tell me."

Persis and Joe walked out into the hallway. Marie was already on her way, clattering down the long, ornate stairway, her thin fingers skimming the rail. Staring at the serpentine banister, Persis wondered how many times Alex had felt its smooth, worn surface beneath his hand.

* * *

"I gave that girl—Marie—five dollars and told her to go and tell Angus you'll be staying with us," said Alma, slapping the reins of the light, two-seated buggy. "I know five dollars is a lot, but she looked as though she needed it. And I wanted Angus to know where you'll be staying. It doesn't hurt, having a friend like him."

"No, it certainly doesn't. He is a fine man. And thank you for helping Marie. We can only hope for a better future for her."

They rode along in silence for a few minutes. Persis noted gratefully that Alma took the side streets to avoid the traffic and social commerce of Last Chance Gulch. She couldn't bear the thought of seeing any of their acquaintances.

"I know this may be hard to believe, Alma," Persis began, "but I don't believe I am in great danger just now. Alex is unlikely to be violent right away. A great calm settles over him once he has given vent to his aggression. Usually I don't see any hints of it for at least six weeks."

"How lovely."

Persis compressed her lips and said nothing. She rummaged through the pockets of the wool coat Charlie had loaned her and felt the reassuring texture of the money. The saddlebags, containing the gun, lay on the buggy floorboards beneath her feet.

That evening, as she and Alma sat in the Bradley kitchen, Persis picked up a lemon peel and twisted it with the fingers of her left hand. "It's working much better today," she said, extending her discolored fingers and closing them again.

Lifting the lemon peel to her nose, she breathed in the clean, sharp scent. Slowly shaking her head from side to side, she stared at the tabletop.

"Alma."

"Yes?"

"I am not as afraid of Alex becoming violent with me as I am afraid of my own inability to resist him. I have always responded to him. Once I give him the slightest indication that I care for him, we go to the bedroom, where our love—well, perhaps it isn't love—but whatever it is, we rekindle it into a roaring blaze. But people like you and John, or Pete and Nora, or Charlie and Constance, God rest her soul, none of your marriages are like this. What I am coming to, Alma, is the question of whether or not Alex and I truly even know what love is."

Alma, who was at the stove, returned to the table and crouched next to Persis's chair, speaking into her friend's downturned face. "It's very likely that you offered him real love. But I believe Alex did not know what to give you in return. Somehow, his fears outweigh his ability to love. I have seen you with him, Persis. In all honesty, while Alex did appear to dote on you in some ways, I never saw your level of caring reciprocated in kind."

"I was often disturbed by the vacant look I saw in you," she continued. "You, who are such a passionate person with so many ideas and an enormous sense of purpose. It didn't fit. Somehow, he managed to keep you intimidated and confused."

"This will make you shudder," Persis said grimly, "but the easiest thing to do would be to go back to him. Easy, that is, if I don't count the loss of my self-respect. Yes, it would be infinitely easy to go to him now, to let him persuade me to try again."

"What's going to stop you from doing that this time?" Alma took Persis's hands into her own.

"I just don't think it's going to go the same way anymore. Somehow I have found my place in the world. I see that I must not dishonor myself, any more than I would choose to crush a beautiful flower beneath my foot. I cannot say if God values me above the flower, but I imagine so, maybe a little bit."

Tears filled her eyes. "I am all I have. I am all the children have. This life together is all we have." She pulled her hands away from Alma's in order to wipe her wet cheeks.

"What I feel for Alex may be love, but it now strikes me as a peculiar kind of craving. An obsession. That word fits the best. Believe it or not, I think I wanted to see myself as responsible for his episodes. It was a curious self-indulgence—me imagining I had such influence over him, enough power to lay low the dashing Alex MacKinney."

In bed that night, Persis listened to the wind sigh in the trees. What will happen to Alex if—I mean *when* we are divorced? He'll move on, of course. There are thousands of women out there who would gladly attach themselves to him, each thinking she will be the one to make him happy. But will anyone ever fill the void in him?

Tomorrow, after I go to the telegraph office, I'll go to the barn to see Angus, she decided, Alex or no Alex. If I see him, then it was meant to be. She stretched her arms and legs out into the pleasantly crisp sheets, breathing deeply. Something made her think of snowflakes falling on the spruce trees around her home in Mill Creek. "Maybe I will dream of snow tonight," she whispered, "and of the girl I used to be."

30

Borrowed buggy, borrowed green shirtwaist and borrowed brown skirt, she ruminated, looking down at herself. But not for long. She had plenty of money in her purse and a large bank draft from Charlie, with promises of more to come. The need to find a place to live both weighed on her and excited her. Wrestling with Alex over the ownership of 610 Gilbert was repugnant; that was clear. She wanted a new life.

She had inspected Charlie's six-shooter the day before, feeling the heft of it and wondering what it would be like to shoot a bottle off a fence. She had done some target practice as a child, under her father's supervision, but that was many years ago.

Because she knew the sequence of Alex's behavior so well, she doubted she would need the gun to ward him off. Words were his most effective ammunition, anyway, she reflected. No debate with him was ever a fair fight. He was a prodigy of coercion. It came completely naturally to him, like blood. While he did not view himself as a tactician, his instincts were virtually infallible. With a sinking feeling, Persis remembered the many times she had seen him savor his polemic victories the way he savored a fine brandy.

So she had brought the gun. If he comes toward me, she decided, I will brandish it. If nothing else, he will think I have gone mad.

The morning sun was already hot, shining down on her black buggy and on the men constructing a new warehouse on Jackson Street. As the ringing of hammers filled the air, their honest toil made her think of Angus. Tears stung her eyes as she eased the buggy to a halt in front of the stock office.

"Angus!" she called out. There was no answer. I wanted him to be here, she thought, wiping her damp hands on her skirt. The gun was a heavy, dragging lump in her right pocket. Glancing over her shoulder, she scanned the street and the footpath she used to use. No one.

She walked quickly to the barn to look for Skye. There, in the best stall, stood the little bay. "How is my princess?" Persis ran forward, stepping over a heap of hay and reaching out to touch the delicate Arabian nose. Opening the stall's half-door, she went inside and ran her hands over every inch of muscle and bone, mane and tail. "You *are* all right, aren't you?"

Skye butted Persis's shoulder with her head. Persis grabbed a halter off a hook and led the horse out into the yard, walking her and checking her gait.

"We'll go for a ride tomorrow," Persis said, leading her back into the stall. "But where is the chief ostler? I need to talk to him."

She closed the stall door and turned around. There, in the shadows, about eight or ten yards away, stood Alex. She caught her breath audibly and took a step back.

"Hello," he said softly. "How are you?" He held his mouth just so, his full lips gathered in supplication. How well she knew that cast of countenance.

"I'm fine," she said, too quickly.

"It is good to see you," he said, in his most dulcet voice.

She did not, could not, reply. Her heart thumped. An aspect of her had already rushed into his embrace and his long, healing kiss.

A deep twinge went through her viscera. I must be conscious of it all. Conscious of my entire life with him. That life was more than the appeal of those amber eyes and the temporary oblivion of his arms.

She forced herself to think about him striking her, shaking his finger in her face, telling her that she was cold and selfish, reminding her of how poorly she handled nearly every thing, nearly every day. She clung to these thoughts like a bird clings to a slender branch in a storm. I told him I was fine, she reflected. My arm is broken, my lip is smashed, and I have another black eye, although I used half a tin of powder to cover it up.

"Those aren't your clothes," he said gently, "but you look more beautiful than I have ever seen you. You remind me just now of that New Year's Eve at your mother's house, on the stairs. You in your green silk. I thought I would die if I couldn't have you. I wanted to hold you close then and I want it now. I can do anything if you'll stand by me, Persis. We have a beautiful life ahead of us." He paused, watching her. "I thought you felt tenderly toward me. What has become of my compassionate darling?"

Tears collected in her eyes, tears she did not want him to see. It will be the worse for me if he does, she thought fiercely, girding her spirit.

Alex was not one to implore, but this was as close as he had ever come. The ghost of a smile curved his lips. "You remember, don't you? You remember how good it can be between us. The good times can come again. I know I have been—fractious. But I also know how much I need you."

"Go ahead and make your pretty speeches, Alex," she blurted out. Instantly, she frowned at herself. I mustn't be acid, she thought. *Honesty*. Nothing but pure honesty. It is what I have lacked for three long years. I owe it to both of us.

She took a deep breath. "If you think you are having an effect on me, you are right. Since the day I laid eyes on you at the Dunkirk dock, your soft inducements have been honey to my soul. I have been ceaselessly and thoroughly intoxicated by you—and by your adoration of me." She didn't know where these words were coming from, but they were pouring magically, effortlessly out of her.

Alex's smile grew broader, more sympathetic.

"Your adoration meant everything to me," she went on. "I confess I did everything I could to sustain and perpetuate it. I dressed and ornamented myself for you, I arranged my days, the children's days, our lives, our dinners, everything for you. I waited for you to come home so that I could entice and enliven you with every charm I possessed. I not only enjoyed it, I thrived on it. It was my chief pursuit."

She sucked in her breath. Her words hung in the air, luminous as the morning light pouring in from the high windows of the barn.

Alex began to look baffled, even suspicious, as if Persis were somehow possessed. "Persis, you've just given me a lovely description of all women who love their husbands. A fine testament," he added in his most generous tone, "to what we have built together, and what will carry us forward."

"Do you honestly think that is proper? For a woman to live the way you suggest?" she asked him directly. Then, she murmured to herself, "Why am I asking *you*?" She watched him watch her, and for a moment, she exulted in his confusion.

"I have come to realize that feminine refinement—the artful practice of the attractive graces to which you attribute such immense value—all that is far, far inferior to the attainment of real human virtue and the unfolding of my own faculties and spirit."

He rolled his eyes. "What is all this," he caviled. "Who have you been talking to? The ghost of Constance?"

She saw and ignored his increasing desperation. "Did you—do you—honestly fear that I might develop *too much* courage or fortitude? Perhaps you did. You must have. And I suppose you had reason to fear it."

"I don't care for your tone, Persis. You are han—"

"I know, I know, Alex. I am handling this very badly. That is nothing new, is it? But I am not finished handling it, badly or not. As I was saying, I gladly spent my day in domestic trifles in order to please you. By remaining childlike and giving you the impression that I was completely and utterly dependent on you, I increased your tender feelings for me. I wanted that tenderness more than anything. As long as you adored me, I could still bewitch you the way I did when we first met. What artifice! And on top of these ridiculous, exhausting efforts of mine, I have had to live with your rage.

"I have colluded in my own injuries," she added slowly, letting the words sink in.

Alex glanced away.

"Not only that," she resumed, "I have compounded the corruption in you that leads to your violence. By effecting the kind of weakness I presumed would bind you to me, I have encouraged your role as a tyrant." The admission made her ill, but the truth of it ran up her spine like an iron rod.

He was scowling now. "This is the biggest load of nonsense—"

"I have been false to you, Alex," she interrupted. "In accepting your view of me, your view of everything, I spared myself the labor of thinking. I am ashamed."

Alex turned a tiny degree to the left, looking at her not quite straight on. Sorting, sifting, he was trying to make out exactly to what sin she was confessing.

"I—" he began cautiously, groping for a chink in her armor, "I still love you."

She wanted to laugh out loud. He was trying to forgive her. The irony of their different perceptions was astounding. Instead of laughing, she said evenly, "You may love me, Alex. But something has changed. I don't believe I love you. I feel something, but it is not the stuff of which a lifelong commitment is made. What matters, Alex, is that we are very clearly not *friends*."

She wanted to say that she did not like him, but instead she said, "I do not like—who I am when I am with you. I am different now." This was a lie. Her transformation was only partial. But more than anything, she *wanted* to be different.

"You're trying to leave me," he said, glowering. "Do you really think I am going to let you?" His voice had shifted to the familiar, threatening timbre she knew so well.

She saw the tense set of his jaw and watched his eyes darken. Her feet were slipping at the black, gaping maw of submission. With extreme effort, she flashed their hideous history of violence on her mind's eye. The darkness disappeared.

"You can't leave me, Persis," he was saying. "It will never happen. We are bound together. Don't you feel it?" He ran his hands through his thick hair and took a step toward her.

"You are wrong, Alex," she said, slipping her right hand into the pocket of the borrowed skirt. She wrapped her fingers around the gun and slowly withdrew it.

"What is this?" he said with a laugh.

Persis shook her head slightly. Even in the white heat of this standoff, Alex's bravado was unfazed. He was dazzlingly handsome, grinning at her in an affable, patriarchal way.

"A gun?" he chided. "A six-shooter, no less. What is this? Is my pretty little wife going to send me to my heavenly reward?"

The blood roared in her ears. She wanted to bind him with the spell of her exploding anger. Yet to her confounding anguish, braided into that rope of anger was a silken cord of something else: her weakness for him, for his swagger, his audacity. This rope stretched out before her, pulling on her heart like a sinew threaded through her rib cage. Why can't I feel indifferent toward him, she raged silently. If that were only the case, I could pull the trigger right now.

Alex took another step forward, smiling. Suddenly, as if she had been slapped, she remembered. This is how it goes. That smile is not a smile of affection, it is a smile of control. Her right hand trembled and she feared she would drop the gun. Despite the fact that her left wrist was in a splint, she placed both hands firmly on the gun, pulled the hammer back, and cocked it. The click of the hammer cut the still morning air.

Alex stopped short. "Don't be a fool," he said.

"Alex, it is you who is being a fool. Stop where you are."

His lips lost their softness. He took another step forward.

"Alex," she said. Her heart beat wildly. She could scarcely focus. All she felt was the gun and the clear, pervading knowledge that she was in danger.

"Percy," he began.

"Don't call me that!" she said, and fired. The bullet whizzed past his shoulder and went into a thick pine column. One of the horses snorted and kicked the wall.

"Put that down and stop behaving like an idiot! You are my wife, for God's sake. Your little exercise in rebellion is over. You've made whatever point you were trying to make. We—we'll talk more when we get home."

He stalked toward her, fatherly and scowling, reaching for the gun. She quailed, and for a moment nearly proffered it to him like a frightened girl.

But her field of vision went teal-green and liquid like the river at the Double Diamond. She saw the translucent husk of her old life dissolving on the pebbly bottom, and she was filled with a vibrant, overwhelming energy. That energy coursed down her arm and into her hand and curled her right forefinger around the trigger. She fired and Alex spun around, struck in the right upper arm. He stopped, dumbfounded.

A shadow drifted across the far end of the barn. Had a horse moved across the corral? Had a crow flown down from the eaves?

More than anything she had ever wanted, Persis hoped it was a person. Please, God, let it be someone, she thought. Someone who knows us. Someone who knows the whole ugly history of our short life together, who knows about my bruises, my broken dreams, and my captivity.

Clutching the wound with his left hand, Alex shook off his surprise and came inexorably toward her. She saw the shadow race past the windows on the north side of the barn. Alex saw it too. The dark shape moved into the bright rectangle of light forming the broad doorway to the corral. It was the tall, broad silhouette of Angus Blaylock.

"Ah, Angus!" laughed Alex. "My wife is—well, shall we say, a little indisposed this morning. She has shot me, for Christ's sake! If you would be so kind, please restrain her."

Angus stood silently in the doorway, holding a hayfork.

"Is there any help you're needin,' Mistress?" he said.

Alex stared, open-mouthed. "Angus, get the damned gun! She's irrational!"

Angus looked at Persis and then back at Alex. "Nae, I think she is just fine."

"What is going on here?" Alex's face contorted in a sneer.

Persis watched a slow spread of recognition come over her husband's face. He is only just now realizing that Angus knows. The great Alex MacKinney is trying to comprehend the fact that someone knows he beats his wife.

There was a feverish look in his eyes. "Well, Persis, you've commissioned quite the dreadnought, haven't you? He has nothing to do with us. If you care anything for me, you will ask him to leave."

"Alex—" Persis said, lowering the gun. She knew the words she was about to say, especially in the presence of a witness, would cripple Alex more than any gunshot. "I have filed for divorce on the basis of extreme cruelty. Our marriage is over."

Alex turned toward Angus and raged, "Damn you to hell, Angus! Leave us! Have you no common decency?"

The rays of the sun beaming through the windows touched Persis's shoulders, filling her with warmth and peace. She nodded to Angus. "It's all right," she said. "You can wait outside."

Angus's large silhouette was perfectly still for another moment. His gaze shifted to Alex and back to Persis, whose golden hair was suffused with sunlight. "I'll be right out in the yard. Oh, and Mr. MacKinney, I don't work for you nae more."

Alex's eyes darted from Persis to Angus and back again. "I'll deal with you later," he muttered as Angus walked away.

"It is you, Persis, who is the cruel one," Alex said, resuming his efforts. "If you do this, you will be the one who is destroying our only remaining chance at happiness. You are creating an unhealthy disruption in the lives of the children. How can you possibly hope to provide for them? Unless, of course, you've taken a lover. I wouldn't put it past you. Nothing I have given you has ever been enough."

Persis looked away. He was ranting, just as he had on so many nights, lecturing her until she was in a complete stupor and would have agreed to anything. Her spirit rose into the rafters and viewed the two of them standing there on the sawdust and straw, she with her two hands on the gun and Alex with scarlet ooze trickling from between his knuckles, down the fine cotton lawn of his sleeve. She felt a strange, cool tenderness toward him, nothing like the visceral stirrings of the past. His wound would need attention.

"What have you got?" he was saying. "A pitiful mining claim that could play out any time. All our difficulties stem from your preoccupation with interests outside our home. I literally begged you to reconsider the choices you were making. There was a chance for us, and now you're destroying that chance." He paused, breathing hard. "Perhaps I never really knew you at all," he said bitterly.

"No, you didn't," she said, lowering the gun and turning her face toward the doors.

"Persis, if you leave now, I will never speak to you again. Do you hear me?"

Tears filled her eyes as she felt Alex slip through her fingers. Her girlish hopes and dreams slipped with him. The broad doorway and its rectangle of sunlight beckoned like a gateway. Uncertain future or no, I must go, she thought. Letting her arms fall calmly to her sides, she turned away from Alex and walked into a golden morning of truth.

31

"It only seems right to me that you should have it all," said Charlie. "You've had my son since he was born, and that's where I would want my money to go anyway. Legally, the mine is yours."

Persis smiled. "Well, the Porphyry belongs to me and Marcus Daly, if you want to get purely legal about it."

Charlie waved his hand. "Well, regardless of the details, the next two and a half years will go by so fast you won't believe it. You'll be the Copper Queen."

"That sounds like the name of an alehouse," she said, wincing. "I want you to be my superintendent, Charlie. But don't worry that I'll heap everything on you. I'll be coming to Butte once a month. I want to be as much of a manager as I can. I'm not good with figures, but I can learn."

Grace was in the next room and Persis knew full well she was listening to every word. Grace called out, "You can do it, Miss Percy. A new broom sweeps the corners best."

Persis leaned over and whispered to Charlie, "She is such a darling—when she wants me to take on something new, she says 'a new broom sweeps the corners best.' When she wants me to continue doing something I have always done, she says, 'an old broom knows all the corners.'"

Laughing, Charlie grabbed his hat and stood up. "I'm going home by way of Anaconda. George Hearst and James Haggin came through with the funding for the land. They weren't too happy about Alex's—I mean, Clark's trickery, but that's behind us now. Someday Clark will wish he'd asked ten times that amount for the land. We're already selling some of the downtown business lots. Just sold one to a fellow named MacGruder. Didn't you know a MacGruder—through Alex, I mean?"

"The MacGruder I knew has gone back East," Persis said. "Of all Alex's companions, I liked him the best."

"Speaking of going back East, are you still thinking of it?" Charlie asked.

"I am, yes. Grace and I have decided that if we go, it will be after Christmas. Mother needs to know these little ones, or they won't be little anymore." She reached out and fluffed Rose's blond ringlets.

"The Northern Pacific is supposed to be built all the way into Livingston by Christmas. You could go east to that terminus and try out the new railroad."

Persis raised her brows. "That's true, we could." The idea of travelling on a railroad that did not remind her of Alex was appealing. While her animosity had begun to fade, her tendency to recall their life together in euphoric terms was still a daily challenge.

"How's the arm?" Charlie asked, walking toward the door.

"Much better. Almost as good as new."

He put his arms around her and kissed her on the forehead. "Take care of yourself."

She watched him go, then surveyed the domain of her new residence. Grace had heard about the place via Helena's domestic grapevine. The former owners, a couple named Ritter, had moved to Missoula. Persis struck a deal with them to rent it for several months and then discuss a purchase.

It was a step down—numerous steps, in fact—from the opulence of Gilbert Street and the Butte townhouse. A white-painted, rambling farmhouse, it sat on the west fringe of Helena, its nearest neighbor a half mile away. When she first saw it from the Bradley's carriage, Persis nodded. "It's clean and neat, with a yard, an apple orchard, and a barn for the horses. If the inside is all right, I'll take it."

The Ritters had left many furnishings behind. While not new or elegant, they were well-kept and clean. Long banks of simple, small-paned windows ran across nearly every wall, and each cluster of rooms had its own fireplace.

"I like picturing you here," said Alma.

John Bradley nodded. "It's got a woman's feel to it. Nothing fancy, but it's real nice. And you'll be glad of having three fireplaces. Not to mention that fine stove in the kitchen."

Persis named the place Orchard House, then Grace set to work, shaking every rug, putting quicksilver on every bedstead—"kills the bedbugs, if there happen to be any"—and finding a man to fix the kitchen plumbing. Persis bought new linens and down ticks for every bedroom. It was late September, and the nights were cool.

"We could use a little more help around here," Persis said one evening as they sat together at the kitchen table, exhausted. "Someone to look after the children and help us tote things," she mused. "A combination of a man and a woman would be just right," she said with a tired laugh.

Several times, as they lifted furniture or moved some old wagon pieces out of the barn, she thought of Angus. But Angus had gone to the new brewer, John Weinschmidt, with a glowing recommendation from Persis, and was now in charge of the teams and delivery routes.

Persis watched Grace deal the cards. They still played poker for matchsticks or dried apples. "We need a strong young woman, that's what we need," she said. "And it should be someone who lives nearby. We aren't crowded here, but with one more person in the house, we would be."

* * *

October seventh, the date of Nora's wedding, approached. Persis tucked the corners of Winston's bed sheets into place and let her mind drift toward the happy event. Do divorced women even attend weddings? It would mean seeing Avery. By now he must have heard most of the sordid details of my life, she thought with a grimace. As she shook out the quilt and let it settle into place, she shoved the wedding from her mind.

In the afternoon, she sank bone-tired into the chair on the side porch and looked out at the apple trees. She and Grace had picked and preserved most of the fruit, but a few pieces had fallen to the ground. Their cidery fragrance wafted past her on the warm air.

She touched her scarred lower lip, thinking, I'll have this remembrance of Alex forever. She shuddered, remembering the first two weeks in September when he drove his phaeton past Orchard House every night, stopping in the middle of the road and just sitting there for a quarter of an hour. The haunting had finally stopped, but Persis was not at ease. She wouldn't be, not for a long time.

She rested her head on her hand. Visions of a lonely future floated before her. She had no desire to get acquainted with any man, but she knew she must begin living life again. Ruby's words came drifting by like the scent of the apples: "For what cannot be cured, patience is best." Ruby, she thought. I would like to see her.

By sundown, she had resolved to go to Nora's wedding, but to take a room at a hotel in Deer Lodge, to which she would retreat as soon as the ceremony was over.

* * *

Wearing a veiled hat and slipping into the church unnoticed, she sat in a shadowy pew. It was not a good seat, but she was able to see the bride in her simple gown of white tafetta. In the nave, barely distinguishable through the crowded pews, stood Pete and Avery. The late afternoon sun passed through the little church's simple geometry of stained glass and shone brilliant rainbows of color on the ceremony.

Persis tiptoed out just before the recessional. It was a short walk to Putnam's Hotel, where she would board the stage early the following morning. Grace would be out most of the evening, Persis knew, so she retired to her room and before long, fell asleep over her book.

* * *

"You've taken the shame that is Alex's due and you're wearing it like sack-cloth and ashes," Ruby said. It was mid-October, and they were sitting at the kitchen table at Orchard House.

Persis looked down at her hands. "He failed in his way, but I failed in mine too."

"You failed to change him. Isn't that what you mean?"

"I failed to *heal* him," Persis said, annoyed.

"What makes you think you could have healed him?"

Persis put her hands up to her forehead and stared at the pattern of the tablecloth. "I thought if I loved him enough—"

"Nature is trying hard to teach you the limits of your power, Persis."

"I just need time to let the dust settle."

Ruby looked out the window at the yellowing cottonwoods. "Grace told me you hired a new girl."

"Louisa," answered Persis. "From down the road. She has her own horse and comes over every morning. She's a good-hearted girl. Swedish. Most important, she works hard and the children adore her."

"You can afford it?"

"Our standard of living is certainly not what it was, but frugality and common sense are carrying us along just fine. I shall not live as I did—in the lap of luxury and ennui—but I have more than enough."

* * *

Thanksgiving night, after dinner with the Bradleys, Persis sat again on the side porch, this time in her heavy coat, her legs swaddled in a wool blanket. She watched as leaves fluttered to the ground and the northwest wind bore an occasional snowflake into her little domain.

Alex's magnetic pull had at last begun to fade. The good memories were sharply visible, but the painful ones were there too. The canvas of her past was finishing itself, with all its darks and lights. As Ruby had predicted, her soul was moving on.

She smiled as she thought of Alma's whispered words over the long process of washing Thanksgiving dishes. "John and I are expecting a baby."

Persis had nearly shouted with delight. "When, when?"

"May."

"What, Mama?" Winston tugged at her arm.

"Mrs. Bradley is going to have a baby, Winston."

He nodded slowly, his lips puckered in thought. "Where is the baby?"

"We have to wait to see the baby, darling."

"Oh, all right," he said crossly, sitting back down on the floor.

He was past tired, Persis realized, and within minutes she had both children bundled up and piled into the carriage. As they spun along the smooth, hard streets, the fathomless indigo of the night sky stretched out before them. Then, to the north, she saw a ghostly flicker.

"Oh! I think I saw the aurora borealis! Over there."

"No, mama," scolded Winston, pointing at the sky. "That's fire."

She laughed and hugged him. "You and Rose and I will discover the world together, Winston. Everything, even the fire in the sky."

Now, with the children in bed, she was free to sit alone with the northern lights. From her seat on the porch, she saw the lamplight go out in Grace's room.

I'm not the least bit tired, she thought, standing up and walking out into the orchard. The opal-colored curtain of light shifted and billowed among the stars. With no one to hear and no censorship coming from within, she blurted out, "I can't stop thinking of Avery."

There had been no word from him, although a letter had come from Nora and Pete, on Double Diamond stationery, thanking her for her gift of yard goods. Persis didn't want to be thinking about a man, especially Avery Burke. She didn't want to wonder what Avery thought of her, or *if* he thought of her. She kicked at a frozen apple and leaned against a tree.

The image of him in the barn last August, when he towered over the miserable Baron Coleman, slid over her like a piece of silk. It had stunned her to have him champion her in a way Alex never had. Alex would have suspected her of arranging some assignation with Baron, seducing him into the haymow, or some such thing. In Alex's mind, it would never have been Baron's fault. For that very reason, she had never bothered to tell Alex about it.

Avery astride his horse, or pouring himself a cup of coffee in the morning, or enthusiastically pointing out the aurora borealis Thanksgiving night a full two years ago—every aspect of him came back to her. Yes, her heartbeat quickened when she thought of him, but the thing she treasured most was the complete trust that had always infused their friendship.

She gave her head a frenzied little shake. These are clearly the workings of an agitated and lonely female mind, she chastised herself, flinging the trailing edge of the blanket up over her shoulder. My life grows fuller every day, and the very thought of being courted fills me with malaise. I'm leaving on Monday for Butte, anyway, to begin my tutelage in the Porphyry's ledgers. That's more than enough to be thinking about.

* * *

The Porphyry office was a board and batten shed a scant ten yards from the mouth of the mine. Persis pulled a rickety stool up to the desk and opened the green, cloth-bound books. Taking a new quill pen out of her bag, she set to work.

After two and a half hours of copying, she wiped her ink-stained hands. She had found and corrected a few errors in the old ledger and had copied an entirely new one for her own use. My life is dull indeed, she thought with a crooked smile, if I am entertained to find cable spelled "cabull" and stake spelled "stayke." But this mine is my life right now, and that's all right.

Copper Queen I am, I suppose, although I'm a tiny fish in this slaggy pond. And I don't see myself sitting down on the board sidewalks of Centerville like old Marcus to share a chaw of tobacco.

Butte is as smoky as ever, she thought, her eyes smarting from the work and the ubiquitous fumes. The office was warm and the light was good, so she postponed the trip down the hill for a few minutes. Reaching into her satchel, she pulled out the half-written letter to Bess Daltry she had begun a few days earlier. She wanted to tell Bess what had happened, but more importantly, she wanted to invite Bess to join her in a special project.

She had conceived the idea of paying rent on a special back room at Joe's Coliseum, a room for women who needed shelter and secrecy the way she had desperately needed it. Joe was willing, and Persis needed just a few more dollars a month to make it happen. She had a feeling Bess would be an easy sell.

When the letter was complete, she packed everything into her satchel, dusted her sleeves, and started on foot down the hill toward Charlie's house. A buggy rattled up behind her. She turned to see her brother at the reins.

"I'm just coming from the Anaconda. Good timing. Climb aboard," he said, dusting the seat with his hat. "So, how bad was the ledger?"

"Just awful."

Charlie's head swiveled to stare at her. "That bad?"

Persis laughed. "I'm teasing. I guess you know a thing or two after all. The mistakes I found were old ones, made by Cyrus Dern's manager two years ago."

Charlie rolled his eyes. "There'll be a pot of something on the stove when we get home," he said. "Schumann's cooking is pretty good, although I am sure her repertoire isn't what you are accustomed to."

"I'm so hungry I'd be happy with a glass of milk and hunk of cheese," Persis said.

As they began cleaning up after dinner, there was a knock at the door. "I never get any guests," Charlie muttered, his forehead wrinkling.

Persis didn't feel social, so she swiftly made for the kitchen. The only thing she wanted was a bath in Charlie's huge copper tub. She heard a woman's voice but kept up her work, drying the steaming dishes. If Charlie had a female caller, she wasn't about to interfere.

"Percy, come out here," he called. There was a peculiar note of enthusiasm.

She entered the front room and there, in the small foyer, stood Mabel Trask.

"Oh, Mabel, you darling!" Persis rushed forward and nearly knocked her friend over with a hearty embrace. "I am so happy to see you. How are you? What news? Come in, come in and sit down. Would you like some tea?"

"Persis, Persis," Mabel said, holding her at arm's length. "Let me look at you! There is something about you—a light in your eyes that was not there before." She paused. "I heard you petitioned for divorce. I confess I am not sorry. Probably the smartest thing you have ever done. You are looking quite well."

As they sat down and began talking, Charlie quietly disappeared.

"And what about you? What is happening in your life?"

"Well, quite a lot, actually," said Mabel, looking uncharacteristically shy. "I got married."

"Married? This is so sudden! It must have been a whirlwind courtship," Persis said. Fear swirled up. The very thought of a hasty love affair turned her stomach. "Are you sure about this? Who is he?"

"It's Artie," Mabel said, her eyes shining with tears.

"Artie! You and Artie? He has come back?" Then she remembered Charlie saying something about a MacGruder buying land in Anaconda.

"He decided he couldn't live without me, I guess," Mabel said, blotting her eyes with her handkerchief. "He left the Ohio farm—and his former fiancée—for good. We got married at the end of October."

Persis stared at Mabel, shaking her head, trying to piece it all together.

"I would have told you," Mabel said, grasping her friend's hand, "but I knew you were in dire straits. How are you, really? I wouldn't have known anything about your situation, but Artie ran into Alex and Jack. He has seen them once or twice, although he is cultivating a new group of friends. He quit drinking."

"I am so glad. I—I suppose he heard a rather biased version of the demise of my marriage," Persis added softly.

"Don't think for a minute that Artie places a high value on Alex's view of anything," said Mabel archly. "He knows what I know. We tell one another everything."

"I've learned—or rather I am trying to learn—to let go of the shame I feel. I am starting over. I am the bookkeeper for the Porphyry." She smiled proudly.

"Bookkeeper and owner," said Mabel. "Praise God for that windfall. But you are the kind of person who would have survived—no, not just survived—*prospered*, no matter what."

Mabel told Persis the story of the boarding house she and Artie were building in the new community of Anaconda. "It's so huge, we've taken to calling it 'The Ark'."

Persis listened with pleased disbelief. Remembering the cruel things Alex had said about Mabel, it filled her with joy to watch the blossoming life he had seen fit to condemn.

As Mabel took her leave, Persis said, "I'll be seeing you soon. Have no doubt. I'm going East after Christmas, and then I want to visit Anaconda."

The next morning, watching Charlie's neighbors make ready for the Christmas holiday, she longed for Orchard House and the children. As Charlie drove her to the stage station, she saw residents of Dublin Gulch tacking juniper and fir boughs on their doors. Last year, she thought, all hearts were turned to the advent of the Utah and Northern rails, and now the long-awaited spur was taken for granted. Talk centered on the progress of the "real" railroad, the standard-gauge Northern Pacific, which had reached Livingston in early December.

As they bounced down the frozen streets, a delivery wagon rolled past, its harness jingling with sleighbells. She let loose a long, exultant sigh, thinking, this Christmas will be the most peaceful one of my short history on the territorial frontier.

When they neared the stage depot, her eye was drawn to an attractive woman climbing into a fashionable, coupe-style buggy. Once the woman was aboard, out from behind her stepped a striking, elegantly-attired man. Alex.

It had been three months since she last saw him. Her throat thickened and her heart began to race. Gathering her pride, she straightened her spine and arranged the lavish gray fox collar on her own new cloak. With a neutral expression, she stared at him as though he were a stranger. No wonder I was smitten by him, she thought. He *is* incredibly handsome.

As if he sensed her presence, Alex looked up and their eyes met. He turned away so quickly that for a moment, it seemed that perhaps he had not recognized her, but she knew he had. Charlie stiffened. Persis prayed he would not urge the horses on. Thankfully, he continued at the same unhurried pace.

She knew that appearing unruffled in the presence of her former husband was an important first step. He had shown so little interest in the children, even in his own daughter, over the last several months, that she knew she did not have to worry about him insisting on frequent visits. This filled her with a churning mix of gratitude and pain.

Ever the boulevardier, she reflected, he was promenading in a stylish buggy, mingling with the *beau monde* and winning the affections of beautiful women. For an eerie moment, she wondered if she would someday feel compelled to reach out to this attractive stranger, as Bess had reached out to her. Her eyes traveled quickly from Alex back to the woman. Their gazes locked and Persis sensed in her the same impudent hauteur she herself had once affected. Ornamenting Alex's arm does that to a woman, she thought. A trace of a smile on her lips, she turned her eyes to the street ahead.

* * *

She was glad to get home and warm herself before the simple stone fireplace at Orchard House. They still had no Christmas tree, she observed. Winston had not commented on this situation, at least not yet.

The next morning, their lack of Christmas greenery had approached a crisis, in her opinion. She drummed her fingers on the windowsill.

Grace was kneading bread. "It's only the twelfth! Angus may yet bring us a tree."

But Persis could stand it no longer. With a pair of pruning shears, she trudged across the snowy field to a long windbreak of spruce trees. Half an hour later, she marched homeward with an armload of greens. The air, still and cold, nipped at her cheeks as she slogged through the hardened furrows and white fluff. Inhaling the clean fragrance of the boughs, she threw her head back and laughed. "This is a time for rejoicing!"

Up ahead, the apple trees around Orchard House were silhouetted like webs against the white afternoon sky. Chickadees whispered among the bare branches. Here and there, wizened bits of fruit dangled like ornaments.

Tree or no tree, she thought, we'll have a splendid Christmas. With Orchard House and with the Porphyry to provide for us, we have everything we need. And the greatest blessing of all is the peace in our lives.

She spread the boughs along the mantle, punctuating them with russet pinecones and twigs of red dogwood. Holding a fan-shaped bundle of greens for the front door, she dug out the hammer and a nail. Swinging the door open, she stepped out onto the stone threshold and raised the hammer.

Wagon wheels rumbled on the road. Slinking back into the shadows, she craned her head around the jamb to look, but could not make out the wagon or the driver. It must be the Darbys, she thought, turning back to her task. She hammered the nail into the door and strung the pine swag over it. It needs a bit of ribbon, she decided, but I'll get to that later.

The rhythmic sound of the wagon wheels slowed and stopped, right in front of her house. As the long-legged driver stepped down, Persis realized it was Avery Burke.

"I brought you a tree," he called out, grinning at her. "Hope you like Douglas fir."

"Oh!" She stood rooted to the spot, her arms slack at her sides, still holding the hammer. "Merry Christmas," she said at last, managing a smile.

"Merry Christmas to you, too, and to everyone in this house." He brought the tree up the narrow stone walkway, avoiding her eyes. "All proper homeowners have a saw," he said to the air.

"A saw. Yes." She turned and hurried into the house. I may be unable to converse, but I can certainly find the blasted saw.

She went quickly to the toolbox in the kitchen and while there, put the teakettle on the stove and grabbed a washtub in which to stand the tree. I haven't completely lost my wits.

Within ten minutes, the tree had been cut to the right proportions and hauled into the front room.

"Would you like some hot cider?" she asked. "We canned some this fall, from our own trees." She looked around for Grace, but the woman had mysteriously disappeared.

"That sounds real good."

He slung his buckskin jacket over a chair and stood against the dry sink as she heated the cider and set out two cups.

"How are Nora and Pete?" she asked, grateful to have her senses return from the ether.

"Just fine. It's a pleasure to watch them together. Nora never loses her sense of humor. Well," he added after a moment, "almost never."

"Oh, I know Nora very well," Persis said, smiling. "She has some spunk, but her heart is a mile wide."

She filled the mugs and set them down on the table, then pulled up a chair to sit across from him. As soon as she sat down, she wished she had sat at an angle so that they would not be looking directly at one another. Finally, with the fire crackling in the stove and the wind sighing softly beneath the windowsill, she began to relax. They talked about the Double Diamond, the success of the fall roundup, who would stay up on the Sun River with the herd over the winter, about Pete and Nora's new house, and about Sparky.

Persis realized she was talking more than she normally would, but she was excited. She wanted him to know how interested she was in his life and how glad she was to see him. She wasn't sure, but it seemed to her that he might be in a similar frame of mind.

Thumping in the hallway heralded the children, who ran in with Louisa panting after them. As soon as they saw the visitor, they doubled back to Louisa, nearly tripping her as they burrowed into her skirt.

"It's all right, Winston. This is Avery Burke," said Persis. "You remember him from the Double Diamond last summer."

Winston grew thoughtful. "Where's Sparky?" he demanded.

Avery laughed. "No one ever forgets Sparky. I think it's the close association folks have between him and all that good food." He leaned toward Winston slightly and added, "He's back home making Christmas cookies. You can come and visit him any time you want."

Persis blushed. Standing up, she said, "Why don't you children come out into the front room and see the surprise that Mr. Burke brought us?"

Seeing the tree, Winston squealed and Rose immediately began tugging at the branches.

"No, no, Rose," said Winston.

Persis and Avery looked on, lost for a moment in the scene. Then Avery said, "I have one more thing for you. We should probably go out to the wagon to get it."

Persis threw on her black cloak and realized that for once, she had not even thought about her appearance. There was no way to stop and look in the glass without being obvious, so she refrained and went outside.

"Look," she said, holding out her hands. "Look at these snowflakes! They're huge."

"Perfect Christmas snow, isn't it? I remember it snowed just like this at last year's Cowboy Christmas Ball."

She followed him to the wagon and watched as he made his way to the rear. There, tied to the tailgate, was Music, the dapple-gray. He took her by the halter and brought her up to Persis.

"Merry Christmas from the Double Diamond," he said softly.

Persis raised her hands to the halter. Pushing her hood back, she leaned into Music's soot-colored, velvety face. Tears streamed down her cheeks. All she could do was hold her head against the horse's muzzle and struggle for words.

"Oh, Avery," was all she could muster. Finally she looked up at him. He was standing at arm's length from her. Her mind raced over everything from her scarred lip to the tears on her face. How do I look to him, and what does he think about the stories that have gone around?

But then she didn't care. Avery saw beyond her face and into her soul. Without a word, he stepped forward and wrapped his arms around her, holding her snugly against him. They stood there in the softly falling snow as Music occasionally pawed the frozen road and tugged at the halter.

Persis's heart was beating fast. She trusted Avery, but she didn't trust herself, not one bit. What was worse, she didn't know when she would. She didn't know what it all meant, especially the twinges in her belly. They frightened her more than anything. Here she was, a few months out of a disastrous marriage, standing in the middle of the road in the arms of another man. What expectations might Avery have of her?

Quelling her confusion, she slowed her breathing and acknowledged their friendship, which had clearly stood the test of time. He wouldn't be here if he didn't want to go on being my friend, she counseled herself. And as much as I don't know, one thing is certain. I want him in my life. But in what capacity, neither one of us can probably say.

When he finally released her, Avery held her by the forearms and said, "I would do anything to keep you safe, Persis. If I had only known—"

"Hush, now. It's all over," she said.

"Don't spend one minute worrying about me or what I am thinking," he said firmly. "If I thought I was causing you one grain of anxiety by being here, I would disappear. I don't want anything from you, Persis, except your friendship. Maybe someday it could be more, but that's a ways off. We both know it."

She nodded, longing to let loose an enormous sigh and hoping her relief was not too visible. Her heart overflowed with gratitude for this man, who perhaps, just perhaps, truly understood her.

"It's so good to be your friend again," she said.

"It never stopped. *I* never stopped. I've thought about you a lot. I hadn't better say how often," he added dryly.

Music nickered. "Let's take her to the barn, shall we?" Persis said.

They walked the horse down the lane and opened up the barn door. "Hope she gets along with Skye," Persis said, raising her brows.

Music nickered again at the sight of Skye, who promptly answered.

They watered and fed the two horses, then closed the barn doors and walked back out into the late afternoon. The western sky was tinted a soft pink, and a tiny star stood out like a silver pinprick.

"Pete and Nora are downtown shopping," Avery said. "We'll stop by tomorrow on our way out of town so they can say hello. We've got to get back so I can get up to the Sun for a few days, just to check on things and take some gifts up to the lonely bunch."

Persis smiled. "I do want to see Nora. And Pete, of course."

"They'll be back in town for the Cowboy Christmas Ball," Avery added. He was quiet for a moment. "I think I'll skip it this year," he said at length.

Persis nodded. She was not ready for such an outing and was glad he understood.

"It's a little far ahead to be asking," Avery said with a wry smile, "but maybe we could go together next year."

"Thank you for giving me adequate notice," Persis said, laughing. "Maybe we could."

* * *

As she and Grace watched Genevieve skating on the public rink at Canaqua Lake, pulling the children behind her on a sled, Persis knew she had done the right thing by coming East. She upbraided herself for not doing it sooner, but remembered Ruby's old aphorism: "Cut no rods with which to beat thyself."

Finally, after six weeks of family dinners and visiting old friends, it was time to go home. "Home," she said aloud as she returned from buying her tickets in Dunkirk. "That's what Montana Territory is. I can't wait!"

The new railroad, as everyone called the Northern Pacific, more than measured up to the standards set by the Union Pacific and its territorial spur, the Utah and Northern. She was glad not to have to make the transfer in northern Utah. As quaint and scenic as the little narrow-gauge was, it would always remind her of Alex.

As the train slowed to a stop in the Dakotas to let a herd of cattle pass over the frozen tracks, she looked at the western horizon, beyond which lay Montana Territory. She loved everything about the Territory, from the undulating prairies studded with sage to the purple mountains and their crashing cataracts. It takes a brave heart to love such a rugged land. And that's what binds all Montanans together— a great, common, intrepid heart.

The Porphyry was on her mind a great deal. Last fall when Charlie first said, "Copper is our game," she had felt a wave of disappointment. Compared to gold and silver, copper was a base, unromantic metal. But as she listened to Charlie talk about the richness of the copper deposits, she grew passionate. Daly reported to Charlie that his overseas experts in Swansea, Wales, had never seen ore of such quality. If there was a copper world, Marcus was setting it on its heels, and she would be part of it all.

She had collected and read every book she could find about mining and accounting. Her satchel grew so heavy that she was forced to buy a new trunk in Dunkirk just to lug her books. She eagerly learned about electrically-powered stamps and about a new patent on heavy-gauge copper wire. A market! A market that meant an improved life for America and prosperity for Montana Territory. With all this knowledge, she cautioned herself, I'll either make friends or enemies quickly.

The excitement of having made the Porphyry a tenable business operation surged through her like an intoxicant. Even after withdrawing enough money to make the trip East, she was able to leave twice as much in her Butte account as she had hoped. The thought of standing up and being counted among the likes of Marcus Daly and Will Clark filled her with apprehension and excitement, but she was ready.

As the train entered Montana Territory, she sighed with relief. On they sped, making brief stops in Glendive, Forsyth, and the settlement of Billings on the Yellowstone River. From there they bent due west, toward the Rockies and Helena.

Night was falling, but in her mind's eye, she could see April stringing green buds like beads on the gray branches of the apple trees. Her chest ached with desire for her children to be safe, now and always. She whispered a private entreaty that they might be unstained by the tumult of the past.

Leaning against the thick velvet drapes, she looked out the window at the limitless night sky. The train was moving swiftly through the deep canyon east of Bozeman. A black fringe of pines stood high on the granite ridge, so high that the treetops seemed to brush the Milky Way.

Only months ago I could not have had solitude of this quality; I could not have spent this quiet moment without feeling the cold wind of dread and shame whistle through my coat and nip at my skin. I have saved myself; I have given my children a future. No longer do we await life, even the next day or the next hour, with foreboding. Our future is like the glorious, forgiving heavens, and faith is our lodestar.

Her heart soared and she laid her cheek against the cold glass. The mystery and wonder of life pulsed through her, and for a moment she thought she saw the stars in the frosty arc above her swell with brilliance, welcoming her home.

ACKNOWLEDGMENTS

The single greatest piece of assistance to me in writing this book was the unconditional support and love of my husband Douglas Mackay. Our two daughters Ashley and Shari were busy enough with their teenage lives not to mind my constant sequesterings, but they gave me their love and encouragement too, for which I am grateful. I must also note the irony that, more than anyone else, these young women taught me the unexpected lesson of possibilities—that people grow and change in ways I never imagined they could.

My father Julian Naetzker gave me his passion, a gift beyond price. The wonderful staff of the Montana Historical Society provided assistance over a period of several years. Friends Jeff Slavick, Kent Williams, and Jeff Okerman, as well as writers Lila Schow and Susan Regele, all helped in unique ways. Judy Gilats of Peregrine Graphics was an indispensable guide and Stanley Gordon West deserves a very special thank you for taking my hand as I leapt off the self-publishing precipice. I must acknowledge too, the inspiration given to me daily by the artists, musicians, and authors who keep the landscape and romance of The West alive in their work. And I thank Mary Ann, wherever she may be.

The support of creative and loving women enables me to persevere, which any author finds is the key to success. I give deeply heartfelt thanks to my dear friends Ann Clancy and Linda Collins for their steadfast love and coaching, and to my mother Patricia Hanna for both her love and for sharing that core of independence that flames like a bright, strong wick down through the generations of our Montana family.

www.ingramcontent.com/pod-product-compliance
Lightning Source LLC
Chambersburg PA
CBHW070403260626
47161CB00001B/255